What Readers Are Saying About

Night's Gift

Night's Gift is a page-turning twist on the classic vampire novel. Virginia's plight is modern and fresh, while the count and his cast of characters are enduringly timeless.
—Kim Makarchuk

Mary M. Cushnie-Mansour blends the real and the arcane seamlessly, taking an ageless fantasy and bringing it alive, quite literally in what could be your own backyard. Beautifully written, a must-read for any vampire lover.
—Bethany Jamieson

Absolutely stunning and intense, *Night's Gift* is the first in what promises to be a gripping series.
—Mariette Havens

I enjoyed the historical aspects to this Gothic romance.
—Brenda Ann Wright

Mary M. Cushnie-Mansour is an excellent storyteller who weaves a wonderfully suspenseful tale, one I found difficult to put down. Her eloquent description and plot design bring her characters alive and make us care what happens to them as the story unfolds. A great read.
—Judi Klinck

Night's Gift brought the myth closer to reality. It is an excellent display of human emotions. The humanizing of evil is interesting and leaves one pondering. Virginia is the ultimate normality.
—Jerusa Hunter

Night's Gift tells a good tale and tells it well. I particularly liked the humanness of the characters—their strengths and weaknesses. They were believable, even though they existed in a parallel world—real and occult.
—George Hatton

Night's Gift

To Kim
Enjoy the gift of the night
Mary M. Cushnie-Mansour

Also by Mary M. Cushnie-Mansour

Poetry

Life's Roller Coaster
Devastations of Mankind
Shattered
Memories

Short Stories

From the Heart

Coming Soon:

Night's Children

Night's Return

Night's Gift

Mary M. Cushnie-Mansour

iUniverse, Inc.
Bloomington

Night's Gift

iUniverse Star
an iUniverse, Inc. imprint

iUniverse books may be ordered through booksellers or by contacting:

iUniverse
1663 Liberty Drive
Bloomington, IN 47403
www.iuniverse.com
1-800-Authors (1-800-288-4677)

ISBN: 978-1-936236-89-3 (s)
ISBN: 978-1-936236-90-9 (e)

Library of Congress Control Number: 2011960413

Printed in the United States of America

iUniverse rev. date: 11/4/2011

To all those who believed in my dream

Contents

Acknowledgements

First, I would like to thank my husband, Ed,
for his patience over the years as I pursued my dream.

Secondly, thanks go to friends who supported me along the way:

Judi Klinck and Joan Jenkins,
for reading some of my first drafts and encouraging me to continue.

George Hatton,
for editing my manuscript
and looking at it with the eyes of a teacher.

Bethany Jamieson, Brenda Ann Wright, Lisa Mallette,
who took time to assist me with editing
and offered some wonderful ideas.

The members of the Brantford Writers' Circle,
for their continued support and encouragement.

The Talos family,
for allowing me to use photos of their property, Wynarden, for my cover.
Wynarden was built in 1864 by the Yates family.
It has often been referred to over the years as Yates Castle.

And last, but certainly not least,
everyone who has believed in me.
There are too many names to list here, but you know who you are!

Introduction

Dear Reader:

I am relating this story to you through my eyes … for it is only my eyes that are capable of seeing into hearts that did not exist; my eyes that can weep for that which was lost; my eyes that are capable of showing any emotion beyond nothingness. It is only my pen that would dare to tell such a story—for those I resided with for a time would not want such secrets to be known.

This is a story that must be told. It is a story that, as you read it, you might believe was written as a Hollywood movie script. It is a story that you'd never dream you would actually ever live. It is my story—a part of my life that can never be erased from my memory—which will live on for eternity. For eternity itself has sealed it within its pages.

Despite all that he could not do for me, I shall be forever grateful to Max for the scraps of paper he provided me with during my sojourn at the house. I have gathered together the scattering of scribbles I was able to write, and I have managed to decipher the majority of my words. However, many of my pages were written beneath a torrent of tears, smearing a great many of the letters into unintelligible scratching. As a result, some of my story has been recreated, a little at a time, from whatever memories I have managed not to suffocate.

I believe it is all here—the love, the hate, the lies, the deceptions, the pain, and the sorrow. There was no hearty laughter where I have just come from, for there were none truly alive, save I. And even though there were moments when I laughed with *him* as we talked and bantered issues past and present, his laughter was never really authentic. Mine was, but at this moment I cannot bring genuine laughter to surface after what happened to me inside that house.

Are you one who loves to take a risk? Are you willing to turn the pages and discover the truths about my life? Then read on. I will share my moments with you in the hope that I might save at least one person from becoming immersed in such evil as I was. Before becoming overly curious about what appears to be an abandoned building, you might think twice. Before you risk a look beyond *any* window sill, read my story!

—Virginia

Chapter 1

Mystery House

The day had been solemn and drab—much like my mood. Storm clouds had threatened to disperse their anger upon the earth. Thunder had rumbled in the distance. Flashes of lightning had lit the far horizons. Yet, with all the impending warnings, not a drop of rain had fallen on Brantford. I had procrastinated long enough for my evening walk, and I was restless, even though the hour was late. I would take an umbrella with me, just in case. Such was the night I had chosen to check out the mysterious mansion at the end of Buffalo Street …

I had only been in the city of Brantford for six months. I had yearned desperately for a small-city atmosphere in order to slow down after the fast-paced life that had devoured me in Toronto. I was tired of big-city lights, big-city noise, big-city dirt, big-city violence—and, most of all, big-city men! However, I could not possibly leave all my conveniences behind. I knew I could never survive in some backwoods town where most modern luxuries would be too inconveniently located or, worse yet, non-existent. In my opinion, those types of places were only meant for weekend getaways, not permanent residences. As a result, Brantford, with its population of 91,000 people, appeared to be the answer to my prayer.

1

Thanks to my former employer, I was fortunate to obtain a position with a large law firm on Wellington Street. One of the partners was a friend of my boss's. Maybe he owed him a favour—no matter really; it was none of my business. I ended up with a good job and was given the opportunity to settle into a very obscure lifestyle. I appreciated Lady Luck looking out for me.

My mother must have had some sort of sixth sense into my future. She had always warned me about my looks, saying that good looks were the downfall of most girls. "Get your education the right way," she had said. "Use your brains; don't give something out to receive good marks." She used to go on and on endlessly, hoping to implant some of her ideals into my head. I used to consider her old-fashioned, but the reality of it was that she had been raised quite strictly, and she had adhered to her upbringing right up to the day she died. I cannot remember a week going by in which my mother did not attend Mass at least four times.

With Mother's words of concern echoing in the back of my mind, I always went to considerable lengths to detract from my natural beauty. I wound my long red hair into a bun every day and wore the most conservative wardrobe I could possibly find: greys and blacks, colours that would help me fade into the shadows. I wore straight-cut skirts and plain blouses, clothing that would not be given a second glance. I even steered clear of wearing makeup and noticeable jewellery.

Well, I guess I should be truthful here and admit there was a time in my life that I did not totally heed my mother's advice. It was the "John time." John was the main reason I had escaped to Brantford. My time with him had been justification enough for wanting no intrusions into the secluded little world I was trying to create for myself. He had treated me like a princess at first, and then he just left me for greener fields.

I met John the first day I began working for Mr. Carverson, a partner in a large law firm in Toronto. I was fresh out of secretarial college and had been sent by an employment agency to fill in for the regular girl, who was on maternity leave. For the first few weeks, I worked at the reception desk. A senior legal secretary spent a few hours with me each day, showing me the ropes on how to be Mr. Carverson's personal assistant. It was sure a lot different from college!

When John walked into the office, my heart went *pitter-patter*—you know the way a heart does when you see someone very extraordinary! He looked as though he were lost. He had the most desperate look on his face—a perfectly formed face it was, too, with tanned skin contrasting sharply against bleach-blond hair. He was a girl's dream just waiting to be realized!

"I need a lawyer!" he demanded. He stopped and stared at me for a second or two. His piercing blue eyes were sparkling—reading my dream! "Has anyone ever told you that you have the most beautiful red hair and shining blue eyes?" He reached over and touched the severe bun at the top of my head. "Ever thought of letting this down, pretty lady?"

He was fulfilling my dream. You must be familiar with the vision—where the prince lets down the hair of the simple maiden, and she becomes the most beautiful princess in the world. Yes, that's the one!

I fell instantly in love; well, that is what I thought it was at the time. I swallowed my blush. "How may I help you … uh …?"

"John," he assisted. "John Tanner, at your service, miss. I do hope it is 'miss,'" he added with a mischievous smile.

"Mr. Tanner," I needed to remember to be professional so chose to ignore the "miss" reference. "What kind of a lawyer do you need?"

"Lawyer? Oh that was just pretence to get in here and meet you." John had the cutest smile. "Your red hair was shining so brightly through the window that I had to come in and see who it was that had such a crown of gloriousness." John perched himself on my desk, crossed his legs, and stared straight into my eyes.

The dream was overcoming my common sense. "Mr. Tanner, please, I have work to do. This is my first day on the job. In fact, this is my first job since graduating from college, and I would like to keep it."

John jumped off my desk. "Oh, excuse me, miss … I didn't catch your name."

"Miss Manser," I answered politely.

"Is there a first name to go with that?" The eyebrows rose seductively.

"Virginia."

"Well, Virginia, what time is lunch?"

"Twelve."

"Good! I will pick you up at twelve."

Before I had a chance to protest, John was out the door. He returned sharply at 12:00, and our whirlwind romance began. I saw John regularly; in fact, after only a month of romancing, John moved in with me. My mother would have been *horrified* at such behaviour from her daughter!

"Hey, Virginia, baby," he had said one day after a long session of making love, "you know how I'm in between jobs at the moment? Well, I can't really afford my apartment right now, and since I am over at your place most of the time, do you think maybe I could ..." John threw me his puppy look.

I smiled naively. "Of course," I answered, for I still tingled when he touched me, and I was still living in my dream world.

Everything in my life appeared to be falling into place. I had done so well at the firm that Mr. Carverson had kept me on after his regular girl had decided to stay home with her baby. I had enrolled in some night courses to expand my knowledge of the law, with the hope of one day becoming a paralegal.

John, as you might have guessed by now, never did find another job. In fact, there were many moments when I wanted to ask him if he had even tried, but for some reason, I never opened my mouth. I just continued to support both of us. I figured it was okay, because every night when I came home from work the apartment was spotless, the laundry was done, and the greatest meals were laid out on the table. Life was good. I was in love. The dream continued.

The months turned into a year and a half. John never mentioned marriage, and I was too scared, or maybe I was just too busy to bother bringing up the subject. My job was going really well, and I had been given several raises. Overall, at the time I would have said that life could not get too much better, despite John's not working. Of course, there were moments when I thought to myself that if he'd had a job we could have afforded to buy a house.

Then came the bomb! I had been naturally blessed with good health and never took days off work, but on one particular day, I felt extremely ill. I asked Mr. Carverson if I could leave early, and of course, he said it was no problem. There have been fleeting moments when I have wished he had told me I couldn't, that he needed some document finished or needed me to file some paper at the courthouse, but that was not the card that life dealt me. I headed home to my apartment, to the love of my life, to my dream world.

Crash! There was John, cosily tucked into bed with some blond bimbo! I did not bother to ask her name—Dream Shatterer is how I think of her. I ordered John to pack his bags and get out, and then I sat down and cried. I tried to piece my life back together, but I just could not seem to manage. Finally, I asked Mr. Carverson for a temporary leave of absence.

"I think I know what you need," he said, leaning back in his chair and folding his hands behind his head. "A change of landscape."

I thought, at first, that he was going to send me to some little out-of-the-way cottage on a deserted island to heal for awhile; that would have been ideal. But I guess what he offered me was something much better.

"A lawyer friend of mine, in Brantford, is in need of a good legal secretary. In fact, he just called the other day and asked me if I knew of anyone. I can give him a call right now, if you like, and see if the position has been filled." Mr. Carverson waited patiently for my answer.

"You can always come back here if you don't like it," he prodded. "I will keep your position open for six months. How does that sound? Brantford is a small city, and it might do you good to get out of Toronto. You really are not a 'big-city gal,'" Mr. Carverson stated, a fatherly tone to his voice.

I sat for a few more moments, contemplating the offer. It was one that I knew I should not refuse, because the reality of my life was that I could not afford to be without a paycheque. I knew I had to close the book on this dream-turned-nightmare before I could get on with my life.

⌒

I located a small, secluded, one-bedroom apartment in the upper back part of an old house on Broad Street. Since it was summer, and I did not reside too far from the downtown core where I was employed, I decided to walk to work every day. There was no sense wasting money on a car. I had planned to save money to continue furthering my education, but it was something I had neglected after John had cheated on me. Even though my aspirations were leading me in the direction of becoming a paralegal, I was also toying with the possibility of studying criminal psychology and profiling. People interested me, especially their behaviours.

Every day on the way to and from work, my footsteps took me past a certain house—a house that I had finally nicknamed Mystery House. I called it this because never once in passing had I noticed a living soul on the premises. The house just stood there, seemingly isolated from the world, aloof behind an army of formidable trees.

It did, however, flaunt a stately demeanour that appeared to be cultivated by the most experienced of horticulturalists, and it looked as if, in its loneliness, it was daring someone, *anyone*, to step past those trees and behold its wonder. I guess I was that someone. Several times I had stood by the trees at the perimeter of the property and gazed at the scene before me. Everything in the yard was in the most perfect order, and I was constantly baffled as to when such tedious work was performed.

The windows were shaded with thick, white lace curtains, which I presumed were meant to filter out the direct rays of the sun. My mother had always drawn her curtains during the day to keep the sun from fading our furniture. I wondered if whoever was living behind those curtains was similarly inclined.

Large white lounge chairs with rose-coloured cushions were scattered on the great wooden veranda that surrounded the house, but I never noticed anybody sitting in them—at least not in the daytime when I passed by. What a waste; they looked invitingly comfortable. I thought it might be nice to stretch out on one of them, on a sunny afternoon, with a good book and an iced tea by my side—maybe even a glass of bubbly wine. I was beginning to dream again.

The flowerbeds were manicured to perfection, displaying an exquisite spectrum of colours. Bright red roses crowded the lily-white trellises that were attached to the side veranda. On each corner of the veranda were huge stone flowerpots filled with pink, red, and white petunias. It was difficult to tell, from a distance, exactly what the pots looked like, although they appeared to be shaped like some sort of animals. What animals, I could not quite tell, but I assumed they were probably the cute kind that most people would purchase: squirrels, rabbits, chipmunks, and so on.

The lawn was mowed in exact, even rows, which created a checkerboard effect. The ancient trees that surrounded the entire area were gnarled by time, and when the breezes blew, they whispered a century of secrets to passers-by. I had yet to hear one of those secrets, but my imagination was ready to conjure up what they might be.

The large, rambling house actually looked like a miniature castle. It appeared to be a replica of the larger monstrosities that dotted the countryside in Europe. The bricks sparkled with a strange shimmering lustre under the rays of the daytime sun. I had wondered many times if it were a sleeping castle waiting for its—and then I would shake my head, discarding such juvenile fairytale thoughts. Silly me—waiting for what? I could not allow the dream to go that far, not yet.

My deep-seated curiosity continued nagging at my better sense—the sense my mother had always told me to keep at the forefront of my priorities. Why I chose such a potentially stormy evening for a late-night walk to discover who lived in that house is still beyond my comprehension. I have rationalized that the night had been unusually hot for the month of October and my apartment very stuffy. My landlord did not believe in wasting electricity on an air conditioner, particularly in the fall. Instead of taking that stroll, especially at such a late hour, I should have been content to stay home, where I would have been safe. I could have had some popcorn, watched a good movie, put my feet up, and relaxed. How different my life would have been had I done that!

However, as I reflect back on the events now, I often wonder if it was the *night* that had chosen *me*.

I found myself creeping stealthily up to the main door. Should I knock? *Don't be silly*, I thought to myself. What would I say? *Hi, I was just passing by. I'm new in the area and just want to meet my neighbours.* For God's sake, by the time I had arrived at the house it was after 11:00—almost midnight, actually! What could I have been thinking? Who would want to be bothered at this ungodly hour?

I let my hand drop back down to my side. Curiosity still pestered me, though, so I proceeded to move slowly along the wall toward the large bay window that jutted out of the front part of the house just to the right of the main door. I noticed a small night light flickering through the curtains. Maybe there was someone still up reading or watching television. After all, the hour was not that late for those who liked to catch the evening news. Maybe just a glimpse of a human entity would satisfy my inquisitiveness.

I inched slowly over to the window and peered into the shadowy room. The flickering light, to my surprise, was a candle, and its light glowed on a massive figure that appeared to be dressed in black. Not that being dressed in black was strange—lots of people wear black. But there was something strange about the figure sitting in the armchair. Whoever it was, was wearing something with a high, stiff collar that covered half their face, making it extremely difficult for me to distinguish any features. And there was no late-night news on the television. There was no television. The figure was just sitting there, with not even a book in hand to pass away the time.

Once again, I found myself conjuring up foolish thoughts of *what* might be sitting in the chair. Of course it was a human—what else could it be? People were entitled to eccentric tastes, especially in their own homes. After living in Toronto for so long, I had seen things that would make my great-grandmother's poker-straight hair curl, and I had a tendency to over-sensationalize things. My mother had mentioned, on many occasions, that my imagination would probably land me in trouble one day!

I continued my vigil, nervously waiting for more clues of who resided in this mysterious house. Another shadow entered the room and walked over to the figure in the chair. The two images appeared to be having a quarrel, but from where I crouched against the thick brick wall, I was unable to hear a word. The house seemed quite soundproof. Besides, the noisy night melodies of the crickets kept any other sounds from my ears.

The standing figure waved its arms and turned to leave the room. I observed long black hair sweeping around the body as it moved, but she, as I now presumed by the hair, did not get far. The figure in the chair stood up. He, as I presumed by the height, was wearing a cape! He grabbed the woman by the wrist and spun her around to face him. By the looks of things, I had landed myself in a family squabble, and I felt a twinge of guilt for being a "peeping Tomasina."

I was unable to pull my eyes away from the scene. I stared more closely at the figures, and my heart leapt into my mouth. "It can't be," I stammered. "It just can't be!" I pinched my arm. I was real. I ran my hand along the window ledge. It was real. I peered through the window again. I watched as the man snarled at the woman, and when his mouth opened I saw the two grotesque fangs protruding from within! They looked so real. But how—how could this be? He threw his head back and let out a hideous laugh. At least that is what it looked like to me!

I started to shake. Halloween around the corner or not, that man in there was too real for comfort! I had to get away. I panicked, spun around, and began to run. I did not get far, though. I half-turned to get another glimpse of the house I was fleeing from. Whatever it was I ran into was a lot harder than my body. All I remembered later was that I felt myself spinning down a tunnel of darkness, into a deathly blackness, deeper than the deepest of sleeps.

CHAPTER 2

Her

Upon awakening, I found myself enclosed in a beautiful canopy bed. Heavy red curtains hung from the overhead wooden bar that extended around the perimeter of the bed. I reached out to touch the material, and my fingertips sank into the lush velvet. The dark wood on the headboard and bedposts was distinctive. I was sure the bed dated back at least to the 1700s. I was slightly startled when I noticed the wood was grooved with intricate carvings of creatures.

The creatures were diabolical. They could be considered human if one were to stretch one's imagination, yet there was an even greater animal-like form to them. If I looked at them from a certain angle, the creatures could be a pack of wild wolves. I also detected the strangest thing—each one had two enormous incisors protruding from its snarling snout, much like the incisors I had noticed on the man in the room. I was aware that wolves had fangs, but not like these ones!

I dared to peer through a crack in the curtain. Sitting in a chair, not far from the door, was a lady. She had long black hair, like the woman I had seen through the window. I assumed it was the same one. She turned her head toward the bed as she sensed my stirring. I tried not to breathe. I did not feel ready yet to encounter anyone. Too late.

"Finally, you are awake." She rose from her chair, walked over to the bed, and drew back the curtain. "You have slept long. It was a nasty blow you took when you ran into the statue in our garden." She sat down on the edge of the bed.

I tried to catch my breath. Earlier, I had only observed the lady from a distance. Now, up close, I could see that she was beautiful, more so than I thought possible for any woman to be. Never, and I mean never, had I ever witnessed such perfection of body and face.

Her hair was of the deepest ebony. It lay in ripples down her back, falling far below her waist, tickling at her calves. Her eyes were deep pools of darkness, and I could not help wondering what secrets they concealed. Her cheeks and lips possessed a natural rosiness that was not created by human touch; it could only have been produced by the mistress of all beauticians, Mother Nature. The ivory smoothness of her skin only emphasized the colour more strongly.

Her body curved in all the fitting places. The sash enclosing the petite waist was slightly loose, as though there were no belt made that was diminutive enough to fit her snugly. Finishing the picture were the hips that curved out softly from the waist, adding a bountiful perfection to the lower extremities.

Then why, I wondered, was this apparently perfect woman dressed in black? With her colouring, she could have worn a deep shade of red, or sapphire. Black was such a sombre colour, usually reserved for funerals and evil creatures, or for women who tried to hide their extra pounds. At least that is what some women believed, but I knew it was actually a fallacy, having read an article on the subject. Black could be very becoming on a woman with the right skin tone for it. This woman did not appear evil, nor was she overweight. Possibly she was in mourning, then.

"Where am I?" I finally managed to stutter.

"I cannot say," her voice was a bare whisper. "Only *he* can tell you this—if he wants to."

"What do you mean, 'if *he* wants to'? Who is *he*?" I began to tremble, and it was not just from petty nerves, but from well-grounded, home-grown terror—especially if the *he* she spoke of was the one I had seen in the room—the one with the fangs!

"He is the owner of this house, the ruler within these walls. His word is the ultimate authority in this, *his* domain. Only *he* decides who comes and goes from here, most especially so for those who come without an invitation!" The strange lady's voice had risen to a more audible level.

"What are you talking about? Ultimate authority? His *domain*? We are living in the twentieth century, are we not? Is this some kind of a sick Halloween joke? Time travel is something that only happens in the movies!" My voice trembled with frustration, or was it fear?

"Yes, your world is in the twentieth century," she confirmed. "But ours is not." She paused. "As for this being a sick joke, my dear, I think you will find that joking is one thing the count never does!" There was no mistaking the meaning of that final statement.

I decided to ignore the word *count*, for the moment. Instead of pursuing the suggestion of aristocracy, I dared myself to ask another question. "How long have you been here?"

"Here?"

"Yes, here, in this place."

"I have been here, and there—a bit of everywhere—for what seems to be an eternity." Her lips curled into a peculiar smile as she answered me.

"Well, that is a long time, *eternity*," I retorted with an edge of sarcasm in my words. "Maybe you could translate that into years for me?"

"Years, such as you know them, have no meaning in our world. I have seen thousands of moons ..."

"What about suns?" I choked on the question. I had no idea why I dared such an enquiry; maybe it was because I still held a vivid picture of the man in my short-term memory. The last time I had laid eyes on a creature like him had been in the Dracula movie I had recently watched.

"I don't care for the sun," she whispered huskily.

"Oh, i…i…is it bad for your skin?" I dared to dig further into what might be dangerous ground.

Once again, the peculiar smile. "Something like that." She turned to a long rope that was hanging by the bed and gave it a pull. "Perhaps you would like some refreshments?"

I wondered how long I had been unconscious. My hand moved to my stomach as my innards acknowledged their hunger by growling loudly. I glanced toward the window. It was dark outside. "How long was I sleeping?"

"For a day. As I said, you took quite a nasty blow. Actually, I am surprised you are up this soon," she declared.

There was a knock at the door. The lady stood up. It appeared to me that she slithered across the floor to unlock the large wooden door. The hinges squeaked as the door swung open. A withered old man stood there, apparently awaiting further orders.

His hair was unkempt, reminding me of the style used to depict mad scientists in the movies. His bones bubbled under his skin, giving him the appearance of a gnarled tree trunk that had witnessed too many years of sun and terrible weather.

His body was bent in an awkward position. My first glance of him had suggested irrefutable frailty, but the deeper I gazed beyond the outward appearance, the more I sensed an indefinable strength that could possibly last forever. Elderly people were like that sometimes, I guessed, even though my experience with seniors was quite limited. I had never known my own grandparents, both having passed on before I was born. My only memory of them was their wedding picture, which my mother had kept, well dusted, on the fireplace mantel. My mother had always said that I had inherited my grandmother's long, thick red hair and my grandfather's slim physique.

"Would you please bring us some refreshments," the lady ordered him, a little coolly, I thought.

"The usual, madam?" he droned.

She smiled. "Yes, that will be fine, Max."

I pondered what "the usual" was and also who would be desperate enough to work in what might be a godforsaken place. The lady was a tad weird, and the man she had been arguing with had seemed sinister, to say the least. At that point, I had no idea just how sinister, or how godforsaken, this place truly was!

Max returned a few minutes later with a dinner cart. If I were a betting person, I would have said the cart had been sitting just down the hallway, already fully prepared. "Will that be all, madam?"

"Yes, Max, thank you. You may return for the trays in half an hour." She paused. "Please inform the master that our guest has awakened, and I will be supping with her tonight."

"As you wish, madam." The door squeaked shut as the old man took his leave.

The beautiful lady motioned to the table. "Please, join me."

I stared at the china soup bowls and mugs sitting on a silver tray. Pictures of ancient castles, overgrown with wild vegetation, were painted all around their exteriors. I leaned closer in order to get a better view of the images. Were those wolves hiding in the thickets? Wolves with fangs? They closely resembled the creatures carved on the wooden bed. *How interesting*, I thought to myself, wondering if the castles were actually replicas of real fortresses.

She lifted the lid from the soup bowl. My stomach churned, just about heaving up what dregs might have still been taking refuge there. It was the most ghastly looking food I had ever seen, if one could even imagine it was food.

"W…w…what is that?" I stammered.

"Pudding—blood pudding," she smiled provocatively. "May I serve you a bowl?" The spoon hovered over the pot.

"Ah, no … no thanks. I believe I'll pass, and wait for dessert," I said staring at the liquid in the bowl. It definitely was no ordinary blood pudding, or at least not like the one I had tried while living in Toronto.

A friend had taken me to an Irish pub, and we'd had a breakfast of sliced blood pudding, eggs, and potatoes. When I had asked what the black sausage was on my plate, my friend had laughed and said, "Oh, that is just blood pudding." When she had noticed the startled look on my face, she had explained the pudding was made of animal blood, grains, raisins, and spices. To my surprise, I had found it quite pleasing.

However, such was not the case here; what was in that bowl I could have sworn was honest-to-goodness real blood, the kind that flows through the veins of every red-blooded mammal! I shook my head in an attempt to cast out such thoughts.

"Oh dear, I am so, so sorry! How absolutely thoughtless of me; I should have known better. I will get Max to bring you something else, something more palatable to your taste buds." The lady in black moved toward the bell. Again I noticed that peculiar curl at the corner of her lips.

"No … please … its okay; don't bother yourself, or Max. I should just be getting on my way. I'm not really that hungry. I'll be able to grab a bite to eat when I get home."

"Oh no, I insist you stay! Maybe you just need a bit more rest to regain your appetite. You do look a little pale still. Max can bring something up before he retires for the night." Once again, the peculiar smile.

"If you don't mind, and I don't mean to insult your hospitality, I would really rather just be going on my way. If I don't arrive home soon, my family will miss me. My mother expects a call from me at least every three days, and I never leave for any great length of time without giving her some kind of word." There was no need for this lady to know my mother had already passed away. "If you would be kind enough to show me the door—front, back, any one will do; I'll find my way from there."

I noticed her eyebrows elevate sharply.

"Well," I stood up, not having received the answer I was looking for. "Would you mind just telling me the way out, then?" I said with more firmness in my words.

"Oh no, I cannot tell, or show, you the way out. You may not leave yet. I thought I had already made that quite clear to you. He must see you first. Only he decides who leaves here." The words flowed smoothly off her tongue; soft enough they were, yet at the same time their tone left a weird, creepy feeling in my bones.

"Yes, I know you said that before, but I really must insist that I leave *now*." I was desperately trying to get my point across. "When do you think he will see me?" I inquired.

"When he is ready." There was an annoyed look on the lady's face.

I stood up and started to pace. What kind of a nightmare was this? *The worst*, I told myself. Why couldn't I simply be like normal people? I could have continued to admire the old house from a distance, from the sidewalk by the street. But oh no, not me! I'd had to walk across the yard and up onto the porch. I'd had to look in the window! And for what reason—just to satisfy my insatiable curiosity? What had I landed myself in? Only God knew at that moment, but I wished He had been kind enough to send me a heavenly vision that would have steered my feet away from their path-wandering tendencies that night!

The situation I found myself in was too ridiculous to even resemble reality. In the room with me was an intriguing black-robed beauty! She was true enough to life. Then there was the blood pudding, made with what appeared to be real blood! Finally, there was the tall mysterious man in a high-collared black cape—a man with fangs! Was he the *him* the lady constantly referred to, the man who claimed to be the ruler of this domain? I had yet to find out if this elusive man, who was referred to as the count, was real—or if the bump on my head had been so severe that my overactive imagination had finally taken total possession of my mind.

I shuffled cautiously over to the window and tried to grasp my bearings. I turned and glanced back at the lady. She was eating, or should I say *slurping*, from her mug, and from the looks of it she was relishing every drop of her drink. A bead of blood escaped the side of the cup and dribbled from the corner of her mouth. Her tongue flicked quickly through her open lips, rescuing the stray droplet. My stomach churned, and I felt as though I were going to vomit for the second time that evening. I turned back to my window, placed my hands on the handles, and attempted to open it. It would not budge.

"There is no use trying to leave." Her voice startled me. "As I told you, only he will decide if and when you may go."

Goosebumps ran up and down my flesh. Who was *he*? What did the lady mean by "if and when"? What power did he wield over this beautiful woman; for that matter, what power did he think he held over me? This was a free country. People came and went as they pleased, yet she had said this was *his* domain. Did that mean he was above the law of the land? *This is Canada*, I mused to myself. *Canadians are protected by the Charter of Rights and Freedoms!* Was he so powerful that he could reach beyond even its protections?

My imagination began spinning again. Maybe I had just landed myself in the home of some big Mafia kingpin who thought I was spying for one of his rivals! Oh Lord, if he thought that, then what would my fate be? Didn't he realize I was not a person of any great importance? I would not dare say a word about anything. Besides, I knew nothing to say anything about!

And who was this mysterious woman? Wife? Lover? Employee? I deduced, from the looks of her, that she fell into the category of wife or lover. No man in his right mind would hire such a beauty if he were in a marriage and wanted to preserve its sanctity! She appeared nice, on the surface, but one could never really tell what might be buried deep under all that serene beauty. I had observed women similar to her at some of the office parties I had attended in Toronto. They were all glamour on the surface, but inside, they were rotten to the core.

What motive could there be for holding me here? Who was he? *What* was he? The same questions kept churning over and over in my mind, creating my own internal horror film. I could feel the tears creeping upward, toward my throat, as I considered my possible predicament. All the recent events continued to race through my mind. Halloween character? Mafia kingpin? Would my fate differ in either case? There was a knock at the door. I held my tears in check; maybe it would be him, coming to say that I could go home. The lady opened the door. Max entered.

"Are you finished, madam?"

"Yes, thank you, Max."

"Was everything to your taste?"

"Perfectly—to mine, that is. I don't believe our guest was very pleased, though; perhaps you could fix something more to her preference for later?" she suggested.

"Yes, madam," Max mumbled.

I shuddered again as an eerie sensation gripped me. I watched as Max gathered everything together and ambled out of the room. The lady closed the door behind him and then turned to me, with that smile. I was wondering by now why she smiled like this. It was not really a friendly smile, and yet it was not hostile, either. It was just, as I have been saying, peculiar.

"You look as though you would like to rest awhile longer; you are still so pale." She glanced toward the window where I was standing. I followed her gaze and noticed the sun was beginning to peek up over the horizon.

She certainly was right about the tired part. I could not shake the fatigue that seemed to have overtaken my body, even though I had been asleep for twenty-four hours. It must be the stress. My mother had always said that stress caused turmoil in the system. My mother had never seemed stressed about anything; I had always wondered how she could remain so calm in the most critical situations. Maybe it had been her simple lifestyle.

"I must retire now," she informed me. "As I mentioned earlier, if you need anything, just ring the bell. Max will see to your needs. He will bring something more edible to you, if you wish."

I could not let her depart without one last-ditch effort to get out of there. "I just want to go home," I choked the words out, tears welling in my eyes.

The lady walked over to the door before she returned an answer. "I will inform him that you wish to see him."

"I don't want to see him!" I screamed. "I want to go home!"

"I will speak to him." Her lips shut in a firm line that declared the conversation was over. The door squeaked shut behind her. There was a clicking sound as the lock fell into place. I was left alone to whatever misery I could conjure up in my mind.

I paced around the room. I had to get out! But to where? And how? Everything seemed to be locked. Wait! I ran to the door. Maybe I had only imagined the click. I tried to open it. My shoulders sagged in desperation. How dare she do that to me! I walked, with faltering steps, back to the bed and lay down. I stared up at the ceiling. Painted creatures, evil and unfamiliar, stared back at me.

The tears began to pour, finally breaking free from their restraining barriers. I rolled over and buried my face in the pillow. Sleep would ease my pain and break me out of this horrid dream I had landed in. When I awoke I would be in my own cosy little apartment, asleep on the couch with a TV remote in my hand. The alarm would wake me in the morning. I would get up, get dressed, and go to work—that was reality! That was what I hoped for. That is what I prayed for. Blessed sleep would make the nightmare go away.

～

I awoke with a start. I was still in the locked room. There was no TV, no remote control in my hand, no comfortable familiarity—not even my cursed alarm clock buzzing me into wakefulness. The sun was shining brightly into my room. My stomach rumbled hungrily, reminding me once again of just how famished I was. I could not remember when my last meal had been; I presumed it had been supper on the night of my little walk. I would have to chance eating something, even if it was not totally to my liking. A sixth sense told me I was going to need a plan to escape from this place, and in order to do that, I would require all of my strength!

I pulled the rope, and within seconds there was a knock on the door.

I was not given time to offer a verbal invitation to enter. A key turned in the lock and the door swung open.

"You called, miss?" Max asked.

"Yes. Would it be possible to have something to eat now, please? The lady told me you could prepare something to my taste."

"What would you like, miss?" He said the magic words, confirming that there just might be some food fit for human consumption in this place.

"Do you have eggs, toast, coffee, and juice?" I asked hopefully.

"How would you like your eggs done, miss?"

I breathed a sigh of relief. "Over easy, please."

"As you wish, miss," Max said as he turned and left. I heard the key click in the lock.

Max certainly was not a man to mince words. I wondered what his role was, besides that of a butler. Were there a cook and a housekeeper as well? Would he be passing my request on to some overweight, jolly chef who wore huge grease-stained aprons and worked cheerily away in a bright, spotless kitchen? No matter, I reasoned; at least I was going to have some decent food. It was of no consequence to me who cooked it or what they looked like.

A vision of the lady in black, sipping at the blood pudding, passed before my eyes. I shuddered. I walked over to the window, pushed aside the curtain, and surveyed the gardens, searching for another form of human life. Nothing—only flowers and grass and trees. I turned around as I heard the key in the door. Max re-entered, carrying a tray laden with my food. The aroma teased my nostrils.

"I'll set it here, miss?" Max asked as he put the tray down on a small table by the window.

"Yes, thank you, Max." I paused. "Where is the lady?" I asked.

"Resting, miss."

"But it is daytime," I remarked curiously.

"Yes, miss. That it is," Max replied matter-of-factly, not offering further information.

"How long will she be resting? When will I see her again? She promised to talk to him, whoever he is, about allowing me to leave."

"When the sun goes down, they will both be up. You will see her then. As for him, I cannot say. He will see you when he is ready to see you, not at your desired time," Max articulated.

"Do they work nights?"

"Work nights?" Max appeared puzzled.

"Yes, you know—a job—the night shift?"

"Oh! Yes, sorry. Yes, something like that," was the evasive reply.

Everything was beginning to add up—add up to an incredibly unbelievable story! I thought these kinds of things only happened in the movies or on the pages of a book, thanks to some writer's overactive imagination. I was not ready yet to accept how my suspicions were adding up. I had a pretty big hunch that I had encountered a real live vampire, and I presumed that the lady in black was not the only vampire in this house. I was willing to bet my bottom dollar that *he* was the head honcho, maybe even the king of vampires himself—Dracula!

It was him I was truly terrified to meet! My hand reached up to my throat, brushing against my necklace, and I breathed a sigh of relief. Thank goodness! I had worn the crucifix that had been my grandmother's and been passed, first to my mother, and then to me, when I had gone off to college. I wore it a lot, because it always gave me a feeling of closeness to my mother. I had an eerie feeling I was going to require its assistance somewhere down the line; I prayed it would carry the power I was going to need if that moment arrived.

Max lit the candles that were scattered around the room. "It will be dark soon," he noted. "You will need this light."

"Why the candles?" I inquired. "Do the light switches not work?"

Max smirked. "The switches do not work. The master had them disconnected. He doesn't cater to a lot of modern conveniences; he prefers to lead a simple life."

Max backed out of the room. I heard the door lock click into place. Once again, I found myself alone. I had to think fast. It would be dark soon. There had to be a way of getting it through to the lady in black that I wished to leave right away. I had no desire whatsoever to meet with him, whoever or whatever he was! Could she be my hope of escape, or was she too connected to and controlled by him to be able to assist me?

I sat down at the little table and tried to enjoy my meal. Whoever was whipping up the real food in this place should open a restaurant. Even though my stomach was in a churning turmoil, I had never tasted anything quite so delicious.

My meal finished, I pushed the dishes aside and stared out the window again. The sun was sinking slowly in the west; the shadows were emerging from their hiding places and beginning to dance in the night garden. I stood up, went over to the bed, and lay down on the soft comforter. Just before I closed my eyes, I thought I heard a wolf howl, long and mournful in its eeriness, but that was not possible, was it? There were no wolves in the city—none that I had heard of, anyway.

CHAPTER 3

The First Meeting

I must have dozed off, for I was awakened by a hand gently shaking my shoulder. I jolted up. There she was again, standing there, smiling down at me with that mysterious smile of hers, still so breathtakingly beautiful. She must have slept well, I thought. I wondered how I looked after my dream-troubled sleep. I gazed around the room, trying to locate a mirror. There was not one anywhere in which to observe my disarray.

"You look lovely this evening," I offered.

"He is ready to see you now," she stated coolly, ignoring my comment. "He has sent me to fetch you. We will all dine together tonight." The lady paused. "He regrets any inconvenience that may have been caused you last night, but he had an urgent matter that needed his attention. By the time he returned, it was very late."

You mean early, I thought to myself. These people really had their days and nights mixed up.

"It must be tough having your husband work nights." I was fishing.

The lady tilted her head and smiled her peculiar smile. Once again, she chose to ignore my comment.

24

I decided on another avenue of conversation. "By the way, what is your name?" I thought I should ask, since I was getting tired of mentally referring to her as "the lady in black."

"Teresa," she replied, "and yours?"

"Mine?" I had not expected her to want to know mine, since up until now she had not bothered to ask. "Mine is Ginny, at least that is what my friends call me. Short for Virginia."

"Very well, Virginia." Teresa emphasized my proper name, leaving me to assume that friendship was out of the question. "Follow me, please."

I followed Teresa into a large hallway, which was lit by wall candle-lamps. From behind pieces of furniture, flickering shadows lunged at me from their concealed corners. My nerves were tense as I searched for a possible escape route from the nightmare I seemed to be trapped in.

"Here we are," Teresa said as she opened a large double door and showed me into an oversized dining room.

I was sure, upon entering the room, that I must be mistaken about my theory of vampires living here. Most of the vampire homes I had seen in the movies had been overrun with dust and cobwebs. This place shone immaculately. Whoever lived here must be filthy rich and probably employed several servants. Most likely they were just moneyed people who had some weird fetishes, and they were going to teach me a lesson for having trespassed on their property. Why in the world they would want to keep insignificant me around for questioning was beyond my comprehension. They would probably make their point and then let me go—I hoped.

I was positive the furniture in the dining room dated back to the same era as the bedroom furnishings. It was of the finest quality, in superb condition, and it was arranged quite proficiently within the room. All the woods were dark and shiny, a reflection of the years of tender, loving care.

An ornate candle chandelier hung from the centre of a painted ceiling. Blue porcelain roses hung from each umbrella-like candle holder.

The base of the chandelier resembled a spinning top and was painted with soft pink roses. A gold chain travelled to the ceiling, embedding itself into an arrangement of shimmering gold leaves. The candles cast star-like reflections on the ceiling paintings, radiating a night-time effect in the room. Smaller candle lights were fastened all around on the walls; some were lit, some were not.

The rug under the huge table in the centre of the room appeared Persian in origin. It was adorned with the strangest conglomeration of pictures. As I studied them, I realized that I was looking at a massive tree laden with branches. Each limb had a pale-yellow life form clutching at its tip. There were no leaves upon the limbs. The tree trunk was a mixture of reddish hues. All were scattered across a pitch-black background.

Imposing paintings of old, gloomy mansions and castles and mysterious people hung on the walls. All the individuals in the paintings wore black. All the men were intense. All the women had peculiar smiles. Now I knew where Teresa's smile originated, and I wondered if I could assume she was related to all these women.

Max gave me a start when he entered the room pushing his little cart. *Does the man ever sleep?* I thought to myself.

"The master will be here in a moment, madam," he informed Teresa. "He has asked me to have everything prepared. He also asked me to inform you that he regrets he will not be able to stay long. Things did not go well for him last night, as I am sure you already know. I am afraid he must go out again tonight. However, before leaving, he said he would like to attend to this little matter." Max nodded his head toward me.

Little matter, I thought. I was a little matter! How dare this old man refer to me as though I were some sort of an inconvenience! However, on second consideration, I hoped whatever was going to happen to me would only *be* a little matter, and I would be allowed to go on my merry way once they made their point. It was not as though I had broken into their home and stolen their possessions. I had only foolishly trespassed onto their grounds and peeked in their window. Then, even more foolishly, I had bumped into one of the garden statues while trying to leave in a panic. The "count" was probably just going to make sure I was okay and then warn me never to set foot on his property again. I saw no reason for further detainment.

Max pulled out a side chair near the head of the table for Teresa. I was directed to sit across from her. He did not pull out my chair, which, at the time, I felt was quite rude. Teresa and I stared at each other across the massive table. God, her eyes were mysterious!

My fingers began to toy with the ruby lace cloth. I lowered my eyes, in order to have a better glimpse of the intricately crocheted figures as well as an ample excuse to release myself from Teresa's penetrating gaze. I shivered to see demons of every evil sort glaring at me. They almost seemed real. I looked up again. Teresa gave me a smile. I returned an uneasy one.

I wondered at the need for such a vast dining table; it must have stretched at least fifteen feet. At the head sat a huge captain's chair. A slightly smaller replica mirrored it at the opposite end. Six mates were set evenly down each side, at firm attention, like guarding foot soldiers.

I looked closely at the backs of the chairs, trying to make some sense of their elaborate carvings. Suddenly, it dawned upon me what I was seeing. On the back of each chair were carvings of faces with open mouths, exposing vicious-looking fangs. The faces were all different from one another, but each, in its own way, could freeze the blood of an ordinary person like me. The cushions on the chairs had been designed to match the rug. They were adorned with intricately embroidered tapestries of black and yellow roses, bouncing on a sea of red waves. I shuddered just wondering what the sea of red was meant to represent!

My thoughts returned to the need for such a large table. So far, I knew of only three people living in this house. Were there more? If so, what were they like? Of course, there had to be a cook, as I assumed Max could not do all the work a house this large would require. Regardless, I felt that a much smaller table would have sufficed for the three individuals who would be dining tonight.

A lofty shadow crowded the doorway. "Ah, here we are at last!"

The voice oozed silky eloquence. "Teresa, my darling, how are you this evening? I missed your delectable company yesternight." He strolled over to Teresa. She extended her hand and he brushed it with what looked like a light, rather cold, unemotional kiss.

"And you," he said, turning to me. "How is our unexpected guest tonight? It is not often that we have guests—how shall I say it now?—" He paused and then continued in his smooth voice, "drop in on us. Normally, I like to *invite* my guests; it is less complicated that way for me. I trust that our hospitality has been adequate?" He flashed me half a smile. I did not notice the fangs that I had previously observed. Possibly I had been mistaken.

I returned him a half smile and summoned every ounce of courage I could before replying. "I am well, thank you. Your hospitality has been adequate; however, I would like to leave. My family, especially my mother, will be missing me by now. As I informed Teresa yesterday, she expects a call from me every three days. You know how mothers can be when their daughters are out on their own. My mother is worse than most—always calling, fussing, making sure I am eating properly, that I am getting enough sleep, that I'm not out partying too much. She doesn't have a lot of use for most of the members of my generation—" What was I doing? I could not believe how I had just run off at the mouth. Whatever had possessed me? I hoped he would not detect the devious undertone in my voice. Was there one? I thought there might have been. I would have to be extremely careful, as he appeared to be intensely intuitive to his surroundings.

"Maybe you have a phone, so I can call her?" I continued. Surely there was someone out there whom I could reach to come to my rescue.

My hopes were quickly dashed. "We have no phone here. I have no desire to be bothered by outsiders. As I mentioned, invitations are at my request, and I have my own means of contacting people. A phone is nothing more than an inconvenience for me," the count stated.

"But how do you get along without a phone?" I asked.

"Quite nicely," he grinned, confirming to me that the lack of conveniences was not inconvenient for this man. I shook my head. Damn, his eyes were piercing! I felt as though he were undressing every inch of me as we conversed.

"You must realize, my dear," he began, changing the subject, "there is a time and a place for everything, and now it is time to sup, and we are at the place to do so. We will discuss the possibility of your leaving later. Max, serve the meal now, please." He snapped his fingers and waved his hand at the patiently waiting Max. The subject of my departure was terminated.

I shuddered to think what might be on my plate, not to mention what would be on theirs! Max set my dish in front of me. I gazed at the spotlessly polished silver. Etchings of wild rose bushes were scattered randomly around on the precious metal, their piercing thorns creeping around the exterior perimeters of the plate under the silvery dome.

Max removed the lid. I breathed a sigh of relief as I looked down on a well-cooked steak garnished with buttery baby potatoes and crisp green beans.

"Wine, miss?" Max asked.

"No, thank you," I answered, afraid of what might actually be poured into my goblet.

Max returned my intended wine to the tray and retrieved a different bottle. He approached the count's and then Teresa's place settings and poured the contents into their wineglasses. I was positive, just from observing the texture of the liquid, that Max was not pouring a vintage wine!

I dared to glance over at the dishes Max set before my hosts—just as I expected. I have seen rare steaks before, but usually there is at least a sign of some braising!

The count turned to Teresa. His fork hovered in the air, a piece of red meat dripping from the end of it. "Teresa, my darling, have you filled our guest in on any details yet?"

"No, Count, I have not," she whispered. I wondered why she whispered. I wondered why she did not look him directly in the eyes. Was she afraid of him?

A count? She kept referring to him as "Count." Had I landed myself in the home of some sort of royal family? Is that why he was so careful about who came and went from his house? But where could he have hailed from? That was the million-dollar question! There were not many royals left in the world—of any notoriety, that is—and if there were an enclave in southern Ontario, I was sure a notation would have appeared somewhere in the presses!

Then there was the question of why they would choose a small, out-of-the-way city like Brantford to make their home. There appeared to be a big difference between the way the royal families of France or England, which I had read about in my history books, selected their living quarters compared to those who might have their roots deep within Transylvania! There I went again—imagining them to be vampires!

"Good. Very good," he said to Teresa. He then turned to me. "What is your name, my dear?"

"Virginia," I stated in a hushed voice. I was not going to try to fool myself with an illusion of forging any kind of friendship with this formidable figure—now or ever, I hoped!

"Ah, such a lovely name—Virginia," the syllables rolled off his tongue. "Such a pretty young woman, too. How unfortunate." He reached over and twirled a stray strand of my hair around his finger. He smiled. This time, I saw the fangs!

The balance of the meal was conducted in silence. I had no desire to watch Teresa and the count consume their meat. Just the thought of them eating raw meat turned my stomach—let alone seeing whatever it was they were drinking from their wineglasses! I ate my own meal, quickly and quietly, with my head bowed. I had to eat well. Encountering this man, or whatever he was, I was even surer I would need every ounce of strength I could acquire to get myself out of the house. I also sensed that my fate was being directed on a much different route than the neat little map I had drawn out so meticulously for myself. And what had he meant by "how unfortunate"? Nothing was adding up, but there was one thing I did know for sure—I was terrified!

The count raised a napkin to his mouth, dabbed the corners of his lips, and then placed it back down on the table. I could not help noticing the tiny red spots dotting the white linen. He raised the wineglass to his lips and downed the balance of its contents in one gulp.

"Teresa darling, would you please bring Virginia to my study when you and she have finished your meals?" It sounded to me more like a command than a request, even though he had said "please." The count glanced at the grandfather clock at the far end of the room. "I must go out again tonight, so please make haste. There is not much time left before the sun will rise again. There are times I detest the seasons of this country."

It was nice to hear him use the word *please* when he spoke to Teresa, but I had a sinking feeling that he got his way with or without the use of good etiquette.

"Yes, Max stated that things had not gone well last night. No major complications, I hope?" Teresa questioned.

"None that cannot be handled." The count's tongue caressed his lips, and he smiled at Teresa. "Don't be long." I noticed there was no *please* this time. He stood and headed for his study, I presumed.

I finished my plate and then gazed up to observe Teresa as she completed her meal. I noticed she did not consume her drink quite as quickly as the count had his. Maybe she did not have the same palate. Should I ask for her help? *Dare* I ask her for help? The count seemed to hold some powerful control over this woman. I wondered again what her role in this house was. Wife? Slave? Hostess? Would she be able to help me even if she wanted to? I decided there was only one way to find out.

"Teresa?" I ventured.

"Yes."

"Is it truly necessary for you to take me to him tonight? Maybe you could just show me the way out. You could tell him I pushed past you, knocked you down, whatever. Please, Teresa, I need your help to get out of here! I do not understand the importance of holding me against my will!" I knew I was begging. Even I could hear the terror in my voice. I also had an eerie feeling, or maybe it was a sixth sense of sorts, that if I stayed here much longer my life would never be the same again.

Teresa frowned. "I don't understand, Virginia. Why do you so desperately want to leave? Has Max said something to you? Has he stepped out of line? I will speak to him if you like. You know it is so hard to get good help nowadays. One never knows whom they can trust." She paused. "But then again, Max has been with us for years; I would trust him with my own well-being, so I really cannot imagine he would try to hurt you. It must be something else. Please tell me; what is the problem? Have we not been the perfect hosts? You, yourself, told the count that our hospitality was adequate." Teresa was acting as if there were nothing wrong with being held against one's will!

I had to think quickly. Maybe there was something in what she had said. Maybe I could play her and Max against each other. She had asked me if Max had stepped out of line. If I could force an argument between him and her, perhaps I could slip away unnoticed and find the door to freedom! It was a chance I was willing to gamble on. After all, what did I have to lose?

"Well, now that you mention it, Teresa," I began, "Max did do something out of line. While you were sleeping, he made advances toward me. I was totally shocked! I never anticipated such a move from him. He ... he's so old and grandfatherly looking." I tried hard to keep my voice edgy. If I were going to play the part, then it would have to be an Academy Award performance. Little did I know, then, that it was the premier of many more performances to come.

"Max!" Teresa turned on the poor old man. I felt a momentary pang of sympathy for him. What if he was as much a victim in this house as I was? Maybe, by telling that horrid lie, I was making his plight even worse!

"Max, how could you? You know the master's rules, and you also know the punishment for breaking them!" Teresa's face took on a worried look, and I thought for a moment that there were tears in the corners of her eyes. Did she care for Max? Did I detect an air of concern for what might happen to him? Was his relationship to her more than that of a multi-tasking household butler? Was he her protector from the rage of the count?

Poor Max. Oh God, what had I done? It was not usually in my nature to intentionally harm anyone. His mouth hung half-open. There was such a look of tortured pain on his face that for a fleeting moment I truly felt guilty about what I was doing. But the moment passed quickly, for I realized that, above all else, self-preservation had to be my utmost concern.

"Madame, I assure you, I never touched the young miss. Surely you know I am not capable of such an act!" Max swung his attention to me. "Why would you contend such a deed, miss? I have never in all my years, and they have been many, done such a thing to a woman! How could you even suggest this?" There was a pleading tone to his words. He was wringing his bony hands as if he were trying to squeeze the nervous droplets from them.

"What do you mean?" I retorted. "How can you stand there and blatantly lie in front of Teresa? You are a dirty old man who would have liked nothing better than to put your grimy paws all over me. Admit it; why don't you just admit it?" My voice swelled with anger. "You knew that she and the count were resting and you probably figured I would never dare to tell! Well, I have told! You are a detestable man to take advantage of a defenceless female guest in such a manner!" I ended with a flourish.

Max could no longer control his trembling. I realized he was more than afraid. He was petrified. He groped for my hand. "Please, miss, you don't know him—you have no idea what he is capable of! If he should think for a moment that I had laid even one tiny finger on you, a guest in his home, I could not guess what fury he would inflict upon me. Please, for the sake of all the saints that you believe in, here on earth and in the heavens—for the sake of my soul, of my existence—please confess to Teresa that you are lying. I shall forgive you for this assault on me, because I know it is only your desperation to leave here that makes you accuse me. Ple-e-e-ease," his voice faded away into a forlorn, moaning sound. His face was riddled with fear as he stood there, helpless to stop me as I plunged onward with my deceitful plan.

I ripped my hand away. "Don't touch me, you perverted beast! Even here, in front of Teresa, you use any excuse to touch me with your diseased hands!" Admittedly, pity had tried to stir my heart again as he had spoken, but only momentarily. I had already stepped over the line of deceit and my life took precedence over all other emotions. There was no turning back. Besides, as the allegation had been uttered, I sensed that it was already too late for Max. I had sealed his fate with my first accusation. I also had an eerie sensation that there was another set of eyes in the room, eyes that were taking in the entire scene—*HIS* eyes!

"Teresa, please believe me! I never touched her!" Max turned despairingly back to Teresa.

"She is so convincing, Max; I don't know ..." Teresa's brow furrowed. She turned away. "The count will be most upset at this turn of events. I ..."

I saw my chance. They had their backs to me. I dodged for the door and slipped into the shadowy hallway. I ran. I had no idea where I was going, but I knew I had to free myself from this place. An open door appeared amongst the shadows just ahead of me. Was it the door to my freedom? I had no choice but to enter it and find out. Teresa and Max had discovered my escape and I heard their cries of despair. Any second now they would be running out of the dining room to retrieve me before *he* found out.

I slid through the opening and found myself at the top of a long spiral staircase. Quickly, I turned and closed the door. Hopefully, they had not noticed where I had exited.

I began running down the stairs, taking some of them two at a time. I stumbled several times in my haste, but the railing saved me from tumbling to the bottom. I prayed that wherever these steps led, it would be better than where I had just been. I could smell the moisture from the walls. I could hear dripping water up ahead. All of a sudden I felt a rush of fresh air. I could not believe my good fortune; I had actually managed to stumble on a way out! I wanted to shout for joy but did not dare for fear they would hear me. They were most likely in hot pursuit, and with my freedom but a breath away, I was not willing to take any unnecessary chances.

The stairs exited into a small courtyard, which I presumed had in the past been used for the lords and ladies of this mansion to get into their carriages. Rain poured down, drenching my body. Cool, cleansing rain washed this place from my skin and my clothes. I was free! The smell of freedom was so sensuous to my quivering nostrils, and I lifted my face to the night sky.

CHAPTER 4

Him

Something flew past my face and landed on the courtyard wall in front of me. I imagined I could see two tiny, bright red lights emanating from whatever it was. Could it be? I did not want to believe my eyes. I started to shake. It could not be! How was it possible? I had to find a way out of here.

I knew there must be an exit somewhere. I began groping desperately along the walls. The darkness of the stormy night was making it exceedingly difficult for me to locate the door. The angry heavens opened even further, and the rain began falling in thick sheets, blurring my already limited vision.

The thing fluttered over my head. I ducked, hoping to ward off an attack. Oh my God, just as I thought, it was a bat—a huge one, too! The pieces of this puzzling place were still fitting too conveniently into place. I was tired of the whole game. All I wanted to do was quit and go home. Why would they not just let me go? What reason was there to detain a nobody like me?

A feeling of terror, much greater than I had ever deemed possible, rose within me. Bats blended in too well with everything else I had been bumping into in the last twenty-four hours. But then again, it was an old house. Realistically, I knew that these kinds of rodents could reside in such places. However, the brief sightings of *his* fangs loomed in my mind again, and from all the vampire movies I had watched, I knew that bats were one of the creatures *they* could become!

My fingers touched a wooden plank. Thank God—the door! Now all I had to do was find the latch. I continued groping along, searching desperately. Finally, I was rewarded; my hand bumped against a steel bolt. I attempted to push it across. I could not fail now. Beads of sweat broke out on my forehead, mingling with the rain that was drenching me from above. The bolt would not budge. I strained harder. Why would the latch not move? I got my answer as I drew in a whiff of the aged rustiness of the metal.

"There is no use, my dear Virginia. This door has not been used for years. The latch is quite rusty. I have no need of this gate. There is no escape for you here!" It was a voice that sent unadulterated terror through my veins. It was *his* voice!

I flattened my back against the door and swung around to face the speaker. My eyes darted around, searching diligently for the bat. Logic told me it would be gone and in its place would be the count.

"Virginia darling, what is the meaning of this? Why are you running from us? You said our hospitality was adequate." The count grabbed hold of my wrist and gently pulled me toward him.

I could not take my eyes from his face. His eyes were like two powerful magnets, piercing my soul and drawing every particle of my being to the surface. The features of his face were not so handsome, yet there was a chiselled perfection to them. Compared to the count, John had been a mere boy, far from the age of maturity. At that moment, I had no idea just how far apart they were!

My knees felt ready to collapse beneath me. For reasons unknown to me at that time, I was unable to resist him. I found it impossible to fight whatever power it was this man possessed. I fell limply against his chest. He wrapped me in his cape and led me back up the stairs that only moments before had promised me freedom.

Teresa and Max were waiting in the study when we entered. I glanced at Teresa. There was a tiny cut and a trickle of blood at the corner of her lips. Her eyes were red and swollen. I ventured a look at Max, but he turned away with his head bowed low. What had I done to them? Had he had time, during the short space of my flight, to inflict such a harsh reprimand on them? Teresa had mentioned something about punishment, or had it been Max who had expressed such graphic fear in the dining room? Come to think of it, it had been both of them! And judging by what I was witnessing now, the count's punishments were dealt out quickly, with not a single moment allowed for explanation and not a single consideration of mercy!

"Teresa, Max," the count opened the conversation. "I have retrieved our little bird that you so carelessly let fly from your keeping." He reached over to Teresa and caressed her cheek. "I am so sorry, Teresa darling. I never meant to hurt you, but you, of all those around me, should know how angry I become when I am disobeyed, or worse yet, when someone is careless with their responsibilities. This little incident has cost me much time. I won't be able to go out tonight, and when I cannot get out, we all suffer, right?" He removed his hand from Teresa's cheek. "Ah well, no matter." The count returned his attention to me. "I shall just have to seek solace elsewhere." He threw back his head and laughed. Evil charged the room.

~

Before I had time to think about my next move, Max was ushering me back to my room. I would have given anything at that moment to tell him how sorry I was about what had happened, but he looked so distant. He probably would not have believed me, anyway. As he shuffled along beside me, I could see the marks of four long scratches on his cheek and the purplish-red swelling all around the marks. I wanted desperately to cry out words of apology, to take back every lying word I had said about him, but I also knew that my only reason for remorse was because it had all been in vain. Max and Teresa had been punished. I was still being held captive; I was still subject to an unknown fate. Had I escaped, I would not have been aware of their misfortune and would have had nothing to feel guilty about.

Max opened the door to my room and gave me a shove. The harshness of his action startled me. Despite my earlier accusations, Max had never touched me, except for the grip of pleading in the dining room. I guess he figured I deserved that push after having accused him of a worse assault. He was probably correct in that assumption, and I was only too willing to grant him his small moment of revenge. He shut my door without saying a word. I listened as the lock clicked into place.

I began to pace. I was becoming quite a proficient pacer. I wondered if there was any hope of me getting out alive. There was no escaping the count's all-seeing eyes. And who would even miss me outside this place? I had lied about family. I had none in this city. To be brutally frank, I had none anywhere. I had been orphaned at the age of nineteen, when my parents had been killed in a bus accident while vacationing in Mexico. I had been in summer school the year they had taken that trip. My parents had both been only children, so there were no aunts or uncles to take care of me. Their lawyer had been set as guardian and administrator of their estate. My college tuition had been paid from a trust fund, but it had not been enough for me to go to university and study what I really wanted to.

In essence, there was absolutely no one out there who truly cared what happened to me—no one. John would not care. Ever since I had kicked him and his airheaded blond trollop out of my apartment, I had not had so much as a phone call from him to inquire how I was coping with the scrap of a life he had left me! What a selfish bastard he was, especially after I had supported him for so long. And what a naïve fool I had been to do that! I felt as if I had been orphaned all over again.

Even at my place of employment I was so new that it could be months before anyone missed me or wondered what had happened to the new girl. They would think I was just another secretary who could not take the pressure of a busy law firm and had decided to quit without giving notice so that she would not have to face the boss. I was sure that is what most of them would be saying. Of course, I had been extremely selective about whom I had associated with, or maybe I should say cautious, but the end result was the same—I had not made even one friend during the short time I had been in Brantford. So who out there would miss me enough to instigate an investigation into my untimely disappearance? And if, by a fluke, my new boss did think to call Mr. Carverson, he would probably say to give me some time; he would mention that I had just been through a rough period in my life; I would return to my senses. I was a good girl, worth having on board, etc., etc. Then again, maybe he would not bother to say much of anything at all—out of sight, out of mind.

In short, I was alone. I was even more alone in this strange world I had happened upon. "Oh God! Oh God!" The plea wrenched out between my sobs. Finally, I slept.

I awoke with a shudder; something was standing over me—a dark shadow. I opened my eyes wide. There stood my nightmare. Once again I had that horrid feeling, a sensation of helplessness. I could not control myself. His eyes were melting the marrow in the deepest depths of my bones. I strained to look away from his face, but the magnetism was too intense for my weakened senses.

"Come, my dear," his voice was so soothing. His arms beckoned me. "Come to me."

I staggered out of my bed and fell willingly into his arms. I lifted my face to his and longed for his lips to devour mine. I was totally powerless to arrest these emotions. I hated my desire, but I simply had no command over it. I did not wish for the count to end the moment with just a kiss. It was beyond my comprehension why I yearned for him to consume every inch of me. "Oh God, please forgive me!" I moaned.

A vicious snarl startled me back to reality. I was hurled across the room, and I smashed against the door. Pain seared through my back, and I had to gasp for my next breath. The powerful spell he had cast on me was broken as he stood there yelling furiously.

"How dare you wear that thing around your neck! Take it off! I order you! Take it off!" The count's voice swelled to a roar, and in his moment of rage, I beheld the true ugliness of the creature before me.

His facial skin had turned grey and wrinkled. His eyes were no longer dark and penetrating, but had become streaked with red, fiery lines of fatigue. He appeared to be distraught and totally out of control!

I trembled, not really understanding what he was ranting about. Take what off? The count had undone the top two buttons on my blouse. My hands reached to my neck and brushed against my gold cross. Of course—the sacred symbol—vampires were terrified of crosses! Anything that was holy they could not look upon, or be touched with, for it would sear the very fabric of the skin that covered their dead bones. I knew that much from the various vampire movies I had whiled away endless lonely nights watching. The cross could be my road to freedom! My trump card! I began to breathe easier.

"Take it off! I command you!" The count had raised his cape, trying to hide his face from the religious symbol. If I were to describe his stance then, I would say it bordered on cowardliness—or maybe the fear of something much more powerful than him!

"No!" I shouted. I felt that I was the powerful one now. It was I who held the trump card. This creature, who had terrified and controlled me just moments before, was now cringing behind his cape, his power over me diminished. "Don't be foolish, Count; this cross is my ticket to freedom. Do you think I would be crazy enough to take it off so you could have your way with me?" I have no idea from where I had summoned that moment of courage. Or was it foolishness?

The count seemed to regain some of his composure. He straightened up and began to walk slowly toward me, keeping his face carefully concealed behind the cape. As he got close to me, I thrust the cross out.

It brushed against his hand. His flesh sizzled. He hissed and stepped back. I reached for the door handle. It turned with ease. I was out of it in a flash, out and running. Running and holding tight to my salvation.

I could hear the count's footsteps behind me. I quickened my pace down the stairs. Just ahead of me, I noticed a glimmer of sunlight slipping through beside the curtains on the front door. Another salvation. If I could just make it to that door, I would be free. I could almost smell my freedom, it was that close.

My hand reached for the doorknob. The count was closing in on me. Thank God, the handle turned. The door was opening. My breath was coming in gasps. I was ecstatic. I was winning. All I needed were a few more steps, and the brilliant sun would wrap me in her arms and lead me home. He had no power beyond these walls; not now, not in the sunlight. I was out the door. Foolishly, I turned to take a final look at what I was leaving behind.

The count stood in the hallway, almost at the threshold of the door. He was just staring at me. At first his eyes were filled with anger, and then I watched as the corners of his lips curled into a smile—an extremely diabolical smile.

What was so amusing? I wondered. Out loud I dared to say: "I have beaten you! You can't follow me where I am going now. Within moments I will be free, and you are powerless to stop me!" I was enjoying my moment of victory over the creature standing in his dark hallway.

But the count just kept smiling, and then his lips curled into laughter. His features relaxed, and before me, once again, stood the magnetic individual who had so mesmerized me earlier. The light from a nearby candle reflected off his fangs.

I began to tremble. Why was he laughing? I had escaped. All there was left for me to do was to turn and walk out the door to my freedom. This second attempt could not fail. I turned swiftly—and ran headlong into Max. I had no idea where he had come from; he had not been there moments before. I screamed at the top of my voice. The tragedy of my plight was hitting home. Also, I was praying that someone, anyone, passing by on the streets beyond those trees would hear me and come to my rescue.

My eyes pleaded with Max just to let me go, but he remained where he was, staring at me with a stone-cold look. I knew he was remembering the lies I had told about him and what he had suffered at the hands of the man behind me. I had no doubt who Max feared more as I caught a glimpse of the scratches on his cheek. My shoulders drooped, and my eyes looked down to the floor. Max would be of no help to me now.

The count's voice echoed to me from the hallway: "Where did you think you would fly to, Little Bird? Bring her in, Max, and return her to her room. I am weary now and would like to retire." He turned and headed down a set of stairs, which I presumed led to the basement. "I will see you tonight, Virginia darling," he called back, his voice emphasizing what seemed to be one of his favourite words, *darling*.

I turned to Max. "Please, Max, let me go. I won't tell anyone about this place or that you kept me here against my will. I just want to go home. Please!" I grabbed Max by the arm.

Max brushed my hand away. "I am very sorry, Miss Virginia; it is impossible for me to let you go. If I were knowingly to allow you to escape, the master would not stop at this!" Max pointed to the scratches on his cheek, confirming my suspicions.

"But what is it that keeps you here, Max? You are obviously not one of them; I mean, you are not like those two, are you? If you were, you would not have been able to stand where the sunlight could reach you."

"No, I am not one of them, my dear, but he is my master, and Teresa is my daughter. So, you see, even if I desired to let you go, I would not. He would harm her, and I could not live with that. I would never dream of putting your life over that of my own daughter."

So that was the connection between them. Teresa was his daughter!

I was not ready to give up yet. "But we could go to the police; we could tell them everything, and they would stop the count from harming your daughter. They could even help you and Teresa get out from under his grasp by locking him up where he cannot escape!" I was definitely pleading.

"You think so, foolish one? I think not. They will not stop the count. Not those mere mortals. He cannot be locked up. He has more wit and experience in his pocket than any of them will gather in their entire lifetime. He can only be stopped by—" Max never finished his sentence. We had arrived at my room.

There was no need for Max to push me into the room this time. I walked slowly through the open doorway, my shoulders sagging. I went to the window and stared out at the sunshine. In one night, I had gambled twice, and I had lost twice. The moon had disappeared into the sun's embrace, and I was still a prisoner.

After awhile, I lost total track of time. The sky started to darken. Angry black clouds rolled in. We were in for another vicious storm. The day was promising to be a match for my despondent spirits.

I ambled aimlessly over to the bed and lay down on the soft coverlet. I stared up at the canopy ceiling. No matter where I was in this house, I was surrounded by diabolical figures. Was there nothing sacred here? I closed my eyes to shut out the evil that surrounded me. I might as well sleep. Everyone else in this house was sleeping now, at least Teresa and the count were. I was still unaware of who all might reside here, and I was still not sure if Max ever slept. Sleep would help me regain my strength and sharpen my wits. Unconsciousness descended quickly on my tired mind and body.

Chapter 5

A Story from the Past

I awakened to a light knocking on the door. "Who is it?" I called out. "Teresa."

"Come in," I summoned. I sat up in bed, gazed down at my rumpled clothes, and realized I had not changed since I had stumbled into this place. I badly needed a bath and a new set of clothing.

Teresa entered. As though she had just read my mind, there she stood with some clothes draped over her arm. "I am sorry not to have brought you a change sooner, Virginia, but you must admit, you have not been the most congenial of guests. You are rather, how shall I say it, 'hard to keep tabs on'? If you will follow me, I will take you to the bath. I'm afraid, though, that you will not be allowed to have privacy. The count is furious at your escape attempts. You are never to be left alone again, unless in a locked room, of course," she added with her peculiar smile.

I followed Teresa into the hallway. My first impulse was to run; logic told me I would not get far. Teresa led me into a large room. In the centre was a massive round marble tub, which had already been filled with water. I noticed I would have to climb up three steps and then descend four steps that were immersed in the water. Heavy red velvet curtains hung on all the windows in the room. Two dark mahogany dressing tables—without mirrors, I noticed—were sitting against one of the walls. The rest of the room, with the exception of a decorative wooden partition in the far corner, was bare. The bath chamber smelled heavily of flowers, reminding me briefly of the time I had attended a friend's funeral—a forewarning?

I glanced around, searching for the fragrant bouquets. There were none that I could see, so I assumed the pleasant odour was from scented bubbles in the bath water.

Teresa came up to me. "Here, Virginia, let me help you off with your things."

"It's okay. I would rather do it myself, thank you," I stated curtly, backing a few steps away from her. I resented her offer. Had she not heard of privacy while bathing? I glanced around the room. "If you don't mind, I'll change behind that," I said. I scooped up one of the towels that had been set out by the tub and headed for the partition.

"As you wish," I heard Teresa say as I walked away from her.

As I was undressing, I studied the workmanship on the dark wooden panels. These pictures, like all the rest in the house, sent an eerie sensation through my body. They were full of strange night creatures, such as bats and wolves, but the figures were not *totally* animals either—there was a human trait to them. There were vast castles where great stones had been chiselled with the utmost precision, sculpturing the most evil-looking gargoyles I had ever seen. All of the gargoyles had protruding fangs. Nowhere did I observe windows in the castle walls where the sun's rays would be allowed to enter; however, crescent moons were visible in every corner of the panels. And nowhere did there appear anyone who looked *totally* human. I unclasped my cross and hid it in my clothing. Now was not the time to use it—not against Teresa, anyway. There would be another, more adequate, time for it to come into play.

Even with the warmth of the heavy towel wrapped around me, an icy shudder pulsated through me as I headed for the bath. Was there nothing in this place that did not depict evil?

My exhausted body welcomed the warm water. My pores opened wide, absorbing the heat. The tub was almost large enough to swim in. I lowered my head under the bubbles. Maybe I should just end it all here. Probably that would be a better fate than what the count had in mind for me. Teresa had mentioned that he was furious, and I had already witnessed a sample of his wrath on her and Max. Then again, maybe the reality here was that he and Teresa were some sort of sadistic serial killers who enjoyed toying with their victims before finishing them off! God alone knew what they had in store for me! Or did He?

I came up from under the water and gasped for air. As long as there was a minute hope of escape, I should not even think of ending my life. Besides, it was against my faith to commit suicide. I definitely did not want to end up in hell! I crossed myself, whispered a small prayer, and finished my bath. I pushed thoughts of death from my mind. At the moment, I just needed to reconsider my options and maintain my strength—mind and body.

Tea and biscuits were waiting on the small table for me when we returned to my room. Of course I knew they were meant for me. As of yet I had not seen Teresa sup on anything other than thick red liquids and uncooked steak.

I felt quite refreshed after the bath. The posy-red gown and the undergarments that Teresa had given me fit perfectly, almost as though they had been tailor-made for me. Of course, my figure was quite similar to hers, give or take an inch or two here and there. Before handing my soiled clothes to Teresa, I retrieved my cross and slipped it into one of the gown's pockets, keeping it safe for another time. Teresa set my clothes by the door.

"Shall we?" Teresa motioned to the tray of goodies. "I'll pour your tea, if you like," and without waiting for my reply, she proceeded. I noticed beside the teapot a small covered bowl on the tray in front of

Teresa's chair. She set it aside while she poured my tea. I presumed that whatever was in the bowl was meant to be her sustenance. She handed me the steaming cup.

I decided to attempt a conversation other than my usual begging to be allowed to go home. "Max told me," I stated mysteriously and then took a sip of my tea.

"Told you what?" Teresa asked.

"That you are his daughter."

"He told you that, did he?" Teresa's lip curled into its mysterious smile as she turned and gazed toward the moonlit window. "What else did Max tell you?"

"Nothing much, except that he could never help me to escape, because it would not be pleasant for either one of you, especially for you. He stated he could never place my welfare over yours."

Teresa turned back to me. "You really have no comprehension yet of exactly what you have gotten yourself into, do you, Virginia?" Her head tilted to the side as she asked me this question.

"I have a vague idea," I declared boldly. "But tell me, why did you and the count locate here in such a small city as Brantford?"

"It's a long story." Teresa's eyes took on a melancholy expression.

"That's okay," I encouraged her to continue. I was not so presumptuous as to think I would not have time for a long story. "Judging by my recent ill fortune, I don't believe I will be going anywhere in a big hurry," I added.

To my utmost surprise, Teresa began to reminisce. I had not dreamed she would actually reply to my query. Was there a glimmer of hope that we could become friends and that she would eventually be willing to help me escape?

"Some years ago, in the old country, my father was the personal servant of the count. One day, when my father was running an errand in town for the count, he met a beautiful woman and fell instantly in love with her."

Some years ago, I thought to myself. I wondered just how many years she was talking about. The count appeared to be fairly youthful. But how old would Max be? I was sure he was elderly, but just *how* old was the big question.

Teresa continued with her story. "My father was an exceptionally handsome man back then. He had raven-black hair and piercing blue eyes, I was told. Anyway, he hurried back to the castle and begged the count to allow him to marry the beautiful maiden, or at least give him leave to initiate a courtship to try to win her heart. The count was not pleased with this turn of events. It had been extremely difficult for him to procure good help, despite his wealth. People tended to steer clear of him. He feared he would lose the services of my father if Max's endeavours succeeded and he ended up actually marrying the girl." Teresa took a sip from her drink.

"My father was totally crushed." She went on, "He felt he had served the count well and that he was not asking for too great a favour. He knew many of the count's secrets, and he felt the count owed him, although he never directly told him that! Finally, after much cajoling, he convinced the count to allow him to pursue the maiden, on the condition that, if things worked out, he and his bride would live at the castle, and my father would continue in his service to the count."

"Why could your father not just leave the count and marry the maiden?" I interrupted.

"No one just leaves the count, my dear—no one that he does not want to leave, anyway. And, to my knowledge, anyone who ever did make an attempt did not live to tell the story. People did not dare to cross him; he was a powerful man in his own country. And, as you have witnessed already, my dear Virginia, he still is a considerably powerful man!"

"You keep calling him *count*; does he have an actual name?" I inquired.

"His full name is Count Basarab Musat of Transylvania. He is a first cousin, on his mother's side, to Count Vlad Dracula, possibly better known to you as Dracula."

A long, low whistle escaped from my lips. Shivers raced up and down my spine. A first cousin to Count Vlad Dracula! I knew *he* was a real historical person, but to have him actually linked to vampirism outside of the fictional story written by Bram Stoker—well, that was just bizarre! I had not realized vampires actually belonged to a particular family or that they might have extended families. Of course, I had never before become acquainted with an authentic vampire, either.

"How in the world did your father ever get mixed up with the count to begin with?" I managed to whisper.

"He felt totally indebted to the count. You see, my father was born the son of a Gypsy. When he was about seven years old, he took ill. Weakness was not tolerated in the Gypsy camps—it couldn't be. They were forced to move around so much, and most times on short notice, so there was little time for attending to those who fell ill.

"At the time, my father's clan was passing through Transylvania and had camped just outside the count's town for a few weeks. The townspeople soon tired of them and chased them from the area; this was the usual scenario wherever they went. Gypsy people loved to dance and party, and to drink and cavort freely. The villagers feared for their children, many of whom had disappeared on earlier occasions when the Gypsy nomads passed through the area. They never thought to consider the times when their children disappeared most often—when there were no Gypsies around!

"My father was so ill he was unable to travel. He was left behind for—how shall I put it delicately?—for nature's elements to purge. There was not much else his family could do, for in those days the code of the Gypsy world was the survival of the fittest. A weak man just did not make it."

I wondered for a moment about Teresa's reference to "those days." She had to be going back a long, long time. I would have been truly shocked had I known just how far back that was!

Teresa continued, "The count found my father half-dead in the woods, carried him home, and then nursed him back to health." Teresa hesitated again and stared directly into my eyes. "So you see, Virginia, my father actually owes the count his very existence, and I suppose, in a roundabout way, so do I."

"What happened next?" I asked. "How did the count get Max to stay on in his service?"

"That was easy enough. The count had saved my father's life, and he was not beneath reminding my father of that fact. So my father became an extremely loyal servant. In fact, he was even willing to lay down his own life for the man who had saved his. Many were the times he staunchly defended the count when the townspeople were threatening to do something about certain mysterious events that were taking place in the area. Eventually it did become apparent to the people that some of these incidents could not be attributed to the count, because many of them happened when he was away from his castle.

"The situation over my mother was the first time my father had ever dared to cross paths with the count. He pursued his maiden and finally won her heart. After the marriage, he took his bride to live in the castle, as they had previously agreed. However, a short time into their marriage, my father dared once again to overstep his position by requesting that he and his bride be allowed to live in the little cottage not far from the castle gates. He was becoming disturbed by the strange influence the count appeared to wield over his wife. The count denied my father's request.

"Life went on, though. I was conceived and born within the first year of their marriage, but after my birth my mother showed absolutely no interest in my well-being. It was my father who attended to my needs—fed me, bathed me, clothed me, and rocked me to sleep at night. In actuality, the count had played a part in this. He had ordered my mother to work alongside my father while she was with child. She had learned most of his duties. Once she was no longer burdened with me in her belly, my mother assumed more and more of my father's regular duties. Thus, he saw less and less of her as the days passed.

"Then came the day when she ceased coming to him at all, even during the night hours, when most dutiful wives would be warming their husbands' beds. The count had consumed her, body and soul. My father's heart was broken, and he soon shrivelled into the old man whom you see today.

"He began to stoop when he walked, and his eyes took on an empty, faraway look. The only moments there was ever a gleam in those vacant wells were the moments when he gazed upon me. I became the sole reason for his existence; my mother appeared to be totally lost to him."

"So why didn't Max just take you and run away?" I asked.

"My father told me that he tried once, with me clutched in his arms. He was going to see me to safety somewhere and then return for my mother. He was sure that if he could have a few minutes alone with her that he could convince her to leave with him. However, the count quickly sought him out, and we were dragged back to the castle. The count ordered my father never to attempt such a thing again. If he did, my mother would meet with an unfortunate accident."

Teresa let out a small, sarcastic laugh. "And can you believe this, Virginia? Even with her detestable treatment of him, my father still loved my mother so much that he would not even dream of another escape attempt. Count Basarab Musat is an excessively sinister and self-centred creature!" For the first time, I saw in Teresa's black eyes a spark of hatred as she spoke of the commanding man who appeared to be her husband. "Something no one, no matter who they might be, should forget," she added.

I had another question I needed an answer to. By now I had assumed that the count and Teresa were vampires, but what was Max? "Teresa," I asked, "how is it that Max still lives?"

She tilted her head and then smiled. "I am not privy to exactly how the count keeps my father alive, but I believe it might have something to do with only being partially 'crossed over.' The count still needs someone who can look after certain affairs during the daytime."

Teresa glanced out the window and then up at the moon. "It is time to dine, Virginia. We must hurry. The count will be furious if we are tardy." Teresa headed for the door. Suddenly she turned, and this time I thought I detected a look of concern emanating from her eyes. "Virginia, please remember this piece of advice that I am about to give you: Do not fight him. The more you do, the harder things will go for you. Believe me, I know." A distinct sense of sadness had crept into her words, and a tear escaped from the corner of her eye. I had no idea, at the time, that these creatures were prone to that kind of emotion, or should I say, *semblance* of emotion? I also wondered just how genuine Teresa was.

"Thank you for your advice, Teresa. I will hold it dear," I murmured. I noticed that Teresa had not really answered my question yet of how she and the count had come to live in Brantford. Oh well, another time.

Teresa turned and strolled out of the room. I trailed after her, humbled by the story I had just heard. My heart was feeling Teresa's obvious pain, but my mind was still trying to figure my way out of this mess. I reached into my pocket, pulled out my cross and refastened it around my neck. It cradled itself beneath the material of my gown. Its warmth against my heart was only slightly comforting.

Chapter 6

A Night to Remember

How can life grow from one who has cold breath?
How can life sprout from one who has experienced death?
Yet, inside my body, a tiny seed doth sprout;
It is HIS seed, of that there is no doubt.

"Ah, Teresa darling, and Virginia, my little bird; it is so pleasant to see you at last. I was beginning to wonder what might be detaining you. I am impatient to get on with our meal so that I may attend to my *outside* business tonight." I felt his cold eyes glaring at me. "Without any more unnecessary delays, I hope," he added.

Teresa sat in her usual chair on the count's left. The count waved his hand toward her and said, "No, Teresa darling, you will not be dining with me tonight. I would prefer you to sup in the kitchen with Max. I have—ah, how shall I say it now—yes, some *business* to discuss with Virginia."

Teresa blushed crimson at the count's dismissal. I was not sure whether it was from embarrassment or from anger. She pushed her chair back from the table, stood up, whirled around, and stalked from the room. The count motioned for me to sit in the vacated spot.

A heavy silence filled the room as Max served our meals. I say meals, for I was confident that mine would be quite different from the count's. Max set the count's dish in front of him, along with a goblet of red liquid. He served me broiled chicken, smothered in a creamy white sauce. The chicken was garnished with baby carrots and small, round potatoes, which had been crisped to a golden brown. A glass of white wine was set at the tip of my silver knife. I guessed that was Max's way of assuring me I was not being served the same drink as the count.

The flickering candles transmitted an eerie ambiance throughout the room. This was it, I thought. The count was going to tell me how sorry he was for all the inconveniences he had inflicted on me and then inform me I was free to leave. But I would have been dreaming if I believed that was even a remote possibility. I had an even greater gut feeling that the count would never allow me to leave. If he were going to, he would have already done so.

I knew deep down that I would have to fight him with every ounce of my wits, plus change my strategy in order to find out what it was he wanted from me. I would have to play his game, whatever that might be, and lead him to believe I was mere putty in his hands, soft and pliable, moulding myself in response to his every whim.

However, that thought was terrifying. I remembered those brief moments when I had been under his spell, and I shuddered. It seemed I had no control over my feelings when he projected his certain look upon me. It would be considerably easier to play the game if I did not have to look the count directly in the eyes!

"Virginia darling." There he went with his *darling* again, I thought to myself as the count paused momentarily. "We must reach an alliance. I do not wish to fight with you, Virginia. I want to love you, make love to you—with you. I want to protect you. I am able to bestow eternal life on you. Did you know that, my dear?" The count's steely eyes pierced deep into me.

I searched those eyes for the love he spoke of, but I saw none there. There was no concern, no promise of protection. Those eyes were colder than the ice at the base of a glacier. In fact, they were so cold that I found myself shivering beneath their gaze.

"Why do you suggest this, Count, when you know I do not wish to stay here? My greatest desire is to be allowed to go home. Is that too difficult a request for such a powerful man as you to grant?" I felt a little flattery here would not hurt my chances for a possible release.

"I give my solemn oath not to tell anyone about you, if that is what you are worried about. However, what it is that you are afraid I would tell is beyond me. I know nothing of who you are or what you do. I do not understand why you are holding me here against my will. I would be willing to erase this experience from my memory if you would just let me go now.

"What about your wife, Teresa? Does she not have something to say about this matter? I have no inclination to interfere between a man and his wife. Your proposal to make love to me sounds more like what we, in this Christian country, call adultery. Of course, maybe fooling around with the neighbour is not considered so wrong where you come from!" I added snappily. My statement was a bit too bold even for my liking, but it was out, and now all I could do was wait for his response.

The count's lip curled upward. A deep throaty chuckle burst forth. "Tell someone about me? You believe I fear you could harm me with your little stories? What is it you wish to tell, Little Bird? That I have fangs? That I drink blood? Maybe even that I turn into a bat on occasion?" His eyebrows were raised in sarcasm. I had the impression my game had not gotten off to a very good start.

"Virginia my dear, for your information, there are many people in this city who already know me. I am quite a popular man, who attends many high-society functions. In fact, just a couple of weeks ago I attended a cocktail party at the mayor's house, a fundraiser for the Red Cross, I believe it was. You have heard of the Red Cross, haven't you—what they are about?" His smile revealed those fangs again.

The count dismissed my threat by waving his hand in the air. He sneered. "After all, this city is extremely—how shall I say this—yes, extremely *honoured* to have such a dignitary as me living here. As for Teresa, she understands. She expects these things to happen. She does know, however, that she will always be my number-one lady. She was my bride. She is my wife. Nothing will ever change that. I told you I would make love to you, care for you, and give you something beyond your comprehension—the prospect of living forever. I did not say you would be replacing my wife. Do not even try to fool yourself with such an illusion, my dear. If you cooperate, you will have a pleasant life with us, possibly forever. If you decide to do something foolish again, you will end up like the rest!"

"The rest?" I questioned. I was shocked to think that there had been others here before me. The thought of him and Teresa being serial killers crossed my mind again.

The count's response was sarcastic: "Oh, what a foolish young woman you are! Do you really think you are the first insignificant idiot who has come snooping around this estate, or any other place where we have lived? No, my dear, there have been many over the years, many ..." The room emanated evil as the count smiled at me and ran his tongue along his lips.

"As you might have guessed, we have to move periodically. It is not wise for us to stay in any one place for too long. We have been in Brantford for about ten years; we can probably get away with a few more, but not too many. I have already had the odd acquaintance comment on how ageless I seem to be."

"Why this city?" I asked.

The count looked thoughtful, as though he was pondering just how much he should actually tell me. "Well," he started, slowly, "I met someone who said he could help me with certain needs, but he insisted it would be easier to do that if I moved here, where he lives. It was about time for us to leave where we were anyway.

"My friend told me of this place and said it would be ideal for my lifestyle. He said he would introduce me to the right dignitaries and help me to fit in."

"Why would this person do all that for you?" I inquired.

"That is another story, one which I don't feel is necessary to share with you at this point. Briefly, though, he had made it his goal in life to study our kind. He was fascinated with us and thought he could glean more information if he were to help us. Of course, I allowed him to think that, for a time—until we were well settled here. He would not dare to betray us now, because that would mean he would lose the comfortable life he has become accustomed to." The count smiled. "I must be going. I am to meet my friend shortly, and having missed him the last couple of nights, I cannot afford to do so again tonight.

"I will return within a couple of hours and shall expect you to be waiting for me in your room. Tonight, darling Virginia, you will be mine, willing or not, although willingly would be a much pleasanter experience for you!" With those final words, the count rose from the table and departed.

As I followed him with my eyes, I noticed Max lingering outside in the hallway. There would be no escape attempt tonight. Of this I was absolutely positive.

I could not finish my meal. The final morsel of food I had bitten off stuck in my throat. I coughed. My stomach felt queasy. If I fought against him, my life would be worth nothing. If I did not fight him, I would become his prisoner, and my soul would be linked with someone who appeared to be the spawn of the devil. He might be offering me eternal life, but in reality it would be a living hell! What was I going to do? Was I so in love with life that I would be willing to sell my very soul in order to stay alive?

It was a clear night, from what I observed through the barred windows. Stars twinkled dazzlingly. The moon glowed full and bright. There was not a cloud to shroud their destinies. A small breeze rustled the leaves on the trees. The distant street lights reflected eerily on the dancing leaves. I paused a moment longer, searching the shadows, watching and waiting for *my* destiny to return.

I felt like a coward. I had decided I had no other choice but to take my chances with the count. I kept telling myself that it was the only way to remain alive. I was terrified of his anger, having seen what it could do, but I thought if I could get him to fall in love with me, he might let his guard down. And even if it were for just a moment, I might have another opportunity to escape. This was the one and only hope that I could possibly cling to.

Watching a falling star plummet from its pinnacle in the heavens, I clasped my hands together, made a wish, crossed myself, and then whispered a fervent prayer. Somehow I knew, though, deep inside, that there was little hope that my wish or my prayer would ever be answered. I turned around and went to sit on the edge of my bed to wait for *him*.

I was startled by a warm breath on my neck. My first impulse was to struggle, but then my better senses took over as I remembered my plan. I looked up into the eyes of the count. I pushed gently on his chest, feeling the hardness of his muscles beneath his shirt. He stood up and backed away from me, waiting. His presence filled the room with a commanding aura.

"Wait," I whispered huskily. I slipped off the bed and began slowly to undo the buttons on the red gown. I reached behind my head, loosened the ribbon from my hair, and gave a little shake so that my long red tresses could flow freely. They cascaded down over my shoulders and covered my breasts. I had always cursed the thickness of my hair, but now I prayed it would be part of my salvation. I gazed intently at the count, trying to show a facsimile of lust in my eyes and to note what effect I was having upon him. I ran my tongue across my lips and continued to unbutton.

The count was watching me attentively. I sensed—no, I knew—he did not trust me. To this point, I had given him no reason to; therefore, my deception was going to have to be foolproof. The count sauntered over to me, his eyes fixed on mine, penetrating—eyes that were like an inferno as they burned into me, mesmerizing me. He moved with the grace of a panther closing in on its prey. My entire body began quivering. I wished it were with fear, but that was not the case. I was quivering in anticipation. I could not wait for this man to gather me in his arms and *take* me. It had been so long since I had slept with a man. Damn John for betraying me, as he had. And damn the count's eyes; damn them to hell!

I raised my hand and slipped one of the sleeves off my shoulder. As I reached for the other sleeve, my hand brushed the cross. The cross! Oh God, my whole plan could fail! It was too late to conceal it from him. He had detected the crossed piece of gold at the same time as I had.

The count backed away from me, snarling. Quickly I undid the clasp and threw the cross to the far corner of the room. Hopefully I would be able to find it later and place it somewhere safe. The count looked at me, amazement written on his face. My action seemed to have puzzled him. I prayed that I had taken a step toward gaining a fraction of his trust.

I allowed the other sleeve to fall from my shoulder, and the gown dropped to the floor. I reached behind my back and unclasped my bra; it joined the gown on the floor. I slipped from my panties and then stood tall, facing the count. The Count Basarab Musat emitted a pleased whistle.

"I did not realize, Virginia darling, that there was such perfection under that gown. You are beautiful indeed, more so than any of your predecessors. Beauty and spunk, wonderful indeed," he added with a smile. This time, at least I thought so at that moment, he did not appear to be quite so evil.

As I stepped provocatively toward the count, unabashed by my nakedness, he began to undo the buttons on his shirt. Within no time, he stood before me as naked as I was. Such perfection had never been painted on any canvas. Game of survival or not, what I wanted at this moment was this man, or whatever he was. The count swept me up with his muscular arms. I leaned into his massive chest, breathing in his scent, as he carried me to the waiting bed. I was sure I could hear the rhythmic beating of a heart!

When I awoke, I was alone. I glanced toward the window. Of course! Rays of sun filtered into my room, circulating amongst the diminutive particles of dust that danced in their warmth. I started to get up from the bed and then realized I was still naked.

I gazed around the room, searching for my gown. My eyes travelled to the spot where I had disrobed and were rewarded with the sight of a red heap of material on the floor. I began to remember. Every minute. Every second. The count had made love to me as no other man ever had. Of course, I had actually only known one other man in my life, and I realized now what a fumbling schoolboy John had been. The tart he had cheated on me with could have him—I had a real man!

The count had been slow and deliberate. He had been gentle but firm. He had taken my body with a tender lust that I would never have believed possible from a man like him. I had been levitated on clouds of ecstasy, and when one cloud would commence to drift away, another would float in to take its place. Thunder and lightning had spewed forth from those clouds and seared my entire body with a raging fire.

I had responded with a zealous fervour, matching him with all my passion. I had not dreamed that such a level of excitement existed within me. His lust had fuelled mine. I had been like a wild animal unleashed from a lifetime of captivity, as I devoured every inch of his body and surrendered to him every element of mine!

I slid out from under the blanket the count had thrown over me before leaving, stepped into the red gown, and pulled it onto my still-trembling body. I detested myself for the way I was feeling. These emotions were contrary to my well-laid plans. I tried desperately to loathe him for the way he had made me feel, but I could not. All I felt was a fiery desire when I thought of him. I yearned for him to walk through the door, sweep me into his arms, and devour me once again with his endless appetite. The one thing that could have been my salvation—my cross—was totally forgotten in a dusty corner.

I ached only for *him*—with all my body and soul.

Damn him!

Damn me!

CHAPTER 7

The Bargain

I was shaken back to reality by a light knocking on the door. I walked over, turned the knob and, to my surprise, found that it was not locked. Maybe all he had wanted was to have his way with me and then let me go. I did not believe the count to be a careless man. Or had he left the door unlocked on purpose, testing to see if I would attempt another escape? I presumed it was the latter. I swung the door open.

Max stood there with my breakfast tray. It looked as if he had been about to put his key in the lock. I noticed the shocked look on his face as he said, "The door is not locked?" He was scrutinizing my face. "You have an unusual glow this morning, miss," he observed. I could have sworn I saw a shadow of sadness pass over his eyes. He shuffled over to my little table. "Your breakfast, Miss Virginia. The count ordered me to prepare you something special." Max hesitated over the word *special*. He gazed around the room, his eyes resting on the rumpled bed. "It appears you slept very well last night?" There seemed a hint of sarcasm in his question.

I smiled sheepishly and stretched my arms upward to the ceiling. It was useless to try to hide how I was feeling. "Very well, Max; very well indeed." My body still tingled from the burning flames of lust that had devoured me during the night.

To my surprise, the conversation took an unexpected turn. "You realize, I hope, Miss Virginia, that you are just another plaything for the count? You will never, ever, replace my Teresa," Max stated bitterly.

I studied the hunched-over old man. Once again, pity pierced my heart for his plight. "I have already been told that, by the count," I answered back curtly, not wanting Max to think he was informing me of something of which I was not aware.

"Then forgive me if I do not understand your actions. Yesterday you could not wait to flee from this place, and now you have the appearance of a contented little kitten who has just found a warm, secure basket to nestle in. I must warn you, Virginia—the count is not a security blanket for anyone. What he did to you, or with you last night, he has done with hundreds before. Most have not lived to tell the tale." Max took my chin in his hand and turned my head from side to side, gazing intensely at my neck.

"What are you doing?" I demanded, brushing his hand from my chin and backing away from him.

"What do you think I am doing?" Max said. He sighed. "Good, there is still hope. He did not take you in that way." He paused a moment, and a look of puzzlement crept into his eyes. "I wonder why … no, you couldn't be. Yet you do have a rugged beauty, unlike most of the others, but I thought he had given up on that …" Max was rambling.

The full realization of what Max was saying began to penetrate the warmth of what I thought to be my new-found love. A chill raced up and down my spine. "What are you driving at, Max?"

"The count has been searching for some time now for a woman to beget him an heir. You see, Teresa was unable to conceive children, the result of an unfortunate accident in her youth. She was thrown from a horse and certain parts inside her, which are important to bearing a child, were damaged. The doctor who examined her said that she would never be able to have children. The count desires a son, a younger version of himself to follow in his footsteps. To be a true heir, the child must be flesh of his flesh. But the count is exceptionally selective, and few have been acceptable to him, let alone survived one night with him. There was a woman, a year or two ago. I thought she might have been the one, but somehow she angered the count. One night, right in front of Teresa and me, he ended her dreams of becoming his. Then he ended her existence. I had tried to warn her. I tried to warn them all—none ever seemed to listen, though. The shame of it." Max glanced again toward my neck but kept his hands to himself. "The fact that you have not been bitten leads me to surmise he may have a much different plan for you than you think."

My mouth dropped open in amazement. I could not believe that the count was only going to use me as a vessel to carry his child—not after a night of passion such as the one we had just shared. Surely he loved me! A man could not consume a woman's body with the lust he had manifested and not love her—or at least be slightly taken with her! I was not that naïve, was I? Max had to be lying. More than anything right now, I needed to believe that the count loved me!

As for the other women, I did not want to think about them or what might have happened to them when the count was through using them! After all, for all I knew, Max was lying. Maybe he was even trying to make me jealous in order to preserve his daughter's place in the household. I had no idea at that time just how wrong I was!

It seemed as though Max had read my thoughts. "You think the count loves you, Virginia? Wake up! Count Basarab Musat loves no one but himself. He will cast you away like yesterday's garbage when he is finished with you! Only my Teresa will remain—and only because of the bargain."

"The bargain?" I asked. "What bargain are you talking about?"

"You know a portion of the past from Teresa, but she did not tell you all. She did not elaborate on what the count really did to her mother, my wife!" Max's words echoed throughout the room like a cold, bitter wind. His face took on an almost youthful look, as if remembering the woman he had loved and cherished had given him a new spark for life.

"But I thought your wife left you to be with the count? I presumed from your story that she did not love you anymore!"

"My wife, my precious Lilly, loved me dearly, at least she did until he exerted his mysterious powers over her—the same powers, I might add, that he wielded over you last night. At first she begged me to take her away from the castle, for us to flee and begin a new life far away from him, somewhere he would never be able to seek us out. However, I was too weak. Despite everything that he had done to me, I still felt beholden to him for the life that he had breathed back into me when I'd been deserted by my family as a child. You must remember that it was a debt which the count was unwilling to allow me to forget.

"You see, dear Virginia, the count could not tolerate that such a beautiful woman could belong to someone other than himself, especially if that woman was living under his roof. It was not really my Lilly he craved; there were many pretty maidens in the villages, or on the surrounding farms, who would quench his thirst. It was just that he did not wish *me* to have her.

"He began to mock me in her presence. He dangled pretty things in front of her, things I could only dream of giving her one day. I did not work for wages, so I had no cash of my own to buy her the little baubles that so fascinate the fairer sex. I was, in essence, the count's slave. I owed him my life, and as I already said, that was a fact which he constantly reminded me of, especially in front of Lilly. It was just another way for him to humiliate me in her eyes.

"There were moments I wanted to end it all, but I did not have the strength. I always felt that as long as there was a glimmer of hope for me and my Lilly ..." Max paused a moment before continuing.

"As I mentioned, for a short time at the beginning of our marriage, Lilly was able to resist the count's advances, and she remained true to me. It was during these days that Teresa was conceived. The count was consumed by jealousy. He began sending me away on business trips, and then, while I was gone, he would work his wickedness on my Lilly.

"Finally, she succumbed. That day sealed her fate. You see, Miss Virginia, it had been nothing more than a mere matter of pride, a game for the count. Lilly had rejected him far too long, and now that he had her where he wanted her, under his complete domination, he was finished with that part of his game. The prize was finally his! She was compelled to do his bidding, or the baby and I would meet with the harshest of punishments!" Max's face was lined with anger.

"But if he didn't want her anymore, why did he continue to keep her away from you?" I asked. "He had already destroyed your lives, and as you said, there was an abundance of young girls around who would be more than willing to accommodate his needs."

Max's eyebrows rose questioningly as he looked at me. "Girls? Like you, Virginia? Needs? Do you think that you really know, after one tumble on the bed, what the Count Basarab Musat's needs are?"

"That is a low blow, Max. I am doing now what I have to do to survive. I have no death wish at the moment."

I realized, too late, the slip of my tongue. How did I know I could trust this man, even with what he had just divulged to me? After all, he had not denounced outright his loyalty to Count Basarab Musat; he was merely conferring on me a bitter rendition of past events. Yet, despite all that had happened many years ago, Max still remained in the service of one of the most formidable, dominating men I had ever heard of!

"Die, Miss Virginia? Your fate with the count will be an eternal living hell. Only my Teresa has an eternity like his, but he still assumes complete authority over her. She will never have the power, or the ability, to prevail against him. She is nothing more than his queen, his chosen symbol of eternal status and beauty. No other will ever dethrone her. The deal was sealed in blood, and the count, such as he is, will never betray such a bargain."

"You keep mentioning a bargain, Max; what bargain do you speak of?" I queried.

"Now you shall hear the truth, the rest of the story, Miss Virginia. Then you will be able to decide for yourself whether it is wiser for you to remain or to flee this place—if you are able to do so without being caught, that is."

I wondered, because of the statement he had just made, if there was a possibility that Max would turn his eyes for a moment.

Max took a deep breath before he continued, "As I mentioned, Lilly finally gave in to the count's wiles, and once she did, the count treated her as if she were dirt in a pebble-strewn field. However, instead of the quick living hell that he inflicted on the majority of his victims, he tortured my Lilly, making her suffering long, drawn out, and painful for me to look upon. He compelled her to solicit for his 'services.' Beg she did, on her hands and knees, grovelling at his feet with less dignity than a common village whore! And then he would laugh at her and walk away, leaving her weeping on the ground.

"I could not bear the sight of her shame. My heart shattered into a million fragments, yet there was not a thing I could do to ease her pain. All that kept me sane during this time was my little Teresa. I began to live and breathe for her alone, so that I could block out what he was doing to my Lilly. There were even moments when I contemplated taking Teresa far from him, as far away as possible, but something always held me back. I just could not leave Lilly to *him*. Well, I did try once; I believe that Teresa told you what happened then.

"In all truth, Lilly was an innocent in the whole bizarre affair. I should have known better than to pursue a bride, let alone to have exposed her to his treatment. Therefore, I kept rationalizing that it was my duty to stay and somehow see her soul at peace. I felt increasingly helpless as time passed, for I could not conceive of anything that would free my Lilly from his demeaning grasp."

Tears began to seep from the corners of the old man's eyes. His shoulders shook uncontrollably. I poured him a glass of water from the jug he had brought me and placed my arm around him. "Here, Max," I uttered softly, "drink this." He took the water and swallowed a few sips. "Please, tell me what happened next," I murmured.

Max took a moment more to recover his composure. "Next? Right. I decided to approach the count with a plan that would free my Lilly. I was willing to go to any expense, even to sacrifice my tiny daughter's life. I thought at the time that the most important thing was to save my wife; I felt I would be able to save my daughter at a later date.

"Lilly had become a walking nightmare. Where once her beautiful blue eyes had been, there were lifeless holes of darkness. Her formerly silky white skin was grey and lined with the crevices of premature aging. Her once-lithe body was now curved and broken from lack of nourishment. Her walk was that of the living dead.

"She had to be released from that hell. I presented my proposal to the count. For a reason that really has no significance to you, I knew he would not refuse. I had been around the family long enough to see and know certain things about them." Max's voice shuddered to a stop.

"Well?" I pushed him to go on.

"I proposed that he allow Lilly to die in peace, with dignity. In return, I would give him my beautiful daughter as his bride. I knew the count would one day be taking some special lady to be his queen, so why not my Teresa? Even at the age of eight, which she was when I made this proposal, anyone with half an eye could tell she was going to be a goddess amongst the angels.

"The count, as I expected, agreed. You see, he was growing tired of Lilly, and I knew it was only a matter of time before he would either kill her or send her away to a living hell, forever wandering the earth with a lust for blood. I could not bear the thought of some overzealous villager or farmer plunging a stake through her heart, even if that would mean an end to her miserable existence. I was sure the prospect of such a precious and pure bride would appeal to the count. He would have Teresa for his queen, and in return, he would release my Lilly from the hell he had relegated her to.

"However, the count made two stipulations: one, that the marriage ceremony would take place immediately; and two, that I remain forever in his services. I agreed. The legal papers were drawn up and sealed with my blood, Teresa's, and the count's. He also agreed not to consummate the union with my daughter until she was of a proper age to do so. He remained true to his word, for if there is another thing he is good for, it is keeping his word!

"I have cursed myself many times for this transaction, but it did free my Lilly from his world, and she rests in peace now. It was her life in exchange for her daughter's. What a monster I was to have assumed such authority over my precious little Teresa!

"So you see, Virginia, I am a damned man. No matter how you look at it, if he ever decides to release me from this world, I will burn in hell for the cowardly thing I have done to my daughter. I was never able, as I had hoped to be, to liberate her from him!"

"This bargain you struck—was it necessary? What I mean is, could he not have had Teresa anyway, any time he desired to take her?" I asked.

"Of course he could have seduced her, but not to be his queen. You see, with his kind, their queen could not be one of the typical victims. First, she had to come to him of her own free will. This Teresa did at the age of eight. In a child's way she worshipped him, because I had never given her any reason not to. Actually, I dared not for the fear of what would happen to Lilly. Teresa was too young to remember the count's treatment of me when I had made my one attempt at escape. I never divulged to her the true extent of his atrocities toward her mother who, by this time in Teresa's life, was nothing more than a shadowy memory. Besides, the count had doted on Teresa, providing her with the best that living could afford. To her, he was wonderful, the provider of all that was beautiful in her life.

"Secondly, the bride had to be pure and innocent, not yet touched by any other man. Of course, these criteria my Teresa also fulfilled. Adding that to her exquisite beauty, she was the perfect bride. Thus was the bargain sealed—her fate and mine!"

I had asked Teresa why it was that her father was still alive, and she had not been very knowledgeable on the details. I felt that if anyone should know, it would be Max. I decided to ask him. "How is it that you still live, Max?"

He looked at me and shook his head. "If I were to tell you that, both of our lives would be ended. You do not want to know such secrets, Virginia. You really do not want to know!"

"Are there others like you?"

"Yes. But I will not discuss this further. The walls have eyes and ears. Let it go, and do not ask me, or Teresa, again." Max looked away.

I was dumbfounded. What a story! I had thought things like this only happened in the movies. Vampires were not real. They were imaginary individuals made up for the entertainment industry. Vampires were box-office hits. I still prayed that this was all a dream, and yet, somewhere deep within the recesses of my mind, I knew that it was not. It was all as real as the old man who stood before me.

Max cleared away the dishes. "Your breakfast is cold now, Virginia. I will warm it up for you and return shortly."

"Max," I gripped his arm. "Are there others here in the castle?"

"No, Virginia. You are quite alone; *we* are quite alone. On occasion, if the count is entertaining, we have hired help for a day, or an evening, but other than that ..." Max waved a limp hand in the air and left the room.

He returned half an hour later with a fresh meal. "Just leave the dishes when you are finished; I will get them later," Max mentioned on his way out the door. He paused a moment as though he had forgotten something. He gazed around the room, and I noticed that something in one of the corners had caught his attention. My heart did a flip as I realized what was there. Max walked to the place of interest, stooped over, and picked up the necklace. "I almost forgot; the count asked me to retrieve and destroy this," he said as he slipped my cross into his pocket.

I dawdled over the eggs and sipped the hot coffee. What was I going to do! I could still feel the warmth floating through my body from the night before, but somehow, after my conversation with Max, it had turned into a chill that was slowly freezing the blood in my veins. And now I had also foolishly allowed my cross, my possible salvation, to slip from my possession!

I needed sleep. Sleep would refresh me and clear my mind, so I could get back on track with my original plan to escape.

What was it Max had said earlier? I should decide whether it was wiser to remain or to flee. Could that mean that he was going to turn his eyes from such an attempt? I would sleep on that thought. Sleep made a person strong, because it nourished both mind and body with such loving care. That is, of course, if it were a peaceful sleep.

I decided to finish my meal before lying down. After a good slumber I would be able to make some sense of the whole bizarre affair! I hoped.

Chapter 8

Family History

History doth whisper the stories of old
Of why the vampire's blood runs cold,
History whispers of a youthful man
Whose soul the old Gypsy damned;
History doth whisper the stories of old
Why he and his loved ones are so cold,
Of battles won, of loves lost
And of all their horrific costs!

The evening meal was over. Max had served it in silence; however, I could not help noticing his questioning eyes whenever he glanced my way. Teresa had been unusually quiet, too. Only the count had seemed in good spirits, and he had constantly cast his beguiling smile toward me. However, the one thing that nagged at me was wondering whether it was a smile filled with love or one denoting victory.

"Let us retire to the study, ladies. I have some good news to impart to both of you." The count stood, bowed graciously, and then motioned us through the dining-room door.

Once in the study, Teresa and I settled into chairs, one on each side of the count. The count sat down, folded his hands elegantly against the bottom of his chin, and opened the conversation. "It has been some time since we have entertained, has it not, Teresa?"

"Yes, Count, it has been," Teresa answered, an unusual huskiness in her voice.

"I believe it is time for a party, especially now that we have something to celebrate—right, Virginia?" He smiled at me.

I was baffled. Was there something to celebrate that I should be aware of? I was not sure what the count was suggesting, so I simply nodded my head, leaving him the floor so that he could enlighten us further.

The count turned to Teresa. "You see, Teresa darling, Virginia is the one I have chosen to bear me a son—excuse my slip, *us* a son," he corrected. "The time for this event is long overdue, and since you, unfortunately, were unable to bear a child for me before you crossed over, I am forced to settle for an alternate vessel. I am sure this circumstance is of no real surprise to you, since we have discussed it many times in the past."

The count, as though it really did not matter to him what Teresa thought, did not even give her an opportunity to reply, even though this issue affected her life, probably more so than it would his. "By the time the baby arrives," he continued, "all the necessary arrangements will have been made, and we will be able to introduce our son to the world in the true ancient custom of my people."

I was absolutely stunned. I also noticed how the count had referred to *his* people—did that mean that Teresa might not actually be like him? That would not make sense, though.

"But Count," I managed to stammer. "How do you know I am pregnant?"

He smiled: warm and sweet—cold and chilling. "I know, Virginia darling, I know!" His voice had an assuredness to it that could not be refuted. He then turned his attention back to Teresa, dismissing me as if I no longer existed. I had facilitated his purpose, and Teresa was, as Max had warned me, the number-one lady in his world. He said to her, "I will furnish you with a list of all whom I wish to attend the ceremonies. You should be able to get in touch with them well before the eve of the birth of our child. That is when the first celebration will commence. Virginia will assist you as long as she is able. It will do her good to learn of our ways, and it will also occupy her time while she awaits the delivery. However, please remember that you are always to remain in charge."

The count glanced in the direction of the window. "I must go now, or I will be late for the party. I am sure my friends will not forgive my absence twice in a row. They take a great risk for me, even though their rewards are substantial." He laughed sarcastically, giving the impression that he truly did not care what his friends thought. I was also sure that, if need be, whoever these people were, they could be easily replaced—even the special friend he had spoken of to me.

"I will see you both at supper tomorrow evening," he added as he left the room.

A queasy feeling crept over me. I noticed that Teresa was studying me hard. "So, Virginia, you gave in, did you?" Her voice was filled with sarcasm. "Of course, I cannot say I blame you for surrendering yourself to such a man as my husband, but it took you longer than most. What I mean is that all the others were too easy; they succumbed to his spell immediately. None of them attempted the foolish escapes you did. In all truthfulness, though, this reluctance of yours has probably temporarily saved your life, for the count is unable to tolerate such weaknesses as the others displayed. He prefers some spirit in his women." Teresa's tone was harsh. And she was talking as though she did not care that her husband had affairs with other women—numerous other women!

"The count's son must have a strong mother, for she will have to be able to deal with the task set before her." Was that cynicism I detected in her voice? Teresa stood up from her chair. "I have matters that need my attention. Please," she waved her hand around the room, "make yourself at home, for that is what this place shall be to you for awhile. There are many books here on the shelves, should you enjoy reading. I do not particularly enjoy such a pastime. There is quite a variety here that might be of interest to you—especially this one."

Teresa pulled a book off the shelf and handed it to me. Unlike the other hardcover books, this one was bound in leather. I glanced inside it. It appeared to be a diary of some sort. "I shall see you tomorrow evening," Teresa stated. "And don't even dream of attempting another escape, for Max, or I, shall never be far away," she added as she strutted from the room, leaving me alone with the book in my hand and with my thoughts.

Alone? No, I was not alone anymore. *It* was there. His seed grew within me. My plan had not succeeded. Unlike Teresa's insinuation of my resistance to his wiles, I knew the count had conquered me without any real immense struggle. I felt sure that, wherever he was at the moment, if he were even thinking of me, he was most likely mocking me. He was probably laughing at the foolish little trollop who had thought she could con such a powerful man.

I glanced at the title of the book Teresa had selected: *History of the Musat Family.* How interesting, I thought as I opened it up and began to read.

~

The fate of our family has been sealed with that of Vlad Dracula. Time, action, and blood have forged our souls together for an eternity in hell. Now that this fact has been confirmed in my mind, I feel it is time to record certain events that led up to the horrific demise that has befallen our royal families. The God that we once prayed to in the great cathedrals of Wallachia, Transylvania, and Moldavia has totally forsaken us, and the witches of Satan have cursed us with a never-ending night.

My name is Atilla Musat. The year is 1480. I was born in Moldavia in 1434. My parents were Ilias and Maria Musat. My first cousin was Stephen, also known as Stephen the Great, whose parents were Bogdan II and Oltea. Not only was my Aunt Oltea related to the Dracul family by blood, a cousin I believe, but my Aunt Eupraxia, a sister of my father, was married to Vlad Dracul, the father of Dracula, who in later years became known as the Impaler. With all of this intermingling of families, one could say that we, Stephen, Dracula, and I, were cousins. Therefore, we spent many of our early years together being educated in the fine art of becoming true princes of the land.

Our fathers were all members of the Order of Dragons, an organization sworn to the preservation and protection of Christianity. However, when I think about my childhood, I realize that neither my father nor my uncles exhibited much reverence for the Christian church, other than homage just sufficient to obtain her eternal blessings and the abundant benefits of her purse. Of the three, my dear uncle Vlad Dracul was the worst. He became so obsessed with his power that he even minted his own coin. The sons of the men of the Order of the Dragon inherited all that went with that symbol, and more. Of the "more" I will speak later.

Stephen and I grew up in the same court, and on many occasions, because our Aunt Eupraxia was married to Vlad Dracul, Dracula would join us for schooling. I was the youngest; Stephen was two years older than Dracula. There were many times those two treated me as if I were a baby, but their demeaning me only encouraged my inner strength and forced me to grow up wise beyond my years. People in the court were always pointing at me and saying things like, "poor child, so old for his age" or "poor little thing, always trying to live up to the expectations of those two older boys."

There passed a long period when Dracula was not able to come to our home. His father had made some sort of pact, as I was later informed, with the Turks. As an insurance policy for Vlad Dracul's word, Dracula and his younger brother, Radu, had been sent to the palace of Sultan Mohammed II of Turkey.

That happened in the summer of 1444. I remember it

vividly, because it was the year I turned ten, which meant I would be able to join Stephen and Dracula at the family table for mealtimes. Age ten was our initial step into manhood. The stigma of being a baby who had to take his meals in the nursery would be lifted from me; I would be able to socialize with my cousins, not only as their equal, but as the man I felt I was.

However, Dracula never arrived—not that summer, nor the next, nor the next. In fact, Dracula was not returned to his homeland until 1448, and he was changed. He had taken on a look and mannerism that Stephen and I could not fathom. Dracula was a young man of eighteen, yet sometimes he appeared, when he thought Stephen and I were not watching, like an old and hardened man who had seen more than his share of the world's cruelties. Stephen and I worried about these drastic changes, and when we were alone we discussed, at great lengths, the metamorphosis of our dear cousin.

In addition to whatever atrocities Dracula had endured while residing at the Turkish court as a guest—actually, a political prisoner, if I were to say the true meaning of why he was there—he had also had to deal with the death of his father. Vlad Dracul was murdered by Mircea, one of the traitorous boyars, in November 1447. To make matters even worse, his father's body was never found. We three cousins were mystified about this. Stephen and I prayed for the burial plot to be found, if for nothing more than to settle Dracula's state of mind. We noticed how this lack of knowledge ate away at his soul and the darkness in his eyes deepened with each passing day.

During Dracula's stay, from September 1448 to December 1451, we studied together, rode together, eyed and chased girls of the surrounding villages together, and practised the art of fighting.

Dracula developed quite the reputation with the young maidens; however, it was not one that had them flocking willingly into his arms. Mothers would lock their daughters inside, and fathers would keep axes by their doors. Dracula would laugh and state that these girls were nothing to him—just playthings to pass away some meaningless time. And any of them who had fallen to his wiles were never quite the same again—some even succumbed to insanity.

I clearly remember an event that happened during the summer of 1451. Our tutor had decided to give me, Stephen, and Dracula an afternoon off from our studies. Possibly it was because of our unexpectedly good behaviour, as we had been studying hard as of late, but I think it was more due to the fact that our tutor had some other planned entertainment for his own afternoon. Not one of us was about to question his good intentions, though. We headed for the meadow at the farthest point of our estate.

It had been a scorching day, but we knew that the pond near that particular meadow would offer our feverish bodies a cool haven. It was nestled inside a grove of ancient trees and was fed by an underground mountain stream.

We stripped and swam, lay naked in the sun, swam some more, and then fell asleep on the green carpet beside the pond. Stephen and I were shaken awake by Dracula, who was suggesting that we seal our brotherhood in blood. I thought at the time it was rather peculiar but, along with Stephen, agreed that it would be a fun thing to do.

Dracula passed us his knife and told us what to do. Stephen and I sliced tiny cuts on our index fingers. Dracula did likewise. As we reached forward to mix our blood in the traditional manner of blood brothers, fingertip to fingertip, Dracula grabbed hold of our wrists and stopped us. Then he took Stephen's hand, raised it to his mouth, and sucked the blood from the open wound. He repeated this action with me.

I experienced a peculiar sensation as Dracula drank the

blood from my opened flesh. I felt, for a moment, that there
was an aura of evil surrounding him. He motioned for us to do
the same to each other, and we did. Dracula informed us that
we were now true blood brothers and that nothing or no one
would ever be able to break our blood bond. This event, as I
learned later, was the first substantial step that sealed our souls
together, forever in darkness.

In October of that year our lives were ripped apart once again
by the assassination of Stephen's father, my dearest uncle, Bogdan
II. Dracula became deranged. His eyes assumed the crazed look
of a man possessed. He took to taking long rides over the fields.
He would ravage the land, scarring with his blade whatever
crossed his path. A few of the maidens who were unaware of his
atrocities and attempted to accommodate his sexual desires met
with untimely and grizzly deaths. Dracula was out of control!

One morning in late December, as the three of us were
enjoying a hearty breakfast, Dracula announced his desire to
leave. He told Stephen and me that enough was enough—first
his father had been brutally murdered and then his precious
uncle, who had given him shelter since his return from Turkey.
Both deaths were without reason. He informed us that he was
going to get to the bottom of their murders, no matter how
deadly the game became. He would flush out the culprits and
avenge the deaths of his father and his uncle, if it was the last
thing he ever did.

Dracula had never spoken much of the events or the things
he had been subjected to in the Turkish courts; however, he
informed us that now the time had come to use the knowledge
he had obtained from the Sultan Mohammed II to benefit his
own people.

His intention, as well, was to return the rightful heir to the
throne of Wallachia, namely himself. He described to Stephen and
me how corrupt the rich boyars were and how he planned to put

them all to shame for their treachery, for they, Dracula believed, were the ones responsible for the deaths of our loved ones.

Stephen and I both cautioned him to be careful and to turn his back to neither friend nor foe. Stephen told me of his fears when we were alone. He could not help worrying about Dracula. "He has changed so, little cousin," he would say. "The demons have possessed him; I am afraid this is one time that even we cannot reach him."

I, still being young, just listened, and watched, and prayed. I prayed that time would heal my cousin and that God would save him before it was too late. That, of course, was during the time that I could still pray to the God in the heavens.

Within the week, Dracula departed.

Max found me in a deep slumber when he brought my breakfast to the den in the morning. The book lay open on my lap. Max shook my shoulder. There was a worried tone in his voice as he called out my name.

"Miss Virginia, wake up," Max ordered gently. "Are you okay?"

Was that concern I detected in his voice? My eyes fluttered open. I was wringing wet. I had been dreaming of the three young men who had grown up together. I had been dreaming of Lilly, the walking nightmare, but it had not been her face I had seen beneath the flowing cape—it had been mine!

"Thank you, Max. I am fine; just a restless sleep, I guess," I murmured as I gathered myself and the book and walked out of the study. I clutched the history of the formidable family close to my bosom. I was hungry for more, yet I was terrified of what else I might find written on the upcoming pages!

Max stepped aside to allow me to lead the way. He followed closely with my breakfast tray as I went up the long stairway that led to my room on the second floor.

CHAPTER 9

The Seal of Blood

For the next while, I filled my waking hours with reading. The count's father had kept such an accurate account of the happenings that at times I almost experienced pangs of sorrow and pity for the plight that had befallen such a proud royal family. His writings humanized them for me; I was getting the sense that they were victims of a fate totally out of their control. The story continued.

Stephen and I waited patiently for a letter from Dracula. It was not forthcoming. However, we did hear news of his escapades, and the reports we received were that Dracula had become a bloodthirsty, diabolical monster. He was wreaking such havoc on the people that even the few friends he had left began to wonder about their safety. It was rumoured from town to town that Dracula no longer feasted on the food of the land; instead, he drank the blood of his victims—at times even before their breaths had fully expired from their bodies!

Stephen was even more uneasy than I. He, as the eldest,

naturally held added authority, especially since his father's death. He wrote several letters to Dracula, pleading to the sanity that he knew, or felt, had once been there. It was a futile attempt. Dracula did not reply, and the horror stories grew more appalling as they spread throughout the land.

Dracula became known through all the regions as the embodiment of evil. No boyar in the land could roam at will, for fear he might cross the path of this bloodthirsty demon. We heard stories that when the older members of that distinguished society of boyars were so unfortunate as to happen upon Dracula, they were impaled on high poles around the dinner table of Dracula and his followers. Impaling was Dracula's favourite method of eliminating whomever he thought to be his enemy. It was also said that Dracula drank their blood as it dripped into waiting goblets.

Others met torture, such as the severing of noses, ears, sexual organs, and limbs. Some were blinded with burning sticks, strangled, boiled alive, or skinned while breath still rustled in their lungs. There were even more gruesome things, which I feel I cannot mention here, for they would turn the stomach of even the most seasoned warriors. The younger boyars, along with their families, were enslaved and put to work rebuilding Dracula's castle. Some of the more fortunate boyars escaped from the country and did not return until the reign of Dracula's brother, Radu the Handsome. Some of these same men, it was rumoured, plotted with Radu to overthrow his deranged brother.

Yet even with all this devastation, time after time, the majority of the people of the land seemed to bow to Dracula's rule. It was rumoured that Dracula had great dialectical talents, so great that he could twist the minds of men he thought to be his enemies to confess guilt for events they had taken no part in. He was also able to persuade the lowly people to believe in his great cause—by convincing them it was their cause as well.

We heard the news that Dracula had taken a wife and that he was quite smitten with her. It was said that she was the daughter of a boyar who had all too willingly exchanged his daughter for his own freedom. But it was also said that she was deeply devoted to her husband. I hoped that her devotion might calm the demons in my cousin.

In 1462, Stephen decided to join with the Turks in an invasion against Dracula. I did not follow him into battle—I could not comprehend why Stephen would turn on our beloved cousin. Finally, one night, Stephen explained to me that, first and foremost, his duty was to protect his country. That responsibility had to take precedence above all else, even above his personal oath of allegiance to his cousin. In Stephen's opinion, Dracula was going too far with his revenge.

Even though Stephen had spoken with anger, I knew there was true pain buried in his heart when he wielded his sword against the cousin he loved so dearly. And I always felt there was something else Stephen had failed to tell me at the time. It was something I would not have knowledge of until much later, when the tides turned against us.

Near the end of June 1462, Dracula was defeated by Mohammed II of Turkey, the same man whom Dracula and Radu's father had sent them to as an insurance policy in 1444. Now Mohammed was appointing Radu to be in charge of destroying his brother, Dracula.

If truth be told here, there had never been any love lost between those two. Radu had always been jealous of their father's preference for Dracula, and he was also bitter that Dracula had not been able to protect him from the Turk's lust for young men while they had been political prisoners. There were times that I wondered if the same lust had been inflicted upon Dracula.

I also questioned, many times, where Dracula had garnered the knowledge of such revolting torture methods. It was rumoured that the Turks were masters of such. I remembered that Dracula had never been the same after his incarceration in Turkey.

The few Romanian boyars who had remained loyal to Dracula quickly abandoned their leader when they realized that the Turkish army was stronger than their own. Many of them even took up arms with Radu, because he promised that their lands and families would be safe under his rule and that the Turks would leave them in peace.

Despite all the treason around him, Dracula still managed to gain two victories in July and September, but by November of 1462, Radu was recognized as the prince of the land by the Boyar Council and King Matthias of Hungary. I had tired of waiting for the axe to fall upon my beloved cousin, and I had not yet found it in my heart to agree with or to join Stephen's alliance with the Turks. I gathered a small force of men and raced to join Dracula.

I knew I was too late to save him from losing his throne, but I felt he might be in need of a true friend—a friend who would watch his back and not stab it. Stephen was home for a short time, and I could tell by the hurt look in his eyes as we bade goodbye that he wished he was riding by my side to the aid of our beloved cousin. His alliance with the Turks was not going exactly as he had thought it would. The Turks were never to be totally trusted. Stephen told me that history would eventually repeat itself, and the boyar's contentment would be short-lived.

I also bade my goodbyes to Mara, my betrothed, for I had grown up and fallen deeply in love with a most beautiful maiden.

"Atilla, I beg you," she cried, tears pouring from her eyes, "don't do this thing; stay here with me. Dracula is lost; he deserves what is happening to him! He is an atrocious man."

I gathered Mara into my arms. "Hush, hush—do not speak so, my love. I go to him as a friend, as a cousin, as a blood brother. I know he cannot be saved—he must relinquish his throne. I go to bring him home, to give him sanctuary when this whole mess is over. As for him deserving this fate, I cannot say that you really know enough of who he truly is to say such a thing. Fate has not always been kind to him."

Mara's sobs subsided. She raised her tear-streaked face to me. "Kiss me, Atilla, love of my life. Let me taste your love just this once, for I fear you shall not return to me."

"I shall return to you, beloved Mara," I whispered before I closed my lips over her trembling ones and then partook of her delicate fruits. The next morning I arose early. I left my love in a rumpled bed and set out to join my cousin.

Dracula welcomed me with open arms. I could tell the fortunes of war were wearing heavily on his spirit. He filled me in on the situation, including the fact that he had taken a wife. I told him we had heard such news and asked if he were happy. Dracula smiled, a rarity for him, and then told me his wife was becoming the heart of his soul. He was tiring of war and wished to spend more time with her. We wept silent tears as we gazed into each other's eyes. Then we turned to await our destiny in the valley of the Arges River, where the Turkish army, along with Radu and the boyars, were fast approaching.

Dracula's enemies were many—not only outside of his ranks, but within them, as well. He had created that state of affairs, though, with his tyrannical behaviour. Unfortunately, an unknown soldier—possibly a relative; we never discovered who—sent a message to Dracula's wife at Castle Dracula. It was a death message, stating that Dracula had been sent to hell and would not be returning home to her arms. She could not bear the thought of losing her beloved husband or the thought of what might be her fate if the Turks captured her, so she threw herself from the high tower window. The river, Riul Doamnei (Princess River), became her tomb. Her body was never found.

Dracula had returned to his castle ahead of me. I had stayed back with a small group of men to try and hold off the Turks. Upon my arrival to the castle I was informed of the sorrowful news about Dracula's wife. I gazed upon a defeated man. Love for a woman can soften the hardest heart in the chest of any man. As I looked upon my cousin, there was no doubt in my mind of Dracula's love for his wife. He ranted and raved as never before. He was a broken man. And as Dracula's grief increased, so did the pounding on the castle walls as they began to crumble under the assault of the Turks on Dracula's private realm.

I knew our time was running out. It would not be long before the walls fell completely. I had no desire to be locked in some Turkish prison and be subjected to tortures that would leave me broken of mind, spirit, and body. I finally convinced my cousin it was necessary for us to flee. Dracula and I escaped, during the night, through secret passages that had been tunnelled through the mountains. What we came upon there, when we exited from the mountain, sealed our destiny. Entering a clearing, we were confronted with a circle of wagons and a group of Gypsy women who were preparing their meal over an open fire. Although we had no great use for Gypsy nomads, our bellies were sorely hungry, so we walked toward the savoury smells.

Upon reaching the enclosure of wagons, we hesitated. We felt there was something peculiar going on. There were no Gypsy men. This was strange—strange indeed! Suddenly, one of the hags turned to us. "At last, you have come," she shrieked. "I have waited many moons to curse your bloodthirsty ways! You and this pup that runs at your side are not worthy to walk in the healing rays of our Mother Sun!" She cast something into the pot she was stirring. A thick, grey smoke billowed into the air.

Dracula regained some of his composure. "What power do you think you wield over me, you sack of broken bones?" he demanded arrogantly.

There was a long, pregnant pause before the creature spoke. The others ceased their activities. They began to form a circle around Dracula and me. We were trapped. The only way out was through their knuckled fists. They began to chant, a droning sound, as the old hag picked up from where she had left off. "Vlad Dracula, better known to all those less fortunate than you as the Impaler, I curse you to an everlasting hell!" the seasoned witch screeched. "Your days shall be spent under closed lids, your nights in horrid shadows. You shall run in the night with the swiftness of the wolf; your eyes shall burn red like a cave bat and you will coerce your victims into submission. You shall be as cunning and charming as the red fox while you lure your victims to your den of darkness. But, at the same time that you are exerting such power, no rest shall ever refresh your soul, and no peace will ever ease your mind. No man shall open his door to you or give you refuge at his table. You, that pup at your side, and all your descendants shall be burdened with this curse from now and into eternity! Those who stand here with me are my witnesses to this blight I cast upon you and yours!"

I dropped the book into my lap and shuddered at the evilness in such a curse. A Gypsy witch had cursed the family—yet it was a Gypsy who served in the home of the Count Basarab Musat—the son of Atilla Musat, who had written the account. As well, the count had married a Gypsy's daughter. What a web had been woven of the lives of these ancient people, who had lived through centuries of aimless wandering as they literally sucked the blood of the land.

Chapter 10

The Curse of Blood

The vampire stalks his victims in the darkest of the night,
They know not where he takes them or what will be their plight.
The wolves sing their songs of woe for what is to be lost,
But all their master's secrets they protect at any cost.

The victims are now lying in the lair of their rebirth,
Far beneath the ground they are, in the vampire's earth.
And the wolves sing praises to their master's great might,
For they, like him, are the children of the night.

The story of this family was fascinating—there was no stopping me from reading on. Nothing like this had ever been portrayed in the movies. I could sense myself feeling empathy for their plight. I could not put the book down ...

As soon as the Gypsy women dropped their hands to their sides, Dracula and I fled that clearing as quickly as possible; the old hag's screeching still echoing in our ears. There are moments, even now, when I think I hear her evil cackle, and then vivid memories of that fateful day rush back to consume me. In truth, I am not sure who the truly evil creature is in this whole mess, for our curse was placed upon us through no choosing of our own.

Our flight led us back into the tunnels from whence we had come. Soon my breath ran short, and I grabbed Dracula's arm. "Please, dear cousin, I must rest."

Dracula laughed. "You are weak, Atilla. Whoever thought to bestow you with such a mighty warrior's name?"

The mockery in his words was belittling. Once again I found myself the child trying to live up to the older cousin. How soon he had forgotten who had come to his aid and who had stayed by his side during his moment of great grief. "It has been a long day, cousin, one filled with many disappointments, not only for me, but for you as well. We must sit a moment, gather our thoughts, and decide what we are to do now. On one side we have a castle destroyed; to the other we have a group of cursed Gypsies. We must lay low for awhile; you can be sure that your enemies will be searching diligently for us, especially for you."

"I apologize if I have touched a nerve, cousin," Dracula smiled. "I meant no harm. You are quite right; we must take cover for a time, until the winds blow safe again."

"What do you think the old hag meant by all her blabbering?" I questioned.

"Just an ill wind we came upon. More gusto than gusts, I am sure," Dracula replied. But there was a troubled tone to his voice, one that did not often creep into my cousin's words.

Days turned into weeks and weeks into months. Dracula and I foraged from the land and drank from the rivers. The heavy forests became our refuge, day and night. At one point I mentioned we should seek refuge at Stephen's, but Dracula was not yet ready to put any trust in a cousin who had sided with the enemy, against him. I tried to defend Stephen, but

Dracula perceived my heart was not in the words I spoke. I knew, though, that the day would inevitably arrive when we would both have to go crawling to Stephen for protection and shelter. Trust would be there, confirmed with Stephen's open arms—of that I felt certain in my heart.

Finally that day arrived. I had convinced Dracula that there was no other way. We found ourselves sneaking to the back entrance of Stephen's castle. The moon was resting elsewhere, and the stars were hiding amongst the clouds. Even the guards were not careful of their obligations on the night we chose.

Once we were inside the castle, we found our way around with no problem. What Dracula had forgotten, I had no trouble remembering, as I had lived there most of my life. We meandered through tunnels and passageways until we reached the top floor of the castle, where I knew Stephen had his quarters.

I tapped lightly on the door. No answer. I tapped again. Still there was no answer. Had my cousin come to be such a heavy sleeper that he could not hear a knock on his door? This was very dangerous for one in such a high position. Dracula decided to just enter. We could not take the chance on being caught standing in a hallway.

The door squeaked open. We hesitated. Dracula pushed his way in further. To our surprise, Stephen was not alone. There were two in the bed. The squeaking of the door must have awakened Stephen. He leapt from his bed and drew the sword that lay close by.

"Who dares to enter my bedchambers unannounced?"

"Hush, Stephen; it is I, your cousin Atilla. Look whom I have brought with me—Dracula."

There was a moment of silence, and then Stephen dropped his sword and rushed to embrace us with open arms. Nothing else mattered for those brief seconds of welcome. We were home, and everything was going to be all right.

"Come," Stephen directed, "we must go elsewhere to speak. I do not wish to wake my wife."

We were ushered out of the room and led down the hall. Stephen pushed a brick in the wall and an opening appeared before us. He motioned for us to follow. The revelation was startling; I had had no idea this particular passage existed. At the end of it we entered a small sitting room. It was scattered with books and papers, old family paintings, and four large chairs, one behind a small mahogany desk, the other three distributed randomly in front of it.

Stephen motioned for us to sit down, and then he sat in the chair behind the desk. "Where do we begin?" he asked, opening the conversation, but directing us to take the lead.

Dracula caught me off-guard. "We begin with why you sided with the bastardly Turks," he demanded.

Stephen surprised me with his calmness. "I, like your father before me, had no choice, my dear cousin. I had received a letter from the Turkish court stating that if I did not join forces with them, then all whom I loved would meet with a dreadful end. Princess Evdochia, of the Ukraine—whom, as you know, Atilla, I was courting—had been taken captive by the Turkish emperor. My mother's life was also threatened and yours, as well, Atilla. I had no choice. As much as I wanted to tell you, I dared not, for fear of what you would do or, worse yet, what might happen to you." There were tears in Stephen's eyes. I saw them; I hoped that Dracula saw them, too.

He did. He calmed down. I could tell, from his facial expression, that the pain of his own recent loss still weighed heavily on his heart. "We only wish to have temporary sanctuary, cousin; are you able to provide that?"

"Yes, but I shall have to keep you well hidden, for there are some, even in my own court, whom I can no longer trust."

There was a pause in the conversation. Stephen's eyebrows

were creased in thought. Finally, he reopened the dialogue. "I and my wife are finding great sensitivity to the daylight hours, and our appetite for food is decreasing at an alarming pace. How do you find your health to be, or is this just happening to us?"

I shuddered. Dracula and I had been experiencing similar symptoms. The old hag's curse came rushing back to my mind. "We and ours have been cursed!" I burst out.

Dracula threw me a warning glance, but it was too late. Stephen pushed for an explanation. "What kind of a curse?" he demanded. "Who would curse our family like this?"

Dracula motioned for me to respond. I proffered the reply. "We have been cursed by the Gypsies—a specific Gypsy, that is. It was a strange curse, though. She said we were a bloodthirsty lot and not fit to walk in the rays of our Mother Sun. She said our days were to be spent under closed lids, our nights in the shadows. She compared us to such creatures as the wolf and the bat; she spoke of us having to lure our victims into our dens of darkness. She said no rest would ever be on our souls; no peace would ever be in our lives. This is the curse she cast, not just upon Dracula and me, but on all our family and on all our descendants. She even said it would be unto eternity."

Heavy silence filled the small room. I could barely breathe, the pain of having to speak of the curse being so great to bear. "Then that is the reason behind this strangeness I feel," Stephen began. "There is something I must tell you; my wife is pregnant. If what you are saying is true, this curse is also on my unborn child."

"On yours and on any that may one day be born to us," I replied.

Dracula spoke up, anger filling his words. "I shall consult the Order of the Dragons—"

Stephen cut him off. "You can consult with no one. As soon as you step out of the shadows, you will be captured and then hung. Your brother, Radu, is on the throne now, and that

is the way many in the land wish it to be, Vlad Dracul—for
that is what some are calling you now, after your father, and it
is a name many wish to forget." Stephen turned directly to me.
"As for you, Atilla, your name is not so linked with his; there is
something I can still do for you. It will also be good to have an
ally by my side, one whom I can trust completely." He paused
before continuing on. "By the way, Mara, awaits your return.
She is here in my castle, weeping every day, thinking that you
are dead and your body is buried in some unmarked grave or,
worse yet, thrown to the elements to be eaten by a wild animal.
My wife tries to comfort her, but Mara feels her heart will not
be mended until she is in the arms of her beloved Atilla." For
the first time since entering the room, Stephen smiled.

"Mara, my beautiful Mara—she still waited for me."

"And one more bit of news that I must add," Stephen
continued. "She is heavy with child."

I was dumbfounded. Heavy with child! How could that
possibly be? Suddenly, realization swept over me. It must have
happened on the night before I had left to join Dracula, when
I had held her to me, and she had closed her arms around me.
I remembered her words, whispered through her trembling lips
as I covered them with my own. "I could not bear to have never
known you in this manner," she had whispered. "If anything
were to happen to you during this war, and I never saw you
again, I would surely die. Give me a child, my beloved Atilla,
so that if you do not return, I shall at least have a replica of you
with me forever. But if you do return, then we shall have a son.
If you are long in this thing that you must do, I shall speak to
him every day, so that when you come home and walk through
the door he will know you are his father!"

It had been a night of urgent passion. Both of us had been
spent. Neither one of us had considered the dilemma Mara
would find herself in if I failed to return and she was found to

be pregnant. She would have lived in disgrace forever. Thank God for Stephen.

"How is she?" I asked.

"She is doing well, in spite of all that is happening."

"When is the child due?"

"In two weeks."

I was shocked. Had Dracula and I been gone that long? "I must see her."

"I shall take you to her in the morning, but I must warn you of one thing. This curse must be striking her as well, for she, too, lacks appetite and has taken to hiding behind the castle walls in the daylight hours. Many have been the moonlit nights when Mara, Evdochia, and I have walked the garden paths so that we might breathe the fresh air outside of the castle walls."

It was settled that I would be reunited with Mara in the morning, and a small wedding ceremony would be celebrated as soon as possible. Dracula would be kept hidden for the time being, at least until we came up with a solution. Stephen, now that he knew that what was happening to him, Evdochia, and Mara was a curse from the Gypsies, promised us he would talk to the one priest he could still trust, Father Mihail. Stephen mentioned that even though Father Mihail remained faithful to the family, he had had to remove all the crosses and holy water from their personal chapel. The sensitivity to such religious symbols was also increasing by the day!

"I shall return for you in the morning." Stephen rose from his chair. "You two may rest here for the remainder of the night; I shall see about more appropriate accommodations for you tomorrow."

My reunion with Mara was a joyous moment, but only for an instant. I gazed into her heavy eyes and knew that Stephen's description of her well-being had been kind. She was a ghost of the vibrant young woman I had made love to a few short months before. But her arms were firm as they embraced me, and her eyes still told me how much she loved me.

"Look, Atilla," she said, placing my hands upon her belly. "Your son is a hungry one, so much so that he leaves me weak and with little spirit. Maybe now that you have returned you can tell him to treat his mother with greater respect," she laughed. It was a good sound to hear.

"I shall have the doctor, Count Balenti Danesti, look in on you," I replied. "He has looked after our family for years. He will know what to do."

"He has been attending me, and he, too, is baffled about what is happening to all of us, my love," Mara informed me. "But he is working on a drink, something filled with nutritious herbs that will restore my strength, he mentioned to me. He says it is almost finished."

"I shall still speak with him and encourage him to hurry to finish his solution before you waste further away. And we must have a ceremony. I shall speak to Stephen about having Father Mihail marry us immediately."

"Stephen has been wonderful to me, Atilla. When you did not return, I feared for so many things: your safety, the unborn child, my reputation being soiled and me being cast into the streets, and then, worst of all, I feared losing our child. All these things weighed heavily on me. Stephen and Evdochia took me in and then informed the court that you and I had been secretly married the night of your flight. Even though many did not believe that story, no one dared to refute the word of the lord and mistress of this castle. The wagging tongues were hushed; it is only Father Mihail who knows the real truth. He is the one who is supposed to have performed our wedding."

"Then, this time, it shall be for real."

Mara and I were married in the secret room within the week. There were three witnesses: Stephen, Evdochia, and Dracula. Our son was born three days later. We called him Basarab.

CHAPTER 11

The Lightening of the Curse

I continued reading ...

Life was becoming progressively more difficult for all of us. Mara, after delivering Basarab, grew weaker by the day. Dr. Balenti was still working on his special drink. I thought he would never finish.

"Yes, here it is," he cried excitedly one day. "This should sustain our precious Mara and bring the rosy glow back into her cheeks."

Dr. Balenti held a glass up to Mara's lips. She sipped at the liquid and screwed up her face. "This is terrible, Doctor," she sputtered.

"You must drink it, Mara, for Basarab's sake." Dr. Balenti knew Mara would do anything for her son.

Mara heaved a deep sigh, held her breath, and kept trying to down the strange concoction. Slowly the liquid disappeared from the glass. She lay back on her pillows.

"There, there now, Mara; now you can rest awhile, love." The doctor's voice was gentle.

Mara's eyes closed. Sleep overtook her. The doctor stood up and left the room. I had been watching him from the hallway, not wanting to distract his effort to get Mara to take the drink.

"How is she, Count Balenti?" I asked.

"She will be fine, I hope."

I looked closely at his eyes. "You are unsure?"

"Yes. I must be honest with you, Atilla. Mara is very weak. The most I may be able to do, at this point in time, is save your son. In all my years of practice I have never come across such a malady." There were tears in Balenti's eyes as he admitted what might be inevitable.

I soon had to face the realization that, even with the benefit of the drink, there was little hope for my Mara. Each day that passed exacerbated the circles around her eyes, the cavities in her cheeks, and the extrusion of her bones. Her milk dried up as well, and there were moments we worried how we would be able to sustain the child if something happened to Mara. Doctor Balenti decided that we should start giving Basarab some of the drink—he thrived on it. He started to fill out, and a healthy child blossomed before our eyes.

Finally, I'd had enough. I approached Dracula with a plan. "I must go and seek out those Gypsies. I have to try to convince them to lift the curse. That may be the only way to save my Mara." I believe that, at the time, I was not really asking my cousin for permission to do this.

Dracula pleaded with me, "Atilla, I do not consider that a good idea. You may worsen the curse. As it is now, none of us are able to look into the sun; properly prepared food tastes disgusting, and we have taken to eating raw meat and drinking the blood of animals to satisfy our appetites and sustain our bodies."

"I must try, cousin—I must try! You, of all people know what it is to love and lose your heart!" I turned and left the room.

⌒

The next evening I kissed Mara goodnight, put Basarab to bed, and left Stephen's castle. Since I could no longer tolerate the sunlight, I waited until its last rays disappeared before heading for the mountainous area where Dracula and I had happened upon the Gypsy hag. I had packed two saddlebags with four containers filled with animal blood. There would be no sense in stopping in towns, for I knew that no one in them would be willing to serve a man his supper in the middle of the night—especially the kind of meal that would sustain a man like me!

I kept to the forested areas. When the sun began to creep over the horizon and burn my skin, I sought shelter in amongst the trees, tethered my horse, and slept under the branches of the great cedars.

Two days passed without incident. I reckoned I had about two or three more nights of travelling before I reached the area around Dracula's castle. I wondered whether Radu had decided to live there or if he had built his own fortress elsewhere.

I was gathering my belongings together to set out on my third night of travel, when I heard wagon wheels and Gypsy music. Had God finally thought to bless me by sending the old hag to me without my having to travel any further? Of course, there was the possibility it would not be the group of Gypsies that I was seeking.

Instead of mounting my horse, I led him through the trees toward the sound of the music. I came upon a moonlit clearing; the Gypsy wagons were just completing their circle. And there she was—the old hag! She was directing the others on setting up camp, from her self-made throne.

"I smell a pup," the hag cackled out to her charges.

One of the older Gypsy women returned an answer. "You always smell dogs, Tanyasin. What we need to do is find you a young man to settle the stirring in your loins!" She laughed. It was a musical laugh, not spoiled with the same malevolence as the hag's.

"I don't need a man, young or old!" the hag retorted sarcastically. "Is it not because you have loved too many men in your lifetime that you finally came to me, in order to give your bones a rest?" This was spoken with an evil grin.

The other woman smiled but said nothing. She went about the business of setting up camp, holding her head high and keeping her back straight. I could tell that she did not fear the hag. In her I might find an ally—maybe even a friend.

I know it was a hasty move, but I felt I had no choice. The sooner I dealt with this, the sooner I would be able to return to Mara and Basarab. I tied my horse securely to a tree branch and then boldly approached the clearing.

I watched the old hag sniff the air, and then she turned toward me like a crazed animal. "It is you—the pup! Where is the dog you run with—hiding like the coward that he is?" she shrieked. "How is life for you? Are you enjoying your long days in the sun?" She exuded malevolence like none I had never known.

Unabashed, I began my request, the one I had rehearsed a thousand times in my mind. "I have come to beg your forgiveness, for whatever sin it was I committed against you and yours, and to ask you to release me and my family from this horrid curse you have wreaked upon us.

"My beautiful wife is dying because of your curse. Her eyes are lifeless, her skin is dull, and her mind is slowly slipping away. She has never hurt anyone in her life; she does not deserve such a death." I was pleading.

"So, tell me about the boy." The hag's question took me by surprise. "What is it you have called him—Basarab?"

Her question shocked me! "Yes," I replied, not daring to ask how she knew that I even had a child, let alone what I had called him.

"Well, how does he fare?"

"At the moment he is healthy, but only because of a drink our doctor concocted. The child still needs his mother."

The hag stepped down from her perch and walked toward me. I held my stance. She came close and pushed her face up to mine. I was overwhelmed by the foulness of her breath.

"Basarab will not need his mother—nor anyone else, for that matter—to survive. He shall be the most powerful of your kind, for he is the firstborn of your kind. How ironic, eh, pup, that you should be the one to sire the leader of your people?"

I could not understand, then, exactly what she meant. I would not know until much later, when Basarab began to grow and mature in his—how do I say it?—in his "lifestyle" as he passed from childhood into manhood.

"Get out of here, pup," the hag yelled to me. "Get out! Crawl back to your dog. I have nothing to offer you. And next time, tell the dog to come himself—or is he not man enough to show his face to me?" Tanyasin smirked wickedly.

"He has nothing to do with why I am here. I have come to beg you to find it in your soul to help my wife." I grovelled, falling to my knees. I kissed the earth at the hem of her rags. "For myself, I ask nothing; I will accept whatever the curse has in store for me. But my Mara—she is an innocent in all of this."

Tanyasin spit on the ground beside me and then turned and walked to her wagon. "I have no soul, pup, something you should remember in the future! And another thing you should remember—the dog has everything to do with why you were compelled to come here. He is the reason for the curse upon your families. Don't forget that fact when you embrace him at your wife's funeral!"

I was totally broken. My Mara was going to die. My mission had failed, miserably. Gradually I stood up and then headed back to my horse—back to my fate. I noticed something move in the trees, but paid no heed. I was a broken man, ready to face death myself if I lost Mara. Stephen and Dracula would raise my son. Basarab would be in good hands.

"Pup!" I heard an anxious whisper. "Come quickly, over here!"

I turned toward the voice. There was the woman who had stood up to the hag. I ventured to her hiding place.

"Listen carefully," she began. "I cannot undo what Tanyasin has done to you, but I do have the power to allow your kind some release should you ever decide to leave this world."

"What do you mean by 'decide to leave'?" I asked. "Everyone dies eventually."

"You are a new breed. Because of the curse, you are not meant to die," she replied straightforwardly. "Tanyasin failed to inform you of that one little bit of information."

"What can you do for us?" I probed, defeat weighing heavily upon me.

She laid her hands upon my head and pushed me gently down to my knees. Then she closed her eyes and began to hum, a soft, sweet music, not harsh and evil as Tanyasin's had been.

"You will take to sleeping in a coffin during daylight hours. In your coffin you must place some earth from your homeland. That, as well as the drinking of blood, is how you shall be sustained. Take care, though, of what kind of blood you drink—that of an animal will nourish you as well as a human's; however, some of you will be tempted to partake of the human kind. Remember, that will only lead to disaster. Tanyasin said you would run with the swiftness of the wolf; your eyes would be able to see like those of a cave bat—I will give you the power to become a wolf, or a bat, when there is need for you to camouflage who, or what, it is you are to become under this curse. Both of these creatures are feared by man, and both are night creatures, as you, too, will soon be. And, like them, you will grow incisors that will be strong enough to feed upon your prey; although it would be better for you to draw the blood in another manner, if possible. Learn the art of butchery, for it will aid you in your new life.

"To end your existence, should it become too burdensome for you, someone must drive a stake through your heart, sever your head from your body, and then seal your remains in your coffin. The head, however, must be buried separately, for your life can be restored if someone opens the coffin and pulls the stake from your heart. If both body and head are together again, you will rise up and be even more powerful than you were before!

"There is a place in the mountains, close to Count Dracula's castle. It is filled with caverns—an ideal refuge for you and yours. You will be able to live in society eventually, but this should become the soil of your final resting place if death should ever happen to you, either by choice or by deliverance from another's hand.

"Lead everyone to this place, gather your wits about you, and then begin your new lives. Tanyasin has not realized that in her anger toward Dracula she has actually created an extremely powerful creature. Also, she has created a potential evil even greater than her own. Mankind will refer to you as 'creature' from this day forth."

"What is it that my cousin did to Tanyasin to embitter her so toward him?" I was still trying to figure it all out.

"She watched her husband, and her son, die at the hands of your cousin. She watched as their bodies were hung upside down and their flesh was stripped from their bodies, sliver by sliver. She listened to their screams of agony as each new slice was carved. She watched as their blood dripped into the waiting cups. She watched as your cousin drank their blood. She heard his evil. She saw his evil. She vowed to avenge that evil! She would rant to us, saying that if Dracula so loved to drink blood then why not curse him with it—only make it so that blood was *all* he would desire! Remember this, Atilla: it is not for Dracula that I grant this lightening of Tanyasin's curse; it is for all the other innocents that have been touched by his evil ways. He might deserve this fate—the rest of you do not!

"Tanyasin, after death finally gave rest to her loved ones, went to the mountains to seek out an old witch who was said to reside there. When she found the witch, Tanyasin begged for her help. In exchange for the power of revenge, Tanyasin had to forfeit her beauty—"

"Her beauty?" I interrupted.

"Yes, her beauty. She, at one time, was one of the most beautiful Gypsy maidens ever to set foot inside a circle of wagons. You see, Atilla, what revenge can do to your soul?"

There was a long pause, during which I wondered why this Gypsy woman had decided to risk Tanyasin's wrath by helping me.

"You may wonder why I assist you now," she began as though reading my thoughts. "I, believe it or not, am much older than Tanyasin. I have my own powers, ones that I do not often wield. Had I been in the clearing the day you and Dracula entered it, I would have stopped the curse then. But fate decreed a different destiny for you and yours. I am sorry for that. The best I can do now is to give your soul a chance for respite."

I looked up into her eyes. Tears began to stream down my cheeks. "What of my Mara? Will she live?" The pain in my heart made me desperate for a positive answer.

The Gypsy lady shook her head. "At this moment, your Mara is drawing her final breaths."

"You are able to see this?"

She nodded.

"How?"

"It is one of my gifts."

The tears continued. My body shook. The Gypsy helped me to my feet. "Come, Atilla; I will show you something."

She led me to a clearing. She approached the edge of a pond laden with water lilies, knelt down on the perimeter of the languid waters, and gently pushed aside a few of the flowers. "Come closer, Atilla; see what I am able to reveal to you."

I knelt beside her, and there in the water was a reflection of my Mara. She was lying on her bed, with a content smile upon her face. Basarab was nestled beside her. Stephen, Dracula, Dr. Balenti, and Evdochia were standing around her bed. The men's faces were etched with sorrow; Evdochia's face was streaked with tears. Mara's lips began to move. To my surprise, I could hear her voice.

"Please, Stephen, tell my Atilla I have loved him to the end. Tell him to take good care of our son. He is a fine, strong boy, and I feel he is destined for great things. Tell him I am sorry. Tell him that this new life that has been inflicted on us is one that I am unable to endure."

Mara reached her hand to Basarab and stroked his dark crown of hair. "And to you, my little son: please grow strong and wise. Be a leader amongst your people; rule with authority and with the wisdom of your forefathers. See to your father; never leave him alone, for one day he will need your strength, as you now need his."

Mara leaned back upon her pillows and stared up through the waters, directly into my eyes. "Farewell, my Atilla, my beloved."

"Mara!" My agony reverberated in the forest.

The Gypsy woman gathered me into her arms. I wept like a baby. She rocked me gently. Time passed—as did the storm—eventually.

"Thank you," I finally managed to speak. "I shall never forget what you have done here for me. If ever you should be in need of refuge, do not hesitate to come to me." I stood up and began to walk back to my horse. Her voice followed me.

"Remember, Atilla, be strong and be careful. Many will seek you out—the evil souls to obtain this power you have and the righteous ones to destroy it! Be wise as to your preservation. Never forget the sweet gentleness of your Mara. You will have many moons to draw upon it all." The Gypsy lady turned and headed back in the direction of the wagons.

"Gypsy lady," I called after her, "I don't even know your name. How are you called?"

"My name is Angelique," she replied as she disappeared into a mist that had not been present seconds before.

When I reached the castle gates, Father Mihail greeted me. "Atilla, my son, I am so sorry; it is about Mara ..."

"I know, Father. I know. Take me to the others, please. I have been given a vision—and a mission. There is much to do and very little time to do it."

Father Mihail led me to my cousins and I told my story to them. Dracula was silent when I related the full reason for the curse. Stephen's face became grim.

"So, there is no way to ease this burden on our family?" Stephen inquired.

"Not completely," I replied. "Here is the rest of the story; it is what we now must do in order to survive."

I finished my tale. Dracula, I noticed, had that old familiar look in his eyes. It was the animal look, the one Stephen and I had seen after the deaths of his father and his uncle. I worried that it could be trouble, not just for him, but for us, as well.

"Perhaps I should pay this hag, Tanyasin, a little visit?" Dracula spoke up for the first time.

"No," I answered quickly. "I do not believe there is anything any of us could do to reverse the curse—most assuredly, there is nothing you could do! Angelique has only been able to give us a way out—should we desire it, of course."

"I shall begin preparations to close up the castle," Stephen said, willing to take charge of the situation.

"Good idea," I replied; "but only temporarily. Angelique said we would eventually be able to assimilate back into society, but we will need some time to adjust to our new way of life, if that is what we will call it. Stephen, is there anyone here, besides Father Mihail, whom we can trust?" I asked.

Stephen rubbed his chin thoughtfully. "There are a couple of servants who have been with me since birth."

I paused. Something had been nagging at me ever since I had left the clearing. If this curse was affecting us to such a great extent, then was it also affecting other family members? Tanyasin had cursed Dracula and all of his relatives. We needed to contact them in order to find out what was happening in their lives.

Stephen noticed my perplexed look. "What's wrong, Atilla?" he asked.

"We must get in touch with anyone who is of our blood in order to see how far this curse has spread," I answered him. "If the spell the hag cast is true—you and all yours—then they, too, will be experiencing these symptoms."

Dracula spoke up, "What of your half-brother, Vacaresti, Atilla; do you know where he is?"

"I am not sure. The last I heard, he had been travelling around, trying to salvage his sanity after his time in the Turkish prison. Our family eventually lost all contact with him."

"It is time to find him, I believe," Stephen added, a serious tone in his voice. "If any of our relatives have also been touched by this curse, it will be those who are closest to us in blood." Stephen had always been wise.

We decided to send out couriers to the homes of as many of our kin as possible, requesting their presence for a family gathering, to be held at Stephen's castle within the fortnight. That would give us time both to prepare our speeches to explain the situation and to gather together whatever belongings we would take with us into the mountains.

⟳

Few of the relatives bothered to reply. Some even refused the couriers entrance through their doors when they realized they were there on behalf of Dracula and me. Word had spread that I had assisted my cousin when things had been falling down around him, and the new powers that be were not pleased. They made sure to tag my name beside Dracula's. Some still felt pity for Stephen—but not enough to come to his castle, especially if Dracula would be present.

However, to our great surprise and delight—especially mine—Vacaresti showed up at our door the night before our planned leaving. I had the great pleasure of being the first to greet him.

"Vacaresti?"

"Atilla?"

"How did you hear of our gathering?" I took my brother by the arm and drew him inside the castle, not wanting the wrong ears to hear what he had to say.

"The news is spreading throughout the land that all the relatives of Dracula have been summoned to the castle of Stephen the Great. Rumour has it that the people are hoping Stephen will be able to exorcize whatever devil has taken possession of this family, even though I doubt that any will show at the door for the exorcism. Are you able to enlighten me at all, little brother?" Vacaresti raised his eyebrows.

"What is it that you already know, Vacaresti?"

"Rumours of a Gypsy curse. I actually came upon some Gypsy wagons with men, women, and children. I was tired, having travelled many miles through the forest that day. They welcomed me to their fire, but then one old woman cringed as she served me a goblet of wine. She began to shriek that I was one of them—one of Tanyasin's cursed! Everyone backed away from me as though I were diseased.

"I had no inclination to stay longer, so I slipped quietly into the shadows and gathered my horse. Before I mounted, one of the Gypsy women approached me and told me I would find you here at Stephen's castle, if I hurried. In case I missed you here, she gave me directions to some caves in the mountains. She told me all would be explained to me then."

I sat my brother down and told him, as briefly as possible, the events that had taken place. His face should have been etched with disbelief, but when I saw it was not, I knew Vacaresti had been experiencing the same symptoms as the rest of us.

"So that is why," he whispered, "why I lust for blood … why I cannot sleep at night … why I cannot travel in the sunlight … and you say there is a way to lift this curse?"

"No, not to lift it—only to end our lives, if we should wish to do so. I am told we have the ability to be released from it. I am told we also have the ability to live for eternity, should we desire that, but that we are some sort of creature, not totally human anymore."

Vacaresti stood. "So, what is your plan, Atilla? To go to the caves, and then what?"

"Once in the caves, we will discover the extensiveness of our curse, how to deal with it, and the power that will come with it. We must be conscious of the fact that some of our relatives may not be aware of all the details, and they may inflict the curse on others outside our family. We must do our best to contain this thing for as long as possible and, if I might be so bold as to add, to end the life of anyone who abuses the power."

"What of Dracula?"

Vacaresti's question surprised me. "What do you mean?"

"Will we be able to contain him? Has he not gone off before and stirred trouble? Is it not because of his deeds that we find our families in this predicament?"

"Only time will tell," I replied cautiously. "For now, brother, I have something very precious to show you."

"Something more?"

"My son."

Vacaresti burst out laughing. "Who ever would have thought you would be a father before me?" He slapped me on the back. "Show me this boy of yours, brother!"

My reunion with Vacaresti was a joyous, yet sad, moment for me. I was happy to be reunited with my brother; I was distressed to have it confirmed that Tanyasin's curse had spread beyond our immediate perimeters.

I feared greatly for the others. Once we were in the caves, we would have to try to reach them again. On our designated departure night, we set out on our journey: I, Atilla Musat, and my son, Basarab; Stephen and his wife, Evdochia, who was heavy with child; Dracula; Vacaresti; Dr. Balenti Danesti; and the two male servants whom Stephen trusted.

Father Mihail was left behind to tend to matters until such time as we were able to return. We had arranged a way to have messages sent back and forth. We knew, at the time, that we had no one else we could put our trust in—quite ironic, isn't it, that we had to put our trust in a man of God, when it seemed that God Himself had reached down from heaven and allowed Tanyasin to curse our family!

To our surprise, upon reaching the caves, we found them fully furnished and stocked with provisions. Silently, I thanked Angelique. None other would have provided this for our arrival. We settled in and then sent one of the servants back to Father Mihail to give him news of our situation. We requested the same be returned from him.

Unfortunately, the servant did not return to us. Dracula became restless. One night, he left the caves and went in search of the servant. He found him lying alongside the roadway that led up to Stephen's castle. A note was attached to his mutilated, naked body:

"All who think to pass through to this cursed castle and its lands

Shall see the wrath of God's most powerful and holy hand!"

Dracula brought us the note and the body. He informed us that the one who had mutilated the body had been dealt with, and he reported that fact with a mysterious, satisfied smile.

⌒

Life settled. Evdochia's child was born. Doctor Balenti had made sure to bring along a good supply of herbs to make the drink. Evdochia thrived on it—as did my son, Basarab. Stephen was enthralled with his new daughter. "A bride for Basarab," he said to me one day as we walked through the caves.

"Have you thought of a name?" I asked.

"Oltea, after my mother."

"Good." I was thoughtful for a moment. "We should perform some sort of ceremony for the children born to us. The church baptizes with holy water, but somehow I don't believe that is possible for us anymore."

"Why don't we baptize the children in our blood?" a voice approached us. "Better yet, we will perform a ceremony and have the babies drink our blood!" Dracula finished with a flourish.

"Don't be absurd, Dracula," I stated.

"They will be like us; that is a fact that cannot be undone—so I understand!" There was a hint of anger in Dracula's voice. "Therefore, it is up to us to baptize our children into our new way of life. It will be a means to survive and to keep our kind, especially our family line, pure. Eventually, I am sure there will be enough rogues for us to deal with. We will need to be strong in order to manage them."

Stephen spoke up, "Dracula might have a point here, Atilla. It may be a way of protecting our children. Who knows what elements will try to obtain our power or try to destroy it? If anyone gets hold of any of our secrets, we could be doomed."

Thus, it was settled. Stephen, Dracula, Vacaresti, and I gathered to discuss a ceremony to seal our children into our family circle. Unfortunately, I am unable to disclose any of those details. They must remain our secret, for the protection of our kind. You understand, I hope. To write such in this account could mean disaster for us. Only trusted family members can be privy to the details. I guard this book with my life, because there are other details in it that could bring disaster upon our heads—literally.

Another sorrowful event followed. Basarab was robbed of his bride. Oltea, Stephen's daughter, did not flourish on either

her mother's milk, or the drink that Doctor Balanti created. No matter what we tried, she got weaker and weaker. Oltea did not see the end of her third month. She did not live long enough to be put through the ceremony her father and uncles had so carefully articulated. Not one of us was able to pray anymore, either, for just saying the word *God* seemed to burn our throats. Even the writing of the word has been painful. But I could still hope, and I did. I cannot speak for the others, for they were all silent when it came to that subject.

We decided that even though Basarab was a strong, healthy baby, we should perform the ritual on him. I remember him smiling through the entire event. He did not shed a single tear. I am not sure if I would have been that courageous.

⁓

We spent two long years in the caves. Dracula left us frequently, sometimes not returning for many nights. Stephen mourned his daughter's death and the barrenness of his wife, Evdochia. Vacaresti and I renewed our brotherhood.

One night, Dracula returned with the news that he had found his two sons, Vlad and Mihail. They were in fine health. Their nursemaid, who had begun to notice peculiarities about the boys, had kept them hidden and had tended to their new needs. She had heard a great many rumours about the Dracul family and all those associated with it.

"Will you be bringing them here to perform the ceremony on them?" Vacaresti enquired.

"That does not appear to be necessary," Dracula replied. "They are no different from us now, and they are fine, healthy boys." He smiled—something Dracula did not do often.

"Then, bring them here for their safety," I suggested. "It will be good for Basarab to have children around him."

Again Dracula smiled. "I am yearning to get out of these caves. I think it is time; we have been here long enough. I have located a castle far to the north. I believe it will soon be vacated; I will go there and then send for my sons."

At the time I did not think much on his statement, but later I heard the rumours going around the countryside of how the owners of that particular castle had mysteriously disappeared. It was only then that I realized in what manner the castle had been vacated!

I have little time now to keep this account, so details are sparse. We have all decided to leave the caves and seek a home in society. Things were under control, or so we thought at the time. We promised to meet once a year at the caves, on All Hallows Eve. We each had fashioned a special coffin that could only be locked from the inside and had layered it with earth from the caves. These we would transport on wagons, under cover, to our homes.

Vacaresti, Stephen, and I embraced, and we wept. The doctor, Count Balenti Danesti, knew he could be with any one of us but chose to come with me for the time being. Basarab looked on with excitement in his eyes. He was anxious to see the world. His Aunt Evdochia hugged him tightly.

"I shall miss you, Basarab," she whispered in his ear. "Be a good boy for your father, you hear?"

Basarab stared straight into her eyes. "I shall, Aunt Evdochia; I shall look after my father, for I am Basarab Atilla Musat, and one day I shall be a great count, and I shall rule over all of my people!" There was power and authority in my son's words! The room was silent. Then I remembered the old hag, Tanyasin. I remembered her statement, which had declared that Basarab would be the most powerful of our kind because he was the first born to us.

All this happened on the day my son turned three.

⁓

Here the diary stopped. I wondered if there was another book somewhere that might continue the tale, but I could not find one in the library. I felt unfulfilled—left in limbo. There were so many more details that I would have liked to know. Now I would have to beg someone to tell me more.

But this much I did glean from the final chronicle: I truly had landed myself in the home of the king of vampires—Basarab Atilla Musat! Also, I was bearing the king a prince. So, where did all this leave me? I still had no idea!

CHAPTER 12

Settling In

When the count had first informed me that I was pregnant, I had not wanted to believe him, but as the days went by, symptoms of my condition emerged. I was constantly nauseated and fatigued. I needed to look for something to occupy my time when I was awake, especially now that I had finished reading the family diary. I was hungry for knowledge and felt it was time to make use of the vast library the count had in his study.

I asked Max if he thought the count would mind if I took some of the books up to my room. Max took the liberty of telling me to help myself. I was particularly interested in the law books and wondered what the count was doing with so many.

After the evening meals, I began heading to the study in order to select my reading material. Sometimes I would even sit in there for awhile before heading back to my room. Teresa and the count would disappear elsewhere, but I always had the feeling that Max was never far away. And it was Max who always appeared in time to escort me back to my room, as though he knew my every thought and what I was going to do next.

One evening, the count followed me into the study. "The previous owner of this place was quite a collector of books. I see you are enjoying them."

I turned—swiftly—nervously. "Yes, I enjoy reading very much, especially law," I finally answered when I recovered from my shock.

"Why law?"

"I worked in a law office and was planning to become a paralegal. Actually, I would like to study criminal psychology and profiling." I paused a moment and looked up at the count. "Why do you ask?" I inquired. I wondered what he was up to, what he wanted from me now.

"I am curious to know you better," the count said. He walked over to a set of shelves that were enclosed behind glass doors. He opened one of the doors, pulled out a book, and handed it to me. "This is one of my favourites," he smiled. I did not notice any fangs when he did so. "These shelves are where I keep my books."

The book he had handed me was Bram Stoker's *Dracula*. It was very old. I ran my fingers over the yellow cloth cover. The title, in large red lettering, stood out boldly.

"It is a first edition," the count informed me.

I opened the book. The pages were discoloured and very brittle. They had an *old* scent to them. "How did you come upon this?" I asked.

"I was living in England at the time. The story was making quite a stir." The count laughed softly. "I actually met Mr. Stoker at a function." The count reached out and took the book from my hand. He opened it to the first page and pointed to the signature. "My own personally signed copy. Stoker had no idea how close he came to the truth on a number of things about our kind. He was fascinated with me, and I, in turn, enjoyed toying with him, leading him along with little titbits of useless information about what I thought a vampire might be." The count laughed again. "We had lunch a couple of times, but things were getting complicated at the time, and Teresa and I had to leave the city."

"What happened?" I inquired.

"Some people actually began to believe what they were reading in Stoker's book. There was quite an interest amongst some of the people as to whether there really were vampires. And there was another problem—there were several very brutal and mysterious deaths in the back alleys of London. Teresa and I had lived quite obscurely for a number of years, and I had thought we were safe there. But, to be truthful, several of those deaths could be attributed to our kind—not us directly, but rogues. I was aware of that. I knew who some of the rogues were, but I hesitated to do too much about it because of the attention it might have brought to those of us who abided by our laws. One night, a couple of constables knocked on my door and told me that they needed to search my residence. I asked why. They would not say. I did not let them in." The count smiled, but it was not warm, as the previous smiles had been. "Later that night I instructed Max to pack our things, and we left on a ship bound for France."

It seemed, during those moments with the count, that all my fear of him had disappeared. I was thirsty to learn more of what he was all about, where he had been, and whom he had met in his travels. We were just two people sitting in a study, talking of the past, and getting to know one another. "How long were you in England?" I asked.

"Twenty years. We could have stayed longer had it not been for Stoker's book and another series of unfortunate events, which I will not go into at the moment. People are so superstitious—something that has not changed over the centuries." The count placed the book back on the shelf.

"Would you mind if I read that copy?" I asked.

"Have you not read this story yet?" The count looked shocked.

"Well, yes, I have, but not a first edition."

"And what would make this so different from the one you have read?"

I really was not sure, but I felt that it would be different to read a first edition of *Dracula*, to turn each fragile page, to breath in the age of it. When I did not answer right away, the count pulled the book from the shelf again and handed it to me. "Be careful with it. I do not believe I will be able to get another signed copy." He laughed. I caught a glimpse of his fangs.

The count walked over to the window and drew the curtain aside. "I must go now; I have matters to attend to. Meet me here tomorrow night after supper. I would like to know more about why you want to study law and about your interest in criminal profiling. I have never had too much use for lawyers, having found only a handful of honest ones over the centuries. But criminals—I have bumped into more than a few of those!" He laughed. He stood in the doorway for a moment, studying me. "You are a most interesting woman, Virginia." And then he was gone.

I stood in the middle of the study holding an original copy of *Dracula*, in my hands. I had just watched a real, live vampire leave the room. I sighed and began to walk toward the door. I was not even thinking about escape. Max was waiting in the hallway.

At the supper table the next evening, I noticed that Teresa was looking very dour, especially when she glanced at me. The count was quite cheerful, though. He turned to Teresa. "I will be spending an hour or so with Virginia after supper, before we go out tonight. I trust you will be able to occupy your time elsewhere."

Teresa nodded her head. And then she glared at me. Was that more than anger I saw in her eyes? Was it a warning for me to be careful? I looked away from her gaze and continued to eat my supper. The count was the first to finish his meal. "I shall be along shortly, Virginia," he said as he left the room.

I sat in one of the high-backed chairs in the study, waiting for him. What I was going to say, or what he was expecting out of these encounters, was beyond me, but I assumed I would find out soon enough. He entered the room. My heart raced at the sight of him. I blushed.

He reached out his hand and tenderly stroked my cheek with his fingers. "You are not feeling well?" he asked. "You are flushed."

"No ... no ..." I stuttered over my words. "I ... I ..." my tongue lost its ability to speak. I prayed he could not read my mind, because all I really wanted, at the moment, was for him to take me up to my room and make love to me as he had done on the night he had planted his seed in my womb.

He laughed—as though he had read my mind. The count sat down in the chair opposite me and folded his hands on his lap. "So, my dear Virginia, how is it you decided you would like to pursue law as a career?"

"I don't wish to mislead you, Count; I was not going to be an actual lawyer."

"Paralegal, you said, right?"

"Yes."

"Why not a lawyer?"

"I didn't have the funds to put myself through seven years of schooling."

The count leaned forward and stared deeply into my eyes. My blood began to race again. "Would you have preferred to have been a lawyer?" He leaned back in his chair.

"At times I considered that possibility, but I went to college and got my degree to be a legal secretary. While I was working at a law firm, I took some night courses that I would need in order to get my paralegal certificate. Once I had accomplished that, I intended to start studying criminal psychology."

"I see." He paused. "So what is it you would be allowed to do as a paralegal that a legal secretary would not be qualified for?"

I began to wonder where the count was leading me with all this questioning. Was he in some kind of legal trouble and hoping to see if I might help him out of it? If that were the case, would I be able to bargain with him—knowledge for freedom?

"So?" There was a slight impatience to his tone as he waited for me to answer his question.

"It is different all over the world. In Canada, paralegals are not just law clerks, as they might be considered in some other countries. We can represent matters in provincial offences court, summary conviction criminal court, and small claims court. We are even allowed to work on tribunals and boards. Some have become commissioners and notary publics, and I even heard of the odd one acting as a justice of the peace."

"Technically, then, you are just a step down from a lawyer?"

I laughed. I had no idea why I was feeling so comfortable in the count's presence. Maybe it was because he was taking a genuine interest in *me*—in *my* life—in what *I* was all about. The fact that I was technically a prisoner in his house was not even crossing my mind. "A step down from a lawyer, to say the least!" I answered. "In more ways than one. We are not allowed to practice in any areas that are reserved for lawyers, and of course, we definitely do not enjoy the same income!" I paused. "Many paralegals do a lot of the grunt work for lawyers, but then the lawyers take all the glory. Paralegals get paid less per hour, too, although I believe most lawyers charge the client *their* fee. I know a couple of my classmates from Toronto intended to open their own offices, so they could specialize in the specifics allowed them under the law and keep all the profits."

"Interesting." The count stood up and walked around to the back of my chair. He put his hands on my shoulders and massaged my muscles. I could feel the electricity from his fingers shooting through me. "So, Virginia, did you aspire to have your own office one day?" His fingers dug deeper into my muscle tissue. It felt so good.

"I hadn't really thought of it," I finally answered. "Like I mentioned, my long-term interest is in criminal psychology and profiling."

"You should have your own office." The count walked around to the front of my chair, placed his hands on the arms, and leaned toward me. His eyes were penetrating right through me. I melted. "That way, you could earn more money and reach your ultimate goal sooner, right?"

I continued melting. I was baffled as to where the count was leading with all of this, but at least this conversation was giving me hope that after I gave birth to his child I would be released to go on with my life.

I was startled by the sound of someone clearing her throat. The count stood up abruptly and turned to face his wife. Teresa's face was dark with anger. "I hope I have not interrupted something here," she stated with a sharp edge to her words.

"Of course not, Teresa. Virginia was just telling me about the career path she was trying to follow in her former life." The count's voice was smooth, but my mind clung to the words *her former life*.

I stood up and walked to the back of my chair, resting my hands on it for support. My legs felt like jelly. The possibilities I had just been foolish enough to be dreaming about had been fractured with Teresa's entrance. The count chuckled as he looked from Teresa to me and then back to Teresa. "I trust I do not detect some jealousy, my dear," he said to her.

Teresa was quick to recover. "No, Count. I only came to see what was detaining you. Have you forgotten that *we* have a party to attend tonight?"

"Oh yes, I had almost forgotten." He turned to me. "Please forgive me, my dear Virginia; I must take my leave. But I think you should seriously consider pursuing more than a career as a paralegal. There are plenty of law books here, as you have already seen, and it would be a good way to spend some of your time while you wait for the birth of my child. Think on it. And you never know when I might need some legal advice," he added. "Until tomorrow evening, then," he said. He put his arm around Teresa and said, "Shall we, my love?" And they were gone.

What an idiot I was! There was his interest in me, the something more he might glean. I felt empty.

Max entered the room. "Are you ready to retire, miss?"

"Yes, Max; I think I have had enough for one evening." I followed Max up to my room.

"Is there anything I can get you, Miss Virginia, before I go about my other affairs?"

I shook my head. Any words I might have wanted to say were

trapped in my throat. I wanted to say to Max that he could let me out of this place, that he could just turn his back while I slipped out the door. I wanted to say that I was nobody of any importance to anyone. I wanted to say there was no reason to keep me here. My hand went to my stomach. Inside me was the reason I was here—*his* reason for keeping me. I turned and headed to my bed; I heard the lock click into place. I picked up the book *Dracula*, and began to read.

I was awakened by the weight of someone sitting on the edge of my bed. It was him. He was just staring at me. Smiling. He picked up the book, which had fallen to the side of me, closed it, and then set it on the floor. He lay down beside me and took me in his arms.

When I awoke in the morning my body still tingled, but the bed was cold. He was gone.

For the next week I did not have the privilege of the count's company after supper. Teresa must have intervened, for each evening when the meal was finished she would stand up and mention some event they had to attend and maintain that they really should get going before it was too late. For the first few days, I used my time to flip through some of the law books, but then I decided to check out the count's collection. I ran my fingers over various titles before hesitating at *Vlad Tepes*. I pulled it out.

"This should be an interesting read," I said out loud as I headed to a chair. "I wonder how it compares to Attila's account of the events that took place during that time."

I lit a couple more candles and spent the next few hours reading. I found that much of the information in the biography of *Vlad Tepes* corresponded with that in Attila's diary. Of course, there were no referrals to a Gypsy curse, but I had not expected there would be. I heard the front door open and glanced out the study window. The sky was beginning to lighten. The count and Teresa must be returning home. I heard laughter from the hallway, and footsteps. And then *his* voice.

"I shall be along shortly, Teresa; I wish to check in on Virginia."

I did not hear her reply, but I doubted it would have been a pleasant one. I had no idea what she feared. I had no intention of usurping her place. I was a victim here—a hopeful one, though. Once the child was born, I assumed I would be on my way, and then they could all be a happy little family again. I looked up and saw him standing in the doorway.

"You are still up?"

"I have been reading."

He walked over to me. "And what is it you are reading tonight?"

"I thought I would read the biography of your uncle Vlad Tepes."

"I see. You are not reading the law books?"

"I looked at some of them, but I am much more interested in the books you have in your cabinet. I thought to start with this one."

"I see," he repeated. The count glanced to the window. "Well, after supper tonight we shall discuss your findings. There are many stories and myths about my uncle. You understand how things get changed as they pass verbally from one person to another. Unless one was *there*, how does one know the real truth?" He smiled. "Until tonight, then. Rest well."

I decided to take the book up to my room with me. I stepped out into the hallway. It was empty. I glanced to the stairs leading to the upper level. I glanced to the foyer where the front door was—the door that might lead to my freedom. I hesitated. What did I really want to do here? *Flee*, my inner voice encouraged. I half-turned toward the door.

"Ah, there you are, Miss Virginia; I was just going to bring you your breakfast." Max appeared out of nowhere.

My feet turned toward the stairs.

"Your uncle was an atrocious man," I pointed out near the beginning of our conversation that evening.

The count chuckled. "That all depends on whose view you are looking at—the families of the ones he impaled or tortured, or the families of the ones he assisted."

"Is he still alive?" I enquired.

"Yes."

I do not know why it should have surprised me to hear that, but it did. I think I was still trying to look at the count as just a very powerful man—not as a vampire who had lived for hundreds of years. If I considered him an ordinary human, then that would negate the fact that any of these other people in Count Attila's diary were still alive, including Dracula. My face must have shown my shock, because the count reached out and laid a hand on my knee. I shivered.

"Virginia, we all still live, if that is what you would call what we do. Is it not in the basic nature of man to cling to life?"

I nodded.

"We once were human. Even I, who was born into the curse, had to adjust, because when I was conceived, my parents were still totally human." He heaved a sigh. "We learned to cope with the curse. It has not been easy. It definitely was not easy for my Uncle Vlad—Dracula, as you know him and as my father referred to him. He felt a great deal of responsibility to his people—to the *real* people of the land, not the rich boyars who ran with whatever tide of fortune might come their way!"

"But his methods of dealing with things—" I began to protest.

"Were no different than many others of the time. And where do you think he learned such techniques?"

"Yes, your father's diary mentioned he learned them while in captivity at the Turkish court." I stood up and walked around to the back of my chair. My knees were shaking, and I did not want the count to see how nervous I was. I still could not understand why he was taking

such an interest in me—why he wanted to talk with me like this. I
pushed on with my feelings. "If he so disliked what happened to him
at the Turkish court, why did he inflict such things on his people? And
was it not because of *his* torturous ways that Tanyasin cursed his family
and all of his blood for generations to come? How did the rest of you
handle that? I am not sure I would have been as sympathetic if I had
been Stephen, or your father. Your father lost his wife—your mother.
She died because of the curse, remember?" I had no idea where I had
found the boldness to speak such words, but they were out of my mouth
before I could stop them!

The count stood up. He walked to where I was standing. He put
his hands on my shoulders and gently moved me away from the chair.
He peered into my eyes. "I was born into this curse, and as you know
from the diary, I have been burdened with the leadership of my kind. I
have no idea why. I want you to understand one thing though, my dear
Virginia—my father and my uncle would never betray their family, and
Dracula was even more than that to them. He was also revered amongst
the poor, because he stood for honour and honesty. Merchants who
cheated their customers were punished. Women who cheated on their
husbands were punished."

"What of the men who cheated on their wives?" I dared to interrupt.
"Were they punished, as well?"

The count's eyes took on a dark countenance. I was beginning to
think I had overstepped a line, but then he smiled. "It is understood
that men sometimes must seek solace elsewhere, but that is not what
we are discussing here, is it, Virginia?" He took me by the hand and led
me over to the window. "Out there is your world," he began, "a world
that we have had to try to fit into, over and over again. Men in your
society seek solace outside of their marital beds—you call it adultery,
I believe?"

I nodded.

"So, what do you call this then, my dear?" The count leaned over
and pressed his lips to mine. His fingers played a melody up and down

my spine. I dissolved into him. Suddenly he pushed me away and began to laugh. It had a mocking tone to it. "How do you think my wife would feel if she were to come upon us at this moment?"

His question took me by surprise.

"What do you think your punishment should be for cavorting with a married man?" The count was still laughing at me. I could tell from his eyes. He went on, "Do you think she might be justified in impaling you, as my uncle did to those women who cheated on their husbands?"

My mind was spinning. Where was this line of questioning leading? I decided to stand up to the count—I felt that was what he wanted me to do. "I am not married; therefore, I am not cheating on a husband!" I stated haughtily.

He laughed again. "Well said, Virginia—well said. But *I am* married."

"True. But, with your way of thinking, there is no cheating here, right? Besides, I am actually a victim—you have kept me here against my will—you have forced yourself upon me. What would your cousin's punishment have been for someone like you?"

The count did not bat an eye as he quickly answered me. "It was a man's world. And whether you want to admit it or not, Virginia, it still is. I see it all the time. It is the women in your society who are oppressed, especially those who cannot turn their eyes the other way if their husband strays once in awhile! The women demand fidelity, and when they cannot have it, they leave their husbands. And then, as I see in many cases, these women are once again ravaged by a society that treats them like second-class citizens. So, is it really worth it for them to cast aside their men because of their *needs*?"

"How is it that you have figured all of that out?" I asked.

"I know much more about your world than you might think. I make it my business to get to know … certain circles."

"And what circles are those?"

"The ones I need to know." The count was being evasive. He was

toying with me, and judging from the look in his eyes, he was enjoying
every minute of it.

His statements about women having to accept their lot in life if
they had cheating husbands had angered me—especially after what
John had done to me! "Anyway, how dare you judge those women?" My
voice had risen to almost a shout. "What do you know of honour? Of
integrity? You, with all your fancy mannerisms and traditions. Times
have changed since your uncle's era—maybe not as much as some of
us would like them to, but they have changed. Your uncle would never
get away today with the atrocities he inflicted on his people back then!
He was a monster. I was looking at one of your books on serial killers,
and Vlad Tepes was right there, one of the first in the book!" I was so
angry that I found it difficult to control my breathing.

The count backed away and studied me for a moment. I could not read
his face. I was certain I had overstepped my limit this time! I had no idea
how much longer I could stand there under his scrutiny; my legs felt like
rubber. Suddenly, he burst out laughing again. "This has been wonderful,
my dear Virginia. You are a spark. Teresa would never dare to—"

"Teresa would never dare to what?" Teresa entered the study. She
looked furious. I wondered how long she had been standing there.

"Ah, Teresa darling, won't you join us? Virginia has been trying to
convince me that my Uncle Dracula is not a very nice person. What
do you think?"

A look of disdain crept across Teresa's face. "I think you are foolish
to be discussing such matters with someone of such little significance!
Within a few months she will be out of our lives, and then, what will it
matter what she thinks of your uncle?"

"I am just passing time with her," the count said. "What harm is
there in a little friendly banter?"

"Pass time with your wife!" Teresa glared at me as she spoke to her
husband.

"Jealousy does not become you, my dear." The count strode over to
his wife. "Well, I am glad you came in now, anyway; I have had enough

chitchat for tonight. I think I fancy a walk in the gardens." He extended his arm to Teresa. "Care to join me, my dear?" At the doorway, he turned to me for a brief moment. "Till next time, Virginia. I have enjoyed this. Read a bit more about my uncle, and try to examine what is between the lines, so that you might come to a point of understanding."

After he left with Teresa, I felt so alone. I had been enjoying myself; in a way, it had actually been fun to have a stimulating conversation with someone. Neither Max nor Teresa ever seemed up for one—Teresa, I had the feeling, because she did not care for me; Max because he just did not have that much time to spare. I felt a stirring in the pit of my stomach. A reminder of what was there. A reminder of why I was here. I left the study and headed to my room. I could sense the presence of someone close by, probably Max. I really did not care. It was not me that the count was walking with in a moonlit garden. It was not me who would be sleeping in his arms tonight. It was *her*—his wife.

By the time I arrived at my room, I heard footsteps coming up the stairs. I knew it would be Max. He looked at me and shook his head. "Don't get too comfortable with the count, Miss Virginia. He is just playing with you."

"What do you mean?" I asked.

"Just what I said. I overheard some of what you and he were talking about. He enjoys baiting people, although I think you had your moments and stood up to him quite admirably a couple of times. Just heed my warning though: You are only temporary. Now, if there is nothing you need, I will just lock your door and be about my business."

I stepped through the doorway. "I don't need anything, Max. Thank you, just the same." As I lay down on my bed, I heard the lock click into place. I closed my eyes and surrendered to sleep. And to dreams ...

Of men, women, and children impaled upon poles ... Of a crazy man drinking their blood ... Of the count and Teresa jeering at me ... Of Teresa walking toward me with a wooden stake, a sadistic smile on her lips ... Of Max shaking his head and wagging his finger as he said: "I told you so; you should have listened to me!"

CHAPTER 13

Revelations

For the next few days I holed up in my room. I was not feeling well. I asked Max to bring my meals up to me and to send my regrets to the count and Teresa. I have no idea why, but I thought that maybe the count would come to me—but he did not. I continued to read the account of Vlad Tepes and began to get more of an understanding of the times and of what he was all about. Still, it did not take away from the fact that he was an atrocious individual. I made a few notes of things I wanted to discuss with the count the next time we got together.

On the fourth evening, there was a light knock on my door. I knew it would not be Max, because he had already retrieved my supper dishes. I heard the key turn in the lock, and the count entered. He closed the door and leaned up against it. His eyes surveyed the room, finally resting on me where I was sitting by the window. "I have missed your company," he began.

I did not reply.

"Are you still not well?" I thought I detected concern in his voice.

"Just tired, I guess," I finally replied. "Part of the condition."

"Condition?"

"Yes, my condition."

"Ah, yes—your condition." He laughed. "Is there anything we can do to make you more comfortable?"

What I wanted to say was that he could let me go home—what I did was shake my head, no. Something told me that asking to leave would not bode well. Then I thought of something I would like: "Would it be too much trouble for me to be able to take a walk in the gardens with you, or with Teresa. I miss the fresh air."

"I see." The count came over and sat down in the chair opposite me. "I shall think on it," he said. He picked up the book that was lying on the table and turned it over. "I see you are still reading my uncle's biography; care to discuss it further?"

I really was not in the mood for another heavy dialogue. In fact, part of the reason I had been avoiding going downstairs for my meals was to avoid just that.

"You hesitate," the count prodded. "Maybe I misunderstood your feelings the other night. It seemed as though you were enjoying our chat—perhaps I was wrong, although I seldom am."

I realized that I was going to have to stay in the game. If the count enjoyed debating with me, then maybe that was one way I could reach him and eventually convince him to let me go. "No, I enjoyed our time together very much; it is just that, as I said, I have been exhausted."

"Good." The count reached his hands over and took mine in his. He lifted them to his lips and kissed the backs of them, lingeringly. "I think I know what you need right now," he said as he stood up, still holding on to my hands.

He drew me to him, lifted me in his arms, and then carried me to the bed. "We will discuss my uncle later," he uttered as he began to undo the buttons on my gown.

The next evening I went downstairs for supper. I could not help but notice the pleased look on the count's face when I entered the room. I could not help notice the disappointed look on Teresa's. I smiled as I sat down. I looked directly at the count. "I feel much better now. Last night was wonderful." I turned my eyes to Teresa, hoping she would understand what I meant. She did. I noticed the muscles in her face tighten, and her eyes clouded with anger.

The count did not appear to notice what was going on between Teresa and me. He motioned for Max to serve the meal and then said, "I shall meet you in the study after supper, Virginia?"

"As you wish." It was at that point that I decided there was no use alienating Teresa completely. If my plan to win over the count did not work, it might bode better for me if I had Teresa on my side. "Would you like to join us, Teresa?" I asked. "Another woman's opinion might be of great value—" I did not get a chance to finish my statement.

"I don't think so," Teresa retorted. "The count knows exactly where I stand. You go on, dear; have your fun for now—it will all be over before you know it!" Her smile was not warm.

I began to protest, "I did not mean anything—"

"I know exactly what your meaning is; I know exactly what you are doing, Virginia. I am no fool. And, just for your information, neither is *my* husband!"

Her statement took a bit of the wind out of my sails, but I recovered rapidly. "As you wish, Teresa."

The rest of the supper hour was conducted in silence. Teresa finished her meal quickly and then excused herself from the table. The count waited patiently for me to finish my dish and then came over to me and pulled my chair out. "Shall we?" he motioned toward the doorway. "I have an appointment with some friends later, but I am anxious to have you reveal what you think of my uncle now that you have read more of the book—if you have changed your opinion of him."

I decided to take a chance and ask again if we could walk outside in the garden. It had been a warm December, and there was no snow yet. "Might we walk outside?" I proposed.

"It is not too cold for you?"

"I am sure the fresh air will do more good than harm. And you must have a coat or something around that you could throw over my shoulders," I added.

The count turned and asked Max to fetch one of Teresa's capes. I had won. I was going to be stepping outside into *my* world. Hopefully, I would have an opportunity to slip from his grasp—but I knew that was a highly unlikely possibility!

We walked around the inside perimeter of the trees. I observed the thickness of the tangled roots and bushes. There was no easy or quick way through them. The night was very still, with not even the sound of a car passing on the street beyond. I caught a glimpse of a couple of street lights, but no people were out walking, that I could see, anyway. I was alone, with *him*.

"So," the count opened the conversation, "you think my uncle was a serial killer?"

"What I said was that history has recorded him as such. And what I think is that the atrocities he committed confirm such."

"It does not matter to you *why* he did what he did?"

"If you are going to tell me that he did those things because he was tortured in the Turkish court, I don't buy that theory. He did not seem to discriminate with his maltreatment—he brutalized his own people, not just the Turks!"

"War is war, even if it is from within your own ranks. Traitors deserve the same punishment as the enemy. There were far too many traitors who had lived off the fat of the land for far too long!"

"Who set Dracula up as judge and executioner?" I dared to ask.

"He was the rightful heir to the throne. Over the years, many of the boyars had repeatedly undermined the princes of the land, and they could not be trusted. My uncle wished to secure his throne, so, in order to do that, he promoted men from amongst the free peasantry and the middle class."

"So you agree with what they say in the book, then, that he was trying to strengthen and modernize the government?"

"I do. The nobility had to be taught a lesson—and what better lesson than to take away their power?"

"He did not have to kill them," I stated. "He could have put them in prison."

"What other way was there during those times? Remember, there was a war going on—a costly war that just never seemed to end. The Turks were persistent in their endeavour to conquer, and Dracula was a great thorn in their sides. As you know from my father's diary, my uncle was *changed* when he returned from the Turkish courts. He refused to ever bow down to the likes of them, again.

"But back to the reason for not putting the boyars in prison—prisons cost money. To incarcerate all the traitors would have been impossible, and my uncle needed to keep close to him the men who were trustworthy to his cause." The count's voice had a sharp edge to it. "You did not live in the 1400s, my dear. The best way to *make* an example was to *set* one. Did you read the part in the book that described how a person could set a bag of gold overnight in the town square and return for the gold the next day?"

I nodded.

"Can you do that today, or would someone steal it?"

"As in your day, I am sure some would steal it, others would not. But to impale someone or to mutilate his body—bit overboard, if you ask me."

The count stopped walking, put his hands on my shoulders, and turned me to face him. "Do you believe everything you read, my dear?"

"No. Most history books are written from someone's point of view, and it all depends on whose point of view it is and what that person's perspective was when he formed his opinion," I responded.

"I am sure you have heard of propaganda?" The count's eyebrows rose questioningly.

"Of course. Propaganda is used on a daily basis to influence people as to what the governments want us to be convinced of."

"My point exactly." The count took my hand and we commenced walking. "Do you really think that Dracula impaled thousands of people at a time? Did you read the section in the book where it stated he impaled 10,000 people in the Transylvanian city of Sibiu and that he impaled 30,000 merchants and officials in the Transylvanian city of Brasov? Do you believe that he would do all that and then sit down amongst the staked corpses and eat their flesh and drink their blood? Or might you consider that the atrociousness of the massacres was inflamed by lies fabricated by his enemies, in order to put fear into the hearts of ordinary men, so that they would turn upon their leader?"

"Are you saying that Dracula did none of these things?" I questioned.

"No, I am saying that he was not as horrible as many would have him be." The count began heading back to the house. "It is getting cold for you, I think," he said. "Shall we continue this conversation inside?"

I nodded.

The count did not take me to the study as I had expected. He led me up to my room, instead. I caught a glimpse of Teresa in the hallway as we ascended the stairs. She definitely did not look pleased.

It appeared the count had forgotten that he had an appointment, for we spent the next hour discussing the fact that Vlad Tepes was, and still is, a national hero in the country of his birth. The count even pointed out that some research was indicating that Vlad was not the true inspiration for the novel written by Bram Stoker.

"Then who was the muse?" I asked.

"Have you ever heard of Elizabeth Bathory?"

"No."

"She was referred to as the 'Blood Countess.'"

"Wait," I interrupted. "I do remember coming across her name, now, when I was going through one of your books. She killed hundreds of girls, and she bathed in their blood to try to make herself look younger."

"Yes, that is the one. One of her ancestors, Stephen Bathory, actually fought against the Turks alongside my Uncle Vlad. The Bathory family was one of the richest and noblest in Hungary at the time. Elizabeth was born in 1560, just over a hundred years after the curse was cast on our family. Some of us had worked hard to assimilate into society, but actions like hers damaged our efforts and kept us forever watching our backs. Our family became quite concerned about the rumours of her lust for blood. Even Dracula was disturbed, for he realized that even though she was not one of us, she might have been a rogue vampire. There were many of them, a problem that had arisen during the early years of the curse, when we were trying to adjust. It is a problem we are still dealing with."

"So you think it is Elizabeth's atrocities, not Dracula's, that Stoker used as his main source of material for his vampire story, even though he used your uncle's name?"

"Yes. The book would not have been a good seller if he had used a woman as his main character. Women just did not do those kinds of things. The story, as it stood, was unbelievable."

Much like my own, at the moment, I thought. "Why was she so evil?" I asked out loud.

"I believe she was actually insane, and from a very young age. She suffered extreme mood swings and violent rages. Some accredited this to inbreeding, which was common amongst the nobility at that time. But it is also my understanding that she was never disciplined properly. She was married off, at the age of fourteen, to a man who was known as a sadist—although even he was disgusted with Elizabeth's actions when he found out what she was doing. While her husband was away at war, she became involved in the occult and took up with some very depraved individuals, who educated her in the fine arts of torture and witchery."

"Much as Dracula had been educated by the Turks," I intervened.

"Possibly. But my uncle did what he did to protect his country and his crown. He was at war. She was not. She did what she did to try to maintain the beauty that was slipping away from her."

"Is there a difference?"

"Yes. You don't see one?"

"A fine line of one, I guess," I admitted. "What happened to her?" I asked.

"What really happened? Or what do the history books say?"

"What really happened?"

"Because of her noble standing in society, she was not put to death as her accomplices had been. She was sealed up in a room and fed through a hole just big enough to slip a plate through. History says that is where she died. I know better, though." The count smiled.

"How so?"

"The authorities did not want to tell the people she had escaped. It was better to say she had died."

"She escaped?"

"Yes—with help, of course."

"From whom?"

"Let us just say that if Elizabeth was not already a rogue when she was slaughtering those girls, she is now!"

"She still lives?"

"Yes." The count leaned back in his chair.

This story was getting more bizarre by the minute. I had had enough for one night. I stood up from my chair and walked over to the window. Slivers of light were beginning to creep through the branches of the trees. My time with the count would soon come to an end. I walked over to him and put my arms around his neck. No reason for him to always be the one to instigate our lovemaking.

"So, we are finished our discussion for tonight, are we, Virginia?" He stood and faced me. I smiled, took his hand, and led him to my bed.

⁓

Time was passing much quicker for me now that I had my nightly discussions with the count. Teresa continued to be surly toward me when the count was not present. Max continued to drop little warnings that I was playing a dangerous game. I continued reading, and I also started a diary of my own, describing the everyday events in my new life. It was my way to maintain my sanity as well as to keep a record of all that had happened to me, should I ever manage to escape or be released. Max graciously supplied me with paper and pen, and he never questioned me about what I was writing. I found that a bit strange, but I guess there was no fear that I would throw a message through an open window, because all the windows were sealed shut. Besides, I still had not seen anyone passing by close enough to respond to my plea for help. If perchance I came across an opening to throw a note from, and I was lucky enough that the wind picked up my scrap of paper and placed it in someone's hands, who would believe such a story as I had to tell?

I would most likely be labelled insane, pumped full of drugs by some well-meaning doctors, and then be thrown into a sanatorium to rot away what life I had left. On the other hand, maybe I had already lost my mind. No, that was not possible. Everything around me was as real as the baby who grew inside my womb. That is why I was compelled to write all the particulars down—every minute detail I could remember. Doing so would be proof enough, at least to me, of my sanity!

Christmas came and went. I knew because I had seen Christmas lights in the distance when I stared out my bedroom window. But the season was different for me this year—there were no Christian celebrations within the walls of the home I was in. I did notice that the count and Teresa went out more in the evenings, probably for Christmas parties. Sometimes they did not have their meals before leaving, and I had to eat alone. On those nights I asked Max if I could eat in my room. I used that extra time to catch up on my diary notes.

January burst through with a big snowstorm. I watched the flakes as they fell and covered the grounds with a thick, white blanket. The tree branches bent from the heavy burden of snow that covered them.

It would be senseless for me to attempt an escape in this weather, even though the thought had crossed my mind that it might be more difficult for Max to catch me. The first week of the new year was quiet. I was beginning to wonder if the count had tired of our conversations. But then he began coming to me again—for conversation, and more!

I was in the study, looking through his books and trying to decide which one I was going to read next, when he entered.

"Ah, Virginia, here you are. What is it you are reading now?" His voice sent a shiver up my spine. It had been a little more than two weeks since we had last met alone.

I turned to him. "I have finished your uncle's biography, and also one on Elizabeth. She really was crazy. I made some notes of the similarities between her and your uncle, and also the dissimilarities."

"You are thinking of writing a profile on them?" he asked.

"Yes, but with my limited knowledge on profiling, I thought maybe I would read some of these other volumes you have here and take notes on them. I think it would be better to try to see the parallels between more than two serial killers at a time," I added.

"Who else did you have in mind?" the count enquired.

"I was thinking of some who lived in this century, like Richard Chase, who was nicknamed the Vampire of Sacramento, or the German fellow, Peter Kurten, dubbed the Vampire of Düsseldorf. But I actually thought to begin with this fellow; he seems to interest a number of people because he was never actually caught," I said as I pulled a biography of Jack the Ripper from the shelf.

"You have set yourself quite a task," the count expressed. "Jack was a demonic character."

My face must have shown shock at his statement, for the count said, "Why are you surprised that I might have known Jack? I know Richard and Peter as well—both rogues. I am familiar with a great many of the individuals who have gone down in history as serial killers—and some of the current ones as well."

"Was Jack one of you?" I inquired.

"Not one of *us*, but a rogue—a very dangerous and uncontrollable one, though." The count paused; he seemed to be considering how much more he should tell me. "Teresa and I were living in London at the time; actually, my father, Uncle Vacaresti, and Aunt Emelia were, as well. We had purchased a large house near the Whitechapel area."

"The same one you were living in when you met Bram Stoker?" I asked.

"Yes." He paused again and then motioned to one of the chairs. "It would probably be better for you to hear this story sitting down." The count remained standing. "Elizabeth had decided to come to England. We heard rumours of what she had left behind as she passed through the countryside—we had our own people keeping tabs on her. But then she decided to come to London. Her thirst for blood was unquenchable, and of course, the pickings were greater in the big city. It was in London that she met 'Jack,' as we shall call him."

"That was not his real name?" I queried.

"No."

"So, you know who he was?"

"Yes."

"And you did not turn him in to the authorities!" I cried out. "That makes you an accomplice."

The count's face turned very serious. "What would you have us do, Virginia? Think about it. Elizabeth had come upon this young man at the hospital. She had taken a job there, cleaning in the morgue at night. He was studying to be a coroner. She watched him closely. One night a young woman was brought in and laid out on the slab. She looked dead enough, but all of a sudden, just as Jack was getting ready to perform his autopsy, she began coughing. Obviously, she had just passed out somewhere and had been taken for dead. It happened a lot in those days. Elizabeth was sweeping at one end of the room when she heard the girl. She watched as Jack leaned over and whispered something in the girl's ear and then, with a smirk on his face, he slit the girl's throat!"

"How do you know all of this?" My mind was telling me that the count, or someone very close to him, would have had to be present.

"We have our means. Working in hospitals was a good way for us to obtain certain things we needed for our existence. Now, back to why we did not turn Jack in to the authorities. Elizabeth saw an opportunity, and she took it. For a long time she had been looking for someone to do her dirty work for her. She sauntered over to Jack. At first he was shocked at having been caught, and he was ready to use his knife on her in order to cover up what he had just done. But Elizabeth was quick, and she was very strong—we all are.

"When our contact—we shall call him Gregory, for the sake of a name—came upon her and Jack, *she* was *feasting*! Gregory hung back in the shadows; he knew how dangerous she was. When she was finished feeding, he watched as Elizabeth held Jack's lips to the wound on the young woman's neck, encouraging him to drink the blood that was still flowing warm from the wound he had inflicted. Gregory heard Elizabeth tell Jack that she had been watching him. At first he did not believe her, but then she described exactly what had happened—that is how I know such detail.

"And then Gregory heard Elizabeth's proposal to Jack. She promised him eternal life if he would supply her with enough *fresh* blood to meet her needs. Jack already had the seeds of darkness inside of him—Elizabeth just pushed him over the edge. At first, Jack was very careless—most rogues are when they first turn. His killing spree made the news headlines, but eventually he settled into his new way of life and kept away from exposure. He was Elizabeth's puppet, as she is someone else's. Someone much more powerful than she is pulls her strings. She does not like that, but there is naught she can do about it."

"Is that individual a rogue?"

"No."

"Do you know who, then?"

"Possibly, but there is no need for you to know that information." The count leaned over my chair and stared directly into my eyes. "So you see, Virginia darling, with what we are, how could we go to the authorities with this kind of information? How could we expose *them*, because that would mean revealing what *we* were? Do you understand this?"

I nodded. I did not want to understand any of this. I was not even sure if I wanted to know anything more. These events just kept getting more and more bizarre. What was I really trying to do here? This man standing in front of me was the leader of his kind, according to his father's diary, yet he *feared* to expose the rogues created by his kind. Was that really the case, or did he truly not care and just kept turning a blind eye? And who was it that was giving rise to the rogues? That was a question the count had avoided answering, even though I had asked. I did not think I was ready to have it answered, in any case!

As though the count had read my mind, he answered some of my inner questioning. "We deal with our own matters, Virginia. That is the way it has to be." He took hold of my hand and pulled me up and into his arms. "And now, the matter I think that needs to be taken care of is the nourishment of my son." He smiled.

As much as I yearned for the count to sweep me away to my room at that moment, I was also very hesitant after what I had just heard. This was a world I did not want any part of. I had been playing a very dangerous game, and it could get even worse—how much so, I had no idea yet! But if I resisted him now, what would the count do? I decided it was better not to—much as the count had decided it was better not to tell the authorities who Jack the Ripper really was. It is called self-preservation!

I followed the count, unwillingly—willingly—up to my room. That night, as we lay in each other's arms, I felt our son move within my womb for the first time.

CHAPTER 14

The Sixth Month

The weeks continued to speed by. Before I knew it, I was entering into my sixth month of pregnancy. My body swelled with the child whom the count had predicted he had implanted in my womb that one rapturous night so long ago. I did not know whether to hate the child that grew inside of me or to love it. I did not even know what it would be. Would my child be like him or, by some quirk of luck, would it escape that fate? Somehow, I doubted the latter.

The count came to me often. We would talk, and then we would make love. Some of our conversations precipitated a more lusty union than others, and I soon learned which issues could really turn him on! He claimed our coming together would give nourishment to his son. Many were the mornings I would wake up hating myself for my promiscuous weakness. I would swear never to submit to him again, but each time he entered my room, my blood would begin surging through my veins, and then he would take me on wings of fire into a hell of ecstasy such as I had never known before. It was a perdition that burned me to the very pit of my soul. I ached for more, so much more. As much as I detested my situation, I could never get enough of the Count Basarab Musat. I damned him when he was not with me;

yet, I opened my arms to him whenever he pleased to walk through my door.

I also damned myself. Physically he nourished me, but the count still had not shown me the emotional attachment that I was hoping for. I had thought that would be possible because of the conversations we continued to have, but it had not happened yet. He kept the conversations at a comfortable distance, and at times, when he felt I had stepped over a line, he would remind me of who he was! In order to escape I needed to gain his full trust, and the voice inside of me kept reminding me I had not yet done that. Time was running short. Escaping was my ultimate goal. At least that was what I kept telling myself.

Teresa busied herself with the preparations for the upcoming celebration, the birth of my child. She had decided my help would not be needed, so I had no idea what was actually in store for me. The invitations had been sent, and the replies were beginning to arrive—all positive, she informed us at supper one night.

The count was elated. Max was busier than usual. One evening, I overheard him telling the count that he might need some assistance when all the guests arrived. The count assured Max that his relatives would be bringing their own servants, so it would be a good idea to prepare some of the guest rooms for them. There would be no need for outsiders, especially at such a crucial time.

I was surprised at how healthy I was during my pregnancy. Max supplied me with a special drink each day, one he said I must consume, not only for my health but the baby's, too. He said it was fortified with vitamins and that it was an ancient mixture that had been used by the family aristocracy for centuries. He always stayed to make sure I drank the liquid to the last drop. Actually, his attendance was not really necessary, because the drink was surprisingly tasty. At the time, I did not even think to connect it to the one Mara had consumed. After all, she had found hers not to be very tasty.

Teresa had started hovering over me when the count was not with me. Max constantly asked me how I was feeling when he brought my meals. They seemed to have accepted the fact that I was there to stay for awhile, especially Teresa. Of course, in a roundabout way, she never ceased to remind me of the fact that my baby would be her child one day. For that reason, amongst others, I did not fully trust Teresa's good intentions. I assumed she had an ulterior motive—I just did not know when she was going to present it!

Finally, partway through my sixth month, I observed the side of the count that I had come to believe was not possible for him to possess. On that particular night, there had been such a genuine gentleness about him; also, there had been a sensitiveness that I could not comprehend coming from the cold, distant man he had continued to be throughout the months. Even our conversation that evening had a different tone to it. It made me wonder if his mother had reached up from her grave and touched him with a breath of humanness.

"Virginia, my darling," he whispered huskily, as he cradled my face in his hands. "Are you not feeling well today? You are so pale."

"I am fine, Count." I forced my focus away from his penetrating eyes.

"Then there must be something bothering you. Is there any possible way in which I would be able to ease the pain I detect behind those beautiful eyes?" The count seemed to be trying to flatter me. Despite the number of times our bodies had been one, he had never spoken quite like this before.

"Well," I began, still unsure of whether I should ask. I had been feeling so penned in. I had not walked outside since that one night in December. I needed to breathe fresh air into my lungs. I needed the sun to sink her rays into my pores. I was a human, not a creature of the night, so how could one like him understand such a need?

"Continue, Virginia. What is it that you desire? If it is within my power, I shall grant your wish." The count's hand grasped hold of my chin, compelling me to look into his eyes. It was a gentle forcefulness.

"I need to get out," I stated. I felt his fingers stiffen on my face. Quickly, I added, "No, no, Count, not away—out into the fresh air. I miss the sun and the fresh breezes on my open skin. From my window I can see spring in the making ..." I forced a tear to escape from the corner of my eye. It trickled slowly down my cheek. *Is he capable of sympathy?* I wondered. I hoped.

The count released his hold on me, straightened up, and strolled over to the window. He stood for what seemed like ages, just staring out through the glass. Finally, he returned his attention to me.

"Would you like to walk the grounds with me tonight, Virginia? I am afraid it is impossible to allow you out in the direct sunlight during daylight hours. You are carrying my son, remember. I do not desire him to have any exposure to the sun, even while still in your womb. In fact, the sun's rays penetrating your body would be most detrimental to his well-being."

The count paused a moment, as though he were still contemplating how he could help alleviate some of my pain. "I shall leave instructions for Max," he continued, "to move you to a room in the tower at the back of the house. It has a door that leads out to a flat, enclosed area of the roof. I believe it is referred to as a 'widow's walk.' I will instruct Max to allow you to take air in the late evenings, once the sun has set. He will have the key to the door, so he can open it for you at the appropriate time and relock it when you are finished. That will eliminate any exposure to the sun's rays and still allow you some fresh air. It is also perfectly hidden so, while you walk, you will not be out in the open. Anyone who might be passing by on the nearby streets will not be able to see you."

"Why the move, dear Count? Would it not be simpler to take my walks in the yard or the courtyard?" I asked.

"Out of the question!" A hint of his old cynicism crept momentarily into his voice. I decided not to pursue that avenue any further. I knew he still did not trust me not to attempt another escape if I were on the ground. Where could I run to from the roof?

I nodded my head. "I am sorry if I touched a sore spot, Count. I was not thinking clearly. I thank you for your consideration of my feelings. And, yes, I would love to walk with you in the gardens now." I went to the closet and retrieved the cape I had worn before—Teresa had not wanted it after she had found out I had worn it.

As I tried to don it, the count's warm hands took control. Do not ask me how a vampire could have warm hands, but *he* did; at least I thought so on that particular night. Maybe it was only the illusion created by the personal warmth he appeared to be extending to me. "Here, Virginia darling, allow me."

Before I had time to react, the cape had been secured around my shoulders, buttoned into place, and I was being escorted out of my room on the arm of the man I hated, loved, and desired all at the same time. He guided me through the gardens, cradling my hand close to his bosom. I took no note as to whether there was a heartbeat beneath my trembling fingers. It was of no consequence to me; I was walking alone, with him. His arm was around my waist. Teresa was nowhere in the picture!

Max must have been in the yard planting flowers—I assumed it had been Max. I had yet to see any other servants around the house. I could not figure out, though, how he had the time for all the matters he attended to. Maybe the count had a gardener who came in once in a while—one to whom Max would just hand an envelope of money after each visit. I would have to pay closer attention now that spring was here. Of course, I had often thought there was the possibility that someone else actually lived in the house and helped Max—someone who worked in an obscure part of the building, where I would never be able to see them. Maybe it was even someone like Max, but of a lower station. But Max had said that there was no one else. I shuddered. The count drew me closer, most likely thinking I was chilled. Good that he could not read my thoughts—or could he?

We approached the statues. During my last walk I had been so engrossed in our conversation that I had not observed them very closely. Now I saw their true diabolic symbolism. They were grotesque-looking creatures, and in my opinion, they did not belong in a garden full of beautiful flowers. However, the thought crossed my mind that the flowers were nothing more than a distraction, so that the world could not see through to the true ugliness that lay behind the walls of the mansion.

I thought back to some of the older buildings and homes I had seen in Toronto. They, too, had had diabolical gargoyles placed on and around their grounds. Was it just a sign of a certain era, or were there a number of vampires out there that people were not aware of? If so, were they like the Count Basarab Musat, or were they the ones "created" over the centuries by the rogue vampire?—the one name that the count would not say. Had some of them, as the count had done, moved to small towns, or cities like Brantford, pretentiously posing as upstanding members of society? If so, how many were there? I shuddered again. The count drew me even closer. He did not seem in a talkative mood.

From the statues, the count led me down to the row of ancient trees that stood like sturdy castle guards around the property. Their branches knitted together, many of them dragging on the ground, leaving no obvious open passage for an escape to the outside world. My eyes searched earnestly for such an opening, but in the pale light of the moon, I could detect none. Their assignment was to let no one pass, in or out, and they did their job well. I wondered why the trees had allowed me in on that fateful night not so long ago. I also wondered why the count was taking me so close to the trees now. Was it to show me I had no way to escape, that I would never make it through the tangled roots? I knew he did not fear I would cry out—how could I, with him beside me? And who else, besides curious twits like me, would be on the streets in a residential area at this hour? Even most teenagers would be home, snug in their beds!

We turned and headed back toward the house. The count became talkative, but it was different from our usual subjects. He talked of his homeland. He described the rolling hills, the mountains, and the castles. There was a dreamy tone to his voice as the words poured out. He talked of the relatives who would soon be arriving. I thought I detected a hint of childish excitement in his voice, too, when he mentioned the guest of honour, his father. This was the man who had so painstakingly written the diary detailing the unfortunate demise of the Musat and Dracul families. "My father has waited a long time for this event," the count stated as he touched my swollen belly.

He released my hand and then gathered me into his arms. The shadows of the trees seemed less eerie as I basked in the strength of his embrace. He leaned over, and I felt the warmth of his breath caress my neck. His lips moved lingeringly over my eyes and then moved on to my waiting lips. His tongue explored the confines of my mouth, and the flame in my loins was ignited once again. Should I be experiencing such desire at this point in my pregnancy? I pondered as we descended slowly to the dew-damp grass.

There, under the light of the moon, on nature's fresh new green carpet, we made love. Our witnesses were the stars, the moon, and whatever creatures might inhabit the ominous darkness of the night. When the moments climaxed, he wrapped the heavy cape around me, gathered me gently in his arms, and carried me into the house and back up to my room.

"Come, Virginia darling, I will draw you a bath. You must be chilly from the dampness of the night. I dare not take a chance on your becoming ill at this point in the pregnancy," he articulated as he selected a white negligee and matching robe from my closet. Like an obedient lamb, I followed him out of my room and down the hallway to the bath chamber.

I was shocked—mesmerized by what Count Basarab Musat was doing for me. I was being treated like a queen—his queen. He was playing the part of a lowly servant as he poured the water into the huge tub. He carefully slid my clothing from my body and then gently directed me into the warm, inviting bubbles. I walked up the three steps and then down into the water, all the while with my fingertips resting in the palm of his hand. The water felt so soothing to my tired, aching body. I closed my eyes and leaned my head against the edge of the tub.

I was startled by hands suddenly touching my abdomen. The count had joined me. He was caressing his child—our child. I smiled. All my fear of this man evaporated.

We resumed our lovemaking, there in the water. He was gentle. Yet, at the same time, there was a ferocious powerfulness to him, which made every inch of my flesh tingle. And the baby, our baby, moved within me, dancing our dance of love. My entire body trembled with our passion.

Too soon for my liking, the count lifted me up from the foamy waters and laid me gently on an enormous white towel he had laid out before he had joined me in the water. He wrapped me in its softness and patted the beads of water and soapy bubbles from my skin. He took my hand and drew me to my feet, and then he slipped a silk gown over my head. I felt the richness of the material on my freshly cleaned skin.

Once again, I was elevated into his powerful arms. I rested my head on his shoulder and sighed contentedly as he carried me back to my room. Tonight, I did not think of it as a prison. Tonight, we had flown together—I was all his and he was all mine!

We continued to enjoy each other until the sun began to creep through the cracks in the curtain. But that was the last night of passion I was to experience before the birth of our child. It was a night to cherish above all others; it was the first time he had shown me there was a possible human side to him ...

So I thought.

My belongings were moved to the room in the tower, as the count had promised they would be. I had no idea how Max managed it by himself, but two days after my request, upon finishing the evening meal, I was led to my new quarters. They were not much different from the old ones; there were still bars on the windows.

Life continued. I read. I waited for him to come to me, but he did not. So I read some more. I made notes of all the vicious people I was reading about, trying to profile them, so that I might have a better understanding of their way of thinking. I had found a book on profiling in the law section. It was interesting to read about some of the fallacies of profiling that my television generation had been exposed to. Motivations for becoming a serial killer were not always clear, and it could not be assumed that there was just one motive. Once a possible motive had been identified, that did not mean the killer could be identified. The book went on to say that most serial murderers committed their crimes because they wanted to; exceptions to that theory are those who are mentally ill. There was a list of usual motives: anger, monetary gain, power and thrill of the kill, ideology, psychosis, and of course, the sexually-based killings. I made as many notes as I could, writing in shorthand, so that I would not have to use so much paper. If I ever got out of this place alive, I would have a good familiarity with the courses I might take to get my degree in criminal profiling—that is, if I still wanted to do that. For now, it helped to pass my time—a sinister distraction for me, immersed in a gloomy world!

When I was not doing that, I wrote in my diary. I had to use candlelight in the dusk hours and even in the daytime, now, for very few rays of sunlight managed to enter this room because of the extra-heavy window tapestries. I had been given strict instructions not to open them now, and I dared not disobey; I never knew when someone might walk in. At night, I strolled in the moonlight, around and around the widow's walk. Max would open the door and then leave me alone, but as soon as I stepped back into my room, he would reappear with the key and relock the door.

I had read about widow's walks in a library book. This was where women would go to watch for their husbands' return from the sea. I wondered at the creation of this particular one, since there was no sea in the vicinity. Was it truly a widow's walk, or was it just where some young bride had made her husband a widower when she jumped to her death? I had fleeting moments when I thought of doing that myself, but then my child would move within me, and I would just continue walking. Of course, there was another logical explanation—it was just the fashionable architecture of the time.

Thoughts of screaming out into the empty night, with the hope of being heard, constantly crossed my mind as well, but I knew from experience that either Max or Teresa was always lurking close by— possibly the count, as well. Besides, if there were even the slightest chance of me being detected, I was sure the count would never have agreed to allow me such a luxury as these nightly strolls!

So I just walked and paced—and prayed. No one from my world ever noticed the lonely figure walking on top of the old mansion; if anyone did, they took no notice. Why would they?

And I yearned for *him* to come to me.

But he never did. I would see him briefly at out meals, but he was aloof, never directing any conversation in my direction. Had I done something to offend him?

Teresa seemed smug.

When I returned to my room, I would cry.

And then, I would damn them both!

CHAPTER 15

The Outsiders

Near the beginning of my seventh month of pregnancy, I noticed that Max was unusually stressed. I knew it was too soon for the relatives to be arriving. Teresa had informed me they were not scheduled to arrive until just before the actual birth.

Max was constantly working, cleaning everywhere. The other clue that something might be going on was the tantalizing food aromas filtering up to my room. In all my months of captivity, that quantity of savoury smells had never penetrated my nostrils. This state of anxiety had been going on for an entire week, but every time I asked Max if he was all right, he would brush me off with a nervous wave of his gnarled old hand.

Saturday morning arrived. Would this end the confusion I was feeling and the tension Max was displaying? The usual light knock sounded on my door, and Max entered with my breakfast tray. I had thought he was nervous during the past week, but this morning he was more jittery than ever!

"Your drink, Miss Virginia." Max handed me the mug. Even though it tasted okay, I longed for a hearty breakfast of bacon and eggs, toast, coffee, and juice. No breakfast like that had been served to me since the end of my first trimester.

I studied Max closely as he moved nervously around the room, straightening the covers on my bed and picking up stray items of clothing. He went to the windows and did something that he had never done before. I was used to the curtains being drawn back at night, but Max took a roll of tape and secured them in place all around, so absolutely nothing could penetrate through—neither sunlight nor moonlight.

Perplexed at this unfamiliar action, and upset with the loss of what little sunlight the cracks at the sides of the curtains had allowed through to my room, I blurted out, "What are you doing, Max? Why are you sealing the curtains so tightly? You know how much I enjoy those few rays of sunshine throughout the day! Even though it is not much, they are something for me to hang on to. So why, Max, why?" I was extremely upset, so much so that tears welled up in my eyes.

Max looked rattled by my reaction. "I am sorry, Miss Virginia. I do know how much you enjoy that bit of sun and being able to open the curtain at night, but I assure you, it is only a temporary situation. The curtains are to remain sealed until after tomorrow. The count has left very strict orders."

"But why, Max?" I pleaded for an answer.

As though Max had not heard me, he continued with his own line of thought. "You, Miss Virginia, will be dining in your room tonight." Max turned to leave. "I will return later with your lunch."

I ran to the door and blocked his exit. "Why, Max? Just tell me why! I won't allow you to leave this room until I am given an explanation. There has been too much going on here all week, too many nervous twitches, too many secret looks between you and Teresa. I want to know what is going on!" My voice rose in anger, and I stamped my foot.

Max scrutinized me closely. I could tell from the look on his face that he was shocked at my outburst. I had become a relatively passive hostage, once I had realized there was little chance of escape, and when I was enjoying the count's company in the evenings. Max's seemed nervous. After a lengthy hesitation, he answered me.

"The master is entertaining tonight," he stated blandly. Max was trying to be nonchalant about the fact that the count was entertaining—something I had not noticed him doing since I had been in the house. "Therefore, because of the circumstances surrounding your stay here, you are to be kept locked in your room for the duration of our guests' visit. You are not to try anything foolish that would bring attention to your presence. You are not to knock on the door, scream, cry for help, or look out the windows.

"Any attempt at disclosure will only cause considerable humiliation for you, and your attempt to escape will be futile. The count has ordered your seclusion. His wishes, as you know by now, are always obeyed." Max finished his deliberation with a knowing look. Or was that a warning glance he threw my way?

I dared to pose another question. "Who is the count entertaining, Max?

"These guests are not his friends, Miss Virginia. Tonight is strictly a business meeting of sorts; however, some of the guests may be spending the night. They have travelled from north of Toronto and will most likely not leave until tomorrow afternoon. The dinner party will go on until quite a late—or should I say early?—hour. No matter. It all depends on who you are as to whether the hour is late or early, doesn't it, Miss Virginia?" Max grinned at me as he drove his point home.

I wondered what kind of business the count was involved in. In spite of all the conversations we'd had, he had never actually informed me how he maintained his household. And I had been so enthralled with the subjects we were discussing that I had not thought to question how the luxurious trappings I was surrounded by had been obtained. I had not thought to question where the food for my meals came from or how it was brought into the house. The biggest mystery of all was where the blood came from that Teresa and the count drank every evening at the supper table. I had not dared to ask about that! But I also wondered how many doctors would scratch their heads in speculation every time they noticed that the blood bank was not as full as it was supposed to be and how many people were affected by that loss—if that is where the blood was coming from!

What did all this really mean, then? Once again I wondered if I were in some kind of dream world. Did this house and the creatures within it truly exist, or were they only figments of my imagination? Were the stories the count had told me about individuals he knew just that—stories from his overactive imagination, stories told just to pass away some idle time? Somehow, I doubted that—the people he had mentioned and whom we had discussed were in the history books—they were real. And then there was the child within me—I felt him kick, catapulting me back to the reality of my present situation!

Max put his hands on my shoulders and gently moved me away from the door. I allowed myself to be shifted. "You will have your little bit of sunshine back tomorrow, Miss Virginia. In the meantime, please remember what I have said, and all will go well for you." With that final warning, Max left. I heard the door lock click. Once again, I was alone in my prison.

⁓

I began pacing. Pacing had become a form of exercise for my body as well as a release for my tensions. What kind of business was the count involved in? Who were these people who were arriving tonight? Were they like him? If not, would they be safe here during the night hours under the same roof with a—with *him*? Oh, God! What if they were humans and the count tried to ... I had no desire to entertain that thought any further. I still wondered at my own fortune of having been spared such a fatal moment. I grew tired of my restless thoughts and lay down on my bed, praying that sleep would ease my pain.

And I dreamed. I dreamed of escape. I dreamed the guests came. I dreamed that they demanded the count release me. They were such kind people, all of them. They crowded around me and assured me of their protection. They came closer and closer. They wrapped their arms around me. Their faces pushed ever nearer to mine.

Suddenly, the loving expressions turned into looks of jeering contempt. I became frightened. I tried to run, but they laughed and held me fast in place. My legs were flailing aimlessly in thin air as I attempted to distance myself from the faces. They taunted. They pulled at my swollen body from every direction, each trying to grab a piece of me. The laughter increased, hideous and grotesque. Their mouths opened wide; they hovered even closer to my trembling body, and then, there they were—the fangs! I screamed, and screamed, and screamed!

"Miss Virginia! Wake up, Miss Virginia!" Max was shaking my shoulder vigorously, trying to arouse me.

I opened my eyes and stared at him, terrified of what I might see. My body was soaked with perspiration. Max gathered me into his arms the way my father had done when I was a child having a nightmare. He cooed softly in my ear. I did not understand why he was doing this for me, but it did bring a sort of serene comfort to my troubled mind. I allowed my tears to flow freely. It had been a dream—at least this time. Thank God!

"Come, Miss Virginia, I shall pour you a bath. You look as though you have just been in quite a battle. You can eat your lunch after freshening up."

I nodded and followed Max to the bathing room. I felt that this was one night I would not be seeking deliverance from this place. The dream had wiped freedom's lure from my mind!

⁓

As evening approached, I watched intently through my covered window for a sign of car lights. Why I bothered, I cannot explain. My dream still terrorized my conscious mind, and I was not willing to jeopardize my life with any unknown entities. Besides, Max had made it perfectly clear that there would be nothing but humiliation in store for me if I were to attempt anything. Of course, that humiliation probably meant that I would be made to look like a fool. Probably it would be pointed out to the guests that I was just a silly and distraught pregnant female. Maybe the count would say I was a widowed sister who had temporarily lost all sense of reality as a result of losing her husband while in such a "delicate condition"!

But still I vacillated; there was another emotion gnawing at me. A tiny voice kept trying to tell me that this just might be my opportunity to free myself from this house and all those in it. I tried desperately to silence that voice, but it continued to wrench at my mind, launching visions of freedom into my tormented thoughts.

I began to reason that if there were a way—any way at all—it would be in the early morning light, when Teresa and the count had lost their imposing powers. It would require little effort to overcome Max, if I could catch him off-guard, and if the guests were cooperative, or even still awake at that hour, it was possible that they might assist me. However, I reasoned that my best chance to escape would be when everyone was sleeping.

Thus the matter was settled, in my subconscious. I would rest now, wake early, and then prepare. It might be my last chance, my final opportunity to save my child from the destiny that awaited it. And, of course, to save myself from whatever fate awaited me, because I still had no idea what the count had planned for me once the child was born.

My door opened slowly, and Teresa entered with my evening meal and drink. She looked stunning! She wore a gown of crimson-red silk, adorned with shimmering red sequins from the neckline to just above the knees. From there, the material, like wild waves on a rugged shoreline, swirled freely to the ankles, where it touched upon her dainty red silk shoes. The gown clung to her perfect body like a silken glove. It was such a change from her usual black attire!

Her cheeks harmonized with the red material, reflecting a lustrous hue on the otherwise pale skin. Teresa's lips appeared smooth and moist, resembling the colour of freshly drawn blood. Her luminous raven hair tumbled, with stunning contrast, over the rich, red material of the gown. What a shame such beauty was wasted on the horrifying creature I indisputably knew her to be!

Teresa set my tray down on the table beside my bed, walked over to the windows, and checked the curtains to ensure they were securely in place. She also checked the lock on the door that led to the roof. "There will be no walking this evening," she informed. "I understand Max has given you a brief summary of tonight's events?"

"Yes, he pointed out my situation quite clearly." I wondered if she noticed the contempt in my voice.

Teresa smiled. I could have sworn it was a victory smile. I knew, even if I did not want to admit it, that her position in this household was secure—regardless of who grew inside of me. She knew it, too. She was the wife of the count, Basarab Musat. I was not. She would be his hostess tonight. The curious little fool locked in the tower, whose body was swollen with his child, would remain incarcerated, as though she were a fruit forbidden to be gazed upon. I experienced a twang of jealousy.

"Then, I trust you will oblige us and not cause any unnecessary scenes?" Teresa continued.

"Whatever makes you suppose I would do something as foolish as that, Teresa?" I answered, slyly. "I am quite content to be here. After all, you must remember, I am the one who carries the count's child." I drove my point home with what I felt to be a ruthless truth. "I would not think of doing something that would jeopardize *our* son!"

I had definitely succeeded in striking a tender nerve. Teresa flinched as though I had driven a stake into her heart. I noticed the anger flash through her dark eyes. She had come here to taunt me with her power and position. I had thrown it back in her face. I smiled sweetly.

"Just heed my warnings. You will be the loser, not I, should you attempt something foolish tonight!" Teresa retorted as she stormed out of the room. In her fury, I saw with amazement, she had failed to lock my door!

What a break—I had certainly not anticipated this! I closed my eyes, clasped my hands together, and prayed that Teresa would not remember her carelessness and return to lock me in. I sat on the edge of my bed and tried to calm the butterflies in my stomach. I picked at my supper. I sipped my drink. Perhaps this would be the last one of its kind I would have to consume.

At the moment, time was on my side, but could I wait patiently for my juncture with freedom? Maybe I would not have to delay departure until the sun rose. Maybe I could slip out of my unlocked cell and sneak away during the festivities, disappearing into the night shadows and out of his clutches, forever!

As I waited, my impatience grew. Time passed too slowly. Finally, I detected a pale reflection of light through the curtains. This light could only mean one thing: the guests were arriving. I walked across the room, placed my ear to the crack in the door, and listened for the strangers' entrance. I was rewarded, moments later, with the sound of voices. All were male voices, so far, and pleasant enough. The count's accent, as he greeted his guests, was quite distinctive.

Then I heard Teresa greeting some women. I detected the names Mrs. Stinson and Mrs. Lawry. That meant that there must be at least two couples. The fact that there were women could improve my chances of escape—if I were caught, that is. Women would be more sympathetic, as long as they were not vampires. That was what I most dreaded. Thoughts of that aspect crept back into my mind, shattering momentarily the hope of my elusive freedom.

I continued listening as the guests entered. Smidgens of incomprehensible conversation, mixed with laughter, filtered up to my tower room. The count's voice continued to ring out, like an imminent warning to me. He was power itself—above all others' his tone stood out. I dared myself to imagine how the other men compared to the count. I was filled with guilt, as my heart told me there would be no comparison.

He was the ultimate man, the total male. Once a woman had been consumed by his fire, she would be his forever. These thoughts were very real to me. They were also very scary and rang too obviously true in my heart. Thank God, I still had some will left to fight the fantasies within my bosom! Hopefully, logic would be enough to propel me away from this place in the early light of the morning that would follow this night.

The night dragged on. I was restless. I was nervous. I paced. I listened. I paced some more. Would they never retire?

From what bits and pieces I could hear, it sounded as though these people had something to do with real estate. Was the count selling the property? Or was he buying another one, somewhere else? Maybe both. But why would he want to move, if life was so good here? Or, was it? I should remember to ask Max—if I were still here in the morning. Of course, there was the possibility the count was preparing to move again, having been in Brantford long enough. Moving around was something he had mentioned he needed to do regularly, before the locals questioned his failure to age.

I grew weary of eavesdropping and plunked myself in the armchair by my bed. I dared not lie down for fear I would sleep too deeply and miss my chance at freedom's lure. Just a catnap would suffice, I thought as I shut my eyes for a moment's respite.

I awoke with a start! I jumped from the chair, disregarding the sharp pain that knifed me in the abdomen. Despite my resolve not to, I had slept deeply. I prayed I was not too late. I prayed that everyone, the guests especially, were still cradled beneath their covers—or wherever. I prayed that Max slept—him most of all, because it was Max who always seemed to be there, lurking around some hidden corner. It was Max who seemed never to sleep. It was his detection I feared in the daylight hours, even though, as I mentioned earlier, I felt he might be easily overpowered if I caught him off-guard. Then again, if all the guests still slept, I would have no one to turn to for aid if things did not go as planned.

I prayed it was well before the hour when Max usually brought my breakfast. I walked over to the door. It swung open easily. Good! Teresa had not noticed her carelessness. I listened intently. The house was deadly silent. I crept out the door of my prison. My entire body trembled. I went quickly down the stairs. At the bottom, I considered which direction I should take. Would Max have locked all of the outer doors? I hoped not. My footsteps turned automatically toward the front foyer. I began to run, as fast as my swollen body would allow.

All was going well. Nothing but the sound of my slippers on the carpet disturbed the silence. I reached the front door. The knob turned easily, and I stepped out onto the large wooden veranda. The sun was just peeping over the horizon, sending slivers of light through the ever-guarding trees. I started to run, slowly at first, and then picking up my pace as I proceeded across the lawn.

I dodged the statues and flower beds. I skirted around the bushes and entered the grove of ancient trees. I stopped and glanced back for a final look at the place that had been my prison for what seemed to have been an eternity. "I'll expose you for what you have done to me," I shook my fist defiantly at the house!

That was my fatal mistake. As freedom's arms beckoned to me, I tripped over a large, protruding tree root. Darkness, once again, covered me with his veil.

When I came to I was in my bed, the one in my prison. I began to weep. Max was sitting in the chair beside me, the same chair that I had rested in through the night. He studied me intently, and there was a worried look on his brow. He noted my waking.

"Foolish girl, Virginia. It was an imprudent thing you tried to do. I am at odds as to what I should do about this," Max commented, shaking his head back and forth, as though he were trying to weigh the situation he was faced with.

I had to think quickly. "Who knows, besides you?" I asked softly. It would not do to anger Max under my present circumstances.

"No one."

"Then all is safe, right? There is no need to tell him." I prayed my nervousness did not show.

"No, I do not have to," Max paused for a moment as a deep, wracking sigh shook his tired body. "But if the count were to find out—if anyone else were to have seen you and informed him of your attempt—" Max seemed too frightened to finish his statement.

I sat up in the bed, reached out, and grasped Max's arm. "Please, Max, if not for my sake, think of the child. Think what his wrath could do to the baby still growing inside me. We cannot take such a risk at this stage of the pregnancy. Remember this child will be Teresa's. She is unable to have one of her own. Don't you want your daughter to experience motherhood?" I wondered if Max would buy into my plea. At this moment, it was *my* life I was concerned for.

Max rose from the chair. He gazed at me with a sad face, a face that was drawn and tired-looking. I wondered if he was growing weary of life with Count Basarab Musat, and if so, would he assist me in my flight to freedom?—after the child was born, of course.

"Okay, Virginia, for the sake of the child, I will say nothing." He paused again. "But there is no guarantee that I will not reveal your attempted escape after the child is born."

I swallowed nervously. "One more question, Max: How did you know I was gone? The house was silent, and I presumed you were sleeping along with the rest."

"I was bringing you your drink before retiring for a few hours. I noticed your door was open—"

I interrupted him. "Teresa forgot to lock it," I mentioned, contempt creeping into my voice. I had to emphasize that point in order to ensure that Max would not expose my attempted escape to the count. If the count knew it was Teresa who had failed to lock the door, then her fate would be no less than mine; it might even be worse—I was convinced of that fact.

"I see," replied Max. "So that is how it was and is to be?" His face showed defeat. "Now to tell you how I detected you. When I found you were gone, I went to your window and peeled away some of the tape that was holding the curtains down. I saw you running across the lawn. It would have been fruitless for me to pursue; I would never have been able to catch you. For a moment, it appeared that you had finally made your escape, even though it would not have been for long. The count would have tracked you down and brought you back here to give birth to his son. After the birth, and when you were no longer needed, he would dispose of you. I would think that by now you have realized that you cannot hide from one such as him.

"But you foolishly looked back, tripped, and did not get up. I knew you must have been hurt. All that was left for me to do was to pick you up and carry you back here, before anyone else detected your flight. It was difficult, because you are heavy with child, and a few times I almost stumbled. But the thought of my grandchild gave me added strength."

"You could have left me to be found by someone else who might have been passing by," I suggested.

"To have left you there for a passerby to find would have created a greater disaster for us all, should you have decided to mention certain aspects of our way of life here. On the other hand, had you gone unnoticed by outsiders, and the count had detected you, well, who is to say what would have happened then!" Max ended with a very thought-provoking possibility.

"I would not have said anything, to anyone," I vowed.

"We cannot take that chance—the count will not take that chance."

I knew I had lost. "Thank you, Max," I whispered humbly. "Then this will be our little secret—yours and mine, right? It must be this way, for all our sakes," I added as I ran my hands across my bulging abdomen.

"Yes, Miss Virginia, for now, for all our sakes," Max replied, wearily. He handed me my drink before shuffling out of the room. He was the picture of a broken old man. His sagging shoulders told the tale of one who had witnessed many defeats and would probably witness many more before he passed from this world, if he ever did. Max's existence was still a mystery to me, but one that I would not push to know, especially after he had told me it would not be healthy to have such knowledge.

I sipped slowly at my breakfast, and I pondered my situation. Where was God? Why had He forsaken me? Was it because I had given myself so wantonly to the count? Because I had not fought hard enough against his wiles? *Why?* I had touched and breathed freedom more than once but had always been stopped short and returned to the uncertain fate that awaited me. What had I done during my short life to deserve this ill fortune?

I slept once again, exhausted from my ordeal. I would see him later. We would debate. I would gaze upon *his* magnificence, and *he* would ease my pain. For this my heart longed. For this my body craved. Against this, my will still tried to fight—but in reality, it never tried hard enough!

CHAPTER 16

Time Draws Near

It was near the end of my eighth month that my fears resurfaced, especially after a conversation I had with Teresa. She had never mentioned anything about my attempted escape, but it was quite obvious to me that Max had informed her of the episode. One evening Teresa presented me with some food for thought.

"It won't be long now, Virginia—about four weeks?" she raised her eyebrows questioningly.

"Yes, I would say about that." I hesitated a moment before asking the question that was bothering me. "There is one thing I have been wondering about, Teresa. Will there be a physician present when the baby is delivered?"

"Of sorts."

"Just what do you mean by *of sorts*?" I felt the butterflies in my stomach again.

"What I mean is, you will be well-looked after, dear Virginia. There is a family physician coming from Transylvania. He is quite versed in the birthing of a child."

"Tell me honestly, Teresa, if you are able to, what is going to happen to me after I deliver this child?" I had finally summoned up the courage to ask the dreaded question.

"After you give birth, you will still be needed to nurse the child for a short time. Once he is weaned, the count will decree what your destiny shall be."

"What if the child is a girl?" I asked.

"Pray to that God you worship that it is not, not only for the sake of the child, but especially for you!" Teresa's words were harsh. "This child must be a son! The count demands that, and what he demands, he gets! If the child is a girl, I may be able to wield some influence and save its life, but as to your fate—I have no influence over that, nor do I really have any desire to help you!"

There it was, in black and white! I had known I could not depend on Teresa. She hated me so much that even if she could have swayed the count to let me go, she never would have. I tried to pretend I had not heard her last statement by striking back at her with some scientific, biological facts.

"But, Teresa, we have to face facts here; we are not dealing with demands. We are talking about biology, maybe something you have little knowledge of. There is a fifty-fifty chance I could have a girl." I paused. "Besides, it is the male who decides a baby's gender," I added.

"You are correct in saying that I know nothing of this *biology* you are talking about. However, if you say that the male decides the gender of the child, then we are both correct. The count is a male, and as I already told you, it is the count who decides what the child will be. That is the extent of my knowledge," Teresa retorted haughtily.

I laughed, inside, at the irony of the situation. The count was definitely a male, but what Teresa appeared not to understand was one of the finer points of biology. Sexual orientation was a matter of nature's choice—not man's *or* a creature's.

I wondered about her education, but then it dawned on me that during her youth biology had probably not been studied extensively in the schools, unless a young man had been interested in a career in medicine. Girls would never be privy to such a subject. To my knowledge, Teresa had been under the count's tutelage from a very early age, so what she knew was only what *he* permitted her to know. She also did not appear to me to be the type who would seek out information beyond the count's world. That was something Teresa had proven over and over again by choosing not to be around when the count and I were having our conversations. She had attempted a couple of times but had not said a word. She had just sat there, her mood becoming more agitated as our discussion went on. Finally, she had just stood up and left.

I wished Count Atilla's diary had continued, so I could learn more of him, how he had educated himself so well, and how he had educated those of his household, including his son. I also wished the diary had gone on to give details of how Atilla had raised Basarab and what the count had been like as a child. Foolish me—why should I care? Hopefully I would be out of here soon and not have to worry about any of that.

Teresa continued, "As I warned you, dear Virginia, you should just pray, for your sake, that it is not a girl! Come now; we will be late for supper. And I know for sure that would not please the count. He is restless of late, and impatient, while awaiting the birth of his son." Teresa emphasized the word *son*. "Also, the count is anxious for the arrival of our guests. It has been many years since he has seen some of them."

"When will they be here?"

"Soon—within the next two weeks. Sometimes a child arrives early, as you with your vast education probably already know, so we must be prepared." Did I detect bitterness in her voice when she alluded to my education?

"Prepared for what?" I inquired.

"For the ceremony."

I wondered if this ceremony was a duplicate of the one referred to in the diary—the one the count Atilla had feared to reveal details of for fear that his diary would fall into the wrong hands. I was not sure if I was ready to hear the answer to that question, let alone be involved in it! Instead, I simply asked, "How many guests are we expecting?"

"Six."

"Are they all … uh?" The exact word escaped me.

Teresa smiled, just enough for me to catch a glimpse of her elongated teeth. "Yes, they are. Let's go now; we must hurry."

I followed Teresa out of my room. She had rekindled my fears sufficiently that I was contemplating another escape attempt. I would have to execute that attempt before my child was born, because if the child was a girl, I had no idea what the count would do to her—or what he would do to me.

As we walked to the dining room, I wondered if the ceremony Teresa had spoken of was the same as the one Atilla had written of, and I wondered if there was anything for me to fear. Would I have any significant part in it, other than delivering the child, of course? What did the ceremony entail? What kind of doctor would be tending to my needs—surely not the count Balenti Danesti? Visions of vampires drinking blood all around me while I delivered the child, covered in my own blood, sprung up in my mind. Oh God! I *had* to escape! I had no other choice!

I felt secure that while the count seemed to have other things on his mind besides me he would never suspect I would attempt to flee again. We had shared so much, and I had become compliant. I was *almost* positive that he had no idea of my last escape attempt. I was *almost* equally sure that the count felt I was completely under his control, because he was still allowing me my evening walks on the widow's walk. An image of the night we had made love in the garden flitted through my mind.

Yes, now was the time. My mind began spinning as I tried to weave another escape plan. If only I could discover a way out other than the front door, or the back stairs that led into the courtyard. I needed a way that would allow me to flee undetected and that had no major obstacles to dodge during my run for freedom. I would definitely have to be more observant. I would diligently search for an alternate route to the outside world.

~

It was a night of obscure darkness. Clouds rolled across the moon, creating eerie shadows that I imagined were creatures of the night. Shivers raced up and down my spine. I had no idea why. Apprehension enveloped me. Then I heard it. Loud and clear. Howling! A chorus of howling, harmonizing together, creating a symphony of such deep sadness that my heart quivered. How could this be possible? Wolves did not make their homes in cities!

The realization of what must be happening seized me. My throat felt as if there were a Vise-Grip squeezing it. The guests were arriving; that meant my time to plan an exit from this place had run out. With so many of them scattered about the house, how could I possibly slip out unnoticed?

The baby moved restlessly within me. It was as though he knew they were coming, and he was anxious to welcome his kin. I caressed my abdomen, trying to sooth the turmoil within. The child refused to succumb to my strokes. In fact, its agitation increased with each note that echoed in the distance!

How, in the name of God, was I ever going to save this child if it was already so affected by *them* from within my womb? Would it be a futile attempt, a foolish thought, to even deem possible such a thing? After all, the count was the father, and even if I were to escape his control, I was quite aware of the fact that the child—male or female—might not! There was also the ever-looming question of my fate after the child was weaned, after the end of my usefulness. So many questions; no logical answers.

A light knock on the door brought me back to the reality of my present situation. Teresa entered without waiting for my reply. Of

course, she hardly ever considered the courtesy of privacy when it came
to entering or leaving my room. Draped over her arm was a white silk
gown.

"Our guests are arriving, Virginia. Supper will be served in one
hour. The count wishes you to wear this, and I am to help you dress,"
Teresa stated as she laid the clothing on my bed.

So the guests were here. I wondered how they would greet me.
Would they rise to the occasion on two legs or bow down to me on four?
"Do you mind informing me who has arrived?" I asked.

"Of course not," Teresa replied. "Not as many as we thought; the
family did not bring any of their servants with them. But the important
ones are here: the count's father, Count Atilla Musat, and two of his
cousins, the counts Mihail and Vlad Dracul. Also, there is an aunt and
uncle, the count Vacaresti Musat and his wife, the countess Emelia.
Last, but certainly not least, the doctor I spoke of earlier, Count Balenti
Danesti."

I breathed in sharply at the mention of the last name. He still lived?
But how? Atilla had not referred to Balenti as a relative, only as a doctor.
"That makes six," I concluded, counting the names in my head. "Which
means everyone is here?"

"Yes," Teresa stated simply. She retrieved my brush from the dresser.
"Come, Virginia; we must hurry. Everything is to be perfect tonight,
including you." I noted the sarcasm in her voice when she said "including
you." Or had that been loathing?

I went and sat in the chair by my window. Teresa followed and
commenced brushing my hair. It had grown quite a bit since my
imprisonment, and despite my pregnancy, or maybe because of it, my
hair was extraordinarily healthy. As Teresa brushed, I went over in my
mind the names she had mentioned. Two in particular bothered me:
Mihail and Vlad Dracul—sons of the Impaler, the one for whom the
curse was truly meant. And why had he not come for this important
event? Did I dare ask? Was he not here because he was the one who
was creating all the new rogues? That could not be possible, I thought,

because the count had never alluded to such; he had always spoken quite highly of his uncle. I thought it might be better if I did not ask about Dracula's whereabouts.

"Your hair feels like silk, Virginia. And the colour is such a lovely shade of red. Not so dark that it is ghastly to gaze upon, but colourful enough that it shimmers in any light. I envy you."

Teresa's compliment startled me. "You envy me? Please, Teresa, do not patronize me with such a statement. You are more beautiful than I could ever dream of being," I confessed to her, even though I felt a twinge of regret at having admitted such a truth.

"My beauty comes out of darkness; it is not real. Yours still has the reflection of light in it." Did I detect a melancholy note in Teresa's voice as she referred to the conflicting shades of beauty? And what did she mean by her beauty not being real?

"Besides, Virginia," Teresa continued, "you should not downgrade yourself; you are an extremely beautiful woman. Do you really think if you were not that you would be carrying his child? No, the count would have discarded you to a living hell, where he has sent many others before you. Take consolation in the fact that your beauty has bought you some time."

I could sense Teresa's evil behind the words *bought you some time.* She finished brushing my hair and returned the brush to the dresser. Inwardly, I cursed the beauty God had bestowed on me. The thought crossed my mind that if I had been plainer-looking, the count might just have let me go. Therefore, I did not truly feel thankful at this moment, when my future was so undecided. But who was I fooling? Teresa had said I would have been discarded to a living hell as the others had been. Was there no winning for me?

Did Teresa believe that I should be content with the extra scrap of time that had been granted me? Was she suggesting that that was all life had to offer? Maybe I should be thankful, because it appeared that scrap of time could open to me a means of escape—without which this story would never have been written!

There were other things that bothered me. How did the child of a vampire age? At what point did the aging process cease? Did they enjoy their eternity, or had many of them eventually tired of such an existence and ended it with stakes through their hearts and swords to sever their heads from their bodies? And who would end it for them—one of their own? I wished I dared to ask someone such questions! I had not even thought to discuss these subjects with the count.

Also, did Teresa presume that I had no emotional ties to the child growing inside of me? If so, then she truly had no idea about being a mother. In her cold, calculating manner, she constantly reminded me that I was being used—so how could I allow myself to suppose she could care? I was a fool to imagine anything different! She was not really her own person; she was merely an extension of the count! And, despite all that had passed between him and me, I still did not understand him!

"Come, I will assist you with the gown, Virginia," Teresa interrupted my thoughts.

I was not willing to let this matter drop. There was too much at stake. "Teresa, you said my beauty has bought me time. What is my fate to be after I give birth to this child and once it is weaned? I must know. I am frightened! It is enough for me to be able to handle all that is happening to me—like a nightmare from a horror novel. But not to know what is to become of me or the child, that is constantly eating away at me!"

I grabbed Teresa's arm. I knew I was still being foolish to think she would care anything about what was going to happen to me physically, let alone what mental torments I was experiencing. My mind had already conjured up a gruesome death when my usefulness was finished. I gazed pleadingly into Teresa's eyes, awaiting my answer, hoping it would be something I would want to hear.

"As I keep trying to tell you," Teresa began, shaking her head back and forth, "I honestly do not know what he will do with you, or when he will do it. As for the child, you will be expected to nurse him; I will have charge of the rest of his care. Max and I keep reminding you: I am the count's wife, not you. You are nothing more than the vessel in which the child was conceived. This you have done, not just for him, but for me as well." There was a definite look of triumph on Teresa's face. "This child will be born, and he will take his rightful place in the world of his father. He will know that *I* am his mother! He will not be with you long enough for him to even have the faintest memory of you!"

"Then, after I give birth, would you help me to escape? Please, Teresa. What difference will it make to you whether I live or die—you will have the child! At least grant me my life; after all, I have given you one!" I was praying that I might have exposed some aspect of humanity within Teresa. "I promise I shall divulge nothing of who you and the count are," I added humbly. "I swear on the life of my child. You have my word that I will be silent, in order to protect him from any harm."

Teresa's face took on a stony look. I truly was fooling myself if I thought she would consider assisting me. She did not understand, or feel, any of the emotions of a human woman. She was nothing more than a feminine version of Count Basarab Musat! I had reasoned within myself, since Max was her father, and he was human—well, at least he appeared to be—that maybe I could reach that part of Teresa's genes. He had definitely, on more than one occasion, manifested human emotions, especially where Lilly and Teresa were concerned. I had no real way of knowing the truth, so putting my trust in her was a chance I felt forced to take. Whatever the outcome, it was my life I was gambling with!

"It is not in my hands to grant you anything," Teresa finally answered. "The men rule supreme in our society. Their word is the law, not as in your world, where I have been told that the men kowtow to their women's every whim." Teresa paused. "Now, Virginia, we have wasted enough time with idle chatter. The count will be furious if we keep him waiting tonight."

Idle chatter? Is that all Teresa thought of my fears and of my life? I dared not let her see me weep; my heart was seeping the tears that should have flowed from my eyes. Teresa assisted me as I slipped into the gown. The silk, as it slid over my skin, felt cool on my hot, swollen body. I wished there were a mirror, so I could observe the full effect and see what had become of me.

A knock sounded on the door, and Max entered, holding a long white veil. Teresa took it and placed it gently on my head. She pulled a section over my face, straightened a few folds, and then stepped back to observe her work.

"The count will present you to his family tonight as the woman he has chosen to bear his son," she stated. "Do not remove this yourself—*he* will lift the veil," she added.

Was I being treated like a bride? Was it not a little late to be getting me to the altar? Besides, Teresa had already been there. So why the white gown and the wedding veil? I was obviously pregnant; in fact, I was almost ready to deliver. I did not present the picture of a bride who was about to take her wedding vows. Of course, no one had actually informed me that I would be taking any vows. Most likely, when all was said and done, I would be attending a funeral—my own.

"What do you think, Max?" Teresa asked, turning to her father. "Will she pass?"

Will I pass? Pass what? How dare she!

Max ran his hand through his hair. "Oh yes, Teresa, she will more than pass. Her condition has added a certain aura to her—she shines. I am positive the count's father will be more than pleased." Max sounded sincere. "But you must go now and dress yourself, Teresa. I will escort Virginia to the dining room. Dinner will be served shortly."

Max extended his arm to me. I laid my hand near his elbow and we swept out of the room. What play-acting—Max the father figure, I the dutiful daughter being led down the aisle to her betrothed. The only problem with the picture was that I knew I was not the glowing bride, and there would be no adoring groom waiting for me at an altar!

CHAPTER 17

Meeting the Family

The dining room shone as never before. Someone must have polished the woodwork for hours in order to create such a shine. The table was set with precision, as though royalty would be attending the evening meal. Pale, rose-coloured dishes adorned a black lace tablecloth. I did not bother to examine its stitches; I suspected there would be creatures as diabolical as those woven into the regular tablecloth.

The faint sound of classical music—Mozart's "Funeral March for Signor Maestro Contrapunto"—resonated from one of the corners. Music had been another one of the elements missing from my life during my months of captivity. I wondered why it was being played now.

Large baskets of multi-coloured flowers lent a sweet fragrance to the room. I had not known Max ever to bring garden flowers into the house before. Why now? To celebrate the guests' arrival, or a parallel to the life that grew inside of me?

Max led me to the chair to the right of where the count would be sitting. He seated me, and then he departed.

Alone again? Totally alone? Why had Max left the dining-room door open? Carelessness? Or was he giving me an opportunity to escape?

Of course I realized, all too well, that he assumed I would not be such a fool, with so many of *them* wandering around the house!

My body shuddered as a strange shivering raced through me. When I was a child, my mother had always said she would get the shivers when she felt someone was watching her. I could sense another presence in the room, hanging over me, haunting the silence. I was not alone! I gazed nervously around the room; searching for—I do not know exactly *what* I was searching for, but I knew that if I managed to find it, I would probably not wish to meet it in a dark alley.

My search ended when my gaze fell upon two tiny red lights in the far corner. I trembled. Just as I suspected, I was being observed. Despite Teresa's warning not to, I lifted the veil off my face and raised my chin. If it was a show they wanted, then I would give them one. Who did they think they were, anyway, spying on me?

"I see you, you know," I spoke up, mockingly. "Why don't you just come out and face me like a man, or a woman, whatever you are? I won't hurt you. I won't even *bite* you." I paused to allow time for the meaning of my words to sink into the mind of the lurking creature. "I do find it rather difficult talking to a ... a ... *rodent*." I emphasized the word *rodent*. I was aware of enough of the folklore that linked vampires to the bat world; I was aware of the curse; I was aware of what was most likely in that corner! And had I not already encountered a bat when I had attempted my first flight?

Silence continued to hang heavily in the room. Suddenly, without warning, the thing flew at me, heading straight for my face. I ducked as quickly as my condition would allow me. I sensed the presence of something formidable behind me. I steeled my nerves. I pushed my chair back from the table, stood up, and then turned to face my assailant. Shock catapulted through me!

There stood a man whose resemblance to the count was flawless. I had no doubt that he was the father of Count Basarab Musat. This was the same man who had written the diary and divulged so much of himself and the plight of the family—Count Atilla Musat himself!

There was a sardonic curl to his lips as he studied me. His eyes were so piercing—like his son's. Finally he spoke, and his voice was as smooth as the soft silk dress that hugged my skin.

"So, you are the one my son has chosen to bear him a son." He extended his hand. "Please allow me to introduce myself. I am Count Atilla Musat, grandfather to this child you bear."

He took hold of my hand and raised it to his lips. I could feel his breath close to my skin. I shuddered from the coolness of the kiss. What was he up to, lingering as he was over my trembling fingers? I stiffened at his slow savouring of my flesh.

"Do not be alarmed, my dear. I wish nothing more than to kiss your hand," he remarked; it was as though he had sensed my discomfort.

I blushed a deep rose colour. The baby kicked, jolting me back to reality. I withdrew my hand from the count's, laid it upon my abdomen, and tried to calm my restless infant.

The count smiled as his eyes followed the movement of my hand. "The child is anxious to meet his grandfather," he laughed.

"Ah, Father, here you are!" Count Basarab Musat entered the dining room. Close on his heels were two other distinguished-looking gentlemen. They reminded me of someone, but I could not put my finger on who that was. They, too, had piercing eyes, but not quite as piercing as the count's or his father's.

"Good evening, Son. I am afraid you have caught me sampling the delights ahead of time. I was just introducing myself to your *little bird*, although I would venture to say that she has the heart of an eagle, not a sparrow! She caught me staring at her from the corner and then challenged me to face her like a man!" The count Atilla concluded his dramatization of the recent event with a great burst of laughter.

Count Basarab glanced toward me, a dark scowl crossing his face. His father noticed his displeasure and quickly intervened. "Basarab, do not be angry. I am rather pleased to see that the mother of my grandson has such spunk," Count Atilla dissuaded his son from admonishing my boldness. "She actually reminds me somewhat of your mother, Mara,

before the curse turned her into a walking nightmare," he added. I
detected wistfulness in his words as he spoke his wife's name. "I just
had to see who was behind the veil; forgive me for not waiting for your
unveiling."

The count nodded stiffly. I wondered why his father had said that
he had lifted my veil. Was he protecting me from his son's wrath? Then
I remembered Teresa's warning.

Count Basarab's cousins joined in the laughter with the elder count.
"I see, cousin, that you have chosen a true beauty to bear you a son, one
who can hold a candle even to your Teresa, no? One with hair of fire,
and I assume a spirit of fire, as well? Just who seduced whom, here, my
dear cousin?" The taller of the two cousins laughed mischievously.

He sauntered up to me and took my hand in his. "Allow me to
introduce myself, lovely lady. It appears that cousin Basarab has forgotten
his manners. He has been away from the old country far too long and is
becoming much too Westernized." He paused just long enough to give
me a small bow. "My name is Count Vlad Dracul." He smiled as he
placed a wispy kiss upon my knuckles. "I am named after my father,"
he added. "And this," he said as he dropped my hand, "is my brother,
Count Mihail Dracul."

The name *Dracul* thrust my senses back to the fearful reality of my
situation. The account written by Atilla Musat was coming alive before
me! I wondered how many family members there were! How many
of the originals were left, and how many had been born of a human
female such as me? However, I did have some sense of relief that the
congregation of guests did not include Count Vlad Dracula himself!
His name had not even been on the original guest list, not that I knew
of, anyway. I dreaded that I might have to come face to face with him.
Would that be another surprise I would have to deal with?

The curse had included Count Vlad Dracula, Count Atilla Musat,
and all their descendants. Had I been so foolish as to think, for even
one moment, that Count Atilla's accounts were not factual, or that
the conversations I had had with Count Basarab Musat had just been

idle chatter to pass some time in the evenings? The proof was standing before me—confirmation enough for me that there was no hope my child would grow up "normal."

Mihail inched forward upon his introduction, and the hand-kissing ceremony was repeated. His smile appeared to glow with warmth, but under my present circumstances, it was not a warmth I could trust, let alone welcome.

"I assume my cousin has not been too harsh with you," he stated. "Back home, Basarab did have quite a reputation, and appetite, when it came to the ladies. A number of young girls felt he was a bit—how shall I say it to one in such a delicate condition? Rough—that is the word I search for. Yes, quite *rough* was the general consensus around the villages when the people spoke of our Basarab. Not that his behaviour ever prevented any of those silly maidens from throwing themselves at his feet, though, the little tramps that most of them were." I took note of the sarcasm in his statement. Mihail smiled teasingly at me. I noticed his teeth. The warmth that I thought might have been there a few seconds earlier had disappeared very quickly into the coldness of his sculpted features. I also still felt the sting from the harsh innuendoes in his words. There would be no ally in the likes of him!

They all laughed, enjoying the levity. I considered their insinuations insolent! I tried to remain composed; I flashed Count Basarab an enchanting smile. I wondered if his cousins and father knew just how gentle *my* count, their leader, could be. Maybe they all were gentle when it suited their purposes.

More shadows entered the room. Count Basarab strolled over to greet a stately looking woman who had paused at the door and was surveying the scene in the dining room. She looked like a typical five-foot-two-inch grandmother, with soft grey curls surrounding a rosy face, but her face was void of the age lines that normal humans develop with the years. The contrast was startling, as was she, in an uncharacteristic sort of way.

"Ah, my dear Aunt Emelia, lovely as ever, I see," the flattering words rolled naturally off the count's tongue. "Your beauty, as always, eludes the years."

I wondered how true his final statement was to his aunt, and also, just how many years her beauty had eluded.

"Oh, Basarab darling, you have not cast aside your golden tongue. Enough of me, though; introduce me to this lovely young lady who has been given the honour to bear your son," Emelia demanded as she walked over to me.

Honour to bear his son! Is that what everyone here considered my condition, or should I say my *plight*, to be? They thought it an honour? Even though I felt love for the child growing inside of me, the circumstance I was confronted with was more like a curse—especially now that I had been told my usefulness would end once the child was weaned!

Emelia gathered me into her arms and planted a kiss on each of my cheeks. She laid her hands on my stomach and paused a moment. I noticed a shadow of concern flit across her face. She gazed up at me, closely scrutinizing my face. Once again, I felt that ghostly shiver race through me. She was just behaving as a typical elderly aunt or grandmother would when meeting a pregnant niece or granddaughter— at least that is what I tried to tell myself. Unfortunately, my nagging inner voice suggested she was anything but typical!

Without further word to me, Emelia turned and whispered something to the gentleman who had entered the room with her. He nodded his head and left, but not before I had caught sight of his worried expression.

Emelia returned her attention to me. "Come, my dear; allow me to introduce you to my husband, Count Vacaresti Musat." Emelia took me by the hand and pulled me over to the gentleman who was still standing by the doorway.

He was an elegant man, at first glance. I detected a slight resemblance to Atilla and Basarab, but there was also something quite different about him. Count Vacaresti had a hawkish look to him. He was not what I would have considered handsome, but there was still something about him that I felt could fatally attract the female gender. His nose was sharply hewn, dominating his other facial features. His jaw was square. His cheeks and forehead jutted out, surrounding the caverns where his eyes were. And there I saw the attraction—like the Count Basarab's—it was his eyes. They were intense and coal-black, with flecks of red. He bowed eloquently over my proffered hand.

"Charmed, my dear," he murmured as he dropped my fingers without planting the ceremonial kiss to my knuckles. I breathed a sigh of relief; yet, at the same time, I felt offended by the omission.

Count Basarab interrupted, "Everyone, please come and sit. Max will be serving our meal momentarily."

Teresa arrived just as the count finished his invitation. I had been wondering when she would make her grand entrance, but of course, I had been the one who had delayed her with my incessant questions. The count strolled over to Teresa and took her by the arm.

"Ah, at last, my darling Teresa. Lovely, lovely indeed. No words can adequately describe your beauty, nor could any other woman's torch outshine yours. Come, my dearest, sit here at the end of the table, so that I, your husband, may gaze upon your perfection throughout the meal." The count motioned to the chair at the opposite end of the table from where he would be sitting. He threw me a mocking look, a *know-your-place* look. My blood boiled angrily, but his words gouged deeply into my heart.

Teresa was more beautiful than I could have imagined. Her hair shone like polished ebony. Her cheeks were the colour of crimson-red roses on a dewy morning, and her eyes sparkled like cultured black diamonds in the noontime sun. Her figure-hugging black velvet gown accentuated every curve of her perfect body. Exquisite and stunning were the best words I could think of to describe Teresa, and despite the many complimentary comments I had received, I felt insignificant in the shadow of her splendour.

"Thank you, my dearest Basarab," Teresa smiled sweetly. As she sauntered to her chair, she stopped at each of the male guests and planted a kiss on each cheek, acting the grand hostess—smiling, flirting—for she was their leader's wife. Her posture informed that she knew that, and it was obvious to me that they did, as well, by the way they welcomed her. When she came to Emelia, Teresa embraced her with an enormous hug and a dramatic, "Oh, my darling aunt, it has been much too long since I have held you in my arms."

Emelia returned the affection. "Yes, but such a joyous occasion it is that has reunited us! And, if I might add, dear Teresa, you are as lovely as the last time I saw you!"

"As are you, my dearest aunt, as are you!" Teresa's laugh tingled through the room. The count pulled her chair out for her and then leaned over and kissed her on the cheek before taking his place at the other end of the table.

The fact that my presence in the room had not been acknowledged by the count's wife seemed to have been totally missed by everyone there. Or was it? Most likely I was the only one who was upset with the obvious exclusion! I was just a woman who had been chosen by their king to bear him a child. That is where my usefulness started and ended. He would have his heir, and I would have …?

Teresa sat at the table like a royal queen, her head held high. Finally she allowed her gaze to turn upon me. Her eyes spoke volumes! Everything I had allowed myself to dream about the count, and about my future here in his house, dissipated. I truly was no more than what Max and Teresa kept telling me I was—a vessel to carry the child. *I* meant nothing to the Count Basarab Musat—nothing at all!

The gentleman to whom Emelia had whispered, and who had left the room, returned. By process of elimination, I presumed he was the doctor, Count Balenti Danesti. He set a drink by my plate. "I believe you will need this tonight," he stated, not offering any further information.

"What is it?" I asked.

"Emelia tells me the baby will enter our world tonight. This drink will be of a comfort to you in your hours of suffering. It is quite similar in taste to the nourishment Max has been serving you during the past months."

I trembled. *Tonight?* It was too soon! The baby was not due for two weeks. My time had run out. If I were going to escape from here now, I would have to wait until after the baby was born, and then I would have to decide whether I could escape with the child or whether I would have to leave it behind. That decision I would need to settle later.

I glanced at the count. He was laughing and talking to his father in a strange language. My heart stirred with love, my mind with contempt. I could not believe, or understand, my foolishness. How could I possibly love such a man? How had I aspired to compete with the likes of Teresa? I thought to myself as I glimpsed her. Teresa must have noticed my discomfort, for she flashed me a malicious smile.

Then again, I do have a powerful weapon, I reasoned within myself. *I am the mother of his child! Not she! He turned to me for conversations of wit. What if I were to become one of them? Oh God—forgive me for even thinking such a thing!* I sighed and began to sip my drink.

I had to keep a clear head. I had to escape, preferably with my child. No nights of lust were worth the eternal damnation that would inevitably follow if I were to join the ranks of those in this room! I had thought I loved him and that maybe he loved me. But, in reality, it had been nothing more than lust, and a game—for both of us! And he, not I, was the obvious victor!

Chapter 18

The Birth

I gaze into his eyes, searching for love
Realizing now, he is not my loving dove.
Do I truly love him, would that be a sin?
Is this my victory, or Teresa's win?
She is his wife; I know they are wed—
Is it really love? The twosome are undead.

Despite the turmoil of my thoughts, the atmosphere was happy and relaxed during the meal. Everyone, except for me, was in a boisterous mood, but I hid my true emotions the best I could. I had finished my drink and was beginning to feel quite squeamish. The baby, I had noticed, had been extremely quiet all day, with the exception of the movement when the guests were arriving and the small amount of turmoil when I had met Count Atilla.

"Aaaaah!" The scream startled me as much as it did the others around the table. I could not help the outburst—pain had exploded across my back!

The count jumped from his chair and raced to my side. He looked over to Emelia. "Is it time?"

"Yes, Basarab, it is time. Balenti and I will prepare the room." Emelia turned to Teresa. "Teresa, could you please walk Virginia up and down the hallway? We will call you when we have everything prepared for the ceremony." Emelia clapped her hands with the glee of a small child. "This is so exciting! I am glad we arrived when we did, or we would have missed the entire birth. Who knows what might have happened if we had not been present to perform the birthing properly!"

Emelia reached over and hugged me as any normal sweet, old aunt would do. "Be patient my dear; it won't be long now, and you will be in the best of hands." With those words, she ushered the doctor out of the room.

Another sharp pain assaulted my lower back. Teresa walked over to me and took hold of my arm. "Breathe, Virginia, breathe through it." I wondered how many other women she had walked in hallways, perhaps thinking that she would never be the one who was walked.

It seemed like forever that I paced up and down the hallway, with Teresa close at my side, supporting me as each contraction battered my body. The pain just would not stop; in fact, it increased its tempo to an almost intolerable rhythm. I was so tired. I wanted to sit down, but Teresa kept forcing me to walk. Had she no consideration at all for how exhausted I was? A woman in labour was usually allowed the dignity of a bed to bear her pain and rest her weary body in between the contractions.

The count appeared in the hallway. "Everything is prepared now. Teresa, if you please, I will have a moment alone with Virginia. Tell the others we will be there shortly," he ordered. Teresa nodded her head curtly and walked away. She knew that even if she were not pleased, it would be of no consequence.

Count Basarab Musat turned his attention to me. "So, finally it is time for the hatching, eh, my little bird? Tonight, you will present me with a son!" He gathered me into his arms. I softened against his body. *Little Bird*, ever since my first attempted escape, had become his nickname for me. "I have waited a long time for this event," he sighed.

"Count?" I ventured into the conversation. "What if we have a daughter?"

He scowled. "You do not carry a girl child, Virginia; please be assured of that!"

Another sharp pain charged through my body. I staggered. He caught me and then drew me even closer into his arms. Was that the beat of his heart that I felt on mine? For a few short seconds we seemed as one. The pain of the contractions ceased momentarily, so I raised my lips to him: "Please, Basarab, may I call you that?"

"Yes—for tonight."

"Please, kiss me before we go in there, before I present you with *our son*." I emphasized *our son*.

Basarab leaned down, and his cool breath whispered close to my waiting lips. Oh God, how good he tasted, I thought as our lips sealed in passion. Despite my present condition, I felt the fire racing up and down my body as we kissed. It had been so long, and I had missed him so. Damn him! Damn me! But he was already damned, and I was not sure yet exactly where I stood. On the threshold of damnation—or of salvation?

The count swept me up into his arms and carried me down the hallway and into the room where everyone else was gathered, waiting. I leaned my head upon his shoulder, breathed in his manliness, and basked in my tiny moment of victory. All I could think of, at that instant, was that the Count Basarab Musat must surely love me, and once I gave him the son he so badly wanted, I would be his queen! Teresa would be diminished to nothing more than a servant girl. I smiled inwardly at the very notion of victory over Teresa. And I wondered why the count seemed unable to display his tender side to those who were in this room.

Was it a game the count played with Teresa and Max? Perhaps it was them he was toying with, fooling *them* into a sense of security. I would love to see their faces when he declared me, the mother of his child, as his new queen! However, there was still the other nagging thought, in the realm of reality, telling me that such wishful thinking was mine alone.

They were all standing around a table, with fixed smiles upon their lips. To me they looked like a lingering congregation of vultures anticipating the death of a victim, so they might fill their growling bellies. A bright red cloth was draped over the table. Candles flickered everywhere, creating an eerie impression. The countess Emelia began chanting in a strange language. It was an ominous sound, yet I felt strangely soothed by the hypnotic intonation. Basarab laid me gently on the table.

"It won't be long now, my little bird," he whispered into my ear, lingering over me for a moment longer than necessary—at least, I thought so. "Be patient; be strong!" With those final words of comfort, he took his place with the others.

The group joined hands and formed a circle around me. I could not understand why they all had to be there: cousins, uncles, aunts, *Teresa*. Were not the doctor and the count enough? They were the only ones *I* would have need of in the next few hours. I especially did not want *her* near me! I tried desperately to cast a contemptuous look at Teresa. No one seemed to notice; they were all in a trance-like state.

The soft lull of Emelia's voice was joined, one at a time, by the others in the group. Soon the chanting inundated the room with a droning that actually began to irritate me. The doctor busied himself at the end of the table. He seemed to be preparing instruments, because I could detect the faint sound of clinking metal.

Another pain shattered my body; it was so intense I could not help but scream again. My body writhed in anguish. I reached out for someone to hold my hand, but no one seemed to care. The chanting continued. I dug my fingers into the sides of the table with the hope that by giving something else pain I would be able to relieve my own.

I never dreamed that the day I would give birth to my first child would be such a lonely one. A few of my friends from Toronto had children, and I had listened to their stories, all different, but all with one common thread—their husbands or partners had been there for them, holding their hands, coaching them through the breathing process, soothing their tortured nerves, whispering endearments into their ears. I had no husband—only *him*, who was but a figment of a love that would never truly be mine. Did I have hope? Only moments. Was the child my only chance for survival?

"It won't be long now," I heard the doctor's voice through my fog of pain. "Draw up your legs, my dear."

I felt a gentle pressure on my legs as they were pushed into a bent position. My gown fell up to my hips. I wanted to cover my nakedness, but another pain rent my body. I screamed again and again and again. I felt a warm gush of liquid expel from my body, and I knew that my water had broken.

"Easy now, Virginia." The doctor laid his hand on my heaving stomach. "I want you to listen to me. Breathe with the pain, my dear, and when I tell you to, push with all your strength. I can see the child's head; he is ready to be born."

Why were they all staring? Another pain. I screamed. I panted. Why did they not just all go away and leave me alone with my count? Another pain. I screamed. I panted. I pushed. *Where are you, my love? I cannot see you!* Another pain. I screamed.

"Again, Virginia. One more push. Now, girl! Push!" The doctor was shouting at me. The horrid chanting would not stop!

I gulped in another deep breath. Again the pain, like a scalpel, tore through my body. I yelled and then pushed with everything I could muster. The assault on my body forced me to rise up onto my elbows. I felt as though I were being ripped open. I heard the crash of thunder from somewhere beyond the walls. Lightning flashed across the curtainless windows. Pellets of rain drove hard on the glass panes. I broke into a cold sweat and dropped back onto the table.

"Easy now, Virginia," the doctor was speaking again. His hands were busy with something—the baby, I presumed. "Breathe again, my dear, breath ... okay now, there are just the shoulders to come out, and then the worst is over. Give me another big push," he ordered.

I obeyed. I felt a warm gush, and then an ambience of relief enveloped me. The chanting ceased. The room was filled with out-of-control shadows, dancing with the candles.

Then I heard the cry. At first small and plaintive, it grew stronger until it filled the room with the glorious sound of a new life. I began to cry—from relief, from fear, from pain—from whatever. I wanted to pray, to thank God, but I was not sure where God was at the moment. My arms reached out for the count … he was there, close, embracing me … covering my face with warm affection. But it was only a hallucination, for there he really stood, off to the side. He was cradling my baby in his arms. There was a content smile upon his face. Teresa stood by his side, sharing with him, and with my child, the moment that should have been mine!

The Count Basarab turned to me. "You see, my dear little bird, you have given me a son, just as I foretold you would." He was smiling at me. My heart rejoiced. I had won! Even if she was the one standing beside him at the moment, I had won! It was a son! And *he* was smiling upon *me*!

I returned his smile through my tears. Inside, I rejoiced. I reached out my arms for the baby. "Please, allow me to hold him," I begged. Someone, I did not notice who, lifted my shoulders and propped some pillows under me. The count placed our son in my arms.

His hand slipped my dress off my right shoulder, and the material fell away, revealing a firm breast waiting to be suckled. At that point, I was beyond worrying who might be staring at my partial nakedness. I raised my infant son to the breast and guided his tiny lips to the nipple. He searched frantically, finally grasped hold of it, and began to suck greedily. My body relaxed as I smiled down at the bunting head of my newborn son.

His head was crowned with a thick mass of black hair. He was beautiful. I ran a finger, gently, down his cheek. He looked like his father. I smiled contentedly, forgetting everything around me as I basked in the warmth of this new life that had just come from my body. I became oblivious to everyone in the room.

The baby cries as he suckles at my breast,
I am a loving mother; have I passed the test?
He catches on greedily, pulls with delight,
But my eyes are aghast at the horrid sight!

The smile froze on my lips when I noticed what was oozing from my breast. All around my son's mouth was a reddish-coloured liquid. I began shaking. I looked up at the count. He smiled at me.

"What is this?" I asked, taking my finger and wiping a drip of the red liquid from my son's chin. It felt sticky and warm.

"It is what you have already guessed it to be, Virginia; it is blood," the Count Basarab answered.

My ever-present flock of butterflies took flight in the pit of my stomach. I wanted to vomit! I was on the verge of hysteria. "But how can this be?" I screamed out.

"The drink Max has been serving you, since the beginning of the pregnancy, has been mixed especially for this purpose. My son must be given a combination of blood and milk in these early weeks in order for him to grow strong and healthy." The count pushed me gently back onto the pillows. "Relax, Virginia. Just relax, and feed our son." He turned to Teresa, who was standing silently at his side. "He is magnificent, is he not, my dearest Teresa?"

Teresa nodded her head. "Yes, my beloved husband, he is. But now, I think we must let Count Balenti and Countess Emelia finish with Virginia and then take her back to her room. Surely she is in need of rest after such an ordeal." Teresa paused. I detected a lack of sympathy for me in her voice. I heard only sarcasm. "And as for us, Basarab darling, we have something to celebrate with your family—*our* family—the birth of *our* son."

Count Basarab Musat threw back his head and roared in laughter. The counts Vlad and Mihail joined in the merriment. Atilla and Vacaresti watched, with smiles on their faces; one was a grandfather, one a great-uncle. I sensed an aura of ungodly omnipotence creep into the room. Even the flames on the candles seemed to freeze on their wicks, as the diabolic laughter filled the room.

The count pulled Teresa to him, and she bent her head back, waiting in anticipation for his lips to join hers. He leaned down and kissed her passionately, right there in front of me. In front of me, in front of his son, he kissed *her*! She cast a look toward me. It was a look that verified the magnitude of the evil within her.

I knew she was fighting for her place with the count. My trump card had been played; she was flushing it away. Even though I was the woman who had presented the Count Basarab Musat with the son he had so desired, Teresa was still his wife, his queen! She was the one in his arms, celebrating the birth of *my* son!

The two of them departed, arm in arm, chuckling with joy. The rest followed, leaving me alone with the doctor, Emelia, and my son. *My* son. *His* son. *Our* son. Surely the count would not forget that it was I who had given him this ultimate gift? Surely not!

I shut my eyes and dozed. Emelia took the baby from my arms. There would be plenty of time to think about things tomorrow, when I was not quite so exhausted. Tomorrow I would fight for what was rightfully mine! Yes, that is what I would do. Tomorrow would be another day, and the sun would surely shine again on me.

I could give more, much more than a son;
He should know; our bodies have been one.
I have tasted his delicacies, basked in his lust,
I have given my all, yet still there is no trust.
And what is to happen to my precious son?
God, forgive me, for I know they have won!

CHAPTER 19

A Woman Scorned

I awoke to the patter of rain on my window. Every muscle in my body ached. I felt sticky all over. My mind was hazy, but as it began to clear, I looked around the room for my baby. My hands caressed my flattened stomach. Yes, I really had given birth last night, and just as the count had foretold, it had been a son!

I eased out of the bed. I was still wearing the white gown I had worn while giving birth. It was damp with blood. Even the blankets on the bed were bloody. I wondered why no one had taken the time to help me clean up properly last night. I wondered where they all were. I wondered where my baby was. I gazed toward the window. Of course—it was daylight; they would all be sleeping.

I walked over to the door. To my surprise, the doorknob turned easily. I gave the door a little push, hoping that this was my opportunity for a sprint to freedom. My spirits fell as I looked down at my clothes. Where I would flee to, covered in blood? However, as the door swung open, my illusion of freedom was quickly shattered by another obstacle. Max was dozing in a chair positioned just outside my room. I took a moment to study him. Had he aged since my arrival? He appeared so tired and drawn. His skin had a grey tinge, and the veins on his skeletal fingers were like thin spiderwebs. He sat slumped in the chair. His breathing was shallow and sporadic. His shoulder bones protruded from his shirt, forming minuscule hills and valleys in the cloth. Even his knees looked as though they were going to poke through the material of his pants.

"What a cruel fate he has been dealt," I mumbled to myself. He was a grandfather now—would he ever be allowed to bounce the child on his knees as most grandfathers would do?

Max must have heard either the shuffle of my feet or my opening of the door, for his eyes fluttered open. "Miss Virginia, how do you feel this morning? May I fetch you something to eat," Max paused a moment and took a good look at me. "Or would you prefer to freshen up first? You fell asleep last night before we had time to clean you up, and the doctor refused to allow you to be awakened," Max informed me.

My stomach growled, notifying me of its preference. However, I knew I would not be able to eat a thing until I got freshened up. "Yes, I believe I would prefer to bathe first," I finally answered. Then, as an afterthought: "Max, where is my son?"

"Sleeping." He paused. "The count asked me to inform you that you will have to begin switching your personal schedule. Your days will become your nights, and vice versa. The baby's eyes will be sensitive to light." Max cleared his throat. "He will do most of his sleeping during daylight hours, as does his father." Max turned and headed toward the bathing room.

"I shall prepare some water for you, Miss Virginia, and while you clean up, I will change the bedding and lay out some clean clothing for you. I have ordered some new apparel for you, clothing that will make it convenient for you to feed the child. Times have changed since I was a lad. How they have changed—newfangled clothing that conceals the beauty of a babe openly suckling upon its mother's breast."

Max disappeared into the bathroom, still mumbling away to himself about the changing times. I wondered if he were dreaming of his Lilly, who had suckled his child many years ago. I wondered if he had visions of her firm breasts giving nourishment to Teresa, and if he ever thought long and hard about how the count had stolen away, and then destroyed, that beauty. I tried to imagine how Max had looked back then. He and Lilly must have been quite a dashing couple to have produced the likes of Teresa.

I gazed around the empty hallway. All I had to do to flee this place was turn in the opposite direction, away from the bathing room. Why should I care about the state of my clothing? I would manage somehow to procure a proper covering. I could hear the water running. Max would not realize I was gone until it was too late. Then again, there was my child to consider. Who would feed my son? Feed my son! Oh God! The scene from the previous night flashed before my eyes, striking me with the force of a harsh gale.

I reached my hands to my breasts. They ached from the fullness of milk. My mind tried desperately to obliterate the other ingredient, an unnatural ingredient to flow from the breast of a woman. It was an unnatural ingredient to be consumed by a suckling child. Blood! How was that possible? The count had informed me that the drink had been responsible for this transformation. He had also disclosed that the drink was an ancient formula created especially for the purpose of nursing a child such as would be conceived by him. It was the drink spoken of in the journal, only the journal had not allowed me any detailed knowledge on how the drink would actually transform the natural production of a mother's milk.

So this was the way it was. The reality of these events finally penetrated my crusty shell, forcing me to accept that there was no possible way to save my son. The count was not only his father, he had also made sure, without me even knowing what was happening, that the child would never be an ordinary human being!

"Oh, God, help me," I cried under my breath. "God help my son! If there is a way out of this mess, please reveal it to me. Help us to escape the path that fate has ushered us on!" I turned to follow Max. As I entered the room, he was just turning off the taps. A couple of towels and a facecloth had been set out on a chair beside the large sink.

"There you go, Miss Virginia. This will have to do until you are able to bathe." He smiled. "If you need any assistance, just call. I shall be waiting outside the doorway as soon as I have set out your clothing," Max informed me before he left the room.

How foolish of me to hope I would be left alone for too long. I was sure that the linens and the clothing were very close at hand. I slipped out of the soiled white gown, letting it drop to the floor. I swished the facecloth in the water and then pressed it to my face. It felt so revitalizing. I closed my eyes and allowed myself to dream.

I dreamed of the night—the first night. I dreamed of the passion—Basarab's passion. I dreamed of the other passion—mine. I dreamed of all the times after that night—the times I had hated him, the times I had loved him, the times I had needed him so badly that it hurt! I dreamed of all our debates, of how he always seemed to love talking with me, and of how I thought I could see a look of melancholy in his eyes each time he had to leave me and return to *her*. I dreamed of the night in the garden, when he had been so kind and tender, and he had shared so much with me—more personal things. I dreamed of our lovemaking in the bathtub that now sat empty behind me. I dreamed of his tender words and of his strong arms as he had carried me to the table where I had given birth to our son. I dreamed of the smile on his face as he had cradled our son in his arms. I dreamed of the love in his eyes as he had gazed upon me ...

Then I dreamed of her—of Teresa! I saw Basarab kissing her passionately, right in front of me, both of them appearing to taunt me. I heard their evil laughter. I dreamed of the blood pouring from my breast into my baby's mouth.

Disheartening nightmares had invaded my beautiful dreams. I came out of my stupor with tears raining from my heart and seeping from my eyes. The bubbles in the sink dissipated as the salty tears touched them. I rinsed the facecloth in the sink; the water turned pink. I wretched what meagre contents were in my stomach into the nearby wastebasket.

The days passed slowly for me. I slept. I paced. I slept again. Waiting. Waiting for the night to come. Waiting to hold my son in my arms. Waiting to see Basarab. Waiting for Basarab to come and sweep me into his arms and consume me as I knew only he could.

Then the night would arrive, and Max would bring my son to me for feedings, and then he would take him away again. I was not allowed to hold my son any longer than it took to nurse him. I was not allowed to talk to him or to play with him. Max would hover over me to make sure I did not step over the line that appeared to have been drawn for me. I realized that I was not going to be allowed to get close to my son's heart. I began to wonder if my child would even be allowed to have a heart!

I could hear the laughter and festivities from rooms beyond my door, but I was never allowed to join in. Teresa stayed away. Everyone, except Max, stayed away. Count Balenti Danesti had checked in on me during the first few days, but when he felt assured that I was recovering nicely, he ceased coming. I was totally alone, more than ever before. I had to break out of this prison they had me in—either to flee or to make an attempt to win the count over to my side. I needed to find the opportunity to claim the Count Basarab Musat for myself so that I could save my life and be with my son. In order to do that, I had to be able to confront him.

An opportunity arose about six days after the birth. Max forgot to lock the door one night after bringing the baby to me for his feeding, and unlike the other times, he had also left my son with me. I had been about to call out to him but had quickly shut my mouth. I wanted to bask in the extra unsupervised moments I had with my child. For some reason, Max did not return to fetch the child or to lock the door. Chance had finally smiled upon me.

I gathered my son in my arms, slipped out of the room, and followed the sound of the voices coming from the dining room. I marched in, clutching the baby to my chest. I could feel his heartbeat strong against my own. I became aware of footsteps behind me, hurried steps, and I detected Max's heavy breathing. He burst through the doorway and was reaching to pull me away, just as everyone in the room turned and noticed me standing there. Fleetingly, I feared for him, but at that moment, I had other more important matters to attend to.

I held my stance. I wanted to present a picture they would never forget. I raised my head and stared straight into their eyes. I am sure it was an epic shot of defiance and victory! I wished someone had been there with a camera to catch the moment. However, it would be a fair guess that none of the others would have shown up in the picture, with the possible exception of Max. I wondered if my child would even show up—probably not. Technically, it would most likely be nothing more than a shot of a foolish woman staring at nothing and looking totally ridiculous!

"Count," Max stammered. "I am sorry. I never thought she would try to leave the room with the child. I thought I heard someone calling me. In my haste, I not only left the child alone with her, I also failed to lock the door. I was running late to serve your meals, and I thought one of the guests might be anxious to sup … but I …" Max stammered over his words. He seemed to have lost track of what he was saying; he looked scared stiff as he stood before the count. His face had turned a pasty white; the blue veins that ribboned through his skin took on a pinkish tone.

The Count Basarab Musat strode toward us, toward the frightened Max and toward me. I glanced at Max from the corner of my eye. Every inch of his body was trembling. I directed my attention to the fast-approaching count and dared to step between him and Max. My moment had arrived—I needed to make the best of it!

"Good evening, Count. I thought I would join you tonight … with our son. I have been bored, and I am in need of adult conversation." I paused and gazed into his eyes. I parted my lips slightly and moistened them with my tongue. "You don't mind, do you?" I whispered huskily. "I am glad Max was careless, but you must forgive him, my dear Count.

He actually did us, I mean me, a favour by allowing me to come here tonight."

Count Basarab examined me with a penetrating gaze. He was most likely trying to read my mind. I, in return, was trying desperately to read his. His face was dark; I was not sure whether it was from the lack of light in the room or from anger. I held my ground, trying hard not to cower.

The baby whimpered and began to bunt for a breast. I cuddled him closer. He quieted. The silence was deafening. Suddenly, the count threw back his head and howled in laughter. "I see our little bird is ready to fly again! Come, my dear Virginia; by all means, join us," he said as he put his arm around my shoulders and led me to the centre of the room. "I trust you are feeling better. Max informed us you were still exhausted from the birthing, so I gave orders that no one was to disturb you until you were fully recovered."

The count's last statement sent a shock wave of anger through me. "Max told you that?" My voice rose in resentment. "I have no idea why he would say such a thing. I never once indicated to him that I was ill. In fact, I have felt quite fine since the birth of our son, my dear Count. The only things missing from my life have been permission to entirely care for our son and to be able to mingle with our guests here ..." I glanced around the room and then returned my attention to the count: "And most of all, I have missed your company, my *beloved* Count," I crooned.

The count looked questioningly toward Max. Teresa moved away from the group to stand beside her father. "You must not be harsh with Max, my dear Count. He was only doing what he thought was best for Virginia. After all, childbirth is not easy, so I am told. Max felt she needed her rest."

So that was it, I thought to myself. It had not been Max's idea; it had been hers! I was furious! For the second time that evening opportunity opened its door to me. "Max felt I needed rest, Teresa?" I turned and faced the woman who had become my greatest adversary. "Or was this just a little ploy on your part to keep me away from the count, the father of *my* son?" Months of anger and resentment rang through my words.

"Oh my, oh my," Aunt Emelia's voice was quivering. She seemed confused. "Gracious me! This is so shocking. This should not be happening."

"What are trying to imply, Virginia?" The nervous tension in Teresa's voice was rather noticeable.

"You know exactly what I mean, Teresa. I have been as well as you are right now. Having a child is not a disease. Women do it every day. One does not have to rest for ..." I paused long enough to allow the next statement to drive home hard: "What length of time was I to be ill for, Teresa?" I inquired sarcastically.

Teresa appeared anxious. "I have no idea what you are babbling about, Virginia. My dear Count, are you just going to stand there and allow her to make such accusations against me, your wife?" Teresa grasped the count's arm. I watched her squirm. What a sweet moment for me!

"Ah, Teresa, I feel you have some explaining to do here. I only gave the order that Virginia not be disturbed because Max informed me she was in need of rest. Obviously, Max was under *your* direct orders in this matter. Therefore, under these circumstances, I believe you do owe Virginia an explanation, as well as an apology for your needless interference!" The count turned to me and smiled most charmingly. Another sweet moment for me!

"I owe her nothing! Nothing, you hear! I owe her nothing!" Teresa snarled. "I will be taking my leave now." She glared at me. "I have had quite enough of this company for one night! Your day will come, Virginia darling—you can bet on that!" Teresa's voice reached a high pitch as she swept furiously from the room before anyone was able to stop her. At the door she turned momentarily and threw me a look of pure hatred!

I ignored her threat and her look. I gloated inwardly, for I knew an open show of mirth would gain me nothing. What a victory! Teresa had lost her nerve and had managed to make a total fool of herself before the entire family. I was back in the game, and I felt I had just won—this round, at least. I turned my attention to the count. He was all mine—for now. Teresa might have manipulated things in order to keep me in my room for a week and a half, but I had managed to beat her at her own game. Plus, I carried the trump card in my arms. I held out the child to his father.

"Would you like to hold *our* son, Basarab?" The words were spoken as smoothly as melting butter on a piping hot pancake. I felt no fear, at the moment. My adrenaline was running high after my recent taste of victory over Teresa. It ran so high, in fact, that I had dared to call the count by his first name. Either no one had taken notice of that or maybe it was just that no one really cared.

Count Basarab took our son from my arms and held him up for all the guests to see. He smiled at me. There was nothing sinister in his smile. It appeared to be full of passionate affection—a girl can dream, can she not?

~

The Count Basarab Musat walked with me to my room that night. Once inside, he shut the door. I felt his eyes studying my every move as I laid our son upon the bed. I turned and faced him. I had won one great victory tonight; I was willing to aim for another.

"Basarab?" I began, slowly. "I would like to ask you something important, something extremely important to me, and for our son." I had made the habit when speaking of the baby to always stress the words *our son*.

The count gathered me into his arms. He seemed more relaxed than I had seen him for awhile. He gave me a look much the same as the one he had given me that night in the garden. It was as though he were always trying to put on a pretext of superiority for everyone around him, but here, with me, he was able to lower his guard and be the man he truly was, or maybe the one he desired to be.

"What is it that is so important to you and our son?" he questioned gently. My stomach fluttered as the words, *our son*, passed through his lips.

"I feel the baby would be better off if he were here with me. I would like his things moved into my room, so that I may tend to his needs all the time. I am his true mother, and it is of the utmost importance for his security and happiness that we be together more, especially for his current emotional stability."

I paused a moment. I was clutching at straws, hoping that I would be able to explain that last statement of "fact" to the count with sufficient proof to satisfy his curiosity so that he would grant my request.

"What do you mean by emotional stability?" The count looked puzzled.

"Well, I do not know how it is with *your* people, but in our society, the mother tries to spend as much time as possible with her infant. This builds a strong bond, plus it gives the child a sense of security. It is not wise for a child to be separated from the birth mother, especially one like me."

I felt that if I convinced the count I was the only one who could really provide for the child's well-being, I might be able to gain extra advantage over what I had already obtained this evening. I continued my line of reasoning.

"Not only am I able to bestow on him life's nectar from my body, I am also able to nourish his mind with a love that no other could ever give—the love of his true mother, the woman who carried him inside her womb for nine months. It will be like the love your mother, Mara, bore for you. My love will give him strength, because he will be secure in my tender and compassionate care. He will have no worries; he will think only of pleasant things.

"I am asking you, my dearest Basarab, love of my heart: For the sake of our son's future, do not separate us. Let me have him here with me before it is too late to change the pattern that may have already begun. I will be the one to hold him close when he hurts. I will be the one to whisper reassurances to him. I will suckle him, love him, and build in him a character that could only be likened to that of his father.

"I will teach him the *human* side of his existence, for he will need that before you send him out to meet this world. There are things I can instruct him on that you cannot." I had thrown my high card on the table. Of course, the fact that the Count Basarab had survived for centuries was of no consequence to me. There was probably nothing I could actually teach my son that his father could not. Even though it appeared that the count had kept himself secluded from the real world over the years, some of our conversations had indicated otherwise. "Our son may want to be part of the action in the real world," I added as an afterthought. "Maybe even take risks that you would be wary of. It would be good to prepare him for such things."

I waited patiently for a sign of approval from the count. Had I been convincing enough for him to fall into my trap and allow the child to remain with me? The count laid his hands on my shoulders and held me at arm's length. He gazed piercingly into my eyes. I knew he was searching for the truth. Would he find it? I prayed not.

Slowly he began to speak: "I do not understand you, Virginia darling. One moment you appear to hate me, yet in the next, I am the love of your heart. Which is it, Little Bird; which is it? Love? Hate? Something in between, maybe?" The count tilted his head to the side.

"What do you think, after all this time, Basarab? Of course I love you, with all my heart. I adore you. I have given you a son. That is the ultimate sacrifice of love a woman can make for the man she loves." I wondered if I sounded convincing enough. I decided to throw another trump on the table. "It is unfortunate for Teresa that she could not bear you a child, and I pity her for not being able to have this same bond with you as I have."

"I know nothing of this kind of love that you describe, Virginia. If I may so boldly remind you of the facts, though, it was *I* who gave *you* the opportunity to bear my son. As for your love for me," he waved his hand lightly in the air, "I wish I could truly consider your declaration of devotion to be an honest one." He paused. "I would like to believe you, yet I am wary of your true intentions. After all, you did try to escape—on more than one occasion, too."

"But not recently—not since I have realized where my heart truly lies—with you," I answered quickly. "And all those times we spent together—not just in lovemaking, but in earnest conversations—did those hours not mean something to you? They did to me. They made me love and respect you even more!" I felt I had nothing to lose by reminding the count of those times.

"That still remains to be proven." The count lingered a moment before continuing on. "It is most unfortunate that my Teresa was not able to give me a child, but I have remedied that for her in the best way I could," he added.

I noticed a faraway look in his eyes. I had dug deeply and touched some distant part of him, of this I felt sure. But the important question was: Had I reached far enough for him to entrust our son to my care?

Why did he have to be such a difficult man to understand? Maybe I should tell him how easy it would have been for me to rid myself of his baby—a fall down a stairway, starving myself . . . I decided against such a revelation. Ending the life of his son would have been the ultimate insult; surely my own life would have followed quickly behind it.

Basarab continued, "As for your request to have the baby here with you, I see no problem with that, for now. If you believe his well-being will be better served and that he will become a stronger man for it, then so be it. But you must remember and fully understand one thing—even though you carried him in your womb, he is *my* son, he is like *me*. He is not your average human. He will never fit into your world. He has my blood running through his veins; therefore he will never truly be yours—*never*! Be assured that there is absolutely nothing you will be able to do about it!" The arrogant Count Basarab had returned.

"And also remember—in the end, it will be me and my kindred who will teach him how to survive in your world. You must keep in mind that this is something we have become quite accomplished at over the centuries."

I was not particularly daunted by the tone of his voice. How quickly he forgot that the child was half mine and that there was a chance he was wrong. Even though I felt I was scoring points in my game with the count, there was always that nagging voice inside me that kept reminding me of what a fool I truly was.

I nodded my head toward the count. "I understand this, and I accept it. I just want to be close to our son. I want to be close to you, as well, and so maybe, when the time is right …" I reached up my hand and straightened the collar on his shirt, "maybe I could give you another son." There—my final bait was laid before him.

I waited for the answer I hoped would come. However, disappointment cut through me, shoving my confidence to the pit of my stomach, as his next words were spoken in the all-too-familiar curt tone. "We will see, my dear Virginia; we will see. For *now*, I see no harm in having the baby's things moved here. Teresa is not going to be pleased; however, after her disgusting exhibition tonight, maybe this will teach her a lesson about meddling in affairs that are not her concern." He paused. "I must inform you, though, that you are still to give Teresa full access to the child, anytime she desires it. Is that clear?"

I nodded, willing to agree to even this in order to have my son with me. My mind also clung to the fact that the count was displeased with Teresa's behaviour—a possible gain for me? I wondered how long the child would be with me. Was it only until Teresa had been brought to heel? Was this man using me and the child as a means to tame his temperamental wife? The count paused at the door and directed his attention to me again.

"I almost forgot to tell you. The baby will be named on the eve of his second week of life. Do you have any ideas for a name?"

"No," I answered. "I have not thought on that subject much, but I will. I had no idea that I would be allowed any input in the naming of my son." Nor did I fool myself that any name I would think up would be considered. I wondered why the count had even bothered to ask me.

"Good. I will see you tomorrow night at supper, then. Max will be here soon with the baby's belongings."

I moved swiftly to the count and threw my arms around his neck in a passionate embrace, before he could take his leave. "Thank you for this kindness you have granted me," I whispered sweetly in his ear.

My lips sought for his and were rewarded in mid-journey. His tongue was like a match as it moved inside my mouth, searching for a place to ignite. And ignite it did, all of me. But physically I was not yet ready for more than this passionate embrace. Being aware of my present condition, I pushed gently against his chest.

"Soon, my love, I will be yours again, body and soul. We can fly together on the wings of a demon fire dragon, as we have many times before."

I slipped from his arms and stepped back into my room. As the door was closing, I caught a brief glimpse of Teresa hovering midway up the stairway. Her face was flushed with rage at the sight she had just witnessed. I wondered how long she had lingered there. I hoped it had been long enough to witness the count's passion toward me, his willingness to greet my fire with his own.

I leaned against the door, breathed deeply, and smiled. I had won more than one victory this night—much more! I whispered a prayer of thanks to the God I thought had forsaken me.

My son whimpered. I walked over to the bed and gathered him into my arms. I hummed a lullaby to him, one I remembered my mother had sung for me when I was a child. He settled.

I smiled. There was hope—on all fronts!

CHAPTER 20

An Unexpected Offer

Where do I run, where can I hide?
For now, my time I must bide.
Where do I turn, whom do I trust
The lady, old man, or the one I lust?
My game increases its tension, its play;
Will I ever again walk in light of day?
Should I heed the warnings freely given?
Is my desire for life too lustfully driven?

The following evening, I heard a light tap on my door. I had just settled down after feeding the baby, and it annoyed me to be disturbed. I was extremely tired. The previous night's events had drained more of my strength than I had realized. To top that off, the baby had been quite restless throughout the day, almost as though he were not sure whether he was to sleep or play; whether to follow in Daddy's footsteps or Mommy's.

"Who is it?" I called out.

"Teresa." There was a pause before she spoke again. "Please, Virginia; I want to apologize for my behaviour toward you last night. May I come in?"

Odd that Teresa should ask—her usual way was a light knock, a turn of the handle, and a grand entrance. I did not trust her after the recent events and knew I would have to be diligent for whatever her next move might be. I would be the biggest fool if I let down my guard for even one second.

"Yes, come in," I finally answered.

I noticed the drawn look about Teresa as she stepped into the room. She turned her face to me, and the candlelight flickered over her. I gasped. Teresa's face was covered with fresh cuts and bruises! Dark circles crowded around her eyes. Her skin was pale beneath the mottling. Her shoulders sagged. She walked slowly, hesitantly. Her usual vibrant beauty was nowhere to be seen. She appeared—old. But she was, wasn't she?

"My God! What has happened to you, Teresa?" Sympathy for her condition prevailed over my common sense.

I slipped out of bed, hurried to her side, and wrapped my arm around her shoulders. I led her to the small table by the window and pushed her gently into one of the chairs. The trauma of seeing such a sight again made me forget, momentarily, what she was. It was as though time had erased my recent memories. We were just two ordinary women, friends who had experienced a terrifying situation together. She was a friend in need; I was the one she had come to for consolation.

"Him!" Teresa finally spit out. "*He* did this to me. Last night, after you accused me of fabricating your illness, he was infuriated. The Count Basarab Musat does not take lightly to being lied to. You, of all people, should remember that fact! You seem to think you have won this little game you are playing. You may believe you have captured his heart, but I warn you now, as I have always tried to do—Basarab has no heart!

"If he ever finds out the truth, or has even the vaguest notion that you are trying to deceive him, he will not hesitate to do this to you as well." Teresa pointed to her face. "Or maybe even something worse," she added shakily. "And I assure you that if he does turn his wrath upon you, your body will not heal as mine does! You will be scarred for the rest of whatever life he might grant you!" I detected the bitterness in her words.

"But I am not deceiving him, Teresa. Why would you even suggest such a thing?" I tried to make my voice sound innocent. I needed to be wary of her possible trickery, especially considering some of the recent events.

Teresa scrutinized me intently. "Well then, as you wish." She shrugged. "But don't say I did not try to warn you. He will discover your game one day; he probably already has. If not, it will only take one little slip on your part, and then—poof! You should realize that he is just using you until your usefulness is over. Have you thought of that, Virginia? I am sure you have; you are a smart woman. I recommend that you constantly be on your guard. I would hate to see such a lovely face as yours scarred beyond recognition. As I said, my scars will disappear—part of what I am. Yours will not, and I assure you, you will *never* be one of us!"

Teresa's lip curled maliciously. She reached her hand up and ran a finger down my cheek. Her nail dug into my flesh, just enough to sting slightly but not enough to draw blood. "And who would look after the child then, should something unfortunate happen to you before he is weaned?"

The pathetic expression that had clouded Teresa's face when she had entered my room had been replaced by a new manifestation. It began to creep slowly into her eyes. It was the same guise that I had observed the night I had given birth to my son. It was a look that reeked with hatred. It was a look that made me glad I had recovered my guard before allowing it to completely fall away. How could I have thought, even for a moment, that we could be just two ordinary women in need of each other's support?

"Nothing bad is going to befall me," I stated, looking Teresa squarely in the eyes. "I am not trying to deceive anyone; therefore, I have nothing to fear, do I? Is there anything else you would like to enlighten me on, Teresa, before you depart?"

Teresa was quick to answer: "Yes. Yes, there is. Actually, the reason I came here tonight was to offer you your freedom; however, it appears to me that you do not desire that anymore."

What was Teresa up to? This was a substantial change of tactic. I was going to have to be extremely careful of what I said next; Teresa could be laying a death trap for me. She would probably like nothing better than to see me as battered as she was at the moment, especially after what she had witnessed at my door last night. It was her turn, I guessed, to deal the hand of cards. It was for me to decide whether or not to pick them up and call her bluff!

"What do you mean, you came here to offer me my freedom? Why would you want to help me—that is, if I were to decide I wanted the help you are offering?"

"You have never made any pretence about wanting to escape from here. I am even aware of your most recent attempt at freedom. I also know how you cajoled Max into silence; you knew he would not breathe a word once he discovered it was I who forgot to lock your door! So I came to you with open arms and an open heart. My only desire was to help you escape from this place before he decides your time is up. Of two facts you can be very sure: one, I will always be his queen; two, your time here will end, despite what the count has done here to me."

She pointed to her wounds, which were already healing. Were the wounds freshly inflicted, just before she came to me? Was it really the count who had struck her, or had she beaten herself in order to gain my sympathy and trust—to play on my emotions? Or was Teresa in collaboration with one of the others, in order to entrap me in her web and expose my true intentions to the count?

"I am his wife. I am his chosen one. I am one with him, for now and eternity. Once the child is weaned, the Count Basarab Musat will have no further use for you. He will gather his son to his bosom, direct him into our fold, and then cast you aside like a piece of garbage. Need I remind you again, *he has no heart*? Surely you realize that fact by now? Also, need I remind you that he is the most powerful of our kind, that he is our leader? He has no time for games and no patience for those who play them—especially at his expense!"

I rose from my chair, wondering just how real this offer of freedom was. After all, she was the same as him, just not as powerful. "Why would you care what happens to me? What is it that you are worried about, Teresa? Is it that you are afraid of me? Afraid of what I might be able to offer the count? *I* could give him more sons. Does he want more than one son, Teresa? Is that what you fear—that eventually he will tire of you and turn to the woman who is able to bear him children?" I paused. "I saw how jealous you used to be when he would spend hours talking to me, leaving you alone in the evenings," I added as another dig at her.

I leaned on the table and studied her face. "Yes! That is it, isn't it? You are afraid of me! It is you Basarab is casting aside! I am not the one who has anything to lose or to fear here—you are! So why should I want to leave? Besides, can you give me one good reason why I should trust you after what transpired last evening?" I threw my ace on the table.

"You are most mistaken in your perception of how things are, Virginia. Your life is in far greater jeopardy than you can imagine. Think hard. Remember that you only bore the child for him. I am the one who sleeps with him in the day, cradled in his arms in the earth of our forefathers. I am the one who sits at his table, as his wife. It matters not that he conversed with you—that was just to pass some idle time away. I am the one who is on his arm when he goes out into society. And I will be the one who will raise his son! You are not one of us, and as I said before, you never will be! Be assured that I shall make sure of that!"

Teresa was putting all of her aces on the table! "Do not be foolish enough to think I have no power to wield within this household! I could, right this moment, *take you*, should it please me to do so. I could make your life, or should I say *death*, into aimless wanderings for eternity. You would never be able to rest. You would never be able to satisfy your lust for nourishment. You would never totally be one of us, though, because

I would never allow you that liberation!" Teresa spewed out at me. "And in the end, should I decide it is time to end your suffering, one of the hunters would track you down and send you to your grave!"

"Just as the Count Basarab Musat did to your mother, Lilly? Is that what you would do to me?" I was hoping to strike a chord of contempt toward the count, the man who had snatched her mother from her at a very young age. However her next statement shattered that hope.

"Even to that extent," she returned, without a trace of emotion. "Therefore, I suggest you do not allow blind stupidity to overpower your common sense! If you think that dangling some semblance of my mother's plight in front of me will soften my position, you are mistaken. She meant nothing to me. The only memories I have of her are what my father tells me.

"There are times when I think he made up most of those nice stories to try to get me to love her as much as he did. Actually, I have nothing but contempt for her. If she had not been so weak, grovelling before the count as she did, then my father would not have had to make the bargain he did. She is responsible for us being damned into this dark world. He is the one who loved her too much, not I!

"As I mentioned earlier, you appear to be an intelligent woman, a fact you have demonstrated on a number of occasions. Don't think for one minute that I was ever far away when my husband spent his time with you. I strongly recommend you take my offer, Virginia. Leave this place while there is still time, while I am still in the generous mood you find me in tonight!" Teresa's voice was rising to a hysterical pitch.

She stood up. Her body was stiff as she marched toward the door. "Think about what I have said. Accept my offer before it is too late. At least you will have your life; this is the gift I offer to you for having given my husband and me a child. If you remain here, there is only one possible outcome for you—death, in one form or another!"

With that final pronouncement Teresa was gone, slamming my door on her departure. The room shook from the vibration. I shook from the impact of her words.

I had little time to gather my thoughts before the baby began fussing. I went to him and peered into the cradle. He was so striking, every feature so perfect. One would never guess that his roots reached deep into a world of darkness. I gathered him into my arms. I wondered: If Teresa cared so much for the child, why she had not even bothered to look at him or ask about him when she was there? Come to think of it, Teresa never really spent much time with the baby.

What was I to do? If I accepted Teresa's offer, I would be leaving a piece of me behind. If I were to stay, I would be taking a chance that Max and Teresa's warnings of my fate would come true. Then again, Teresa could be setting a trap. If that were the case, then all my carefully laid plans would be thwarted by her deceit. The baby nuzzled my breast.

"Yes, yes, little one. You are hungry, I know. Momma will feed you. Your momma will feed you."

I settled myself against the pillows on my bed and put the child to suckle. The flow of blood had ceased to bother me; I had learned to accept it, or maybe it was just that I had learned to ignore the sight of it. He pulled greedily at the nipple, waiting impatiently for his reward to let down. Soon, all I could hear was the sucking sound of a satisfied child. This was the scene that greeted the Count Basarab Musat when he entered my room—the picture of motherhood at its loveliest!

"A charming vision to feast my eyes upon, Virginia," he stated, sitting down on the edge of the bed. His fingers played with the red lace at the bottom of my nightgown. He gazed into my eyes: "When will you be ready for me, my dear Virginia?"

The count's question startled me. I had totally forgotten my parting comments to him the previous night. "What do you mean, Basarab?"

"In the hallway last night, you suggested to me that I would soon be able to delight in the pleasures of your body again. As I understand, from you of course, I have possession of your heart already—correct?" He smiled. I caught a glimpse of the fangs—the constant reminder of evil.

The count wore a white shirt with a wide lace ruffle that fell in tiny waves on each side of the button lines. The buttons had been left undone, allowing a narrow strip of his body, from the neck to the waist, to tantalize my womanly urges. I raised my foot and began to massage his chest with my toes. He gently gathered my foot into his hands, kissing it lightly, following a line from toe tip to the end of my heel, sending shivers racing through my body. The baby at my breast was momentarily forgotten.

"Do you doubt me, my beloved Basarab?" I managed to whisper. "My soul is yours. It was linked to yours the day I discovered our baby grew inside my womb. I love you, and I love the child we conceived together. As for my body, it is yours on the night that we name our son. Come to me then, and I shall be ready to receive you once again! I shall be ready to receive another son of yours into my womb, if that be your desire as well." I smiled at him seductively. I knew that was a bit soon to be intimate after giving birth, but I had to get my cards on the table, before it was too late for me. "By the way, have you thought of a name for our son yet?" I added.

"As a matter of fact, yes. My father has chosen the name. The child will be called Santan Basarab Atilla Musat. Do you approve?" The count set my foot down on the bed.

I wondered if my approval actually mattered. Probably not. Santan. The sound of it was much too satanic for my liking, but I dared not anger the count by saying such a thing. It would be much wiser to agree.

"Santan … Basarab … Atilla … Musat." I allowed the name to roll off my tongue. I shifted the baby to my other breast. He latched on easily and resumed his feeding, making his familiar little grunting sounds. "Hello, little Santan," I cooed at him. I looked up at the count. "Santan—yes, that will be just fine," I managed to smile, even though just saying the name had almost choked me.

"Good, it is settled then. I am so glad you are pleased. My father will also be happy you approve. He has taken quite a liking to you since your first meeting. He has also requested that I make sure you join us for supper tonight. Are you able?"

"Of course," I answered. "I would love to join the family." I stressed the word *family*.

"Excellent." The count raised my free hand to his lips and brushed it with a kiss. "I shall see you at supper, then. Max will see that the child is taken care of during your absence," he mentioned before he departed.

I was alone with the child. His child? My child? Teresa's child? I looked down on the curly black hair of my son; his eyes were closed in peaceful contentment. Not a semblance of evil lined his countenance. Every few seconds he would pacify on the breast, but sleep finally laid its claim on him. I pulled Santan's mouth gently off the nipple and then laid him in his cradle. I crawled back under my covers, stretched out my weariness on the bed, and closed my eyes to rest for a few moments.

I dreamed. Oh, so sweet was the dream. The Count Basarab Musat smiled lovingly at me. His hands caressed me softly, awakening my blood. I arched upward to greet him, opening my body to him, writhing, beckoning for him to enter! However, as usually happened in my dreams, terror tore into my world, shattering the ecstasy. It was no longer his face leaning over me—it was Teresa's. She was chanting: "You should have taken my offer; you should have taken my offer!" over and over again.

CHAPTER 21

The Upset

That evening I prepared myself with meticulous care. Tonight I hoped to look better than ever before. I would make sure Teresa was a mere dying flicker in the brilliance I would cast in the dining room upon my entrance.

I went to the closet, selected a red velvet gown, and slipped it on over my head. I could feel the cool, silky softness of the lining as it slithered over my skin. The neckline plunged in a deep V, exposing my maternal bosom. Below the V, the material gathered in pleats and then fell in ruby ripples to sweep the floor with its hem. The sleeves were crocheted with a fine red silk thread, and intertwining through the patterns were slivers of shimmering silver. They draped freely around my arms, cascading from my shoulders like a swirling skirt.

I brushed my hair till it shone. I noticed how it shimmered against the dress as it flowed through the bristles of my brush, coming softly to its resting place on the red material.

I rubbed my cheeks to attain a rosy colour. Of course, there was no way of seeing how I really looked, since I was without the luxury of a mirror, but a little voice inside of me kept saying, "You are one stunning lady, Miss Virginia, one stunning lady, indeed!"

The baby was sleeping peacefully when I left the room. I knew it would not be long before Max came to check on him. *Eat your heart out, Teresa; I am on my way. Tonight we shall see who the reigning queen is in the house of Count Basarab Musat!*

❧

As I entered the dining room, everyone turned. Surprised gasps began to break the silence that had temporarily held the gathering. I knew my little inner voice had hit the nail squarely on the head. I hesitated in the doorway, a moment longer than necessary, to allow my beauty to have its full impact. I wanted—no, I *needed*—every one of them to admire me, to be obsessed with me. To attain my victory, I had to influence those who seemed to mean so much to the count, especially his father. It was quite obvious to me that the count loved him deeply.

The count's father was first to speak. He walked to me and offered his arm. "Come, my dear; I will seat you. You shall sit here to my son's right and across from me, so that I might gaze upon your beauty. Basarab has told me a great deal about you, but I would like to get to know you better for myself." Count Atilla smiled pleasantly. I took note of the fact that the count had spoken of me to his father. Another win on my side of the table?

I held my head high as the esteemed senior count pulled my chair out for me. My high-school drama teacher would have been proud of me for the natural wit and untiring charm I was displaying as I fought to preserve my life.

I nodded graciously to the count's cousins, to his uncle, and to the doctor. I then turned to the countess Emelia: "Dearest Aunt Emelia ..." I paused. "I may call you aunt, I hope?" I asked in a sugary voice. It was a bold request and a challenge.

Emelia appeared startled, and she hesitated, but only fleetingly. "Yes, dear," she replied. "Go right ahead. Aunt Emelia will be fine."

"Thank you." I breathed a sigh of relief. My stomach felt agitated. I could still hear Teresa's words clearly in my mind: *You are not one of us! You will never be one of us! I shall make sure of that!* I gazed around me and wondered just how genuine the smiles and admiring looks from those at the table were.

"Dear Aunt Emelia," I went on, "I trust you are having a pleasant holiday? I would like to learn more about your homeland, since that is where the forefathers of my son were born. I would love for you to come to my room some evening—at your convenience, of course," I added hastily, "and tell me some stories, maybe even one or two about the count when he was a little boy?" I smiled mischievously.

"After all," I continued, a hint of laughter gurgling in my throat; "sons do often follow in their father's footsteps. I would like to know what I may expect in the future." I spoke as though I would be around forever for my child.

I had often wondered if Count Basarab Musat had ever been a child, in the true sense of the word. The journal had stopped when he was three, but the last entry, that of his farewell to his aunt as they left the cave, had not portrayed the mindset of a typical three-year-old. The details of the rest of his youth were absent. I desired to know more about him. I returned my attention to the present moment.

Emelia threw a questioning look toward Basarab. I wondered if I had stepped over the limit this time, but my fears were cast aside when she looked at me and said, "That would be nice Virginia. I would love to chat with you. But it must be soon; we are departing immediately after the baby's naming ceremony."

"I shall look forward to your enlightenments, dear aunt," I said. "And of course, the sooner the better," I added.

"Look forward to what?" Teresa's voice cut through the tranquil moments I was having with Emelia. Time froze as she stood in the doorway, glaring angrily at me. There was no beauty in her countenance, only a cloak of diabolic ugliness.

I held my head high and stared back at her. "Aunt Emelia was just saying that she would love to come and tell me some family stories," I replied to Teresa's demand. "Maybe I shall hear some of the stories that you have not told and ones that were not recorded in Count Atilla's diaries."

Teresa shrieked, "Aunt Emelia? How could you? How could you divulge any more of our family stories to her? She already knows much more than she should, much more than any other of *her* kind has ever been allowed!" She stepped angrily over to the count's chair and confronted him.

"What games are we playing, my dear Count, my husband? *She*," Teresa continued her assault, "is not of our family—she is not one of *us*! She need know nothing more of our family history. You have divulged things to her that it would be better she did not know—that she has no right to know! I listened many nights, outside the study door, to your conversations. Have you forgotten the dangers that can beset us when her kind is too well-informed? The headhunters become vicious in their desire to eradicate us! Do you so soon forget our torment, our hiding, the scattering of our families?

"Do you forget how difficult it was to get you safely out of the country—how close you came to losing your head? How it was *I* who came to your aid, just as the hunter was ready to sever it? How I sent that man to hell for you? How I pulled the stake from your heart, lay down beside you, and breathed life back into you? Do you forget so soon, husband?"

The room had gone silent again. Everyone was staring at Teresa, including me. What a revelation! I looked at the count. His eyes were blacker than I had ever seen them—was it anger, or distress at having had a vulnerable moment in his life exposed in front of me—a moment that informed me he was not as invincible as he would have had me believe!

Teresa allowed her glance to take in everyone at the table before she continued. "Do you forget so quickly, my dear Basarab, the escape attempts she has already made? She is deceiving you, all of you." Teresa made a sweeping motion with her arm.

"She has you all entranced with her provocative beauty, her unending wit, and last, but certainly not least, the baby. Yes, I know that we have all waited a long time for such an event, the birth of a healthy child to our fold—but I warn you, she is only using your son, Basarab, to try to win a place in our world. This child was meant for my arms, our arms. He is to be nourished in our ways, not hers! Cannot one of you in this room see what she is trying to do?" Tears of torment and frustration streaked down Teresa's cheeks. Her fist smashed down on the dining table, rattling the silverware and crystal with its fury.

The count rose slowly from his chair. He grabbed Teresa's wrist in a firm grip. I noticed the look in his eyes as he contemplated the shrew in front of him. For a brief moment I almost felt pity for her. The moment passed. Even though her face no longer carried the scars and bruises from the beating of the night before, she had become an exact replica of the living dead portrayed on the Hollywood screens. The count's hold on her wrist drained the beauty from her, leaving her flesh a dull, lifeless grey.

"My dear Teresa," he spoke slowly and emphatically. "Must you always cause such scenes as this? You are acting like a jealous vixen, and jealousy is one of the traits you know I cannot, *will not* tolerate, especially in front of my family. You have divulged something here that should not have been spoken of again, and in doing so, you have caused me the pain of remembering that dark moment in my existence. You have also embarrassed me. I will not excuse such demeaning outbursts from my wife again! You were given the honour of being my queen, but I must warn you, my dear Teresa, even though you saved me on that day, you are replaceable if this outrageous resentment persists. It is a show of weakness that is most unbecoming of your position, and I demand you desist from this sort of conduct in the future!"

"Why is it you do not see what she is trying to do, Basarab?" Teresa continued pleading. "She is playing a game with you! Why am I the only one seeing through her?"

"You still wish to play the jealous wife, Teresa? Do you forget that I am no fool, and I am not so easily fooled with one such as her? I will deal with our little bird when the time comes. She should be of no concern to you. She is only the biological mother of the child. You are my wife, and I must repeat, if you wish to remain so, stop this petty display of jealousy at once! You are boring me to no end!"

Teresa raised her head, threw back her shoulders, and wrested her wrist from the count's grip. "I have no desire to dine here tonight. I apologize for my outburst, for embarrassing and upsetting you in front of your family."

She glanced at the guests, and when her eyes met mine, I noted the boiling hatred. "As I have said before, Virginia, your moment will come. Watch closely the shadows. Beware of your moves, because all it will take will be just one tiny slip in your little game. For now, I shall relish the vision of seeing you wandering aimlessly in hell one day!" Teresa warned before she strode angrily from the room.

Despite the fact that Teresa had been disgraced in front of the entire family, I was smart enough to realize she had actually won this round. I could no longer bask in my own assumed acceptance by these creatures. I kept hearing the count's words to Teresa, words uttered only moments earlier: *She is only the biological mother of my child. You are my wife. I will deal with our little bird when the time comes.* How much clearer could things have been pointed out to me?

Yet, he had said that if she continued with her jealous ways she could lose her lofty position as his queen. Was there a way I could continue irritating her, thus forcing her from the imperial perch? How could I win this game? Did I really aspire to win? Was there any chance that I *could* win? What would I do if I *did*? And the final question I needed to ask myself was—what would I become if I won?

Would I be saner to take my chances and attempt another flight before my usefulness as a mother was finished? Questions, questions, but no answers—only a mixed-up muddle of unknowns. I was so consumed by this role I was acting out that I was having difficulty separating reality from fantasy. That was a dangerous line to walk!

I also had to seriously consider that I might have to leave my son behind. If and when it came down to it, could I do that? He was, after all, still very much a part of me. He was my baby—that made him half-human. I had nurtured him within my womb: singing to him, telling him my stories, caressing his tiny body as it had formed within the heart of my body. Surely those intimate moments within the womb would assure some human tendencies. "Oh, God above, why can *You* not give me an easy answer or, better yet, a blessed deliverer?"

"Virginia," the count's voice broke into my thoughts. "I hope Teresa's little scene has not unsettled you. She is just upset at the extra attention you have been receiving of late, because of the baby, of course. You have nothing to fear, for now." He studied me for a moment as he paused, and then he added, "Nothing to fear as long as you are being truthful."

If all the words he had just said had been bricks, I could have built a house. His statements confirmed that I had not gained his trust. How foolish I was to assume I had, or ever would. I had not even dented its exterior. Maybe that was impossible to do. Even in my room, he had stated that he would like to believe me, but he felt there was something amiss. He was such a difficult man to read. The fact that he had survived as long as he had should have told me how difficult he would be to fool!

Once again, I was faced with the sinking feeling that I was no match for him. I began to think I should have been more receptive to Teresa's recent offer of freedom. Now that I had angered and embarrassed her in front of him and his family, the thought of reopening such a bargain with her was a tiny speck on the far horizon. She hated me more than ever now, probably with a fiery passion greater than the furnaces of hell itself!

Count Atilla Musat broke the silence that had enveloped the room. "Basarab, was Virginia happy with our choice of a name for the child?" The elder count smoothly changed the subject.

"Yes. Yes, she was, Father." Basarab still had his eyes glued on me. "She liked it very much."

I wondered at their pretences when I was in their company. I felt, as I had many times before, that it did not truly matter what I thought. My end, even after all my trials and well-laid plans of deception, would be no different now than what had been decided for me from the beginning. I was no match for the kinds of games these men played. Their ruthlessness was of sinister dimensions. Of that reality I was more assured now than ever before!

The elderly Count Musat continued, "Good. There is something else I would like to discuss with you later, Basarab. I need you to return home. There is some urgent business that must be attended to. I am in need of your advice and, more than likely, your assistance as well. Your leadership will be welcomed on the home front."

"What business is of such urgency, Father, that it requires my return home?" Did I detect hesitation in the count's voice at the possibility of having to revisit the land of his birth? Did it have something to do with the recent revelation I had just heard—with his mortality?

"Later, my son. We do not need to bother the others with these trivialities. It is our duty, as the elected leaders of our people, to decide the best course of action for the preservation of our kind." Count Atilla waved his hand aimlessly around the room, but somehow I felt his eyes remained fixed upon me.

He continued, "The outcome of our decisions will greatly affect all our families, at home and abroad. There are also some of our own who have been quite careless with our secrets. They, too, must be dealt with accordingly." He paused a moment, as though considering how much more to say. "Let me just say this much—it has a great deal to do with Elizabeth and Jack, and the one who pulls their strings."

The two names shook me! They were still around! Of course, I should have known it was possible after what the count had disclosed to me. He had never mentioned the name of whomever it was that was creating all the rogues, though; I wondered why not. Was it someone too close to him—maybe even Dracula? After all, *he* was not here!

The elder count clapped his hands. "Enough idle chatter. Let us partake of our nourishment. Max, serve us please; we are ready." He smiled, and I caught a brief glimpse of his fangs. Pure evil—definitely not the picture of the grandfatherly type I was familiar with or would have hoped to have for my children!

I let my mind wander to what mysterious business could possibly be going on that would affect the whole family. Were they being threatened? Were the rogues becoming more powerful than the original family members? Was there really a difference between the two? I wondered if the statement about some of their own being careless with the family secrets was meant to indirectly warn me about the knowledge I had been allowed to glean. What was the fate of one who dared to expose such knowledge? Were the rogues, or whoever it was who led them, trying to usurp Basarab from his role as leader? If the family was in danger and they took my son with them, what would happen to him? And if they left me behind, alive, what could I do to get him back?

Silence reigned as Max served the evening meal, if you could call it a meal. I still could not bring myself to call what they consumed a true dinner delight. I ate meals—they drank blood!

Teresa's accusations had left me uneasy. *Her* words kept swirling around my head. *His* words were doing the same. My game and my pretences were but child's play to what these creatures were capable of. How could my meagre life experiences even compare, let alone compete?

I felt as though every eye in the room was studying me, penetrating and infiltrating my mind. Had they already unearthed the awful truth I was attempting to hide? I was no longer sure how long I could withstand such microscopic scrutiny without losing my composure. I laid my napkin on the table.

"Count Basarab," I bowed my head in a humble show of respect, "I am afraid this entire horrid scene with Teresa has tired me considerably more than I expected. May I please have your permission to retire?"

"Of course, Virginia. If you are fatigued, you may be excused. Shall I have Max accompany you to your room?" The count raised his eyebrows.

"Thank you, but no; I shall find my own way. The baby will be waking soon, anyway; I am sure he will be hungry." I rose from my chair. "I would appreciate it if Max would bring me some supper later."

I allowed my eyes to drift around the table, settling momentarily upon each one of the guests. "Good night, everyone. I sincerely hope you will enjoy the rest of your evening."

"Good night, Virginia," the countess Emelia returned. "Would you mind if I stopped by later to see you and the child? Maybe we could have that little chat we were discussing earlier. I shall save Max a trip by bringing your supper with me when I come."

"That would give me great pleasure, Aunt Emelia," I answered as I leaned over and planted a kiss on her cheek. "Once again, everyone, I bid you all a good night." I slipped quickly out of the room.

Once in the hallway, I leaned against the wall for a moment. My breath gurgled in my throat. I gasped frantically, trying to free it. "Calm yourself," I whispered. "Stay calm and all will be well. Lose your nerve, and you will lose everything!" I took in a couple of deep, shuddering breaths and then released them slowly in order to still my frayed nerves.

I stared into the shadows that always seemed to lurk in this long corridor. Teresa had warned me to watch the shadows. Was she there in the midst of them? Skulking somewhere, watching my every move; waiting for the moment to strike me down?

Damn her! Damn her to hell! But was there a worse hell than the one she was already in? What kept me playing these games? I was no match for them; I must be out of my mind! Why did I continue to fool myself time and time again?

It was *him*. It was the Count Basarab Musat, so outrageously intriguing! He was my downfall, the fiery grate of my passion that would not relinquish its flame. He was so inviting, so enticing! As much as I detested what was happening to me, I desired it, too. It was probably the most excitement I had ever experienced or, for that matter, would ever experience again—if I ever managed to get out alive!

My body ached for him. It anticipated the moment when he would run his hands along my neck and over my breasts, pausing for unending seconds to tease my nipples before proceeding down, down to explore the depths of my escalating lust. I could feel the tingling in my loins as though he were with me at that very moment, stroking me into wanting him above all else!

I shook my head, drawing myself back to reality. I started up the winding stairway to my room on the top floor. I heard the baby stirring in his bed as I entered. I walked slowly to the cradle, gathered him into my arms, and held him close to my heart.

"What are you going to be, my little son?" I whispered in his ear. "You are half mine, half his. If I were to take you away from here, surely I could save you from becoming like your father and the rest of his kind." I rocked the child in my arms as I voiced the thoughts that raced through my mind.

The child did not care about the distant future; his next meal was occupying his mind. He looked and acted like any other normal human baby as he began to wail loudly for the meal that was not as quickly forthcoming as he desired it to be.

"Okay, okay, little one. I shall feed you."

I snuggled down into the chair near the window and exposed my overflowing breast from its hiding place. Santan latched on quickly and began sucking greedily. I watched for a moment as the reddish liquid overflowed his tiny lips. Was that a smile I noticed at the corners of his lips? Tonight, for some odd reason, I discovered I was once again repulsed by this sight. I looked away, staring at the heavily curtained window, searching and praying for a sign of freedom. I reached over with my free arm and pulled the curtains aside. The night was gloomy.

I noticed how the wind was whipping at the leaves of the ever-guarding trees. There was no rain yet, but the darkness of the night suggested to me that we were in for a storm. This evening had turned into a nightmare. Each time I gained ground, or thought I had, my mind was thrown into turmoil worse than before. The game I was trying to play had slowly become my master. It cracked its whip. It told me when to jump. It told me how high. And I, the one who thought she was so smart, continued to ask for more!

I started to weep. The tears poured, falling like a relentless waterfall with no direction. My frustrations oozed out with the tears as they fell down onto the face of my infant son, blending with the overflow of his supper, creating miniature pinkish-coloured runaway rivers on his constantly sucking cheeks. No matter how hard I tried, I could not prevent the torrent from bursting forth. The months of being cooped up in this place were again taking their toll. I was tired of the game I was trying to play—ever so tired. I feared its ending now more than I ever had before. And I damned myself for having tried to stay in it!

This was the condition that the countess Emelia found me in when she came to my room that night. The sight that greeted her was a young woman rocking in a chair, staring blankly, clutching her baby tightly to her chest, and sobbing her heart's pain away.

"There, there, my dear. This has all been too much for you. Teresa should be ashamed of herself for trying to upset you so soon after the birthing. A woman's emotions are fragile enough with the trauma of delivery. It just isn't good for you, or the baby. Of course she would not know of these things, would she, never having had the gratification of birthing a child herself." Emelia rambled on, pausing just long enough, every once in a while, to wipe the tears from my eyes.

"Come, come now, hand me the child. I will give him a bath and change him for you. You just crawl under your covers and keep warm. I shall come and tell you a story about the count when I am finished. Would you like that?" Emelia smiled sweetly.

I nodded. Aunt Emelia was not evil; surely she was not. Someone as nice as her could not really be one of *them*. In my mind I did not want her to be one of them, so I willed her part in their world away. For the time being, I would just bask in her kindness and heal my wounds. I crept slowly under the covers and lay waiting, like an anxious child, for my bedtime story.

But the story never materialized. By the time the countess Emelia had finished attending to Santan and had settled him down in his cradle, I was sound asleep. The battles of wits, the strained scenes with Teresa, the tears—they had all taken their toll on me. I had drifted off into another troubled world, one that I visited often—that of my dreams ...

My dream began on a riverbank. I was holding my son and attempting to cross. I could see the place from which I was fleeing—a stone castle, built into the side of a mountain. I could hear the shouts of men and women as they pursued me; they were coming ever closer. The child was crying. I was crying. I pushed forward into the frigid river water. On the other side was a great, dark forest. I felt the urgency to reach it. My feet were slipping on the river rocks, and several times I almost lost my balance. Then I heard someone shout, "There she is!" I tried to quicken my pace.

But the child was heavy, oh so heavy. My feet slipped again. I felt myself losing control. I was being swallowed by the frothy water. The child was still crying, louder and more anxiously. I placed my hand on his mouth. As I was sinking, I saw a woman's face. I felt the firm grip of her hands as she reached under my arms and then propelled me to the bank on the other side. She did not exit from the deep herself, but she had placed me on firm enough footing that I could catch my balance. When I reached the edge of the wood, I turned and saw the water leaping furiously. The woman was hovering over the waves, her arms spread wide. She was facing the advancing army, and she was chanting.

I saw the army of men and women stop at the edge of the river. I saw the anger on some faces, the fear on others. I saw *him* glaring at me. But then his fury turned into beckoning. I hesitated, almost ready to run back to his arms. A voice from within the woods stopped me. "Hurry, Virginia; there is not much time."

I looked for the woman in the water. She was gone. I turned, ran into the darkness, and saw no more!

CHAPTER 22

Emelia's Story

When I awoke, it was morning. Santan and I spent a quiet, uneventful day; he slept most of it—possibly a sign of things to come? Max brought me the usual breakfast drink and a roast beef sandwich with a side salad for lunch. As the sun began to set, I wondered what the evening would bring. A light knock came on the door.

"Who is it?" I called out.

"Aunt Emelia."

I rushed to the door, forgetting that I could only open it from the inside if it were unlocked. I was surprised when it swung open easily. "Come in, please," I said. I noticed the key in the door. Someone must have left it there for Emelia, but she had been considerate enough to wait for my permission to enter.

Emelia was carrying a tray of food. "I thought to have our little chat tonight, since you were much too tired last evening and fell asleep before I could begin." She smiled warmly. Nothing sinister.

"Here, let me take the tray," I said. I set it down on the table by my window.

"Isn't he lovely?"

I looked back. Emelia was bent over the cradle.

"I think so," I answered.

"He resembles my first son." Emelia paused.

I spoke before she could continue. "How many children do you have?"

"I *had* three," she replied sadly. "Only one is still alive, and I do not know where he is. He disappeared after the last great cleansing. I can only hope he is safe, maybe in the caves."

"The caves Atilla spoke of in his diary?"

"Yes."

"Is that why Basarab came here, because of this cleansing you speak of?"

"I believe so. Of course, his was the head most desired; therefore, the importance of getting him to safety was prevalent in all our minds, especially since we had come so close to losing him, as Teresa mentioned last night."

"But now he is needed again?" I pushed forward, hoping I was finally going to get some answers. "Count Atilla mentioned something about Elizabeth and Jack—is that Elizabeth Bathory and Jack the Ripper?"

"You know of them?"

"Yes. Basarab and I discussed them at great length."

"I see." She frowned and then went on to answer my first question. "Yes, he must return; he is our leader, and there are certain matters that need looking after. Atilla has done his best in his son's absence, but he does not have the same power of persuasion as Basarab. There are too many who will not listen to him. That is why he is asking his son to return to the homeland."

I walked back to the table and sat down. "Come, Aunt Emelia, let's eat. After that, I hope you will tell me some stories. Count Atilla's diaries ended when Basarab was three."

Emelia sat down opposite me. "Yes. There is much to tell. I shall do my best to answer as many of your questions as possible."

I noticed Emelia made no move to touch any of the dishes in front of us. She set aside the goblet, which I presumed was hers. I picked up my fork, dug into the supper, and looked at Emelia. I was like an impatient child, waiting for the story to begin.

～

She began with the day she met Count Vacaresti Musat …

"He was an amazing man. He came one day to see my father. Actually, as he told me later in our relationship, it was me he had really come to see. He had heard a great many rumours about my 'incredible beauty.'

"My father was hesitant to admit him into our castle. The rumours about his family were so vicious, you know. However, the Musat family was also very powerful, and you did not deny them access to anything you owned, should they make a request for it.

"After he had visited my father's home several times, I began to notice something very peculiar about Vacaresti. He never ate from our table. He always excused himself, telling us he had just finished a meal before arriving. He would pat his stomach and say that he never ate after a certain hour; it would upset his digestive system. When I mentioned this oddity to my father, he just brushed it off.

"I remember clearly the night Vacaresti turned to my father and asked permission to walk with me through the gardens. He even said that one of my personal maids could accompany us, if there was any concern for my honour.

"Father was much too compliant. The count's place in society, his concern for protocol—it all added up to one thing for my father. Maybe his spinster daughter would finally be married, and to a count who was more than a suitable candidate, in spite of some of the horrific rumours about his family."

I interrupted. "Why is it, if your beauty was so great, Aunt Emelia, that you had not had an offer of marriage?" I was puzzled.

"Ah, there lies your answer within your question, my dear. Great beauty brings hesitation of hearts. Most men believed that one so beautiful could never be a faithful wife, for all those who laid eyes upon her would seek some favour from her. It was assumed that sooner or later she would succumb to their amorous advances."

"I see," I whispered.

Emelia continued: "Thus the courtship began. Vacaresti came every day, or should I say *evening*. We walked through the gardens, by the river, and sometimes in the forest. He told me tales of the earth and the sky, weaving stories with such romantic imagination that I soon found myself falling helplessly in love. I was mesmerized by his knowledge and by his charm; I am not sure which one of those characteristics fascinated me more. His knowledge quenched my thirst for learning, his charm for ..." She smiled.

"Anyway, no one else thought it peculiar that he came only at night; the man was obviously busy during the day looking after family business. One evening, Vacaresti asked my father if he would mind if we took a moonlight ride on the horses. My father consented. He had no reason to doubt Vacaresti's honourable intentions. Neither did I for, as of yet, he had not made any offensive moves toward me; my honour was still intact. We rode to Vacaresti's castle.

"That was the first night Vacaresti kissed me. That night I fell totally in love, so much so that I took no notice of the stinging sensation on my neck; nor did I feel the withdrawal as my life's blood was being sucked from me.

"I kissed him back, that night, and the next, and the next. I still took no heed as to what was happening to me, until my personal maid mentioned how pale I was becoming. She also pointed out that I was losing my appetite. I insisted it was nothing. I was in love. I continued to see my count. I continued to kiss him and be kissed by him.

"The count Vacaresti asked my father for my hand in marriage two months from our first meeting. I remember my father's smile. He was thrilled to have finally found a good catch for his single daughter. He told Count Vacaresti that he would begin preparations for the wedding right away. I am sure my father's urgency was because he wanted to make certain that I married the count quickly, just in case he changed his mind.

"However, Vacaresti informed my father that it would not be necessary for him to plan or pay for the wedding. He would look after all the arrangements. Some of his relatives would be leaving for abroad soon, and their presence was required in order to have a proper wedding. He explained to my father that it was a family thing.

"My father, who should have been my wise protector, and who should have questioned such a thing, did not. I have often wondered, over the years, whether he was naïve—or just desperate to be rid of me. He did not even question that he would not be attending my wedding. My bags were packed, and my dowry chests were loaded onto the count's carriage. My father embraced me goodbye and wished me luck. There were not even any departure tears for me, at least none that he allowed me to see. That was the last time I saw him alive.

"Vacaresti assured me I would have no need of my maid, that he would provide me with a new one—one more suitable to my new station in life, he had whispered in my ear. I embraced my lifelong friend. We both wept openly; I shall never forget her love for me. She had attended to my needs from the moment I entered this world. It had been a difficult birth for my mother, and she never recovered from the ordeal. She actually became a recluse; there was nothing that anyone, including my father, could do for her. She just faded away, body and mind. She died when I was four. So you see, my maid was not just a friend; she was my mother, too. I could not imagine my life without her." Emelia's eyes were moist with unwept tears.

"It was the most unusual wedding ceremony I had ever witnessed," she continued. "There was no priest present, only Vacaresti's close relatives, and the boy, Basarab. Basarab's father said some words over us as we knelt before him. Before I knew it, Vacaresti assisted me to my feet, kissed me, and told me we were married."

"You mentioned that Vacaresti's close relatives were present. Who were they?" I asked.

"Atilla; Stephen and his wife, Evdochia; Dracula and his two sons, Vlad and Mihail; the doctor, Balenti Danesti; and Basarab were all there."

"How old was Basarab at the time?"

"Twelve."

Emelia raised her goblet, took a sip, and then continued. "I believe I became pregnant on my wedding night. No number of talks with other females, or with my maid, could have prepared me for what happened to me that night. Count Vacaresti moved me into womanhood with such ease that I was barely aware of what was happening to me. It was like a beautiful dream, one which I never wished to awaken from.

"I felt only slight shame for having responded to my husband so wantonly, but I could not help myself. He whispered things to me, and he did things to my body that ignited a lust in me that I had no idea I possessed! I also reasoned within myself that anything so rapturous could not be wrong. I felt sorry for those women who only considered it a duty to let their husbands mount them, so to speak. I began to imagine ways to pleasure my husband. Vacaresti was a most willing participant!

"During those first few months, I learned that Basarab ruled the roost. Atilla was actually quite a gentle man. Still is. I always found him either reading books or writing in his journal. When I asked him one day why it was that he kept a journal, he said it was to ensure that there would be a record of our family, in case of our demise. I did not understand exactly what he meant at the time; I do now.

"Vlad and Mihail came and went often, but they were a pair of rascals who only kept their teeth from my throat because I was Vacaresti's chosen bride. Dracula, Vlad and Mihail's father, was the only one of the group who remained absent for quite some time after the wedding. We heard much of his terrors around the countryside, though. His sons thought he was a hero. Atilla would get a faraway, forlorn look in his eyes when Dracula's name was mentioned. Stephen would just hang his head; Evdochia would tense and walk away. I was still too new in the family to have any reaction to Dracula at all, except for a twinge of fear now and then.

"The first child grew within me. I became quite ill, though, and found I had no desire for food. The count Balenti brought me a drink to replace the meals I could no longer eat. I told him it tasted horrible, but he ordered me to drink it. At the time, it seemed to be the only thing I could tolerate.

"Basarab was fascinated with my condition, so much so that we actually spent many hours together. For a twelve-year-old child, he was most astute. He questioned everything that was happening to me, demanding to know exactly how I felt, both mentally and physically. We became the best of friends.

"Time drew near for the birthing. I became quite agitated. I was terrified. I missed and wanted my old maid. Vacaresti tried to sooth me, but I began to blame him for my discomfort. He would laugh and tease me; then he would hold me close to him and whisper old stories in my ear. That usually settled me, at least until my next fit of emotional distress.

"My first son was born on the second day of spring. He died on the third day. There was no comforting me this time. There was also no Vacaresti to hold me close, because following the death of his son, he rode off to the mountains, taking our dead child with him.

"It was only later that I learned about the caves. Vacaresti took me there and showed me our son's grave. It was also at that time that I actually learned to whom, or to *what*, I was married. Somehow, I had been kept from the truth, or maybe I had just failed to see the reality of the family I was now a part of.

"My husband's grief so overwhelmed him that he almost killed me that night, as his fangs tore into my neck! In fact, had it not been for Basarab, who had followed us to the caves, he probably would have killed me. At the time, I think Vacaresti blamed me for our son's death.

"'Uncle!' Basarab had screamed out. 'She is your wife, Uncle, your chosen one! Do not do this to her! She will bear you another child. Have we not already learned that the woman must still be human in order to bear a child of our kind?'

"Vacaresti stopped instantly and released me from his grip. I crumbled to the earth. Basarab was there, soothing me, rocking away my fear. 'There, there, Auntie,' he kept saying as he stroked my hair. 'Uncle won't hurt you again.' It was Basarab who helped me up onto my horse. It was Basarab who accompanied me back to the castle. It was Basarab who tended the wounds left from my husband's fury. Vacaresti was too ashamed of what he had almost done to me. He did not come home for several days.

"But my husband never hurt me again. When Basarab spoke, it seemed everyone listened, and most obeyed, eventually. It was obvious, even at such a young age, that Basarab was a leader—their leader. My second child was born the following spring; this one lived."

"What did you call him?" I asked.

"We named him Ilias Atilla Musat," Emelia answered.

"Ilias?" I prompted.

"After Vacaresti's father," Emelia answered. She continued with her story. "Vacaresti was getting restless and felt that he and I should return to his castle; we had imposed on Atilla and Basarab long enough. Since Ilias was so young, the doctor moved with us. He wanted to ensure that this child lived." Emelia took another sip from her cup—its contents were a constant reminder to me of what she really was.

I had wondered about the doctor; what was he? One of them, or was he like Max? I decided to ask Emelia. "Is Count Danesti a vampire?"

Emelia frowned at first, and then she sighed. "No, he is like Max; only his station in life is much higher, as I presume you already know."

"You cannot tell me *how* they are what they are?" I inquired, even though I already knew the answer.

"That is correct." Emelia set her cup down. Her story continued.

"We decided to leave after Basarab's birthday celebration. He would be thirteen. Atilla had sent out invitations to as many family members as possible. Many of them had relented over the years and had come to Atilla seeking advice on how to best deal with the curse they found themselves faced with.

"It was a grand celebration, one I shall never forget. Basarab displayed his power and authority, as was becoming his custom. Atilla allowed his son free rein to speak; Basarab opened the floodgate of his future plans for our kind. He said we must settle around the communities peacefully, leave the villagers and country folk alone, and desist from the violence some of our kind had been inflicting on the people. In other words, he was trying to encourage us to live discreetly so that we would not be hunted down like dogs.

"Somehow, the secrets that Angelique had bequeathed to Atilla that day so long ago, when he had sought solace for his Mara, had been revealed to the general public. Too many were seeking us out to kill us by driving stakes through our hearts and then severing our heads. But, to be fair, too many of our kind had ravished the people, leaving many of them to roam the land like walking dead, inflicting death on others. There was no pattern; there was no discrimination. It all depended on the mood. People lay awake at night fearing when their turn would come and their lives become a living hell!

"Actually, it was many of this new breed, the ones who were only half-crossed over, and who hadn't been taught how to deal with their new lifestyle, that terrorized the people more than *our* family members did, with the exception of a couple of them, if I am to be honest. I am not at liberty to say which family member has caused us the most pain over the years."

"Is it the one who is responsible for Elizabeth Bathory?"

"Yes."

I was trying desperately to digest all of this new information Emelia was sharing with me. I had pictured Basarab as more of a warrior-type leader, at least that is the manner in which Max and Teresa had always portrayed him to me—a man who took what he wanted and answered to no one.

"But was not Basarab a bit of a scoundrel himself?" I asked.

"Not at first," Emelia sighed. "But as time went by, his youthful ideals turned into a bloodbath. He began to think the only way our kind could survive was to force the people to fear us so much that they would eventually leave us alone. Then we could return to a more quiet way of life. Many of us fled back into the caves in order to be safe. Ilias was six at the time, Basarab almost twenty—"

"Did you not say," I interrupted again, "that you had three children?"

"Oh, yes; I gave birth to a girl when Ilias was three. She died before the end of her second week. It was then that Basarab came to his uncle and mentioned that maybe it was time to bring me completely into the fold.

"Vacaresti discussed this with me, actually giving me a choice. He said I could grow old and die like all the other humans, or I could live for an eternity with him. It was really not a difficult decision for me to make. He was my husband, the father of my children, and I loved him dearly. And there was my son, who would need me forever, I thought at the time ... so here I am." Emelia glanced out the window. The first rays of the sun were making their way through the trees. Santan began to whimper.

Emelia stood up. "If you like, I shall return tonight to finish my story. I am tired now."

I looked at this woman standing before me. She had enlightened me so much, yet she was one of them. I knew I wanted to hear more. "I shall be waiting for you," I confirmed my desire for her to return. "I definitely want to hear more about the count."

"Yes, yes." As Emelia was leaving, she almost bumped into Max, who was bringing up my breakfast tray. "Excuse me, Max," Emelia said as she slid past him.

"Yes, Countess Emelia," Max returned stiffly as he sidestepped and then entered my room. Was that a look of dislike I saw on his face?

He set the breakfast tray on the table by my window, retrieved the evening tray, and left without speaking a word to me. In fact, he did not even look into the cradle to see his grandson, as he had been accustomed to doing.

"I shall bring Virginia her supper again tonight," I overheard Emelia tell him from the hallway.

"As you wish, Countess."

Once again, I was alone with my son.

CHAPTER 23

Basarab

Emelia showed up, as promised, with my supper tray. "Max fixed you your favourite for tonight," she mentioned as she opened the conversation.

My nostrils twitched in anticipation as I sniffed the aroma of roast beef. "I wonder why he would go to the bother," I said.

"Why do you say that?" Emelia tilted her head questioningly.

"Well, he seemed so distant and upset this morning, almost as though he resented the fact that you were here with me."

"You must understand Max," Emelia said. "He really means no harm. His existence depends on how he is able to serve the count, and Teresa. I have noted a great change in Max since the last time I saw him. He is more tired than I have ever before seen him, even more so than when he fought for his Lilly's life."

"Did you know Lilly?" I interrupted.

"Yes."

"What was she like? Was she as beautiful as Max told me she was?"

"So beautiful that Teresa pales in comparison. And her spirit, at first, was gentle and loving. I remember the first time I saw her, my breath caught in my throat. I also remember thinking that Max would never be able to keep her, because Basarab, by then, had changed so much—" Emelia stopped and drew in a sharp breath.

"How had he changed, Aunt Emelia?" I pushed for more.

Emelia set the tray on the table. Her lips remained in a thin line. She sauntered over to Santan's cradle and peeked in. *That is a question I may have to ask again*, I thought to myself.

"He will sleep for awhile," I stated, coming up to her and placing my arm around her shoulders. "Please tell me more; I need to understand the man to whom I have just given a son."

Emelia heaved a great sigh, walked back to the table, and sat in her chair. "There is so much to tell," she began, "so much to tell."

"Start with the moment you crossed over," I suggested.

"Yes … yes … the moment I crossed over. Evdochia came to me with a crimson gown made from the finest velvet—"

I put my hand out and touched Emelia on the arm. I had forgotten about Stephen and Evdochia. "Where are Stephen and Evdochia?" I asked. "I assumed they would have been here for the birth; were they not invited?"

Emelia wrung her hands nervously before answering. "They had to stay behind. We had to have someone we could trust to attend to matters until our return. Stephen has always been responsible in that way. Now, to continue with my story … Evdochia poured me a bath and filled the waters with creamy bubbles of milk. She scrubbed my body with pumice, until my skin shone a healthy pink. She helped me from the bath, patted me dry with a soft towel, and then slipped the gown over my head. The cool silkiness of the satiny side of the velvet soothed my freshly scrubbed skin. She took a brush and untangled my lengthy strands of hair, smoothing it to a silky shine against the velvet material. She spun me around and smiled at the results before her.

"You are ready," she informed me. "I wish I had your beauty."

I interrupted Emelia. "Describe how you looked to me, please, Auntie."

Emelia got a faraway look in her eyes. Tears crowded the corners, fighting for a chance to be the first released. "I was beautiful, Virginia, as you already know from my previous story. I was so tiny that Vacaresti could encircle my waist with his hands. My hair swept the floor, and it shone like gold in the days when the sun had been allowed to touch it. It was so thick that, when braided, it was as strong as any man's rope. It was quite similar to your colour, but not quite as red.

"My eyelashes were long, dark, and curly; my eyes were a piercing green—sea eyes, some would say when they visited my father's home. The old women used to tell my father that I had a wandering spirit; they could see it in my eyes.

"My skin was porcelain, unblemished, and soft to the touch. I was the envy of my sisters and of all the girls who were courted by my brothers. When I was very young, I had basked in my superior looks, but as each of my sisters married and began to have children, I started to curse the beauty that had been bestowed upon me. Therefore, it was no wonder that my father saw Vacaresti as my salvation—I did, as well!"

I studied the woman in front of me. If I looked closely, I could see some semblance of the beauty she spoke of, but her body had changed. I think Vacaresti would have a most difficult time encircling her waist with his hands now. She was still tiny, but not as petite as she had once been. Her hair had been cropped short and curled, and it did not shine gold; it was more of a dull blond. Her skin was not quite the colour of porcelain, and there were a few darker areas that clouded the youthful perfection that she had spoken of.

But the eyes were still green—sea green—a piercing kaleidoscope of greens that did not allow intruders to see beyond their surface. I wondered what was really behind them!

Emelia laughed when she noticed me staring at her. "Hard to believe, isn't it Virginia?"

"Your eyes are still a stunning green, Aunt Emelia, and you have a beautiful soul, I might add."

"I have no soul." Emelia stood up abruptly, walked to the other window, and stared out into the darkness. "Something, no matter what you think you are feeling for me right now, you would be wise to remember, my dear," she added.

I kept silent. I must have struck a sensitive chord with the mention of a soul. I should have known better. How thoughtless of me to mention she had a soul, when she had been just about to disclose to me how she had lost hers!

I walked over and put my arm around her shoulder. "Come, Auntie. Come, sit down and tell me how it happened. I am so sorry."

"Tsk tsk, Virginia, you are still of this world. You have no idea of how our minds work or what we had to do to survive. You have no idea of whom, or *what*, we really are!"

I waited for her next comment, not wanting to push further. I agreed with Emelia that I only had a general idea of what the family had been through. Emelia turned slowly and returned to the table.

"Where was I now? Yes … Evdochia had just finished preparing me for my initiation into their world. All I can really tell you is this—even though it was a horrible feeling, at the same time it was exciting. It is against our creed for me to describe to you, or any other mortal, the actual particulars of becoming a proper *chosen* vampire."

"Was Basarab there?" I asked.

"Of course. Actually, if it were not for Basarab, Vacaresti would have killed me—not intentionally, of course, but with passion and desire. That is the main reason that I aged, as I am now. What happened that night could not be completely erased. Once again I owed my life to my nephew."

Emelia paused again and looked away. "They ought to pay for what they did to him!" she continued, changing the subject, focusing on telling me about her beloved nephew. There was a hint of anger in her voice. "He was a fine young man. Difficult to read at times, though, as a severe moodiness had begun to replace the youthful rationalism he had once displayed.

"His proposal for a peaceful existence with mankind was becoming warped, as I mentioned yesterday. Those cursed Gypsies would not let the people forget what we were—especially the old one, Tanyasin. She was responsible, as you know from the diary, for cursing Basarab with the leadership of his people. I also believe she was the one responsible for informing the people of Angelique's lightening of our curse—a green light, as you might say in today's world, for men to seek us out and destroy us. I am sure it gave Tanyasin great pleasure to see our kind live in constant fear for our lives. Still does."

"She, too, still lives?"

"I believe so. Anyway, she was angry when she found out what Angelique had done. The last thing I heard of our saviour was that she had been cast out of her tribe and had been forced into seclusion. The other Gypsy women were too afraid of Tanyasin to stand with Angelique. Some say her spirit wanders the mountain caves and helps our people when they are in trouble. Who knows? Maybe she even crossed over and became one of us.

"In some ways, though, her lightening of the curse actually has caused us many problems over the centuries. But she is not to be blamed; she had no idea of the colossal evilness that would grow from both curse and blessing ...

"Anyway, back to Basarab; he more than lived up to his role of leader. He was powerful and fair, and never once did he take his designated position for granted amongst his own kind. He held us together and kept the peace when some would—how should I say it?—become a bit too *rambunctious* out in the real world.

"He insisted we take our nourishment from animals and that we leave the farmers and the villagers alone. If we did that, he could see no reason why anyone would want to hunt us down and destroy us.

"However, as I said, Tanyasin had worked more evil. Every time there was an 'unusual' death, she would stir hatred against us into the hearts and minds of people. The caves became our only refuge. We were driven from our homes, hunted like dogs, and slaughtered without reason.

"As a result, many decided they had had enough of Basarab's gentle ways, and that is when the first real scourge began. Blood was shed on both sides, but we left them with many undead—something that has haunted us over the centuries. With so many to contend with, and with Basarab so angry and frustrated with both worlds, we began to lose control. And there was still the one who had taken control over the *rogues* we had all created—we were constantly at odds with him—still are.

"Because of all this, Basarab decided it would be best to keep our race as pure as possible. We had concluded that a woman who was completely crossed-over could bear children, but the children did not live very long. That is why I never attempted to have any more children after I crossed over. Basarab deduced that the males should mate with human women. That has not been overly successful either, but there are a few out there who have succeeded. These are the vampires who usually hail to a higher standard of morality and are more protective of our ways. I believe that your child will be another success story for us. He is the picture of health and strength."

"What if the females of your kind were to mate with a human male? Would that have worked?" I queried.

"Basarab would not allow that. There was no explanation as to why, but I feel it has something to do with us being the weaker sex. In our society, the males rule supreme. It would not be tolerated if our women were to step outside the family circle. We are their 'possessions.'" Emelia smiled.

"To continue about Basarab, there were many years during this era that Vacaresti and I did not see Basarab. His father stayed with us in the safety of the caves, but our leader would not bow to the masses. I presumed Basarab had found something that worked for him, though, for he settled in an area where there was little known about our kind. He made a name for himself as a hard, but fair, landlord. It was during this time that Max came to live with Basarab."

I decided to interrupt Emelia again. "But I thought he was horrible even then—"

"I guess that depends on your definition of horrible," Emelia cut me off. "Do not misunderstand me, Virginia; the count was no saint. He was a fearsome figure, and he used this fact to manipulate all around him. All of the innocent, noble ideals he had once tried to instil in us were gone. They had been replaced by a need to survive. He did what he had to do! As did we all!"

Emelia settled back in her chair and folded her arms. I noticed the lightening of the room and felt sad that she would be leaving me again. Santan whimpered from his cradle. Emelia stood up and brought my son to me. "Feed your child, Virginia; he is hungry."

I went to my bed, settled back onto some pillows, and put him to my breast. Emelia walked to the door and stood there for a few seconds, a strange smile on her lips as she watched me. I wondered what she was thinking; I wondered what she was really all about. I smiled back to her, hoping that maybe she was *just* smiling at me.

Emelia's features did not change. They were like a picture—like all the women in the portraits in the dining room—frozen in time!

CHAPTER 24

The Knife Twists Deeper

My eyes opened to greet the full morning sun streaming in through the windows. Even though I had been ordered to always keep the curtains drawn while the child was with me, I did not stop to consider that this was strange. Santan must still be sleeping, and I was happy at how considerate he was being to finally allow his mommy to get a bit of extra rest. I must have fallen asleep while he was nursing, and Aunt Emelia probably had put him in the cradle.

Emelia's story had exhausted me. I remembered my last vision of her, standing in the doorway, smiling weirdly. *So how could she have laid Santan in the cradle if she had already left?* I shivered. I turned my gaze to where the cradle should be. Horror dealt me a blow in my stomach. It was gone! I panicked. Fear drove me from my bed and over to the door. I shook the handle, trying desperately to open it.

Oh God! Where was my baby? Had Emelia said she was going to put him to bed? I could not remember! Had I been so exhausted that I had not stayed awake long enough … no … no … *Clear your mind*! It had to have been *me* who had lain Santan in his bed! Of course— Emelia had left while he was still feeding. Could she have returned, after I fell asleep, and taken him? But why? Why would she want to do that?

248

She had appeared so kind, so concerned for my welfare. She had even rebuked Teresa for her rash behaviour toward me!

I fastened the buttons on my gown. I scrutinized my room. Everything to do with Santan had been removed! Everything—his bed, his clothing, his bath things. There was not a trace left in the room to confirm that a child had ever been there!

I began pounding on the door with my fists. I screamed hysterically, but my voice just ricocheted off the wooden door, echoing through the emptiness of the room where I stood.

"Max! Max! Someone! Let me out of here! Max! Where are you? Where is my baby?"

I continued pounding on the door until my strength was totally drained. I slid down to the floor and covered my face with my shaking hands. Uncontrollable sobs overtook my body. Why were they doing this to me? Why could they not just let me take my baby and leave? What had I ever done to them to deserve such a torture? Why the constant charade, the constant changing of my position?

I felt a tingling in my breasts. The milk—the blood—whatever it was I was creating within my body, was letting down. But there was no baby. I did not bother to try to suppress the flow. Soon my gown was saturated with the reddish liquid.

I have no recollection of how long I sat there, but I was jolted back to reality by the rattle of the key in my lock. I jumped to my feet and twirled around. "Max?"

The door opened, and there stood Max, holding my fussing son. He handed him to me and then moved quickly to the windows to shut the curtains. "I apologize for my tardiness, Virginia. I must have drifted off and overslept the hour of the child's feeding."

Max smiled, but I was sure I detected a hint of malice on his weathered old face. "The baby woke me with his crying; I hurried as quickly as was possible for my tired old body." Once again, he smiled. "I trust that you were not too alarmed?"

Max's final statement was issued in an I-don't-need-an-answer tone.

I got the impression that it did not matter one iota that I had been alarmed. Max had said he was tired? Since when had he ever been so tired that he fell asleep while he was on duty? The Max I was familiar with seemed to be available to wait on this family, or me, at any hour of the day or night. Was this the same Max who now complained of a tired old body? Or was it a Max who was up to no good?

"Alarmed? Max, I have been beside myself! Did you not hear me screaming and pounding on this door?"

"It is a very large house, Miss Virginia, and I do not sleep near your room anymore, now that you are up here. As a matter of fact, I dozed off in the baby's room, which is situated in another wing," Max stated as he handed me my son. "Here is the child for his feeding. I shall return shortly for him."

Max offered me no further information as to the exact proximity of my son's room; nor, did he offer an explanation as to why my son had been removed from my room. "Return for him? What do you mean? Where are his things? Why has he been removed from my room? What is going on here?" I was trying to demand a satisfactory answer!

"You have too many questions all the time, Virginia, and you keep asking those who have no answers. All I have are my orders, orders that I must obey, and answer to, if I don't." Max looked worried.

"Your orders? Who is it that gave these orders? The count is the one who allowed the child to be with me. Who has dared to disregard his wishes?" I demanded to know.

"It was the Count Basarab Musat who gave the order. Who else?" Max answered as he turned to leave the room.

"I thought that maybe Teresa—" I did not get a chance to finish my statement.

"No, my dear Virginia; it was not Teresa. It was the man whom you think you have conquered." Max shut the door as he left.

What was going on here? One minute the count allowed me my son, the next he ordered him removed. What kind of game was he playing now, and where was this round leading? To my death?

Santan bunted at my breast and began to whimper. "Okay, okay," I snapped. Oblivious to the sticky liquid that had saturated my clothing, I undid the buttons on my gown and settled my son for his meal. All the while Santan fed, my mind kept racing, trying to figure my way out of the maze I was deeply entangled in. I had thought I had gained so much ground, even to the point that I had actually been anticipating some kind of a victory. Now there had surfaced another heinous force, so potent, so tireless—a force that seemed to have pushed me back to square one, shattering all my hopes!

Max returned, too soon, for Santan. He took him from my arms and left without saying a word. I heard the lock click, closing me once again into desolate loneliness. I turned in my despair to the window and desperately searched the outside shadows for a hint of beckoning freedom.

Nothing. Nothing but grass, shrubs, flowers, and huge, grotesque-looking trees. Their knurled old trunks blocked me from the world I had once known. It seemed I had been here an eternity.

Hours must have passed as I stood there, motionless. The sun bid me goodnight through the top branches of my captive fortress as she drifted away to her other world. With her departure, I remained behind in the dark world that was slowly consuming my soul, piece by tiny piece.

⁓

I whiled away three lonely, desolate days. My meals were brought to my room. Santan was left with me only long enough for his feedings. Nothing more was mentioned as to the reason for this turn of events. Tonight Santan would be two weeks old. I knew the family would be preparing for the naming ceremony. I wondered if I would be allowed to attend, or if I was to remain locked in my room.

I did not understand this roller-coaster ride the count was taking me on. Also, since Santan had been removed from my room, my excursions on the widow's walk had been cancelled. Max told me the count had ordered me confined to my room. Had he become anxious that someone might see me, or I them? Did he fear that I would cry out? I continued to ponder this turn of events. Were these constant changes the count's actions, or just more of Teresa's deceptions?

I glanced out my window. The sun was disappearing behind the trees once again. Dark clouds were gathering in the sky, constructing bizarre-looking figures that scurried along as though in a hurry to be somewhere else. I imagined them to be the ancient gods of Olympus. I wondered if they were mocking me from their heavenly roosts, mocking me for the foolishness of my present predicament. The moon woke up; I noticed his sinister smile as he began the celebration of his most gargantuan night of the month.

Would this also be my biggest night yet? Would this be the night I would discover what my destiny was to be? I gazed around at the walls of my prison. I looked at the bed I had slept in for most of the past year, at the bed where I had made love to someone who had consumed me as I could never have imagined possible. I looked at the large oak door that had kept me prisoner whenever it pleased Count Basarab Musat to do so.

Why did he treat me this way? Was it that he truly did not have a heart, even after I had given him the son he so desired? However, I realized I had not had much of a choice in that matter. I had been impregnated without being consulted. Then I had foolishly tried to use my pregnancy to win him over—to win over a man I should have known I was no match for.

The question now was: What would happen later tonight? Had I not promised the count I would be his once again? Had he not accepted my offer with delighted anticipation? Had he not told me how much he looked forward to our liaison? But dark, evil-looking shadows kept clouding my pleasant thoughts. I wondered if this would be the final sacrifice I would have to make—before my end.

I had heard Count Atilla inform Basarab that he must come home to settle some *business*, and he had made it sound quite urgent. Aunt Emelia had confirmed this. However, I had not noticed any preparations for a trip, so how soon was he actually leaving? And what would this mean for me and my son? Would I be going with them, to care for Santan? If matters were that urgent, most likely they could not wait until the baby was weaned, although there was the possibility that the good doctor had another drink concoction that could replace my milk.

The ideal situation would be if they would leave me here with the child, under the ever-watchful eyes of Max. If I had only him to contend with, perhaps I could manage to escape. As always, I was faced with numerous *maybes*. I could not find one definitive answer to any of the many questions circulating in my mind.

The key turned in my door. Max entered, with Santan in one arm and a crimson gown draped over the other. He paused for a moment in the doorway. We studied one another, as though we were two old friends meeting after years of separation, neither one knowing where to begin the conversation.

I wished I could read his mind. I wondered just how far Max would go in tempting the rage of the count, in order to keep Teresa's place secure in the count's household.

"The baby, Miss Virginia," Max stated as he walked over to me.

He relinquished Santan into my arms. "The count desires your presence at the ceremony tonight. He has sent along this dress for you to wear." Max handed me the gown.

I laid both baby and gown on the bed and then turned to Max. He had to help me; I prayed for just this one little miracle. Surely, in my short life, I had not transgressed against God so much that he would not grant me this one small request! "Max," I commenced to speak—hesitantly, though, for I was still unsure how to approach him, yet again, on this matter.

"Yes?" he replied, much too calmly for my liking. It were as though he knew what I was about to ask.

"What is going to happen to me, Max? Surely you have heard something while passing through the corridors of this house. You have been with the count for so long that you must have an idea of the outcome of a situation like mine."

"What is going to happen to you, Virginia? Honestly, I do not know. Your *situation*, as you put it, is as new to me as it is to you. No other woman has ever borne the count a son. Then again, one never knows what the Count Basarab Musat has up his sleeve from one minute to the next. He is as changeable as the weather: calm and serene for a time, allowing one to grow comfortable in the luxury of his kindness, and then, suddenly, he will turn angry and fierce before one can realize he has changed. He is the master of all the destinies that surround him. He moulds his household to suit his present needs and desires. Past experiences have strengthened his resolve to make sure nothing, and no one, besets his kind again. If they should try, they will not succeed.

"So beware, Virginia; I emphasize this fact to you: *no one person*, no matter who they might be, is ever sure where he or she stands with Count Basarab Musat. He truly is the most powerful of his kind, and he maintains the position of leader not just because of the Gypsy curse! It is not through being soft that he sustains his leadership, either, regardless of Emelia's stories. She has always been partial to Basarab, no matter what he did. But, of course, you know her so well now, don't you—you might even *trust* her?" Max smiled an uncharacteristic smile. "But, back to the count; as I said, he has as many moods as the clouds have designs, and these moods usually dictate whatever his will is at that particular moment!"

Max paused. He drew closer to me and laid his wizened old hands on my shoulders. "Be assured, Virginia, that the count *is* aware of your little game. If both Teresa and I suspect you, do you really believe for a moment that you have fooled him? He has the capacity to read minds—be certain he has read yours! You will never know what has hit you, if he becomes weary of your antics. In the snap of a finger, it will be over!

"In a way, I pity you. You stumbled into this situation purely by accident, out of curiosity, in fact, but we all know what happens to a curious cat, don't we?" Max's voice took on a mocking tone.

Max was constantly emphasizing the count's changeable moods, yet his own seemed to constantly change! One minute he was sarcastic, the next deeply concerned. Then he would mock me. Which of his temperaments was I to put my trust in? Or should I even be contemplating such a thing? Did I have a choice?

"Max, if you overheard that the count was going to *dispose* of me, would you warn me in time? Maybe even help me to escape?" These were questions to which I needed an affirmative answer, but Max was still being difficult to read as to which way his loyalty might sway.

I found that out quickly, when Max's face took on a bitter look. "Why should I help you, Virginia, after all the pain you have caused the only one who has my heart? Your ploys have hurt my Teresa much more than you think. She is fighting for her very existence, especially where the count's father is concerned. He was quite taken by you; but then, you already know that, don't you? The count Atilla enjoys a woman with a vibrant spirit and strong willpower; and like his son, he is not able to tolerate such weak displays of jealous outrage as my Teresa has displayed of late. I actually overheard a conversation Atilla had with Basarab, suggesting that maybe he should keep you around a bit longer. However, if I might add this warning: also like his son, he soon tires of those who insist on playing charades."

"You speak only of the pain I have caused Teresa," I whispered huskily, "but have you forgotten about the pain that the Count Basarab Musat has inflicted upon you?" My mind was working swiftly. I had a sinking feeling that these moments were my last chance. If I could touch that one vulnerable part of Max, maybe I could gain his help.

"Think of Lilly, Max. Think of the life that you could have had with Lilly and Teresa—as a real family. Think of that, and then remember what bones the count flung to you instead, cast as most people would throw scraps to a stray dog at their door! He has made your life nothing more than an existence filled with servitude and loneliness. That is all he gave to you! He *took* your daughter from you, even though you claim you *gave* her to him, as part of the bargain to save your wife. I do not see that she even respects you! I know she has no respect for her mother, your Lilly—she told me so.

"Think of the picnics you three could have had on a quiet riverbank, or outings to the theatre. Think of the passion between you and Lilly, the joy you felt when you shared the knowledge of Teresa's conception, and then the moment of her birth! Think of what a beautiful child Teresa was—*yours and Lilly's* child! And when you have remembered all of this, keep in mind that it was the Count Basarab Musat who ripped it all away from you. And for what? For a whim, because you had something he did not!

"Now ask yourself if it would not be worth it, just once, to take revenge on the count. To taste the sweetness of his pain, by taking something from him that he values. To have victory over him. Would not that be worth it, Max? Wouldn't it?"

"You have no right to speak like this, Miss Virginia! How could you possibly know how I feel?"

I could tell I had struck a chord. Max was visibly shaken by my words. I had disturbed his cobwebbed mind. My mission had been accomplished. Now all I needed to do was add more mortar to the fortress I was creating.

"I do know how you feel, Max, because I have loved. Yes, I admit, without any reservations, that I love him. I also know the count is evil, and that is why I wish to flee from him. I appear to have no control over this love I feel. It is a lust that eats away at my soul night and day. It picks at my brain like crows attacking a straw man in a corn field. When he is with me I have no willpower; I am weakened in both mind and body by what he does to me—just as he did to your Lilly. Then I detest myself after it is over, probably in much the same way as your precious Lilly did. I hate him. I loathe him. I love him. I *need* him!

"Is not love one of the strangest emotions? The Count Basarab Musat did the same thing to Lilly as he has done to me." I reiterated the count's annihilation of Lilly. It was the only way I could think of to keep driving my point home. "He totally confused her mind with his overwhelming powers. She did not know what she wanted anymore, he had so befuddled her. He probably even threatened her by telling her he would harm you should she resist him. I think, because she loved you so much, that threat would have broken down what little resistance she might have had left, leaving her totally vulnerable to his oppressive authority."

I paused for breath and to allow my words to sink into Max's mind. If ever I were to take the plunge, it had to be now. Max's face had drained of all colour, but his eyes were filled with the fury of the eye of a hurricane!

"Yes, Max," I continued. "You and Teresa have guessed correctly. I have been playing a game; it is called the game of *survival*! I am sorry for what has happened to Teresa, I truly am, but I had no choice. Don't forget, Max, I have also given birth to a child. You know what it is like to have your child taken from you! Look at what you have done in order to remain by her side all these years.

"You submit to his anger, and you allow him to humiliate you every day of your existence. I have no idea what would happen to you if you were to help me; I am not even sure whether I would be able to take my son with me, but at least I will have my life. Maybe one day I could set out to find my child, and when I found him, I would tell him that I had not abandoned him by choice. I could tell him that I love him, just as you can tell Teresa every day that you love her. As one parent to another, can you not find it in your heart to do this for me?" My eyes were damp from emotion.

Max spoke slowly, as though hesitant to say what was on his mind. "After your son has spent any amount of time in his father's company, he will be so much like him that he will not care for you any more than he would care for a strumpet on the streets. He will be unable to love, truly love; nor will it be important to him to know that you love him.

"But, if I were to help you, and I say only *if* I were, it would be exclusively my way to thank you for giving my Teresa a child. You would have to flee far from here and start a new life. You should never seek to retrieve the child, not for any other reason either, because …"

Max never finished that statement. He went on, though, rambling off in another direction: "He may decide to leave you alone if you do not take the child. You are still young and very beautiful. I am sure you would have no problem finding yourself a nice young man to marry. You would be able to have more children. Before long, you would forget this entire ordeal. I must consult with Teresa on this matter. She will instruct me as to the right thing to do."

I could not camouflage the shock on my face. Teresa! He was going to consult her! She could not be trusted. What would stop her from going to the count, thus ending my life immediately? She was so angry and upset with me that I feared she might betray even her father in order to see me burn in hell!

"Max, please! This must be our secret! You know things have not been exactly the greatest between me and Teresa. Even if she were to understand that I just wanted to leave, she might slip and reveal our plan. You can do this while they sleep. I am sure you could come up with a plausible excuse for how I got out, and if I leave my son behind, it will go better for you. It is best for both of us if this conversation stays within this room. Please, Max!" I was praying that he would help me and not bring Teresa into the matter.

"I shall think on it, Virginia, but remember—I promise you nothing." Max turned to leave. "I must go. The count will wonder what is taking me so long, and you need to get ready for the ceremony, as well."

Max opened the door. The fluttering sound shocked both of us. Something flew past us and disappeared into the shadows of the dark hallway. Max's face took on a look of total defeat. I stood in paralysed shock as I realized that there was only one type of creature that fluttered around like that in this house!

Max looked at me, tears forming in his eyes. "You see, Miss Virginia, there is no escaping him. And now he knows all. There will be hell to pay for what has passed our lips in this room tonight—if that was him, of course. If it wasn't, only your God knows how long it will take for

the news to filter back to the count! I hope He is willing to aid us both!"
Max's eyes looked upward before he took his leave, shuffling away as
fast as his fatigued and broken body allowed.

I stood in the open doorway, my entire body shaking. Max had felt
so terrorized he had called upon *God* to help us both! Who had been
in my room, and for how long? How much had been heard? Teresa had
warned me to watch the shadows. If it had been Teresa, she would not
tell, regardless of what I had said about her. She would not expose her
father. I felt sure there were two men she would die for: the count and
her father. Of course she did not fear her father, and there was still the
risk that her hatred for me could outweigh any love she had for him.

There were other possibilities, too. It could have been the countess
Emelia. But what would her motive be? She had shown me nothing
but kindness so far. Maybe she was spying on behalf of her favourite
nephew. What was it Max had said? *Emelia has always been partial to
Basarab.* I remembered her telling me that Basarab had saved her life,
not just once but twice. Santan had been taken from my room after
her last visit to me—just how far would she be willing to go for her
precious nephew?

Or was it Count Atilla? Was he spying on me to see how good a
mother I was to his grandson? Perhaps he had another motivation to
snoop on me, one that he would not readily disclose to his son. The elder
count had stated he would like to get to know me better. If it had been
him, he now knew me better than I wished him to!

There was also the possibility that the cousins wanted to play "I Spy"
for the fun of it. They seemed to me like the type who enjoyed playing
pranks. Would their game turn into my nightmare? Would they fly
to tell cousin Basarab about the treason of his faithful servant and the
intended flight of his 'little bird'? Or would they keep their secret, to
use against me at a later time?

But there was no greater fear than that which pointed the finger
at *him*! And how was I to know for sure? The one thing I *did* know
for sure was that the flying creature had not been a figment of my

imagination—Max had seen it, too. The best thing for me to do now was to keep playing my game and to take my chances. No matter which way I turned, I had nothing to lose.

I gathered my son to my bosom. He gurgled contentedly, just like any other baby, but I knew he was not like any other baby!

My life truly was in God's hands now—that is, if He had not totally forsaken me!

CHAPTER 25

The Ceremony

All too soon, Max returned for Santan. He stood waiting for the baby to finish his meal. I could tell Max was still traumatized. I feared to even speak to him. The conversation that had passed between us could mean our demise, if it had fallen upon the wrong ears. The chance of there being any right ears in this place was highly improbable. In fact, someone could be deciding our fate at this very moment. Obviously, I was disposable, and I was sure that if the count needed to, he could find another Max.

"I shall return shortly to guide you to the room where the ceremony will take place. There is not much time left—please hurry," Max stated as he left with Santan. I noticed he did not look at me.

I began dressing. The count knew my size to precision. The dress closed over my body like a glove. I was thankful for my youthful figure, even so soon after childbirth. I brushed my hair until I noticed the ends shimmering. I would have liked to put my hair up, but the count had never seen fit to provide me with such trinkets as clips or ribbons. The one I had had in my hair when I first arrived was long gone. I had noticed Teresa never wore such baubles, either; obviously it was a preference of the count.

Satisfied that I could make no further improvements in my appearance, I wandered over to my window and gazed out into the night. The window seemed to be my only real friend in this house. But it was a cautious and unsympathetic friend, one that never opened up to release me back to the world that had forsaken me. All it would allow me were glimpses through its panes. Was even the window afraid of him?

I noticed the wind was increasing, and rain was starting to fall from the clouds that had formed earlier in the evening. We were in for a wicked storm; I felt it in my bones. I also wondered if it was a warning of what was about to commence in my own life.

"Virginia," Max's voice startled me. "It is time. Follow me, please."

I trailed after Max, out of my prison cell, down the winding staircase, past my old room on the second floor, and down to the long, familiar hallway that led to the dining room, the study, and the front door. *To my freedom?* Near the end of the hall my hopes were dashed as Max opened a door and led me down a set of long, narrow stone steps. For a moment I was foolish enough to think he was going to lead me out to the courtyard and set me free. At the bottom of the stairs, he turned and pushed open another large door. This led us into a seemingly endless, constricted corridor lit by a few flickering candles that were hung, like sleeping bats, from the low ceiling.

The walls were overgrown with green moss. Flecks of black mould had begun their intrusion upon the soft green landscape. The place smelled damp, and I detected the sound of dripping water. I began to get a sinking feeling. I wondered whether I was even going to the ceremony or whether I was to be locked in some cold, dank room in the dungeons of this castle, to rot the rest of my life away in isolation.

My fears of lifelong solitude were alleviated when Max opened yet another door. I heard voices in earnest conversation. I stopped in the doorway and studied the room. This must be where everyone slept. There were eight coffins arranged in a circle. They were all open, and I could smell the earth from within them. In the centre of the circle was a small coffin—the size of a child's. It was shrouded with a black velvet cloth, giving it the appearance of an altar. I wondered if it were a sacrificial one!

Candles surrounded us on the cold stone walls. Clumps of wax clung to the rocks beneath them, concocting eerie figurations. Beads of moisture trickled down the walls, disappearing into the cracks of the cold earthen floor.

All of the men were dressed in full-length black capes with high, stiff collars that concealed most of their faces. The linings of the capes were bright red. Under the capes they wore elegant black tuxedos, starched white shirts, and intense red ties that matched the lining of the capes. They looked majestic—and fearsome.

Teresa and Countess Emelia were dressed in white velvet gowns. Red velvet capes, tied with a black silk ribbon, hung from their shoulders.

Teresa appeared to have regained her old composure since our last encounter. She was as stunningly beautiful as ever. Her long hair glistened, and it cascaded down her back like waves of black ebony. I had never seen her eyes as dark as they were tonight—like polished black diamonds sparkling in a noon sun. Her lips were a moist ruby-red; her cheeks had a crimson gleam. I could see that Teresa had risen to the occasion tonight, for she carried herself like a queen. Her looks clearly stated that her mission here was to lay permanent claim to Santan, and to her husband!

The countess Emelia walked over to where I stood transfixed in the doorway. She placed her arm around my waist. Her fingers dug into my skin as she propelled me into the room. "Come, dear, we are about to begin the ceremony. You really do not want to miss this. It is quite an experience, one that none of us have too often. In fact, I have not been to one since that of my own son, many long years ago. These births in our family are too few and far between." The countess rambled on as though she were nervous about something. Was she hiding something? Or was she just excited?

"Where is my baby, Aunt Emelia?" I managed to enquire.

"The count will be here with him shortly," she replied with a smile.

I glanced over to the group of men and counted them. Five, plus Max. Yes, the count was missing. I had no sooner finished counting, when a shadow filled the doorway. Everyone in the room turned to admire the Count Basarab Musat. He stood there, pausing a moment in the entrance, holding his son in his arms, and allowing the congregation to take in the total picture. At that moment, he resembled a figure carved in stone. Regardless of those special moments we had shared, I realized that the hardest part of him was his heart. I was also sure that none of *their* hearts were any softer. Only a fool would believe otherwise.

"Good evening," he greeted as he stepped toward the coffin-altar in the centre of the room and laid the baby upon it. "I apologize for my tardiness, Father," and before anyone could object to his apology, he turned to his father. "Would you please do me the honour of commencing the ceremony?"

Count Atilla nodded. Everyone moved automatically into a circle around the baby and joined hands. I was forced into a spot between Teresa and Emelia. Count Atilla began a low chant in their strange language. It was the same language I had heard the night I gave birth to the child who was lying on the altar, awaiting whatever providence had in store for him. One by one, each member of this strange group joined in the chant.

The baby began crying. Instinctively, I reached for him, but the grips on my hands tightened, holding me in place. The chanting lowered to a barely audible hum, and Count Atilla commenced speaking, still in the strange language. The only words I was able to comprehend were Santan Atilla Musat.

The doctor broke away from the circle and walked over to a table that was set in the corner of the room. It, too, was covered with a black velvet cloth. I noticed a small wooden bowl and a large hunting knife sitting on the table. He picked them up and returned to the circle. The Count Basarab and his father released their hands to allow the doctor back into the circle.

Count Atilla ceased his oration, but the humming continued for several more minutes. The rhythmic notes were like the pendulum of the old town clock. I wondered when it would cease. I felt my hands being released and then noticed that although everyone still hummed, they no longer held hands, either.

The doctor stopped in front of Count Basarab and raised the knife. The count held out his hand; the doctor slit his finger. The count squeezed some of his blood into the wooden bowl. The doctor repeated the same procedure with everyone, except me. The bowl was returned to Count Basarab. He held it while the doctor cut his finger and added his blood to the bowl. He took the knife and set it at the end of the altar, before resuming his place in the circle.

Count Basarab raised the bowl to the ceiling. Thunder crashed through the stone walls to add to the crescendo of the incessant chanting that had begun again. The count uttered some mysterious words over the bowl of blood, and then he stepped from the circle to stand by his son. The baby was screaming in what I presumed to be fright. His arms and legs were flailing wildly, yet when his eyes rested on his father, the child quieted. The count raised the knife and wielded it over his son. Santan stared up at his father. He gurgled contentedly.

My entire body tensed. What the hell was going on here? What was he going to do to my baby? I was screaming, but no sound came out of my mouth!

The count proceeded to pick up Santan's hand and then cut a tiny incision on his thumb. Santan let out a piercing wail as the sudden pain was inflicted on him. The count paid no heed to the suffering infant as he squeezed the child's blood into the bowl, mingling it with the rest. Then the count stirred the bowl's contents with the knife's blade, raised the bowl to the ceiling, and began chanting again—only this time the notes took on an even eerier sound than before. Everyone, with the exception of me, joined in.

The chanting, along with the thunder, was deafening. I could barely keep hold of my senses. The next sight was that of the Count Basarab lifting the bowl of blood to his lips and tipping it up to receive the liquid into his mouth. He shouted out: "Santan Atilla Musat—long may he live!" before handing the bowl to his father.

The roomful of vampires repeated the count's actions before returning the bowl to him. He walked slowly over to Santan, gathered him into one arm, and put the bowl up to the infant's mouth. Santan struggled at the strangeness of the situation, but the bright red liquid was forced through his lips. I watched as some of the blood trickled down my son's chin. It was almost like when Santan suckled at my breast, only this was not mixed with his mother's milk—this was the blood of *his kind*!

The count removed the cloth from the lid of the small coffin and opened it. Everyone walked to their coffins, and they each drew out a handful of earth. They returned to where the count was standing with Santan and placed their dirt in the child's coffin. The count handed Santan to his father, stepped to his coffin, and did the same as the others. He then took his son back into his arms and raised Santan above his head. A circle was formed again around the coffin. The chanting voices rang off the cold stone walls! My God! What was the count doing? My son was being lowered into the coffin!

"To the earth of your forefathers!" I heard the count roar as he laid Santan inside. And then he closed the lid! I could not suppress myself any longer. I screamed! Thunder crashed in my ears. Perspiration poured from every pore of my body! I screamed on and on and on!

The next thing I felt was Max slapping me across the face, trying to bring me back to the moment. The circle had broken up. Everyone was going up to the count and embracing first him and then the child. Teresa stood by his side—his queen.

All was lost for me. My exclusion from this ceremony—not that I had wanted a part in it!—confirmed that whatever influence I might have thought I had was gone. There was only *one man* in control here. Even God and the devil had no spot in this place! What was in store for me now that I had witnessed this ceremony? I was certain I would never be able to take my newfound knowledge beyond these walls.

Count Basarab's voice cut through the confusion. "Max, please escort Virginia back to her room. She has seen enough here." I detected a look of disgust as he dismissed my presence from the intimate family gathering. He then glanced at me as though an afterthought had occurred to him. "I shall come to see you shortly, my little bird; I believe you promised me something."

His evil laughter, mingled with Teresa's, followed me as Max escorted me out. My son was lost to me forever. I knew only a miracle could save me now!

Max and I wound our way back to my room, neither one of us speaking. I thought to attempt a conversation. After all, what more could I lose? "Max, was it Teresa in my room earlier this evening?" I had to know, whatever the cost.

"No, Virginia, it was not Teresa; of that I am sure," Max stated as he opened the door for me. "I have no idea who it was. Whatever is about to happen to you now, Miss Virginia, I wish you luck." Max's voice sounded distant.

The door shut. The key clicked the lock into place. I was left alone to await my fate. I was no longer going to play the fool in my mind. I had cavorted with someone who was probably worse than the devil, and he, in turn, had entertained himself, and his household, with my foolishness. I had been a toy in his hands, and now I would be cast aside and forgotten, along with all the other toys that had preceded me. I had given the count the child he had desired—*that* had been my only purpose in this house!

I sat on the edge of my bed and tried to weep, but the tears would no longer flow. The wells had dried up. I was completely alone with my misery. I sat and waited for the inevitable.

Chapter 26

The Wings of Hell

I waited for what seemed an eternity. The storm outside increased its intensity. Lightning flashed, zigzagging across the night sky. Thunder followed close on its heels. It was a nerve-wracking night, a night that matched the emotions that crowded my mind. My chances had run out. I was absolutely deserted by all the forces of good that had been the cornerstone of my youthful teachings.

I lay down upon the bed to await the fury that would soon crash through my door. I knew there would be no stopping the impending invasion. My heart and body desired haste, even though I realized I might be partaking of my final draught of life. I closed my eyes, trying to shut down my thoughts and trying to gather some order of calmness to myself before the irrevocable upheaval of my last moments on earth.

The eerie sensation that I was being watched caused me to open my eyes. There he stood, still dressed in his ceremonial clothing. He was overwhelming! How could something so perfect be so evil?

He smiled. It was truly not an evil smile, until I caught a glimpse of the fangs. "Where would you like to fly with me tonight, Little Bird?" the count tilted his head slightly.

Was that a hint of sarcasm I detected in his question? Was he baiting me with what he already knew? Had he been the one lurking in the corner of my room a few short hours before? Was I to be sent to the same hell he had imprisoned Lilly in for so many years?

My stomach was in knots. I felt as though I were going to be sick. I could not find my tongue to answer his question. Was he able to read my mind? I prayed not. Could he detect the terror that I was desperately trying to camouflage? I wanted to fly tonight, all right—but my destination would be a flight *away from* this hell I had faltered upon! Did he comprehend how much I loved him, hated him, and desired him—all at the same time? Did he care?

"You have not answered me yet, Virginia darling." The count leaned over me, one hand on either side of my head. His hawkish eyes stared straight into my own apprehensive ones. They demanded an answer.

"Wh...where would you like to take me?" I managed to stutter.

The Count Basarab Musat laughed. Slowly. Softly. The laughter rumbled up from deep within his abdomen, and his aura of evil enveloped me. "Perhaps," he paused to savour his moment, "I shall take you for a flight on the *wings of hell*!" His breath drew closer and closer until he was breathing fire into my ear. "Would you like that?" he whispered tenderly.

I was not allowed to reply. The count captured my lips with his, and then he launched his tongue deeply into my mouth. At first I tried to struggle; my mind was telling me that was what I should do, but his unrelenting passion began to kindle a flame deep within my body. Soon I was wantonly answering his probing with my own.

The count drew back the covers. His hand reached to my gown, searching for buttons. There were none. I heard the material rip away, and then I felt the familiar firmness of his hand as it grasped my breast. I began to writhe in anticipation of what I knew would follow. He tore the rest of the gown from my trembling body.

He stood on the bed, towering over my quivering flesh. Slowly he began to remove his own clothing, piece by piece, throwing them to the floor. He loomed over me like an omnipotent god preparing to claim his innocent victim; his well-muscled body resembled that of a twisting serpent about to feast upon its prey. He dropped to his knees, straddling my body. The closeness of his manliness called out to all the wild beasts within me. Goosebumps rose excitedly over every inch of my flesh.

"Come fly with me, Little Bird," he murmured as he gently lowered himself onto my nakedness.

My back arched up to greet him. I groaned in ecstasy. He moved slowly, deliberately—teasing me, taunting me with every inch of his being. My arms encircled his neck, and my nails raked across his back, forming a trail all the way down to his buttocks. I had become like one possessed; a tigress in full heat! I begged recklessly for fulfilment.

"Now!" I screamed. "Now!"

The count raised himself slightly off my body. He gazed down into my pleading eyes. An unnatural howl filled the room. Lightning flashed through the curtained window. Thunder followed, rattling the thin panes to the point of breaking. He thrust his fullness into me. I opened to accept the momentum of his fury.

Oh God, how the fire burned, searing me deeper and deeper, pushing me into the flames of hell! I begged for more as he impaled deeper into unexplored depths. My head whirled in clouds of ecstasy and clouds shrouded in flames of lust, consuming me in volcanic moments of rapture. My body exploded, time after time, climaxing to the ultimate that I had never dreamed possible.

His breath came heavier and heavier on my neck. I could hear his desire mingled with mine. I detected his fulfilment as his final deliverance exploded into my body. The storm was spent. All was quiet, except for the rasping sound of breathing from the two exhausted bodies upon the bed.

The count lay still upon me for a moment. Then he rose, slowly. As he moved away from me, I could not help but notice the look of disdain, for the second time that night, inscribed on his face. Suddenly, I felt so very cold. So very used. He picked up a blanket and cast it across my sweating body.

"Did you enjoy the flight, Virginia darling?" His smile manifested evil.

What a cold-hearted question! How could he be so indifferent after such passionate lovemaking? What was the point to all of this? Now the storm was over, would the count drop the bomb? I waited silently for my sentence.

"I must inform you—regretfully, of course—that this was our final union and the last time I will see you. I leave with my father and the others for the old country tomorrow evening." The count pronounced these facts casually as he dressed.

The bomb was being dropped. I was still shocked that it came so soon after the moments we had just shared. Had I been hoping for some sort of human compassion from this man? How many times had I been warned not to expect such?

"But what of Santan? What will happen to my baby? Who will care for him? Feed him?" I asked, desperate now that I realized my moment of fate had finally arrived.

"He has no further need for you," was the cutting reply. "After tonight's ceremony, his needs are the same as mine."

"So what are your plans for me, my count?" I jumped up from the bed and grabbed at his arm as he swung his cape across his shoulders. "I have given you the son you wanted so much; I have done all that you asked of me! Please …" I dropped to the floor, grovelling at his feet, begging for life itself—probably just as Lilly had done. How low I had stooped for the miserable existence I endured! "Please, I could give you another son—we talked of this …"

The Count Basarab Musat regarded me, the cowering, naked figure at his feet. Disgust was still etched across his face. "*You* talked of that, Virginia darling. As for *my* plans for you—I have none. I am finished with you. I thought only to take one last moment of pleasure from your body, as well as to give you a moment of the same. It is my understanding, from having studied human behaviours for so many years, that they desire to leave this earth on a happy note. I trust you enjoyed the symphony I have just played for you?" His words were freezing my blood.

"You have given me a fine son. For this, perhaps I should thank you; but you see, if it had not been you, some other eager female would have happened along eventually to accomplish the same job. I do not really need *you* in particular to produce another son for me. Besides, I do not believe that anything you have done for me has been done with honest willingness, has it now, my darling Virginia? In fact, that is exactly what it has been for you, right, Virginia—a performance?" The count's accusation destroyed any resistance I might have had left.

"I tire easily of insincerity," he continued. "You comprehend, I am sure. You should never have allowed such a thing as trying to fool me cross your mind, not even for a moment!"

I reached out and clutched at his cloak. He plucked my fingers from it. "As for your fate, be sure you will know it before I depart this house." With those searing words, he left me, a crumpled heap upon the floor in the room where moments before he had soared with me to the ultimate ecstasy a man and woman could ever ascend to.

Waiting for him just outside my door was Teresa. She laughed, throwing her head back to reveal the horrid fangs. The count joined in her mirth, both of them laughing at me and my exposure. They embraced. They fondled at each other's necks. I lay upon the floor, staring disbelievingly out my open door at Basarab Musat and his chosen queen, Teresa. They lifted their heads and jeered at me; blood was trickling from the corners of their mouths. My eyes narrowed in on the fresh puncture wounds that dominated the flesh on both necks!

"Come, my queen, *my chosen one*," the count guffawed, "from now until eternity you shall be forever mine!"

My head turned away. When I dared to look again, they were gone.

The realization that I had less than twenty-four hours to live weighed heavily on my mind. My fists pounded angrily on the wooden floor planks. There were only the walls and the furniture there to listen to my anguish, and they were helpless to assist me.

Tears of disappointment flowed freely from my eyes. My body shivered from the cold, and from the fear that encompassed me. I was being cheated out of a normal lifetime, just for the sake of one night of curiosity!

Where was the God my mother had spoken of? Why had He forsaken me?

I dragged myself to the edge of the bed and pulled myself up. My body sank into the mattress that had become cold. My eyes closed. It was over.

CHAPTER 27

The Gift

I awoke to the first rays of morning as they crept through the cracks at the edges of my curtains. Grogginess still weighed heavily on my eyes, as well as my mind. I ran my fingers along the edge of the blanket. I could not remember how I had returned to the bed, for my last memory was of my defeated self pounding upon the floor. I focused my mind on the moments I had spent in the count's arms, but as the fogginess began to clear, the realization of what he had said upon taking his leave, the scene on the landing with Teresa, and the understanding that my fate would be sealed before another sun rose to its fullest height—all of that overpowered the storm that had consumed me last night.

He, the Count Basarab Musat, the lord of this place, had dismissed me as if I were nothing. He had confirmed what Max and Teresa had been trying to tell me all along—I was nothing more to him than a vessel to carry the child that Teresa was unable to bear him. My only chance to escape would be today, in the sunlight. That would have to be done as quickly as possible, and it would only happen if I could convince Max to help me. He was the only other person in this godforsaken place who could be out in the light of day. I had no choice but to gamble on his possible goodness, or perhaps his change of heart. Surely he would be along soon with some breakfast.

I climbed out of bed and walked over to the closet to select my clothing. It would have to be suitable for running, because once I got outside that front door, my life would depend on the swiftness of my feet and, as past experience had taught me, the sharpness of my eyes. To my dismay, I discovered that all of my clothing had been removed!

I glanced frantically around the room. My eyes fell to the rumpled bed, searching desperately for the ripped gown that had been cast aside last night. It would be better than nothing. My reward peeked from beneath the blankets.

I grabbed up the remnants of the gown. It was in shreds. I had not realized, being so caught up in the moment, how the count had torn it from my body. Possibly, if I tried hard enough and used a little of that imagination I seemed to be gifted with, I could fashion the material in such a way to at least modestly cover me. Within minutes I had the dress tied together well enough to cover most of me. I thought of using the blanket but then decided its heaviness would weigh me down.

I ventured over to my door, praying all the way to the God who appeared to have forsaken me—praying that He would have seen fit to unlock this barrier for me and praying that He would forgive me my transgressions with the count, albeit that they were ones beyond my control. My final prayer was that God would somehow soften just one heart in this house, allowing someone to assist me in what I knew would be my final escape attempt. If I failed again, I knew there would be no more chances.

I reached the door. I turned the handle. To my surprise, it opened!

God's first grace!

I took another look around the room I was hoping to leave behind. My journals—I must take them with me! They were my proof that all here had actually happened. I prayed that they had not been removed along with my clothing. I moved quickly back into the room, lifted the bedskirt, and breathed a deep sigh of relief. I retrieved the box containing the ragged pages and then headed back to the open doorway.

God's second grace!

I ventured onto the dimly lit landing at the top of the staircase. All the candles in the lower hall had been snuffed out, and it took a few seconds for my eyes to adjust to the darkness. I hoped this was my first step toward the freedom I so longed for. I glanced around at the shadows, forever aware of Teresa's cautioning words. The very echo of them haunted me constantly: *Beware of the shadows!* Was she laying a trap for me? Would she be lurking in the hall below, ready to stop me, once again, at the threshold of my freedom?

Maybe she had returned after her rendezvous with the count last night. Maybe it was she who had taken my clothing and placed me back in the bed. Perhaps she had left the door unlocked, knowing full well that I would attempt one final escape. Could that be her final gift to me—so she could watch the count's wrath come down upon me, as it had upon her and Max so many times, because of my *game-playing*? I could not blame her for her moment of revenge or say that I would not have done the same if I were in her shoes.

There was no more time to ponder the reason for an unlocked door or the complicated relationships within the household. I moved quickly down the steps, memory guiding my feet. My heart thumped loudly in my chest. Perspiration broke out on my forehead. I reached the bottom and began running toward the light that I knew was at the end of the hallway. My greatest fear was of what I might find there or, worse yet, who would discover me before I touched the doorknob of freedom.

To my utter surprise, I reached the door without mishap. Everything was happening much too easily. I kept waiting for the axe to drop on my head, for someone to drag me back into the house—but this time I was sure I would not be returned to my room. Most likely I was destined for that dark cell in the dungeon of this horrid place, the cell where I would be left to rot, unnoticed, until a day when someone might happen upon my bones while exploring an abandoned old house. Or worse, I would become the next Lilly, cursed to wander in a lifeless existence for eternity, constantly being hounded by the human race to which I had once belonged, and never being able to explain that I could not help what I was—that I was really one of them and had been cursed to such an existence by some evil creatures! How could I explain that I had no control over the urges that I would probably be left to deal with? Why would anyone believe someone who was a murdering criminal in their eyes—a serial killer, like the ones the count and I had talked about so often? Unlike Lilly, I had no Max in my life who would bargain for the peace of my soul. And it would not matter anyway, because *they* would likely wipe out any memories of my time with them that I might have been able to retain.

I thought I detected a noise behind me. I peeped nervously over my shoulder. I could see nothing. I turned back to the door. It opened easily, and I stepped out into the foyer. One more door to get through, and then I would just have to get across the gardens and through those trees. I would be free! I would try to come back later for my son. Perhaps I could even bring the police in time to prevent the count from taking Santan out of the country. Of course, even if they did come to arrest the count, what kind of power could they wield over one such as him?

My hand reached for the other door handle. It froze in mid-air as words ripped through the silence. "Wait, Virginia." The voice was low and husky. I knew it was a woman, but at that moment I could not decipher whether it was Teresa or Aunt Emelia. I turned to face the voice that had stopped me on the threshold of escape. I tried to prepare a speech in my mind, one that would plead convincingly for my life. I was ready to do whatever was necessary to save my life—even more than I had already done over the past months!

"Please—" I began.

The figure stepped out of the shadowy corridor. "Hush, child."

It was Aunt Emelia, and from the sound of her voice and the look of her attire, I sensed she was there to help me. She was totally robed in black, and a black silk veil covered her face. Under the veil, I detected a pair of dark glasses, which I assumed were meant to give even more protection to her sensitive eyes. I sent a fervent thanks to God.

God's third grace!

"There is a better, less conspicuous, way out of here," Emelia whispered. "Follow me."

I had no choice but to trust her. She led me through the den and opened a small wooden door that was hidden behind a thick red curtain. We stepped through into a musty-smelling tunnel. The ground was hard-packed earth. Cobwebs hung everywhere. Spiders were busily repairing their webs from what must have been a recent intrusion. Flies buzzed around, trying to dodge the webs. Piles of boxes, broken furniture, and antique relics were scattered randomly around. I turned to speak to Emelia, but she raised her finger to her lips.

"This tunnel will take you out into what once was used as a schoolroom. I have released all the locks for you. From there, you will find your way to the street, and your freedom.

"I have left a large basket in the schoolroom. Take it with you. Inside the basket are some gifts from me to you, my dear. Go quickly now, before you are found out, and before I am discovered assisting you!"

I was totally baffled. "Why are you doing this for me, Aunt Emelia?"

Worried frustration was beginning to show on Emelia's face. "There is no time for explanations right now, dear. I have left you a letter in the basket, which will make everything clear to you, plus give you further instructions. Now hurry; you must go before Max discovers you are missing. You are both very lucky that it was I who hid in your room that day when you begged him to help you escape. Max still does not know for sure that it was I, but he suspects so, because damnation has not rained down upon him yet. You were very foolish to think that he would help you—he will never ever challenge the count's authority."

"But why?" I continued to plead for an explanation from Emelia, but she shoved me gently down the passage.

"Go!" she whispered huskily. "Go! No, wait just a moment." Emelia removed her cape, placed it around my shoulders, and then sent me on my way again with these final words: "There. You will need a proper covering; your dress is so torn. Go quickly. Use your hands on the walls to feel your way along. The passage will become very narrow further down, and it is dimly lit, but your eyes should soon adjust to the darkness. Do not stop to read my note until you are far from this place."

I still hesitated.

"Go!" she ordered nervously as she glanced back over her shoulder. "There is no time to explain anything now!" And with those words, she disappeared back into the den and shut the door. I was left alone in the corridor to freedom.

I stumbled forward, tripping over something on the ground. I almost dropped the box with my diary notes. I regained my footing, clutched the box to my chest, and pushed on, thoughts of my impending freedom guiding my nervous feet.

As I worked my way along, my heart beat anxiously. Would this passageway ever end? When would I reach the room Emelia had spoken of? Or was she sending me to my death? That was one thing I had not had time to think of, because everything had happened so quickly. After all, why would she cross Basarab, the nephew she loved so dearly?

Without warning, I bumped into a wooden door. My fingers fumbled in the dim light. I found the latch. It opened easily. The door swung open noiselessly, as though someone had recently oiled the rusty hinges. I entered a small, cluttered room.

An antique wood stove, looking very much like the one I had seen in pictures of my grandmother's old farmhouse, sat in the front part of the room. Long pine tables, with hard, backless benches, filled the area beyond the old heating relic. On one of the back tables, close to another door, was a large wicker basket, just as Emelia had promised.

Swiftly, I moved across the room, picked up the basket, and placed my box on top of the blanket. I wondered at the heaviness of the basket, as I stepped through what I prayed would be my door to freedom, but I did not want to waste a precious moment until I was far from this place.

There had already been too many *almosts* for me to take another chance. A soft breeze caressed my face. "Welcome home," it whispered.

God's fourth grace!

I took my bearings. There was a small piece of lawn to cross and then what appeared to be a stone driveway. But those trees were still lurking at the extreme edges, hanging over the end of the driveway; some of their branches swept the sidewalks on the other side. At the moment, I feared those trees, with their grappling arms and roots, more than anything else!

I started running across the yard as quickly as I was able, for the basket was quite heavy, and Emelia's cape was restricting my legs. I ran past the flowers ... past the statues ... onto the pebbled drive, ever gaining on the formidable trees just ahead. The breeze picked up, helping the trees to reach out their branches in the hopes of arresting me until either Basarab or Max came along to drag me back. I prayed they would fail at their task!

Then I heard the whimper from within the basket.

God's fifth grace!

It was all I needed to give me the extra strength to push forward. Past the trees I ran. A huge iron gate loomed behind the swinging branches. I sighed in relief. It would not impede my flight; it was open—my road to freedom was waiting for me! I kept running, running as far away from that house as I could ... past rows of houses ... blindly, to nowhere in particular! Just *away*!

By this time, the crying from the basket had become much louder, and I was weeping with it. Tears of relief and joy poured from my eyes. God had sent me a deliverer, and along with this gift was another gift, much more precious than I could have hoped for.

Fatigue finally overtook me. I slowed to a quick walk. I sat down under a large maple tree, opened the basket, and picked up my son. I cradled him to my heart. Emelia's note was still nestled inside, under a small blanket. There would be time to read it later. For now, I just needed to hang on to this precious moment and drink in the air of an almost-forgotten world. Looking more closely, I realized I was sitting at the edge of a graveyard. West Street was in front of me, and the train track ran to my left. Street life had not yet awakened. At last I was truly alone with my child.

I picked up the basket and walked into the cemetery. I needed to find a more secluded place to rest, and to feed Santan, because I knew the city would be waking soon. When he finished his meal, he settled back to sleep in my arms. I was curious about the contents of the envelope. I laid Santan down, wrapping him in the blanket Aunt Emelia had provided. I picked up the envelope and opened it slowly. I was shocked when a large pile of one-hundred-dollar bills fell into my lap.

God's sixth grace!

I counted them. Ten thousand dollars! Where would Emelia have obtained such a large sum? I picked up the letter and began to read aloud to the trees, to the gravestones—to my freedom.

My Dear Virginia:

By now, I pray that you are far from the place that entrapped you for so many months. If you are reading my letter, then you have attained your freedom, along with both of the gifts I have given you—your child and the money. Use the money wisely, for a fresh start in life.

Now, to answer your question of why I am helping you. I anticipated your curiosity. I was the one who was spying that day when you and Max were in such deep conversation over your possible escape. My heart, such as it is, went out to you. Even as I write this letter, I am not sure that what I am doing is a wise and sensible thing, but then again, maybe I am helping you because there is still a small part of me that is human. Maybe there was a piece of my soul that was not totally consumed in the crossover.

You see, Virginia, as I told you, I was once a lot like you— young, beautiful, and more curious than necessary. I fell into the trap of my own count, but unlike you, I never had quite the same desire to escape. Even after I realized exactly what kind of family I had married into, I was content to accept what fate had offered me, and as you already know, in time I became one of them. But it was different then: my count had chosen me for his bride.

After observing the scene in your room that day, I knew that you would never be allowed to become one of us, even if Attila and I were able to convince Basarab not to kill you. I was also pretty positive Teresa would never allow your life to be spared. Not that I can blame her; we all fight for what we desire, don't we, Virginia?

Somehow, this inner strength that you possess, despite all they have put you through, stirred some sympathy in my heart. I felt I had to try to return a piece of the life that had been so maliciously snatched from you. And in doing so, I thought to include your son. A mother must never be separated from her son. This I know.

I did not get to finish all I wished to tell you about vampires trying to conceive their own children. The peoples of Transylvania were becoming more and more aware of the evil that was spreading throughout their land. Men began tracking down whoever they thought was one of the heinous creatures. They splashed holy water on our sacred earth. They stuck crosses in the ground around the coffins where we took our daily refuge. When they found us, they drove stakes through our hearts and then severed our heads. It was the time of the first great cleansing. Many of our dearest relatives were lost to us. And many of these were not the ones who were wreaking the havoc.

Fortunately, the leaders of the Order of the Dragons, the Dracula and Musat families, were still alive. They had hidden so deep in the mountains that none of the townspeople had been able to find them. They wished desperately to preserve their heritage. They implored Count Balenti Danesti to devise a concoction that would promote both blood and milk to come through a woman's breast. This way, if an infant was conceived in the womb of a human, then the child would get the needed nourishment at birth that would seal him or her to the chosen destiny—or curse, whatever you wish to call it—of their fathers. That is the same drink Max served to you for months. It was also a derivative of the one the doctor had created for Mara.

However, once that was all in place, there were still problems. As I told you, two of my children were born very weak and died within their first month. I gave birth to one strong son, and as far as I know, he still lives somewhere in Transylvania. It has been years since I have seen him.

As I mentioned to you before, we realized that women who had crossed over could bear children, but that these children did not live long. Most vampire women, though, are barren. However, it did appear to be different for the men. Somehow, they were still able to give life, but it had to be with a human—thus the reason for my struggle to keep my babies alive. Vacaresti had been taking a few nips here and there; I was in limbo. Before the conception of my second son, because of his sorrow at the loss of our first child, my husband had pretty much left me alone—thus the child lived. Our third child died because Vacaresti had begun indulging again.

Santan is the first child that Basarab has been able to sire. He has made a few attempts, but they failed. At this point, it appears your son is going to grow to manhood. What I am trying to do, by giving him to you for a time, is to take away his father's fate of eternal damnation! Over the years, that is what I have concluded our existence is. Hopefully, you will have the time to raise him as a human, so that he can live an ordinary life, as it is meant to be. He will not have to hide his face from the world. He will grow up, fall in love, and give you grandchildren. That is the way life is intended to be. Your son, unlike mine, may have the chance to live and die normally.

I have used the words, for a time, because that, my dear Virginia, is all that you have. Beware, for the danger is not yet over. Basarab will be furious at what has been done here today, and he will seek out his son. Maybe not right away, because he leaves for the old country with us today. But be assured the count will return for Santan! *When* will depend on how long it takes to settle matters at home.

Use this time wisely. Try to mould Santan to be truly yours. Lift the evil veil from him, and immerse him with your goodness. Give him your strength, because it is power he will need when his father comes for him. You must warn him, when he is old enough to understand, who and what his father is. He will need to have knowledge of his adversary.

I say adversary because, with his time with you, and with the absence of his father's influence, Santan will most likely take your side of things—at the beginning anyway. This will anger Basarab, but he will not desist in his attempts to reclaim Santan.

Do not fear for my fate, should it cross your mind to consider it. My position in this family will protect me. My husband, if I am found out, will chastise me, and I may fall slightly from grace for a short time, but I have my own ways to protect myself—I *am* one of them.

I must close now. Time draws short. May the God that I once knew protect you both!

Write me just once, to let me know where I may send you the money necessary to raise the child; a secured bank account would be best. Also, wherever you find to live, make sure it is as secluded as possible. Only you must bring up your son, for as you know, he is a special child. You must never—I repeat, *never*—leave him with strangers! You alone must be his guide, his teacher, his confidante—in essence, you must be his very life. Even your choice of friends should be extremely selective, and the fewer the better. Trust me in this matter. Be aware that he will be sensitive to the sun, so take great care as to which hours you expose him to the outdoors, especially at first. Hopefully, this sensitivity will diminish with time. My address is:

The Countess Emelia Musat
c/o Miss Adelaide Georgian
10 West Blvd.,
Kenora, Transylvania.

Love,
Aunt Emelia

The letter slipped from my fingers and dropped to the grass. I wept, partly for my fate and partly for Aunt Emelia because of what she had dared to do for me. I gathered Santan into my arms, cuddled him for a moment, and then laid him gently in the basket. Picking it up, I began the journey down the road to my new life.

I breathed deeply the air of freedom. I wanted to make the best of every moment I had to share with my son, before the count came to claim him. I was sure, deep down, that Aunt Emelia was right; she had only been able to lend me Santan for a small space of time, in the eternity of his life. I knew the day would come when the Count Basarab Musat would return to claim him. And I would have to be ready!

My footsteps hastened down the road. One night of thoughtless inquisitiveness had changed the course of my entire life. But at least my horizons were brighter now than they had been a few hours earlier.

I was free. Santan was mine. For now.

Epilogue

I had no way of knowing that Max had watched, from my bedroom window, my flight across the lawn and out the gate.

I had no way of knowing the wrath that befell the household that night, when the count discovered that not only had I escaped but I had taken *his* son with me.

I had no way of knowing how Max was suspected of assisting me, and how the count was ready to rain his fury down on him. I was not there to see Emelia step in and reason with her nephew without admitting her part in my flight.

I had no way of knowing that Teresa was pleased when she found me gone—that secretly she did not care anything about the child her husband so badly wanted.

I had no way of knowing that it was the count's father who had reasoned with him, telling his son that there was time enough later to find us—that the more pressing matter was to get home and deal with the problems there.

I had no way of knowing. Neither did I worry—for the only thing that I could think of was finding a place far from that house, somewhere secluded from prying eyes, where I could raise Santan as *my* son.

My steps took me as far as the Red-D-Mix factory by the railway tracks on Henry Street. A long, narrow laneway beside the entrance to the factory had a sign pointing inward that said, Apartment for Rent. I gazed up the lane, but I could not see a house—just trees. I turned and began walking toward them. The trees I had just come through had held me prisoner; maybe these ones would help protect me.

Author Biography

Mary was born on November 15, 1953, in Stoney Creek, Ontario, Canada. She is a freelance creative writer who now resides in Brantford, Ontario with her husband, Adel (Ed).

Her love for the written word began at a very early age. Daydreamer was the description Mary's teachers would write on her report cards––little did they know that the seeds of great writings to come were germinating in the caverns of Mary's mind!

In March 2006, Mary completed a freelance journalism course at the University of Waterloo, after which she began writing freelance articles and a fictional short-story column for the Brantford Expositor.

Mary has published, under her publishing company, *Cavern of Dreams*, four poetry anthologies: *Life's Roller Coaster, Devastations of Mankind, Shattered,* and *Memories*; and a collection of short stories, *From the Heart.* She also writes children's stories, novels, plays, and songs.

Mary is active in the writing community. For several years she ran a creative writing program, *Just Imagine,* for the Grand Erie District School Board. Mary is always encouraging those who have a love for writing to follow their dreams.

Web-site: www.cavernofdreams.ca

CPSIA information can be obtained at www.ICGtesting.com
Printed in the USA
LVOW052222200912

299635LV00007B/122/P